Mary Scarlett Hardcastle, Baron John Campbell

Life of John, Lord Campbell, Lord High Chancellor of Great Britain

consisting of a selection from his autobiography, diary, and letters. Second Edition

Mary Scarlett Hardcastle, Baron John Campbell

Life of John, Lord Campbell, Lord High Chancellor of Great Britain
consisting of a selection from his autobiography, diary, and letters. Second Edition

ISBN/EAN: 9783337123604

Printed in Europe, USA, Canada, Australia, Japan

Cover: Foto ©Raphael Reischuk / pixelio.de

More available books at **www.hansebooks.com**

LIFE

OF

JOHN, LORD CAMPBELL

LORD HIGH CHANCELLOR OF GREAT BRITAIN

CONSISTING OF A SELECTION FROM HIS AUTOBIOGRAPHY, DIARY, AND LETTERS

EDITED BY HIS DAUGHTER

THE HON. MRS. HARDCASTLE

SECOND EDITION

IN TWO VOLUMES—VOL. II.

With Portrait

LONDON
JOHN MURRAY, ALBEMARLE STREET
1881

CONTENTS

OF

THE SECOND VOLUME.

———∘✕∘———

CHAPTER XIX.

NOVEMBER 1831—DECEMBER 1832.

CHAPTER XX.

JANUARY 1833—NOVEMBER 1834.

CHAPTER XXIV.

MARCH 1840—JUNE 1841.

CHAPTER XXV.

JUNE 1841—NOVEMBER 1842.

CHAPTER XXVI.

NOVEMBER 1842—JUNE 1846.

CHAPTER XXVII.

JUNE 1846—NOVEMBER 1847.

CHAPTER XXVIII.

NOVEMBER 1847—AUGUST 1849.

CHAPTER XXIX.

AUGUST 1849—MARCH 1850.

CHAPTER XXX.

MARCH 1850—DECEMBER 1851.

CHAPTER XXXI.

DECEMBER 1851—JUNE 1854.

CHAPTER XXXII.

AUGUST 1854—AUGUST 1856.

CHAPTER XXXIII.

NOVEMBER 1856—MAY 1859.

CHAPTER XXXIV.

JUNE 1859—JUNE 1860.

CHAPTER XXXV.

JUNE 1860—JUNE 1861.

LIFE

OF

LORD CAMPBELL.

———•○•———

CHAPTER XIX.

NOVEMBER, 1831——DECEMBER, 1832.

Burning of Bristol—New Session—Reform Bill reintroduced—Letters
from Bristol and Brighton—Alarm about the Cholera—Registration
Bill—Second Reading of the Reform Bill in the House of Lords—
Lord Lyndhurst's Amendment—Resignation of Ministers—Attempt of
the Duke of Wellington to form a Ministry—Passing of the Reform
Bill—Goes to Dudley to canvass the Borough—His Last Circuit—
Trial of the Mayor of Bristol—Death of Lord Tenterden—Is appointed
Solicitor-General—Elected M.P. for Dudley.

Brooks's: Tuesday, November 1, 1831.

Dear George, . . . We are rather in a state of consternation here, and I myself apprehend that we are verging
fast to a state of anarchy. Bristol is still burning. To
make use of a *new* simile, Lord Grey is like Phaëton,
who could not drive his chariot and set the world on fire.
They say Parliament is to reassemble on the 6th of December. An adjournment till after Christmas is now impossible.
Strange to say, Brougham remains in the country and is not
coming to town till Monday. He can never act like another
man.

If I were king I should be a little uneasy, or if I were
a peer; but in a revolution I can take my chance; only
that I am very odious to Hume and the Radicals for certain
speeches I made towards the conclusion of the session. If

Ministers give the least countenance to *armed* associations I leave them. Be your form of government what it may, republican or monarchical, it is preposterous to suppose that there can be a military force in the country not under the command of government; and this opinion I shall proclaim on all occasions and at whatever cost.

Brooks's : Saturday, November 26, 1831.

. . . I sat three hours with Lord Althorp on the new Bill, along with other lawyers, on Wednesday night. God knows what is to happen. No concession!

I yesterday met Lord and Lady Holland at dinner, who are both very unflinching. Lady Holland told me the King did not object to make new peers, but there was a great reluctance on the part of Lord Grey.

Dr. Russell, of cholera notoriety, was of the party, and is a sort of *lion* at present. He seems a modest, sensible man. He agrees that the disease will travel all over Europe, and will probably remain more or less for many years.

Thursday, December 1, 1831.

. . . Everything has a gloomy air. The cholera advances and will cause terrible confusion before long.

I had an agreeable dinner last Sunday with Lord Lyndhurst, who seems to me ready to concede a good deal on Reform. Billy Holmes entertained the party by a story he said he had on undoubted authority, that Serjeant Wilde, Pepys, and Campbell were to draw lots for the office of Solicitor-General.

I have had another long sitting with Lord Althorp on the new Bill. I augur nothing good. It seems to me as if the world were coming to an end and the destinies of the human race were accomplished.

Monday, December 12, 1831.

Dear George,—I have been at prayers and securing myself a place in the House.[1] I have had a copy of the new Bill four or five days. You will be pleased hardly to be able to distinguish it from the old. For my own part I should

---

[1] The session had opened on the 6th of December.—ED.

have been better pleased had there been any prospect of conciliation and compromise.

By order of the King there was a meeting on Saturday between the heads of the two parties ; but, as might be expected, I believe it came to nothing.

Sunday, December 18, 1831.

. . . You will see we had a glorious division last night on the Reform Bill—two to one exactly. The Bill may be considered as now passed. There may be a few alterations in the Lords, but there will no longer be any stout or hearty opposition.

I had an interview with the Duke of Richmond this morning about the Register Bill, some clauses of which he opposes as Postmaster-General. I smoothed him over, but I fear the Bill will not pass as the attorneys are so powerful. I shall get the others through, I hope, without any serious difficulty.

Stanley last night cut up my friend Croker in great style. If I had made the speech I could have said *nunc dimittis.*

Bristol : January 3, 1832.

Dear George,—I am here an idle man. I arrived yesterday morning, being told it was essential I should be present at the opening of the commission. I come 'special' to defend Captain Lewis, who shot a boy in the mob, and is indicted for murder. The city is perfectly tranquil, but anything like Queen Square I never saw, except Valenciennes after it had been bombarded and taken by storm.

Brighton : Monday, January 9, 1832.

. . . I got back here yesterday from Bristol, which I left on Saturday evening at half-past five. . . . I suppose you will see by the newspapers that my client, Captain Lewis, had a triumphant acquittal. I took great pains in getting up his defence, and, though I had no opportunity for public display, I certainly well earned my fee.

Sir James Scarlett is here and dines to-day with the King. His Majesty applied to Lord Palmerston for a situation for Peter, notwithstanding Sir James's anti-Reform principles and votes.

Nothing is known here about the new peers. The Princess Augusta yesterday told Scarlett that she could learn nothing, and that the King never mentioned politics in the family. . . .

Thursday, January 19, 1832.

. . . The King threw out to Scarlett at Brighton a sarcasm against Lord Grey. You know that the saying is that 'the Premier provides for his seventeenth cousins.' Scarlett thanked the King for his condescension in applying to Lord Palmerston in favour of Peter. 'Ah,' said his Majesty, ' I think it a very fair thing for a man to do what he can for a son or daughter; but when it comes to the *seventeenth cousin* it is rather too much.'

House of Commons : Wednesday, January 25, 1832.

. . . Of Parliamentary Reform I am sick, and I am hampered by Scarlett taking an active part in the Committee. Last night I wished to speak; but it would not have been decent to have come into direct collision with him. O'Connell is sitting by me, fuming about there being no House, and saying that it is a manœuvre to defeat his motion about Lord Killeen.

Temple : February 4, 1832.

. . . I have had a very severe week; never in bed till past two, and up before eight. I spoke in the House last night more successfully than hitherto, upon the ten-pound clause. I was loudly cheered in the first two or three sentences, which gave me courage. There is nothing so exciting as fixing the attention of your audience, and the suspicion of being deemed tiresome annihilates me.

Court of King's Bench, Guildhall :
Friday, February 17, 1832.

. . . We are not quite accustomed to the cholera in London, and a good deal of alarm prevails. It is said to be in Piccadilly and the upper parts of the town. I have, while sitting in court here, signed my will, making provision, to the best of my judgment, for those who are dependent on me, and I know not what duty to others I have now to perform.

I do seriously think the House of Commons as dangerous a place as any in London. The cholera is a river or aquatic disorder, and it is certainly at Lambeth on the opposite side of the Thames. What I continue chiefly to apprehend is its tendency to impede commerce, and to throw multitudes out of employment. Thousands certainly will be ruined by it. As a slight example, fruit and vegetables are hardly used, and few venture to ride in a hackney coach. . . . The scarlet fever is raging at the West End of the town, and I am as much afraid of it as of the cholera. I wonder if we shall ever see wholesome times again.

Saturday, February 25, 1832.

. . . Lords Harrowby and Wharncliffe are trying to make converts to the second reading of the Reform Bill, and it is now said there will be a majority for the second reading without more peers, with an understanding that there may be some modifications in the Committee.

Gloucester: April 1, 1832.

. . . You were right in supposing that I should be touched by your description of your meeting with your children,—

Non obtusa adeo gestamus pectora Pœni.[2]

I have myself been most singularly fortunate in domestic life, upon which I am well convinced much more depends than on schemes of ambition. The political cards have turned out badly. Scarlett's secession from the Whigs was a very inauspicious event. He himself is not in the remotest degree to blame, and it was by my advice that he accepted Lord Lonsdale's offer, and was returned for Cockermouth. But the consequences have unnerved me in the House of Commons.

My Committee I believe is going on very prosperously, The best report of the part of Peel's speech in which he alluded to the Registration Bill, I had from Mary, who heard

[2] *Æn.* i. 567.

it from the ventilator. 'He taunted the Government for their want of vigour and good faith in abandoning the learned author of the Registry Bill in the midst of his difficulties when bringing forward a measure which was so necessary and important as a legal reform. Yet the great Reformers themselves, frightened by a host of interested attorneys, dared not support it, and the learned framer of the Bill was forced, by their pusillanimity, to take refuge in a Committee.' . . . I am very wretched here from the slowness of the judges. But I have no remedy. My renouncing the circuit is quite out of the question, and all that I can do is to make them come into court at eight in the morning and sit till midnight. They are abundantly willing and, to do them justice, no men can be more anxious to serve the public. I have this consolation, that I would rather be in my situation than in theirs.

House of Commons: Friday, April 13, 1832.

. . . There is no doubt the English Reform Bill will be read a second time in the Lords. I mean to sit up for the division, which probably will not take place till five o'clock to-morrow morning.[3] Brougham, Copley, and Plunket are to speak to-night.

Brougham continues exceedingly depressed, although I suppose he will rouse himself to make a great speech. He believes himself that his depression proceeds entirely from the melancholy state of his child. But this was nearly as bad last year when he was so much excited. The truth is that the extreme excitement to which he was then subject has exhausted him, and he will continue in his present condition for some months longer, when I expect to see him revive. I have marked this revolution in his spirits several times before.

Ministers altogether are very flat, and there is a strong notion that they cannot long survive. I shall be true to them and never leave the Whig party, unless they should commit greater blunders than they have hitherto done, which I hold to be impossible.

---

[3] The division took place—majority of 9 for the second reading.—ED.

Wednesday, April 18, 1832.

. . . Ireland is now the stumbing block. If you had heard the speeches of Sheil and Stanley the other night you would have despaired of the republic. The common notion prevailing among Liberals in England is that Ireland is wholly incapable of laws or liberty, and must be governed by the sword. I really doubt whether the Irish Reform Bill will pass through the House of Commons, and it is rumoured that Government will abandon it—at least for the present session. But the waverers in the Lords say ' we will not pass the English Reform Bill till we have all the three on our table.

Wetherell has been here to-day to move for a criminal information for a libel on the Duke of Cumberland. He boasts that Ministers are afraid to meet Parliament, and that this is the reason why the Easter recess is so unusually long. This is stuff, but the truth is that Ministers are going on very indifferently. Luckily for them the Duke of Wellington makes himself more and more unpopular, and a Tory government is quite impossible.

Tuesday, May 8, 1832.

. . . The crisis is come.[4] In two hours it will be determined whether Lord Grey goes out, or sixty or seventy new peers are to be made. I was in the Lords last night during the whole of the debate and the division. Down to the actual division the Ministers did not apprehend a majority of more than twenty.

Court of King's Bench : Wednesday, May 9, 1832.

. . . Ministers are out and there will be an immediate dissolution of Parliament. We have had floating rumours all the morning, which are now put an end to by Denman's arrival from the levée. He speaks by the authority of Grey himself whom he saw there. Grey and Brougham went to Windsor yesterday, and told the King they brought the unanimous resolution of the Cabinet that they must resign unless new peers were made to the number of fifty at least. The King gave a doubtful answer, and it was thought he might yield.

[4] An amendment proposed by Lord Lyndhurst in committee was carried by a majority of 5.—ED.

But this morning at nine o'clock a letter from the King was received, extremely civil, but saying that upon consideration he could not consent to the measure proposed, and that he therefore accepted the tendered resignation.

The Duke of Wellington has not been sent for, and nobody exactly knows what is to be done.

House of Commons, six o'clock.—I have just been listening to Lord Althorp's declaration, and the speeches which followed. The Duke of Wellington and Peel, I certainly know, have had no communication from the King. It is said that Lord Harrowby has been sent for, and has agreed to form the new administration. I conceive that he has undertaken what is impossible. Lord Ebrington's motion to-morrow will pledge the House of Commons, and an appeal to the people would be madness. Events are at hand such as have not been seen in this country for more than two centuries. Baring stated that sixty or seventy peers were demanded. I have given you the authentic account from Denman, who, poor fellow, is terribly dejected. I am sincerely sorry for him. The chances were that he would have been Chief Justice of the King's Bench and a peer. Now he is professionally ruined, and his family will be in poverty.

There may be some defection, but I anticipate that there will be a very large majority of the Commons for Ebrington's motion; I shall remain true to my colours. What law arrangements will be made I cannot conjecture. Scarlett must be somehow included, which of course will give joy to those I love. But the change I sincerely and deeply deplore as fraught with public calamity.

I have been in the Lords and heard Grey deliver a very spirited defence of his own conduct.

I had my Scotch Reform speech all cut and dry. The Treasury circulated notes this morning asking us to attend on the second reading of the Bill. The House was a very amusing scene. It was particularly curious to observe the forced smile of gaiety assumed by the Ministers as they entered, and the radiance of real joy on the countenances of their antagonists. The triumph of the latter must be very short-lived. Althorp I really believe is well pleased, and

Jeffrey seems to me very tranquil, but many display the deepest dejection.

Court of King's Bench: Thursday, May 10, 1832.

. . . Nothing more known. There is a report that the King was insulted in going yesterday to Bushey, and that there is a mob gone out to insult him to-day. This, if true, will very much serve the anti-Reformers. Lord Lyndhurst, and no one else, saw the King yesterday. He is not sitting in the Exchequer to-day, having other fish to fry. It is thought the Duke of Wellington and Peel cannot accept office till the Bill is passed. But the vote of the Commons to-night may mar the new arrangements. We had a meeting at Brooks's last night to frame the resolution to be moved to-day by Lord Ebrington. The Tories say Lord Ebrington will not have a majority, but I think they are sure to be greatly outnumbered.

Friday, May 11, 1832.

. . . I know very little, but I had an interview two hours ago with the private secretaries of Lord Althorp and Lord Brougham, who told me that the Duke of Wellington has accepted, and is proceeding to form a Ministry: Leach Chancellor, A. Baring Chancellor of the Exchequer, Lord Tenterden to retire for an earldom, to be succeeded by Lord Lyndhurst. I feel as if some domestic calamity had overwhelmed me. You will see last night's debate in the newspapers.

Saturday, May 12, 1832.

. . . The Duke of Wellington is going on with his insane project. It is said Parliament will be dissolved on Monday. This I still doubt. London remains quiet. There are great apprehensions of risings in the country.

Monday, May 14, 1832.

. . . I hope you will accomplish your visit to London, but you must just wait till you see whether Parliament is to be dissolved, for you might come and find London deserted for the general election. My own opinion is that there will not be a dissolution for the present. We decided that pretty well at Brooks's last night. We had a meeting to determine whether Ebrington should not move a Resolution to-night that 'after the Duke of Wellington's recorded opinion upon the Reform Bill, no administration of which he forms a part can have the confidence of this House or of the country.' There was a great deal of discussion, which terminated in agreeing to abstain, to let the Duke carry through the Bill in the Lords and send it down again to the Commons, and then to accept it, and then to turn out the Duke. It was agreed on all hands that the Resolution would necessarily have brought about an instant dissolution, which would have produced a House of Commons to compel the King to recall the Whigs, but that this would delay and endanger the Reform Bill. Althorp and Stanley spoke exceedingly well, and against the Resolution.

Nothing more known about appointments, except that Croker refuses to accept office as well as Peel, having taken such an active part against the Bill.

Guildhall: Tuesday, May 15, 1832.

. . . I am just returned from Westminster, where I heard, what I expected, that the Duke of Wellington has given up the formation of a new Ministry, and that the King has sent for Lord Grey. The proceedings in the House of Commons last night were decisive, but things are by no means settled with the King. Brougham said in the Lords, in rather a disdainful tone, 'that the communication from the King had had, and might have, no consequence.'

Wednesday, May 16, 1832.

Dear George,—I hope you will not now hesitate to pay your visit to London. Things are not yet adjusted between the King and Lord Grey, but a dissolution is wholly out of the question. Lord Munster declared yesterday that, sooner than create peers, the King, his father, would go to Hanover. He must nevertheless agree to the terms dictated, which I dare say will be severe enough: the Bill to pass without any alteration; and the power to make as many peers as may be necessary for that purpose in case of resistance;—if not further to dismiss Lord Hill and all Tories in office under the Crown.

My own notion is that the great body of the Tories will now secede from the House of Lords, and that the Bill will pass without further opposition. I consider the revolution pretty well effected. From this time the King and the peers can do nothing against the will of the people.

Friday, May 18, 1832.

. . . I am sick of bulletins—not but that it gives me sincere pleasure if I can give you any intelligence or gratification; but I wish excitement were over, and we had again quiet and dull times. The question I believe now is whether Lord Grey shall at all events force the making of peers, or the King can avoid it. The Tories, seeing the Bill must pass, are anxious to prevent the making of a great number of Whig peers who would permanently overwhelm them, and, for this purpose, are willing to secede from the further discussions on the Bill. . . .

House of Commons, six o'clock.—After the prospect of a great explosion all is finally settled. Grey is Minister and Reform is carried. When I came down I found all in a state of alarm. It was understood that the King obstinately held out, and that something frightful would happen. The House was called over on Hume's motion, and Lord Milton was prepared to move another address to the King. But when Lord Milton was ready to get up, the cry came 'It is settled,' and it turned out that Grey had just left the King and that there was a satisfactory arrangement. In a few minutes after, Lord Althorp got up and said that Lord Grey had now a satisfactory assurance that he had the means of carrying the Reform Bill, and that he and his colleagues remained in office. There has since been an explanation from Peel justifying himself for refusing to join the Duke of Wellington.

Lord Milton afterwards showed me his address. What a stormy debate it would have brought on!

[Extract from the Autobiography.]

Lord Grey was reinstated in his office and an intimation

was given on the part of the Duke of Wellington, Lord Lyndhurst, and the great bulk of the peers who had opposed the Bill,
that they would absent themselves from the House in its
subsequent stages, and offer it no further obstruction. The
necessity for making new peers was thus obviated. I think Lord
Grey, under the circumstances, was justified in proposing such
a step, as otherwise some more violent breach of the Constitution would almost inevitably have occurred; but I must confess that a numerous creation of peers to carry a particular
measure against the opinion of the existing House cannot in
my opinion be considered a constitutional proceeding, and
can only be defended as a *coup d'état* to ward off greater
evils.

On the 4th of June the Bill passed the Lords by a majority
of eighty-four, twenty-two peers only voting against it.

The Bills for Ireland and Scotland followed and were
carried without difficulty. In the latter, *ratione originis*, I
took a special interest. I had long felt galled by the state
of political degradation to which my native country had been
reduced. The forty-five members for Scotland were returned
by, and voted for, the Minister of the day like the sixteen
peers, and had regularly changed their allegiance on every
change of administration. Hence the general belief that all
Scotchmen were venal politicians, and hence the popularity
on the stage of such a character as Sir Pertinax Macsycophant.
Sir Robert Peel allowed that the system of ' superiorities' in
Scotch counties, and of self-elected town councils in Scotch
boroughs, could only be excused as a necessary counterbalance to the excess of popular election prevailing in England. I was therefore delighted to assist Jeffrey, the Lord
Advocate, in framing the Scotch Reform Bill, and in doing
everything in my power to further its progress through the
House.

During this session I again introduced my Bill for
a General Register of Deeds. It was referred to a Select
Committee, which I attended most laboriously. I made converts of almost all the members of the committee, but I was
defeated by a combination of the country attorneys, who
thought, erroneously, that the measure would diminish their

business and their profits. They are the most influential class in the country. Lord Grey was against the measure because his attorney in Northumberland told him it was a bad thing. The country attorneys have the borough seats very much at their disposal, and they frighten more members by their threats than they influence by their arguments.

Sunday, June 17, 1832.

Dear George,—I was delighted to hear of your happy meeting with your wife and children at Edenwood, and that you were pleased with your visit to London.[5]

I have been so much hurried that I literally have not had time to write you a scrap. This evening I start for Birmingham, and to-morrow morning I enter Dudley, a new borough in Schedule D, from which I have had an invitation. The thing looks exceedingly well at present. There is no other candidate in the field except a Tory who has no chance. . . .

Birmingham : Monday night, June 18, 1832.

Dear George,—We have had a glorious day at Dudley, and I really think the thing is certain. Sir Horace St. Paul, the Tory candidate, has not the remotest chance, and no other reforming candidate is now likely to offer. What a contrast to Stafford! Our procession was one of the most magnificent spectacles ever beheld. There were in it about twenty large banners with inscriptions, and there were flags in almost every window in the town. A great many came here to meet me, and in Dudley the multitude was said to exceed 10,000. Instead of treating them, they treated me. I was not allowed to put my hand in my pocket from the time I started from Birmingham till I returned. What struck me most was the extreme moderation of the party, although they are called *Radicals*. They received with perfect approbation the exposition of my genuine political sentiments.

I am to sleep here to-night and set off early in the morning for London.

---

[5] His brother, who had lately received the honour of knighthood, had been staying in London, and the correspondence had been interrupted during part of the months of May and June.—ED.

Thursday, July 5, 1832.

. . . The dullness of the times must excuse the brevity of my epistles. There is here the languor of exhaustion. The House of Commons is empty, and politics seem forgotten. I cannot get Lord Althorp and Lord John to bring on the Bribery Bill for a second reading, and I shall be gone on the circuit before it is discussed. This is the only subject about which I now much care.

Mary is going the circuit with me.[6] We are to have a trial for high treason on our circuit at Abingdon, after finishing at Gloucester, but this cannot last more than a single day. The accused is the person who threw a stone at the King at Ascot. I have then only to attend to the registration of the Dudley electors, at which I must be present—then for Scotland.

Worcester: July 25, 1832.

. . . We talk of nothing here but the cholera. Thank Heaven, the assizes are over, and I am yet safe, with my wife and babe. Mary and Hally are at a gentleman's house about two miles off in a pure delightful air. We contrived to get through the business last night and I joined them. The courts had rather a melancholy aspect, no woman or man admitted unless on business, with chloride of lime sprinkled every half-hour. There are a good many new cases here, but it has not been as yet so bad as at Gloucester. One doctor ran away and has covered himself with disgrace.

Stafford is said to be very healthy. Mary is to be at Ingestre (Lord Talbot's), about five miles off. We are going on an excursion to Eastnor, Lord Somers's. In spite of the cholera I never enjoyed life more.

Gloucester: Wednesday, August 15, 1832.

Dear George,—We remain all quite well, but the matter becomes rather serious, and I have despatched Mary and Hally to Stroud, nine miles off. There were last night five deaths, three close by the lodgings where I now write to you, and there are a great number of new cases to-day from the heat

_ His last circuit.—ED.

and moisture. Had it not been for the extreme slowness of the judge, we should have finished yesterday, and I now very much doubt whether we shall finish to-morrow.

The city presents rather a dismal scene, but our corps preserve their *gaieté de cœur*, and I make no doubt that we shall all escape. My clerk was the only craven. When he came into Gloucester he laid himself on two chairs and gave himself up; so I was obliged to send him off to London yesterday. In court we are almost overpowered by fumigations and aspersions. Most men have bottles or charms of different sorts about them. A druggist has made a little fortune by selling what he denominates 'disinfectors.' The walls of the houses are covered with placards advertising remedies, giving cautions, and offering religious advice to the inhabitants.

Clifton: August 20, 1832.

. . . We are again in the midst of the cholera. It has been raging tremendously at Bristol and has come over to Clifton, although it has not yet mounted the down or table-land above the Avon. It has been much worse both here and at Gloucester than the returns published by the Privy Council represent, as the local authorities for the sake of the place, and the Government for the sake of the country, take care that only a part of the truth is told. The most remarkable circumstance I hear of at Bristol is that the people hate the doctors who are labouring for them, and believe that the sick are poisoned and buried alive.

We leave this at six o'clock to-morrow morning, breakfast at Bath, and then push on for Abingdon.

We had a very nice drive from Stroud to Dursley, through the clothing valleys, which are exceedingly picturesque and interesting. We then visited Berkeley Castle, and saw the very identical room in which Edward II. was murdered. The sword which is shown as the instrument is apocryphal, but the room and the whole castle certainly remain as they were five hundred years ago. It is the only baronial castle in England which remains entire and is still inhabited.

Abingdon: August 22, 1832.

. . . I was wrong in saying that none of our corps had been frightened. Charles Phillips the orator (who has fought a duel), finding the state in which Gloucester was on Saturday week, left his briefs and fled from it. . While I was in Bath yesterday, Serjeant —— passed through from Wells for London, being afraid to go to attend the assizes at Bristol, giving up his briefs to his clients. This I consider very pusillanimous and culpable. Where a man's duty requires him to be, there the cholera is to be disregarded.

Our trial for high treason is over and has terminated, as might be expected, in a conviction, but without any notion of an execution.

We are going on to-night to Reading, and to-morrow to Erlwood, near Bagshot, where Loo and little Mary still are. I know not what we shall do during the autumn, but I really consider our visit to you at an end till next year, when I trust we may accomplish it under happier auspices.

Brooks's: September 17, 1832.

. . . No public news. Strong attempts by the Radicals to make Ministers and the Whigs unpopular from the alleged defects in the Reform Bill. We shall now be the Conservative party. The *movement* must be resisted. Think of poor Denman being received at Nottingham very much as Sir Charles Wetherell was at Bristol. I expect to go down to Dudley in a few days. The cholera has been raging dreadfully in that country, but it is rather subsiding, and my presence now is reckoned material. Had it not been for this I should now have been at Brighton, where it is at last determined we are to taste the sea breezes.

Hagley: September 26, 1832.

Dear George,—They have a fast day at Dudley for the cholera. This has interrupted the canvass. Here I am about six miles off for pure air and quiet. I came over last night and return this evening. . . .

The canvass has gone on satisfactorily. There is considerable languor, but the electors seem to remain true. I do not think there is now any danger of an ultra-Radical candidate. The struggle will be with the Tories, who are to try to bring in Sir Horace St. Paul, now member for Bridport, an anti-Reformer, who has large property in the parish. His party have been very active the two last days. They have all Lord Dudley's interest. The peer himself, you know, is under restraint, but his managing agent is giving notices to quit, turning off workmen, and resorting to other violent measures to intimidate the Liberal voters. It is a curious fact that if the franchise had been lower we should have been beaten ; but the ten-pounders are chiefly shopkeepers and independent tradesmen, and set all threats at defiance.

I expect to finish the canvass on Friday, and get back to London on Saturday.

Brooks's : Thursday, November 1, 1832.

Dear George,—I do not know whether you care about the result of the Bristol case.[7] The defendant is gloriously acquitted. Nothing endangered us except Scarlett's Conservative peroration, which I could not induce him to omit. The rest of his speech was most admirable.

Lord Tenterden continues as ill as can be, and I do not believe that he will live three weeks. People hail me as Mr. Solicitor, but I have not the slightest reason to expect promotion. It has just been stated to me by a man who pretends to know, that Wilde has no chance, but that there are two others besides myself under consultation.

I am only anxious about Dudley. The Tories are making tremendous efforts, and although my friends are very honest, I do not rely much upon their conduct.

Birmingham . Sunday, November 4, 1832.

. . . I am on my way to Dudley to be present to-morrow at the revision of the list. The last news I heard before I left London was that Lord Tenterden was dead. Everything will be settled before my return. I must a little regret my absence, though I could do nothing were I on the spot but listen to reports.

[7] Trial at bar of the Mayor of Bristol for neglect of duty during the Reform riots, when a great part of the city was burnt down.—ED.

Court of King's Bench : Tuesday, November 6, 1832.

. . . Denman has had notice that he will be recommended to the King as Chief Justice. Nothing is published as to Solicitor-General, but I hear the report that John Williams is to be the man; I have heard nothing more from any other quarter.

I had a successful trip to Dudley, and was very cordially received. I harangued them assembled in the market-place, and they insisted on taking my horses from my carriage and dragged me nearly a mile out of town, where we parted, agreeing to meet at the same spot when Parliament is dissolved.

[Secret and confidential.] New Street : Thursday, November 8, 1832.

Dear George,—I have had an interview with Brougham, and all is right. I cannot, even with you, enter into details, which it was stated to me are known only to Brougham himself, Grey, Althorp, Holland and Denman. Thus much I must be justified in saying, though not to be mentioned to anyone, that I am to be Solicitor-General. Knowing the lively interest you take in all that concerns me, I should have acted wrong if I had kept you longer in suspense. This was indeed the crisis of my fate.

King's Bench : Monday, November 19, 1832.

Dear George.—Nothing is yet finally fixed, but, under injunction to secrecy, I may mention to you that the object of Government was to provide for Horne, to make me Attorney-General, and a Chancery man Solicitor-General. This cannot be done for the present. A tiresome negotiation has been going on for Bayley to resign. After a great deal of vacillation he has sent me his definitive answer this morning, that he will resign in February and not sooner. I conceive therefore that Horne will now be Attorney-General, and I presume your humble servant Solicitor-General. I have just left Brougham, who is a good deal annoyed about it, but nothing more can be done. I have had a disagreeable negotiation and I am glad to wash my hands of it, whatever may be the result.

I wish this Belgic question were well settled. I know not how our Government could have acted differently; but, as happens to governments and individuals with hardly any blame, they are in a bad scrape. The Tories do not disguise their wish that the citadel of Antwerp may hold out till the three absolute powers take part with Holland, that the French fleet may be burnt, and the English dispersed. There cannot be a better test of political sentiment at present than the question how long can the citadel of Antwerp hold out.— A Whig says, 'ten days at furthest;' a Conservative, ' it is impregnable.'

King's Bench: November 23, 1832.

Dear George,—By the time this reaches you Margaret will be sister-in-law to her Majesty's Solicitor-General. I have had an interview with Brougham to-day and everything is settled. Horne *pro tempore* Attorney-General, with an understanding that he is to become a judge, and that in the meantime I am to conduct all government prosecutions in the King's Bench, and to be consulted separately when necessary. The appointments are gone down to Brighton to-day, and I suppose I shall be sworn in on Monday. I feel a good deal excited, but I shall bear my faculties very meekly.

Yours most affectionately,

J. C.

Brooks's: Sunday, November 25, 1832.

Dear George,—I had my interview yesterday between one and two with Gaffer Grey. He made only one condition with me, that I should not bring in the Register Bill as it might make Government unpopular. I told him I had arranged that William Brougham should bring it in and I should support it. The Gaffer was even afraid that one so nearly connected with Government as William Brougham should bring it in, declaring himself personally hostile to it. I soon refuted the argument he used, but the truth is he knows nothing about the matter.

I called to-day voluntarily on Althorp, who saw me and was exceedingly cordial. I know from a good source that he stuck out for me very strenuously. He told me, what I before knew, that he is to communicate directly and exclusively with me, without regard to Mr. Attorney.

Nothing is wanting now but that the Belgic question were settled and the elections well over. Both are very awkward subjects. If there be a protracted siege of the citadel of Antwerp, there will be a great outcry against Government. Then I am desperately afraid there will be a number of official men thrown out. The Conservatives very confidently assert that I shall be among the number. But I know they have told several specific lies about the Dudley election, and I pay the less attention to their boasting, although I cannot but feel a good deal of anxiety upon the subject.

Parliament is to be dissolved on Monday the 3rd.

King's Bench: Tuesday, November 27, 1832.

Dear George,—I am now fully installed in office. I was sworn in yesterday, ' and took my place accordingly.' . . .

The King does not come to town till Monday. Loo amuses herself by going through the ceremony of knighthood. She, as Sovereign, makes Hally get down on one knee, she then touches his shoulder with a pen, and says, ' Rise, Sir Hallyburton,' on which he immediately springs up and makes his obeisance.

There is nothing new in politics. That ugly General Chasse still haunts us. I expect to hear in a few hours that Antwerp is in ashes. The question, it is said, was referred to our Government whether the French troops should enter the city or not, and all the responsibility will be cast upon us. However I think it was wise to do everything to bring the matter to a speedy conclusion *coûte que coûte*.

. . . Assuming only common prudence, I believe Grey's Government may go on. Most moderate and sensible men see that this affords the best chance of preserving the monarchy. No new-born zeal on my part, for I have often said that I thought it exceedingly desirable for the public tranquillity that the Whigs should remain in office a few years after the passing of the Reform Bill.

Dudley: December 5, 1832.

Dear George,—I intended to have written you a few lines in answer to your exceedingly kind and gratifying letter of November 30 before I left town on Monday; but I was detained at St. James's till past six, and at seven I was in my post-chaise. Brougham took me with him at two, in the expectation of having my business done before the Council; but this could not be contrived, and I was obliged to wait till it broke up, after considering the recorder's report. I had an opportunity of seeing the Ministers, who were all very kind and cordial. The Gaffer condescended to quiz me a little about my knighthood. His Majesty asked me divers questions, among others, whether I was not married to a daughter of Sir James Scarlett.

I made my entrance here yesterday at twelve o'clock. We had a very grand procession, and there were, besides all the flags in the procession, 111 large ones hung out from houses in the streets. There seems a good spirit among my friends, but still there will be a very arduous struggle, and I cannot regard it without considerable anxiety. There are 670 votes registered. My committee say there are 340 on whom they can positively depend, that St. Paul has not more than from 170 to 200, and that the rest are doubtful. The committee are very sincere, I believe, but they may be deceived, and this is not quite a satisfactory state of things. According to the usual rule of electioneering, you ought (that you may be secure) to be able to give all the doubtful to your antagonist, and to have still a clear majority. Luckily we have no bother about pledges, and no division of the Liberal interest.

I am established as the guest of a great grocer in the town, my principal supporter. I shall have a very disagreeable time of it till the election is over, but I shall soon forget all this if I am returned.

Hustings, Dudley: December 11, 1832.
Tuesday, three o'clock.

Dear George,—This is the first moment I could have written you anything at all satisfactory about the election.

I can safely say *we have won!* There is a majority of about 100 for Campbell, and there are not so many votes remaining unpolled. So St. Paul's success is not upon the cards. I presume he will resign this evening. At all events, after the most intense anxiety, I now consider myself quite safe. The Tories continued most confident in their assertions to the last, and spread reports in London which very much alarmed my friends. Every promise has been performed, and I must say there has been a great display of public virtue.

When I am back in New Street I shall enjoy my good luck. I have had time enough to read more than once your very kind letter, which I received on the hustings this morning. I must conclude.   Thine,

J. C.

Court of King's Bench:
Thursday, December 13, 1832.

. . . My letter from the hustings on Tuesday would set your mind quite at rest. Soon after I had despatched it Sir Horace St. Paul gave up the contest, but we could not get through the necessary forms to have the returns proclaimed till yesterday at twelve. The triumphal procession then began and was not over till dark. You can hardly imagine to yourself the exultation of the whole mass of the inhabitants, and it was truly a glorious victory.

I got off about seven in the evening, and reached New Street between eleven and twelve this morning. Mary's happiness was perfect, for her father has very unexpectedly succeeded at Norwich. This circumstance gives me great pleasure.

The elections have gone most prosperously. I rejoice exceedingly that the Reform Bill has worked so well. I was very uneasy about the metropolitan districts, but they have sent excellent men, and fully justified my anticipations when this part of the Act was under discussion in Parliament.

What a deliverance from Stafford! There has been more bribery there than ever, and the new part of the constituency is worse than the old.

Temple : Wednesday, December 19, 1832.

Dear George,—You shall have my first frank as member for Dudley. This is, indeed, a very prosperous time for me. The elections have taken a turn which renders Ministers quite secure. When I was sworn in Solicitor-General, we debated what I should do if there should be a change of government before the circuit. Things then looked very gloomy. The Radicals were getting ahead, and it seemed very doubtful whether the Bill might not end in the disgrace of its authors. The result, however, has been most glorious. The machinery has worked beyond our most sanguine hopes, and almost universally the very men have been returned that would have been wished for. Not one official man has been ousted in England, although the Tories asserted that hardly one would get in. My poor brother Solicitor-General in Ireland is thrown out for the University of Dublin, and this is the only discomfiture of Government. The Tories as a party are annihilated, and the Radicals repressed. Against such a House of Commons neither King nor Peers can resist improvement, or try to restore ancient abuses.

My friends at Dudley behaved most nobly. I never was deceived in any representation made to me. No promise was broken. There was no drunkenness, no bribery. I was a little afraid of what might be attempted in this way ; but I was told, and I believe told truly, that St. Paul could not buy five votes in the borough, for that any man suspected of taking money would be infamous.

I ought to mention to you that there were twenty-five Scotchmen ten-pounders who voted for me. How extraordinary ! There is no reason why there should be Scots at Dudley more than any other town in England. They are all shopkeepers and little traders, exceedingly decent and respectable men, and my warm friends. I was supported by every countryman in the place. Did you read in the Tory papers an account of his Majesty's Solicitor-General having kissed the cap of Liberty, presented to him on the end of a pole in the streets of Dudley ? Hilyard, a Conservative counsel sent down against me, said if the Government had any firmness they would dismiss me for this outrage. It was a blue cap, much more like an imperial crown, a gift from the ladies of Dudley, which Hally now wears on his head crying out, 'Campbell for ever! No Paul! No tripe!' This last cry was very effective during the election, and arose from an attempt of the Paulites to bribe my voters by tripe suppers.

Brooks's: Christmas Day, 1832.

Dear George,—We are in great spirits here upon the surrender of the citadel of Antwerp. The news was first brought us by Lord John Russell, who had just read the Government despatches. Lillo and Liefkenshoek I presume will be ceded immediately, and the Belgic question finally settled. The Conservatives will hang themselves; for this was their last hope.

Thus we have a merry Christmas, and I hope we shall have a happy New Year—*multos et felices*.

Brooks's: Saturday, December 29, 1832.

. . . I have had a prosperous trip to Dudley. I went to Birmingham by the mail on Wednesday night, went over to Dudley after breakfast on Thursday, had a grand dinner, at which, considering that we are the *rabble*, we made a tolerably respectable figure. Yesterday morning I gave audience to all Dudley people, electors or non-electors, who wished to consult me—like a Roman patrician among his clients. You would have been amused to see how I was required to get people large estates and great sums of money—they not knowing how they were connected with the property, and only having heard that they were entitled to it. I was expected, first, to tell what the will was, and then to interpret it. I made my escape between two and three. At Birmingham an early dinner party was made for me to meet the new members, Attwood and Scholefield. I have conversed with these heroes several times before in passing through Birmingham. They are both mighty good-natured, and I believe very well-meaning men. I was obliged to leave the company soon after seven. I came up

by a night coach and breakfasted in New Street. The
children are greatly delighted to see me, and a beautiful
glass cup presented to me by a patriotic glass manufacturer
at Dudley.

I have since been answering government cases, and now
I am going out with Mary to a dinner party. I cannot
complain that at present life stagnates.

CHAPTER XX.

JANUARY 1833—NOVEMBER 1834.

The Irish Coercion Bill—Lord Stanley—Manners Sutton re-elected
Speaker—Mr. Pease, the Quaker—Bills for the Amendment of the
Law—Stafford Disfranchisement Bill—Business at the Bar—Dinner
at Kensington Palace—Stay at Walmer—Tour in Ireland—Marquess
Wellesley—Appointed Attorney-General—Defeated at Dudley—Out
of Parliament for Three Months—Elected M.P. for Edinburgh—Resig-
nation of four Members of the Cabinet—Lord Melbourne succeeds
Lord Grey—Autumn in Scotland—The Grey Festival—Pepys succeeds
Leach as Master of the Rolls—Rolfe the new Solicitor-General—
Burning of the Houses of Parliament.

CHAP.
XX.

A.D. 1833.

[FROM the time of my father's appointment as Solicitor-
General, he had little leisure to devote to correspondence.
His letters to his brother, though not less frequent, are
more hurried and fragmentary. To passing events he
merely alludes, as he assumes his correspondent to be acquainted with them from reading the daily papers. On the
other hand, the Memoir, written in 1842, has now reached a
period within ten years of the time of writing, and the
history of those ten years was accordingly still fresh in
his memory. I have therefore availed myself chiefly of the
Autobiography for the narrative of these years, introducing
letters occasionally when they give an account of matters
which he does not mention in the Memoir. —ED.]

Autobiography.

My foot was now in the stirrup, but still I was in
frequent apprehension of being thrown by unlucky chances
and the imprudence of others. My confidence was soon
shaken in the wisdom and discretion of my new masters, and
I doubted the stability of their power, notwithstanding the

immense majority of Liberal members returned to the House of Commons.

My first 'confidential communication from the Government was a printed copy of the draft of the Irish Coercion Bill. I read it with amazement and grief. It was then still more arbitrary than when introduced into the House of Commons, several very obnoxious clauses having been omitted, or qualified, on my earnest remonstrances to Lord Grey. The Bill no doubt was the measure of Stanley, the Irish Secretary, and very much in accordance with his rashness, wilfulness and determined spirit; but I am now quite at a loss to understand how all the rest of the Cabinet were induced to concur in it. They had not the experience which we have since happily obtained of the good effect upon Ireland of a kind, liberal and confiding government; but that it should have been defended by those who had so often reprobated and moved for the repeal of Lord Castlereagh's *Six Acts* only shows how differently men feel on the same subjects in different situations. They ought to have been alarmed likewise by the apprehension of suddenly turning the tide of popular opinion against themselves, although now they were probably tranquillised by recollecting how essentially Ireland is hated by the English nation, and what a lenient view is taken here of any measure which tends to degrade the mass of the Irish population. For my own part I could only remonstrate and try to mitigate. The Bill, being an isolated measure, was no sufficient reason for my leaving a Government whose Tory opponents most zealously supported it, a Government whose general policy I admired, a Government about to abolish slavery, about to open the Indian trade, about to reform municipal corporations in the three portions of the United Kingdom. I can safely aver that, both before this famous Coercion Bill was introduced and while it was passing through Parliament, I laboured, and in various instances successfully, to mitigate its severity.

I was now acting Attorney-General for Ireland. Blackburne, who filled the office of Attorney-General, would never consent to leave his practice in the Four Courts in order to serve in the House of Commons. Crampton, the Solicitor, had been rejected by the University of Dublin, and there was a difficulty in finding another seat for him. No confidence was reposed in Horne, my colleague. He was never consulted on any measure depending, he was not invited to take part in any debate, and he was seldom in the House except when his attendance was required by the Secretary of the Treasury upon a division.

I then saw a great deal of Stanley, the Irish Secretary, and I can bear my testimony not only to his being quick and vigorous in business, but very courteous and agreeable. If he said sharp things, he was willing to be paid back on a footing of perfect equality. Although afterwards very obnoxious to him when he had gone into opposition and the Church Rates question came up, during this session of Parliament I was a great favourite of his, and, when there was a vacancy on the bench, he declared 'they might make judges whom they pleased so that they left him Campbell.' I was rather at a loss to account for his extreme unpopularity in Ireland, till I saw the excessive *brusquerie* of his manner with strangers, and his carelessness about the opinion of others.

The session of 1833 began with the re-election of Manners Sutton as Speaker, a step said to have been resorted to from the difficulty of reconciling the conflicting claims of two members of the Reform party to the chair (Littleton and Spring Rice); but it was a most inauspicious start for the Reformed House of Commons. The old Speaker had not only been the nominee of the Tories, but was known to all who had narrowly observed him to be, in the chair, an unfair enemy of the Liberals, calling upon those of his own party who, he thought, would serve it, and when he had to go to the other side, liking to select such men as Feargus O'Connor, who he knew would disgrace it. Besides, though he had the reputation of being an excellent Speaker, as every Speaker has for the last forty years,[1] he had nothing

---

[1] I have heard Lord Holland say:—'It must require very little talent to make a good Speaker, for every Speaker in my time has been pronounced a good Speaker; unless one—and he was the only man of talent who has been Speaker in my time—Lord Grenville.'

to recommend him except good humour and gentlemanlike manners, for he had no acuteness of intellect, and he was utterly deficient in constitutional law. While he filled the chair he was talked of for Prime Minister; but as soon as he was ejected from it he fell into perfect insignificance.

My first display as Solicitor-General was on the question whether Mr. Pease the Quaker might be permitted to sit on making an affirmation at the table, without taking an oath. I maintained that upon the just construction of the statutes he might, and the House followed my advice, for which I was much applauded in the newspapers. But my popularity was soon dimmed by the arrival of the Irish Coercion Bill from the Lords, where it had passed almost unanimously. I thought it was gone on the first reading—it was so very inefficiently opened by Lord Althorp, who seemed heartily ashamed of it; but Stanley came to the rescue and showed such nerve, such knowledge, such tact, and such eloquence, that he brought round the House to the opinion that it was necessary, mild and humane. I avoided speaking on the principle of the Bill; but when it came into Committee the labouring oar fell upon me, and I had many tussles with O'Connell, who denounced me as a tool of the 'base and bloody Whigs.'

Early this session I reintroduced my Bills for abolishing 'fines and recoveries,' for allowing brothers and sisters of the half blood to succeed one another, for regulating the law of dower, and for fixing at twenty years the period of possession which shall give a right to real property. They quietly passed through both Houses of Parliament without one single syllable being altered in any of them. This is the only wise way of legislating on such a subject. They had been drawn by the Real Property Commissioners, printed and extensively circulated, and repeatedly revised, with the advantage of the observations of skilful men studying them in their closet. A mixed and numerous deliberative assembly is wholly unfit for such work.

Later in the session I brought in a Bill for enabling creditors to obtain satisfaction from the property of their debtors, and to abolish imprisonment for debt except in cases of fraud. Absurd as it may seem, by the then existing law, neither land, nor gold, nor bank-notes could be taken in execution and applied to satisfy a debt established by the judgment of a court; while without the judgment of a court or the warrant of a magistrate, any man might throw any other man into prison by merely swearing to a debt of 10*l*. The simple statement of such abuses bespoke favour with the judicious for a measure to correct them; but a tremendous clamour was raised against the Bill by tradesmen accustomed to defraud young heirs, and by unprincipled money-lenders, countenanced by some well-meaning people who think that nothing, however oppressive or absurd, can be bad if it has existed while the nation has been thriving; and the Bill met with so much opposition that I was obliged to let it drop.

The only stipulation made with me by Lord Grey when I was appointed Solicitor-General, was that I should not, while a law officer of the Crown, again bring forward the General Registration Bill, lest it might be supposed that the Government supported a measure which he and his solicitor disliked, and which was so odious to a large and powerful class in the community. I acquiesced the more readily as the measure never can be carried without the strenuous support of a strong administration. William Brougham with my concurrence moved for leave to reintroduce the Bill. I seconded his motion, but after it had been once read he abandoned it in despair, and it still waits a more auspicious time.[2]

Much discussion took place during the session on a subject from which I studiously kept aloof,—the Stafford Disfranchisement Bill. It was charged that at the first election under the Reform Act there had been grosser corruption than was ever known in the borough before,

---

[2] *September* 27, 1857.—I thought that auspicious time had arrived in the session of 1851, when, the measure being recommended in the Queen's Speech, I brought it in as the organ of the Government, and carried it triumphantly through the House of Lords; but although Lord J. Russell professed and felt a great desire that it should pass, it was dropped from the paralysis which then seized him and his colleagues. Since then there has been no Government strong enough to deal with the measure.

the ten-pound householders as well as the old freemen, instead of decently waiting for the distribution of voting money, openly putting up their votes for sale to the highest bidder, and the matter was referred to a Select Committee. The object of a preliminary Bill was to indemnify the witnesses who should give evidence accusing themselves. A frightful case was made out, and in several successive sessions Bills were brought in, and passed the Commons, entirely to disfranchise the borough. But the measure met with no favour from Lord Brougham and the Lords, and the borough continues in possession of its franchise, the electors doubtless insisting more strenuously than ever that their ' roits ' shall be respected. Under one of the ancillary Indemnity Acts, Gisborne, my old colleague, was examined as a witness, and ' made a clean breast.' I was strongly advised to follow his example, lest some malicious person should institute an action or indictment against me for bribery; but I preferred running the risk, as it was not very serious, and, although it was well understood that no one for a hundred years had represented Stafford on principles of perfect purity, certain mischief would have arisen from a law officer of the Crown himself openly admitting an infraction of the law.

My business at the bar was now nearly equal to that of Scarlett, and much greater than that of any other man in court. I was generally opposed to him, and, considering the relation in which we stood to each other, there were sometimes rather unpleasant collisions between us. I of course thought that I behaved with great moderation and forbearance, and that the fault was his in expecting that at the expense of my client I should defer to him as in private life. Unfortunately he had now gone over most zealously and bitterly to the Tories. This arose partly from bad luck, by which he gradually and imperceptibly drifted into a false position, and partly from the treachery of Brougham, who when the Whigs took office in 1830 was commissioned by Lord Grey to conciliate Scarlett, and hold out to him the prospect of being made Chief Justice of the King's Bench, but who withheld the communication and forced him from the Liberal side, with the feeling rankling in his breast of having been betrayed and cast off by the party he had long zealously supported.

I had about this time the disagreeable task of conducting the trial of a criminal information filed in the name of Horne, the Attorney-General, against a newspaper for calling on the people to refuse the payment of taxes, and to rise in insurrection against the government because the Reform Bill was so imperfect, and universal suffrage, annual parliaments and the ballot were withheld from the people. I was reminded by the counsel for the defendant of a sentiment uttered by Lord Milton during the fervour of the Reform Bill, that 'when the wishes of the people were disregarded by a wicked government, resistance was no rebellion,' and of a speech said to have been made by William Brougham, the Chancellor's brother, during the crisis in May 1832, to a tax-gatherer who called with 'a little bill' for assessed taxes: 'Walk away, Sir, till our *little Bill* is passed; and when our *little Bill* is passed, I will pay yours.' Why were not these cases prosecuted? I was obliged to rely on the difference between intemperate expressions spoken without premeditation and immediately repented of, and a systematic purpose to excite insurrection and bring about a change in the government by physical force. After some hard blows on myself and my employers I obtained a conviction, and the defendant was sentenced to imprisonment, which he richly deserved, whatever fate ought to have befallen the over-violent friends of the Reform Bill.

Letters to Sir George Campbell in the year 1833.

Court of King's Bench: February 2, 1833.

. . . I give a grand dinner to-day to the Oxford circuit, who rejoice most sincerely in my promotion, but not more so than they did in the report that I had been killed by a fall from my horse at Gloucester. I have got a Court suit for my dinner at Lord Althorp's on Monday.

February 5, 1833.

. . . Althorp's dinner went off very pleasantly. The Speech, which I entirely approve of, was read before dinner.

I wish there had been something in it about taking off taxes.
I introduced myself to Lord Ormelie.[3] He talked very touch-
ingly of his father's regard for ours. I fear the Marquess
will never take his seat on the Marquesses' bench. It seems
he has been extremely infirm for the last two years.

New Street: Sunday night, February 10, 1833.

. . . I have worked to-day above thirteen hours, but the
quiet of my library has rather restored me after the bustling
fatigues of the week. To struggle against Sir James Scarlett
all the morning and sit in the House of Commons all night,
is not an easy life.

March 1, 1833.

. . . I look forward to the termination of the sittings
as the commencement of great enjoyment, but I am in sad
trouble. This Irish Coercion Bill places me in a most distressing situation. My constituents are all in a flame, and I
have petitions to present against it signed by thousands. I
shall not be at all surprised if it prove the ruin of the whole
party. Loss of office I should care little about if we fell with
dignity, but it is rather disgraceful to be turned out for
grasping at arbitrary power.

I have been leading a horrid life for the last ten days. I
have not sat down to dinner more than twice, and this morning
at two I went to bed having tasted nothing since breakfast
but a few gingerbread nuts.

March 23, 1833.

. . . Thank God we have at last got the Irish Bill through
the Committee. I shall have a little trouble upon the Report, and then my cares will be over. The only benefit it has
done me is to accustom me a little to beat the red box on the
table opposite the Treasury Bench. When I first spoke as a
man in office I was embarrassed by my novel situation in the
House, and, as in former times, my mouth suddenly became
parched; but in my late contests with O'Connell I was as
much at home as wrangling in the King's Bench. He and I

---

[3] Son of John, fourth Earl of Breadalbane, who was raised to the
Marquisate of Breadalbane and Earldom of Ormelie in 1831, and died in
1834.—ED.

are great friends now. Last night he acted the *bon enfant* and tried to be amiable both publicly and privately. He is a very extraordinary fellow and certainly has vast powers and resources. I told him some time ago by way of a *reductio ad absurdum,* that he could not have his Parliament in College Green unless he were to agree that it should be subordinate to our Parliament at St. Stephen's, like the House of Assembly at Jamaica. He now says he has been working upon that idea, and he thinks they may agree not to change the succession to the Crown, or meddle with questions of peace or war, &c. But this will not take us in, for no sooner would he have his domestic legislation than he would declare it independent and supreme.

What I have seen of Stanley in these matters has raised him in my opinion. He is most exceedingly acute and of vigorous understanding and flowing eloquence, and, notwithstanding an abrupt, careless manner, I think he is unaffected and good-natured.

March 29, 1833.

. . . I am amused by what you say of dialect. If England and Scotland go on together under the same government for a thousand years, there will be a marked difference between the dialects of the two countries,—even among well educated men; but unless in peculiar situations the Doric is hardly any disadvantage. We have a very barbarous pronunciation from most of the representatives of the new boroughs, who talk of the ' ustings ' and the ' ouse ' &c. This is vulgar, and denotes want of education, and bad company. Not so the national brogue, Irish or Scotch.

The King said to the Duchess of Gloucester the day after the last Drawing-room, ' What a pretty woman Lady Campbell is ! ' I am quite jealous !

May 27, 1833.

. . . I have got my own five Bills through the House. I was obliged to watch for opportunities to forward them between twelve at night and three in the morning.

The Stafford business has annoyed me a little. Till settled, I am prevented from taking any part in the Bribery debates.

We have filed an *ex officio* against the 'True Sun' (O'Connell's and Cobbett's paper) for exhorting the people not to pay taxes and preaching up passive resistance. I am responsible for this prosecution, and I never shall regret it whatever may be the event.

Amidst these pains my public pleasures are going to Lady Lansdowne's and Lady Grey's parties, and dining with the Duchess of Kent.

June 4, 1833.

. . . The dinner at Kensington went off very well. The Duchess was very civil to me and reminded me of our *séjour* at Broadstairs when we were neighbours. I merely made my bow to little Princess Victoria. She is short for her age, but seems in good health and looks lively and good-humoured. She is very graceful in her manners. She appeared in the drawing-room before dinner, and we found her there when we returned. She soon afterwards took leave of the company very graciously and retired. There were thirty-four at table, ladies and gentlemen. I was lowest in rank and sat next Sir John Conroy. He says the Duchess is decidedly Liberal, although she does not mix in party politics. The little girl by accident about two years ago became acquainted with her destinies. Those about her are loud in her praise. Her life is very valuable, for if the Duke of Cumberland were next heir a revolution would be inevitable.

June 5, 1833.

. . . I suppose you have often seen Lady Ormelie.[4] I met her for the first time at the Duchess of Kent's and struck up a great friendship with her. Were not my heart fortified against any such impressions, I should have fallen in love with her. She is one of the most beautiful and graceful creatures I ever beheld, and a great credit to our country.

As I have heard you say you like to see a trait of vanity in me, I must inform you that the Attorney-General is not invited to Kensington, and that my introduction to the Princess was personal and not official.

[4] Eliza, daughter of George Baillie, Esq., of Jerviswood ; married A.D. 1821, died A.D. 1861.—ED.

June 8, 1833.

. . . We had a splendid dinner yesterday at Lansdowne House—the Premier, several Cabinet Ministers and a blaze of fashionable beauty, to meet his Royal Highness (the Duke of Sussex). I said to him, ' Sir, we heard your Royal Highness bestow a hearty imprecation on the bishops in the House of Lords on Monday, to which we said Amen.' ' Ay,' said he ; ' flesh and blood could not stand it.' [5]

June 14, 1833.

. . . The divine creature I saw at Lansdowne House, and who completely effaced Lady Ormelie, was Lady Stafford, lately Lady Gower, a most exquisite production of nature.[6]

New Street : August 11, 1833.

. . . You may be surprised that I am now here. I had prepared everything to start for Walmer yesterday at seven. But the preceding night between one and two Lord Althorp said he should bring on the Bank Charter at twelve. I told him how I was circumstanced, and that I could not attend. He said he could not go on without me, and proposed to the House to put off the Bill till Monday. This they would not agree to, as many members were remaining in town on purpose. Althorp offered to send down a King's messenger to explain my detention to Lady Campbell. I wrote my letter and he despatched it. We got through the Bill and I dined with him.

. . . On Friday night I caused a prodigious laugh at Hume's expense. He put a question to me as Solicitor-General that had nothing to do with the matter in hand. I remaining silent, he reiterated his question very peremptorily. I rose and said, ' If the hon. member for Middlesex would call at my chambers to-morrow and fix a consultation with *proper instructions*, I would look into my books and answer the

[5] ' On the question (Irish Church Reform Bill) being put, all the bishops except one marched below the bar. Somebody observed to the Duke of Sussex, " Look at the bishops," when he exclaimed in a voice to be heard by fifty persons, " G— eternally d— them " '—Extract from a previous letter.

[6] Harriet, daughter of sixth Earl of Carlisle ; married second Duke of Sutherland ; died A.D. 1868.

question to the best of my ability.' This was well understood as an insinuation that Joseph wished *economically* to filch an opinion out of me without a fee, and from the unexpectedness of the turn it told amazingly. ' John Bull ' to-day perverts the story and converts it into a proof of my being surly and sordid.

Brooks's: Saturday, August 24, 1833.

. . . I am on the wing for Walmer. The House has adjourned till Tuesday, and the session may be considered at an end. On Wednesday I rode with Fred [7] from Hampstead to Hendon. He repeated to me beautifully the first fifty lines of Ovid's Metamorphoses, ' Ante mare et terras,' etc. It was a sort of epoch in my existence to hear my son declaim Latin poetry, understanding and relishing it.

Walmer: September 1, 1833.

. . . I got back on Friday evening. We are all well, affectionate and contented. It blows a terrible storm, and a ship was wrecked yesterday evening on the Goodwin sands. I said, ' Polly,[8] suppose you and I had been on board, what should we have done ? ' *Polly* (embracing me). ' We should have put our arms round each other and sunk together.' *Hally*. ' If I were a big man I would put you on my back, dear Papa, and swim ashore with you.'

Walmer: September 5, 1833.

. . . My days pass very indolently and agreeably. We are upon the margin of the sea, on the very spot where Julius Cæsar landed. This really is so, as you will see if you will look at the map and his account of his first expedition into Britain. The cliffs end about half a mile to the south, and here is an open beach for the disembarkation of an army, which Henry VIII. thought it necessary to fortify by Walmer, Deal and Sandown castles. We have had terrible storms, but it was curious to observe on Saturday and Sunday about a hundred ships, that by good luck had got into the Downs, lying at anchor in smooth water as comfortably as if they had

[7] His eldest boy, aged nine, who was at school at Hampstead.—ED.
[8] His second daughter, aged six.—ED.

been in a wet dock. The crew of a wrecked vessel we saw landed on the beach before our door.

Brooks's : September 21, 1833.

. . . I am going by the Holyhead mail to Birmingham to-morrow night. After the King had delivered his speech proroguing Parliament about three weeks ago, he withdrew to uncrown, and while this ceremony was going on he said to the Chancellor, ' I did not spare my voice, my Lord ; sailors and lawyers do not spare their voices. Are you going out of town immediately ? ' *Chancellor.* ' Yes, Sir, this very night.' *King.* ' What, by the mail ? ' I was told this within half an hour of the colloquy by two persons at different times who were present, Brougham not being one of them. There- fore do not consider it derogatory to the dignity of the Soli- citor-General to travel by the mail, when his Majesty was not aware that there would have been any impropriety in his Chancellor travelling by this conveyance.

Autobiography.

After the close of the session I paid a visit to my con- stituents at Dudley to give an account of my stewardship. The Irish Coercion Act was difficult to deal with, but I had a glorious theme in the Abolition of Slavery all over the British Empire ; my own law reforms were trumpeted with effect ; and a delusive vote was carried with hardly a dis- sentient voice, that ' Sir John Campbell deserved the un- abated confidence of the electors of Dudley.'

I proceeded on a tour to Ireland. My headquarters were with Littleton, the Chief Secretary (now Lord Hatherton). He introduced me to his father-in-law, Marquess Wellesley, the Lord-Lieutenant. His Excellency received me with distinction, and in several interviews talked to me of his own history with singular frankness. The ex-Governor- General was at no pains to disguise his own opinion that he is the first statesman of the age, and that he had done more for our Indian Empire than Clive or Hastings. He spoke most contemptuously of the Duke of Wellington as a politician, although he allowed him talents as a military commander. 'But,' said he, 'the public owe Arthur to me. I first discovered his genius for war, and I employed him on my responsibility when he was unknown, and would have remained unknown. Arthur owes everything to me.' He still denied him all 'civil wisdom,' insisted that he was incapable of discerning public opinion, or either following or guiding it, and that he was quite unfit for the post of Prime Minister. The noble Marquess, notwithstanding his disappointment at not being sent back to Ireland in April 1835, nor employed in the Government then formed, appears to have continued of the same mind till towards the end of the Whig rule, when he transferred his proxy in the House of Lords to the same 'Arthur,' being actuated by Lord Melbourne's peremptory refusal to make him a duke —an honour which he most greedily coveted, thinking he better deserved it than 'Arthur.'

I dined with the Lord Mayor of Dublin to meet his Excellency, who delivered a most admirable speech. I was made acquainted with Blackburne, the Attorney-General, and several distinguished lawyers on the bench and at the bar, and I was very much pleased with their manners and their conversation. In point of literature and general information I think they are inferior to Scotch advocates, but they are superior to them in eloquence, every Irishman having *the gift of the gab.*

I passed some days with Lord Duncannon in the county of Kilkenny, and I went by Lismore and Cork to the Lake of Killarney, equal in picturesque beauty, I think, to any lake to be seen in England, Scotland, Swisserland or Italy. I was now near Derrynane Abbey, and I had some thoughts of paying my respects to Daniel O'Connell, but I was afraid of bringing scandal on Lord Grey's Government, then at dire enmity with the 'Liberator.' When he heard I was coming to Ireland he asked me to visit him. I said that if I accepted his invitation it must be without prejudice to my prosecuting him for high treason.

Having gone by Holyhead, I returned by Liverpool, and for the first time in my life travelled by a railroad, then

considered something marvellous, but hardly more marvellous
than was the rapid mail-coach by which I originally travelled
in two days and three nights from Edinburgh to London.
I hastened back to my family at Walmer. This is the
only tour I have ever taken, since my marriage, without my
dear wife, and she would now have accompanied me had she
not been disabled from travelling by the approaching arrival
in this world of my third son. He made his appearance in
due time, and I called him Dudley in compliment to my
faithless constituents.[9]

In the end of 1833 it was thought an opportunity
had arisen to provide for Horne. Judge Bayley, for many
years a justice of the King's Bench and now a Baron of the
Exchequer, had become very infirm and wished to retire.
The plan was that Horne should succeed him. A most
violent controversy arose upon this subject between Horne
and Lord Brougham, the Chancellor. Horne asserted that
Brougham induced him to agree to become a Baron of the
Exchequer on a solemn promise that he was never to go
circuits or sit as a criminal judge, and that a new Equity
judgeship was to be cut out for him in the Exchequer.
Brougham insisted that Horne had unconditionally accepted
the appointment of a puisne Baron. Bayley resigned.
Horne positively refused to be his successor.[1] On the 22nd

---

[9] My youngest daughter was named Edina, in compliment to constituents who ever remained true to me.

[1] By the following letter Brougham wished to make me try to frighten
Horne, but I positively refused to take any part in the controversy:—

'Great Stanhope Street: Wednesday.

'My dear Solicitor-General,—I send the two last letters: one received
at eleven last night, and after I had, as I thought, settled the new difficulty
as to Horne's motion. I saw Lord Duncannon afterwards, but he thinks
his seeing him would do no good, and agrees with me in thinking you
should go to him in order to give him a hint that we are aware he has very
injudicious, possibly perfidious, advisers, and he will do well to listen to
them no longer. I really consider this as useful, if not necessary, for in
the position into which he has brought things I should be extremely sorry
if anything harsh or unkind were done towards him, and I may be forced
to let the affair take its course, which he would be the first to repent of.
Giving him a general warning, as above, and also letting him know that
one of the most eminent (if not the most eminent) men in the Court of

of February, 1834, a patent passed the Great Seal appointing
Sir John Campbell Attorney-General.   Gurney was made
the new Baron.   This was very annoying to me.   I had a
sincere regard for Horne, who had many valuable qualities,
and I grieved on every account to see him thus sacrificed,
even if it were by his own caprice.   He imputed no blame
to me, and our friendship has remained uninterrupted.   We
meet occasionally at the bench table in Lincoln's Inn Hall—
neither of us very lucky as Attorney-Generals— he a Master
in Chancery, I a pensionless peer.[2]

The session of 1834 had begun before this crisis, and I
had been engaged in a sharp debate which arose out of
certain charges brought against Baron Smith, an Irish judge.
I thought they ought to be entertained, and made an
animated speech against judges delivering harangues to
grand juries on politics and political economy, contending
that the foreman has a good right, if he dissents, to get up
and answer them in open court.   The Government, under
my advice, carried a motion for a committee of inquiry.   As
soon as I ceased to be a member of the House, advantage
was taken of my absence ; a motion was made to rescind
the order for the Committee ; the Government remained
staunch, but, being without legal assistance, they were overpowered in argument, and the motion was carried against
them by a small majority.

At this time I was fighting at Dudley, and about to be
defeated there.   My seat was vacated by my promotion.
This is an absurd law.   An officer in the army does not
vacate his seat if promoted to be lieutenant-colonel from
being a major, and the step from Solicitor to Attorney-

Chancery is ready to take the office to-day, would be but fair to him and
kind.   He will be at Lincoln's Inn at ten, if you prefer that to calling on
him.   ' Yours ever,
                                               ' H. B.'

    [2] Sir Denis Le Marchant in his *Life of Lord Althorp* (p. 62) uses the
following expressions : ' Horne was abruptly displaced at the instigation of
Sir John Campbell, who being then Solicitor, was impatient to be Attorney-
General.'   The context gives a very different view of the transaction from
that suggested by Sir Denis Le Marchant,—who adduces no authority for
the statement which he makes.   See also *Life of Lord Brougham*, p. 426.
—ED.

General is equally professional advancement, there being no reason to suppose that a constituency would make any distinction between the two offices. But the result in my case may lead some to argue that the opportunities cannot be too frequent of enabling the people to express their opinion of the existing administration.[3]

On my approach to Dudley I was met by a respectable procession ; but when I began to canvass I discovered the cold shoulder of some of my former partisans, and I was told that the Whig Government had not rooted out corruption in the manner expected when the Reform Bill was passed. Daniel Whittle Harvey had, a few days previously, brought forward his motion in the House of Commons about the Pension List, and my iron-hearted operatives asked, ' Why are the mothers and sisters and children of peers, who have done nothing for the public, to be maintained in luxury at the public expense, while we are obliged to support our poor relatives from our hard-earned wages, or see them sent to the workhouse ? '

I transmitted news to Downing Street of the shadow of my defeat cast by the coming event, and it occasioned great surprise and consternation. This was the first heavy blow which the Whig Government received. I went on resolutely doing my utmost for eight days and nights, but without any favourable turn. My opponent was the same Major Hawkes whom I had twice defeated at Stafford,—a good-natured, silly, harmless fellow, but whose personal qualities were as little considered as mine, he being most zealously supported as the Conservative candidate. On the day of

___

[3] 'A curious expedient was suggested to me whereby I might by the existing law accept the office of Attorney-General without vacating my seat.

'. . . The point which has occurred to me for consideration is whether a new election is quite necessary or not. If you take the office *without* any of the emoluments, &c., thereto belonging, as I did my King's counsel-ship, and as is now generally done in that case, how are you in a different position as to vacating your seat ? I had the Crown briefs on the Northern circuit by virtue of my office—as you have in Customs, Excise, &c. This all assumes the *salary* to be almost nominal also. One should avoid doing it unless there was a strong inducement—but think of it. Yours ever,

'H. B'

election the battle was soon over, the electors being polled
out at the numerous booths in three hours, and Hawkes had
as great a majority over me as I had had over Sir Horace St.
Paul.

The pain of defeat was for some time absorbed in the
apprehension that the town of Dudley would be utterly destroyed. Many thousand pit-men had come in from the
surrounding iron and coal mines, forming a most formidable
mob in my interest; and as they said I had not had fair play,
they were determined to be revenged on all who had voted
against me. They were actually beginning to pull down the
house of the master-manufacturer who had proposed Hawkes.
I wished to go out to them and address them, imploring
them to disperse, but I was assured that this would only
make them worse, and that the only way to induce them
to desist from their enterprise was that they should be
told I had left Dudley. My carriage was accordingly sent
by a private way to the outskirts of the town. I there
joined it and posted off to London. The intelligence of my
departure had the desired effect, and the commencement of
the riot only produced a few trials for misdemeanour at the
ensuing assizes. My inglorious retreat, however, was a
great enhancement of the Tory triumph, and they painted in
large characters on a house at the corner of the lane by
which I left the town, 'Campbell's Flight, 1834.'

I was very generously received by Lord Grey and the
Chancellor, but I found that I was blamed by subordinate
members of the Government, who said that I ought to have
carried the seat at any cost. I would sooner have lost my
office and seen the party at once driven from power than
have attempted to corrupt such a constituency; but my
accusers were afterwards comforted by knowing that an
unauthorised agent, unknown to me and to them, had
actually made the attempt and failed. I trust that this
virgin constituency remains uncontaminated, being still represented by the same Major Hawkes without any serious
subsequent contest. The incipient danger of corruption I
found to arise from publicans and keepers of beer-shops, who
were electors, and, without any notion of receiving bribe or

voting-money, were eager to have their houses opened with a view to the profit on the sale of liquor, and I fear would be thereby influenced in their votes. Perhaps the best practical security against corruption would be to disqualify all publicans and keepers of beer-shops.

An interval of above three months elapsed before I was restored to the House of Commons, a period of my life full of mortification and trouble. The Attorney-General without a seat in Parliament was the fox without his tail, and I did not like to show myself. The Government were very anxious again to have the full benefit of my services. Pepys, the new Solicitor-General, though an excellent Equity lawyer and destined to be a considerable Equity judge, hated the bustle of the House of Commons, could with difficulty be made to attend, and only once while he was in his then office was prevailed upon to speak.[4]

The first place thought of for me was Morpeth, which might easily have been managed, but we were afraid of the clamour that would have been excited about the Whigs reserving a snug rotten borough for their Attorney-General. Tiverton, now held by Lord Palmerston, was nearly arranged for me, but Kennedy, the occupant, who on resigning was to have been sent by Stanley to the colonies, always rose in his terms, and there was no dealing with him. In my distress one day, meeting Billy Holmes, the Tory whipper-in, I said jocularly I must come to him, as our own people could do nothing for me. *Holmes.* 'I will tell you what I will do for you. Get your friend Pollock to resign Huntingdon, and I will bring you in for that, for it is the only rotten borough you have left us.'

At length, what no god nor whipper-in could promise was brought about by the resignation of Lord Craigie, an old Scotch judge. He was succeeded by Jeffrey, the Lord Advocate, who, a little alarmed by the *shakiness* of the Administration, was desirous of securing a safe retreat on the bench. There was thus a vacancy in the representation of the city of Edinburgh, which by the Reform Act had two

---

[4] This was in a discussion on the law of libel.—See *Lives of the Chancellors*, vol. viii. p. 428.

representatives returned by 10,000 electors, instead of one
returned by 32. I was invited to stand, but it was a question
of great difficulty whether I ought to run the risk of another
defeat. I was personally unknown in Edinburgh, the Government had lately been beaten in the county of Perth,
and was rapidly losing its popularity. Sir John Hobhouse,
who had been thrown out for Westminster about the same
time that I was for Dudley, had put forth feelers to try how
a Government candidate would fare at Edinburgh, and had
shrunk from the attempt.

However, I was determined, if I could get the consent of
Lord Grey, to hazard all on this die, to take the box in my
hand and to throw. Lord Grey said, ' It is a very perilous
thing for you and for us. Another defeat would be most
injurious to you individually, and ruin to us as a Government; but you being a Scotsman who in the North may be
thought an honour to your country, there is a reasonable
chance of success to justify the attempt. Go, and good luck
attend you.' He asked me, however, whether the Chancellor
had expressed his approbation; ' otherwise,' said he, ' the fat
will all be in the fire.' Brougham, who, on such occasions,
inspired great awe, or rather apprehension and alarm, in his
colleagues, had consented, although he was evidently a little
disturbed at the notion of my becoming member for the
Scottish metropolis, and would have been much better pleased
to see me filling an obscure dependent seat.[5]

I set off by the mail coach the same evening. As I
approached Haddington, I was little encouraged by the conversation of a gentleman whom we had taken up at the
preceding stage. He had been in Edinburgh the day before,

---

[5] I had received the following note from him, accompanied by a present
of smoked haddocks :—

' Dear A.,—I am puzzled about Edinburgh. I still think you are not
the man, but it is by no means certain. All I have made a point of is that
it *must be a certainty*. Of the other seat the delay is absolutely unaccountable, as a large place for life was offered to one who wanted it, and
no answer had come when I saw Lord G., though it was a week after.

' Yours ever,
' H. B.'

I have sent you the *honoured remains* of three of your countrymen—
from Aberdeen—which arrived this morning in high preservation.

and he gave a very animated description of the confusion prevailing there about the choice of a representative, concluding in these words: 'As for poor Campbell, he has not the remotest chance.'

When I left London I was aware that the state of affairs might be such in Edinburgh as to render it inexpedient for me even to show my face there, and I had made an appointment with my brother, who then lived in Edinburgh for the education of his children, to meet me at Dalkeith. Thither I drove from Haddington, and there my brother soon joined me, accompanied by John Cuninghame, now Lord Cuninghame, and a very eminent judge in the Court of Session, then the life and soul of the Whig party in Scotland, and ever one of the most sensible, friendly and excellent of men. They did not hold out a very flattering prospect to me, but said that I should make myself ridiculous by now retreating, and that, as I had come so far, it would be a less evil to be beaten. So we posted off to Edinburgh and penned an advertisement to the electors, announcing Sir John Campbell as a candidate for their suffrages, and inviting them to meet him next day in the Waterloo rooms, to hear an exposition of his sentiments.

Curiosity drew an immense assemblage, by whom my harangue was not very favourably received. After the meeting we called upon several leading shopkeepers in the Grassmarket, who gave us little encouragement, and I said to my brother (of which he often reminded me), 'This is as bad as my last canvass in Dudley.'

However, the next day things began to assume a better aspect. Instead of the candidate going from door to door, the city was divided into districts, the electors of each district met in a church belonging to the Establishment, or a dissenting meeting-house, within the district; he mounted, not the pulpit, but the *precentor's* desk, and from this he addressed the audience, who were seated in the pews like a religious congregation, and, when he had finished his discourse, any elector present questioned him respecting the topics he had handled, or any other part of his political faith or practice. A friend then addressed the assembly and, after a panegyric on the merits and services of A.B., moved that the said A.B. is the most fit and proper person to represent this city in Parliament. The resolution was then put to the vote, and, being carried, the meeting dispersed. Such a use of a place erected for religious worship in Scotland is not considered in the slightest degree irreverent or objectionable.

My chief rhetorical supporter was Sir Thomas Dick Lauder, Bart., who relieved the gravity of the proceeding with his jokes. I was sometimes taunted with being a lawyer. My Tory antagonist was Mr. Learmonth, a wealthy coachmaker. Lauder on one occasion said: ' I am very proud of the eminence Sir John Campbell has acquired in Westminster Hall, although I must acknowledge that the Tories too may boast that their candidate is a great *conveyancer*, a distinguished *spokesman* and an ornament to the bar—of course I mean the *splinter-bar*.'

I had likewise a Radical opponent, Mr. Aytoun, who was less formidable, as Radicalism has never had much favour in Edinburgh, and he was only to be dreaded from his dividing and weakening the Liberal interest.

One night I was knocked out of bed by the arrival of a King's messenger from London. He brought me letters from the Lord Chancellor and the Secretary to the Treasury announcing that Stanley, Sir James Graham, Lord Ripon and the Duke of Richmond had seceded from the Cabinet,—but that Lord Grey was vigorously to carry on the Government without them.[6] Two hours later the Tories had an express from the Carlton Club to announce these resignations; and they immediately issued an handbill asserting that the Whig

---

[6] Extract from the Lord Chancellor's letter:—'. . . If you are going on half as well as we are here, you are safe enough. Never was king more cordial—I may say so cordial—with servants as his Majesty with us. I was with him a long time yesterday morning, and the same to the fullest extent with Lord G. The vacancies will be easily filled and speedily, though Stanley's is an irreparable loss,—but it is only a temporary one. He has behaved, and will behave, admirably and honestly—only too punctiliously. House of Commons was last night in such raptures, that I should not wonder if they addressed both the King and his Ministers. When Lord A. pronounced the word *confidence*, the roar was so loud and so long that no one ever heard its equal. You must not name names, but you *may affirm unabated confidence of King and increased love of House of Commons* with a safe conscience.   ' Yours ever,
                                                    ' H. B.'

Government was dissolved and calling on the electors to rally round the constitutional party which possessed the confidence of the Sovereign. We published a counter address congratulating the Liberal party on the secession of those members of the Government who had distracted its councils, weakened its efficiency, and impaired its popularity, and foretelling a new course of policy, to be marked by the unanimity, vigour and liberality of those who directed it.

The day of election at last arrived, and I had more votes than both my opponents put together. There was no chairing, but I proceeded in an open carriage through some of the principal streets to my brother's house, where he and my five sisters were assembled to embrace me as representative in Parliament of the metropolis of my native country. In my farewell address to the multitude who accompanied me, I alluded to this circumstance, quoting the Scotch proverb: ' Blood is thicker than water.'

I ought to mention that, though the contest was a severe one, there not only was not a shilling spent in bribery, but there was not distributed a pint of ale or a gill of whisky at my expense. Indeed there was no drinking by reason of the election. The shawl-makers, the fleshers and the different trades met to consider how their favourite candidate was to be supported, without participating in anything except ' the feast of reason and the flow of soul.' The cost of the election was considerable, but it arose chiefly from *agency*. Thereafter the agents acted gratuitously, and the disbursements of the members were confined to the hustings and other strictly legal expenses of the election, a yearly contribution in aid of registration, a subscription to charities and public undertakings, and private benevolence expected in London by all Edinburgh people in distress.

The morning of my return to London I waited first on the Lord Chancellor in his private room in Westminster Hall. He presented me with his great official nosegay, which I carried into the King's Bench as a trophy of victory. On my way I met Lord Lyndhurst, going into the Court of Exchequer as Chief Baron, who said, ' Well, if you had been thrown out, it would have been a great matter for us, but I cannot in

my heart be sorry for the success of an old friend.' When
at four o'clock I took my seat in the House I was received
with very warm cheers by our party.

The prophecy respecting the unanimity and stability of
Lord Grey's Government when he got rid of the sticklers for
the ascendency of the Protestant Episcopal Church in Roman
Catholic Ireland, was by no means fulfilled. Other controversies arose, and in July following Lord Grey ' descended
from power.' I most deeply deplored the event, even when
it was found that a Liberal Administration was formed under
the auspices of Lord Melbourne ; but I rejoiced in the altered
tone towards Ireland.[7] Instead of the Coercion Act being
renewed, I had instructions to prepare a Bill omitting the
trial of offences by court-martial and the arbitrary power the
Lord Lieutenant had enjoyed of prohibiting public meetings
and suspending the Constitution at pleasure. This change
made the Tories very angry, and I had a violent scuffle with
Peel when the Bill came into committee. He alleged that
I had drawn it very clumsily and that its interpretation was
very doubtful, trying to make good his assertions by certain
verbal criticisms and subtle distinctions. In answer I showed
that my Bill was not only remarkable for brevity, but was

---

[7] *Hartrigge : October* 1846.—I must admit that upon reflection my admiration of Lord Grey as a statesman has considerably abated. Against high
principles and great abilities we have to set serious defects and grievous
faults. He was utterly ignorant of political economy, and upon social as
well as commercial questions he adhered to most of the antiquated notions
of his ' order.' His combination with the Duke of Wellington against
Canning in 1827 was wholly unjustifiable. He displayed great energy in
carrying the Reform Bill, but he was unprepared to govern the country
under the new *régime*. He had a childish dislike of O'Connell, and he
never thought that Irishmen were to be treated like Englishmen. He
was now impracticable in the Cabinet, and constantly threatened to resign,
considering it utterly impossible that the party should go on an hour
without him. He was at last so annoyed by the vagaries of Brougham
that he really longed for repose, and thought he should be happier out of
office. Brougham had a frantic idea of becoming Prime Minister, but all
the other members of the Cabinet were earnestly desirous of supporting
the chief. I was employed by Edward Ellice to write a letter to Lord
Grey, urging him to continue at the helm. He capriciously broke up the
Government on a foolish controversy respecting a correspondence between
Littleton, Brougham, Lord Wellesley, and O'Connell.

drawn with perspicuity and precision. This was really true, and no difficulty ever arose in carrying it into execution.

A few days before the prorogation we had a more than usually jolly fish-dinner. The ministerial fish-dinner is a gathering at Greenwich or Blackwall of all the members of the Government in either House of Parliament, superior and subordinate, including the Household, to eat whitebait and all manner of fish produced by European seas, lakes, and rivers, and to get merry on the recollection of past dangers, the certainty of holding office for six months longer, and the probability of reaching another Easter without a serious shake. It is a sort of saturnalia or 'high jinks,' and, with a due observance of parliamentary forms, mock motions, impeachments and bills are brought forward. Although there is a great risk that when men meet for the purpose of being jocular they will be very dull, on this occasion we had some very good fun.

The session being closed, I joined my family, who were settled at Rosemount, a villa about four miles from Edinburgh, that I might cultivate the acquaintance and good graces of my new constituents.

Edinburgh was soon in a state of uncommon excitement. The great scientific meeting attended by Arago, Agassiz, and many other distinguished continental as well as British philosophers, was immediately followed by the famous 'Grey Festival.' The Scottish nation, feeling justly that they owed to Lord Grey their deliverance from political degradation, invited him to come to receive their homage in the capital, and he accepted the invitation. His progress from Berwick to Edinburgh was marked by as much enthusiasm, and was attended with more real glory, than that of Napoleon from Cannes to Paris on his return from Elba. I had the honour to be one of the directors of the solemnities at Edinburgh. Nothing disturbed our proceedings except the unexpected appearance of Lord Brougham from a progress he had been making in the North of Scotland, where he amused the people with accounts of his intimacy with King William and promises to report their sayings in his daily despatch to Windsor; whereas it was truly supposed that of all the members of the

'Government he had become the most obnoxious to his Majesty, and they who were in the secret knew that his Majesty was then talking of him as a madman who had run off with the Great Seal to John o' Groat's House. The difficulty was to bring Lord Brougham into the company of Lord Grey, who at that time was at no pains to conceal his dislike of him, and whose family openly charged his treachery as the cause of the late changes.

The Lord High Chancellor being in Edinburgh must necessarily be invited to the Festival. He himself took off from the awkwardness of their meeting in public by voluntarily coming to Lord Stair's at Oxenford Castle, near Edinburgh, where Lord Grey, Lady Grey and his daughters were residing. I was present at the *rencontre*, and never did I so much admire Brougham's boldness of heart and loftiness of manner. He was fully aware of the feelings of all the Greys towards him, and if he had been before ignorant he must now have been informed by their averted eyes, cold looks and shunning demeanour. But he accosted them and continued to behave to them as if he had believed they regarded him with unmixed benevolence,—only that his approaches were more than usually respectful, and his caresses more than usually tender. He conquered, and to my utter amazement he has since been in confidential correspondence with Lord Grey and invited to Howick. This cordial reconciliation did not take place till both had been a considerable time out of office, and both had a grudge against Lord Melbourne's Government. To reconcile all past differences between political leaders there is nothing so effectual as *idem sentire de republicâ*, i.e. to hate the Minister for the time being from a sense of injury. In this way have I repeatedly seen men harmoniously knit together who, with great reason, had vowed against each other eternal enmity.

The triumphal entrance of Lord Grey into Edinburgh, the presentation of addresses to him from all parts of Scotland, and the speeches in the banqueting hall, were all very fine. Lord Grey's expression 'that he had not fallen but descended from power' was truly felicitous. Lord Durham's speech was the best he ever spoke, though he was not justified on such

an occasion in complaining of the Government for not doing
enough. This complaint drew out Brougham's famous declaration, which he has often denied but which I myself heard,
that 'the Government last session had done too much, and
that he hoped next session they would do less.' He however
showed himself, as he always does, to be a consummate
rhetorician.

At this very time died at Edinburgh Sir John Leach,
Master of the Rolls, who might have left a great name behind
him if he had resolutely stuck to his profession and his party,
instead of becoming a Court intriguer. But with a view to
his own advancement, and to ruin Lord Eldon in the good
graces of George IV., he issued the Milan Commission and
brought on the trial of Queen Caroline, which marred his
own fortune, shook the monarchy, and ensured to his patron
the fame of being the most profligate, the most heartless, and
the most foolish of sovereigns.

According to the usual routine of promotion, I, as
Attorney-General, ought to have succeeded Leach. Brougham
however selected Pepys, the Solicitor-General, little suspecting that this was the man who was to supersede him as Whig
Lord Chancellor. The pretence for passing me over was that
Brougham being himself a common lawyer, it would have
made an outcry if at the same time a common lawyer had
been appointed to the Rolls. This was so plausible that I
found I could not resist the appointment, and I offered no
opposition to it beyond a protest that it should not be drawn
into a precedent.

After a tour in the Highlands and a delightful week at
Taymouth, the seat of Lord Breadalbane, where I met and
established a great intimacy with Lord Durham, I returned
to England and resumed the regular discharge of my official
duties. There was a considerable demur about naming me a
colleague as Solicitor-General. With my concurrence Charles
Austin was first proposed, and I wrote to him strongly advising him to accept. , . . . He was a man of consummate
abilities, and might have made himself a great name.[8] . . . .

* My father adds that Mr. Austin had made 40,000l. in one session
before railway committees, and that his health broke down soon after this.

'The other two deliberated upon for the office of Solicitor-General were Wilde and Rolfe. I was for Rolfe, and luckily for me I carried him through, for I afterwards acted with him for five years most harmoniously, and always received from him most effectual assistance.

Our connection as colleagues was in the first instance speedily dissolved. His patent had passed the Great Seal, and he had been sworn in, but before he kissed hands or was knighted the Whigs were all turned out of office.

Letters to Sir George Campbell in the year 1834.

Brooks's : January 1, 1834.

. . . Lord Holland is the only Minister in London. I dined with him on Sunday, and met in the evening Talleyrand, Dedel the Dutch Ambassador, &c. Nothing memorable except that Lord Holland heard the King say on the morning of the dissolution of the last Parliament, when a difficulty was made about the state carriage, that he would go in a hackney coach.

House of Lords : March 29, 1834.

. . . Here I am again in my wig and gown, forgetting my misfortunes.[9] I have been debating whether the English Attorney-General or the Lord Advocate of Scotland has precedence. The Chancellor was for giving it hollow in my favour, but I candidly stated a fact which induced him to suspend any decision, and, bowing like Noodle and Doodle in the play, we mutually protested for our respective offices.

I dined yesterday with the Chancellor. He said that an arrangement must and would be made for bringing me again into Parliament immediately after the recess. He was pleased to observe that there had been no Attorney-General since Perceval whose presence in the House of Commons was so important to the Government, and that the measures in contemplation could not be got through without me. There is some flourish in this ; but, notwithstanding insinuations

date. These statements must refer to a later period, as Mr. Austin did not retire before the year 1846.—ED.

[9] Having lost his election at Dudley on being made Attorney-General.
—ED.

I have heard to the contrary, I believe that he and all the others are sincere in their wish that I should be restored.

. . . If the security of Ministers is endangered by their own folly, they are set up again by the folly of their opponents. The Duke of Wellington's speech about 'the Thirty-nine Articles of Christianity' has placed us on a pinnacle.

Brooks's: Friday, August 22, 1834.

. . . I am going to Boyle Farm, on the banks of the Thames, to pay what may be considered a whimsical visit to Sir Edward Sugden. If Brougham knows of it he will certainly think that I have entered into a conspiracy with his enemies to defame him. The truth is that Suggy and I, by an interrogatur of the First Division of the Court of Session, are called upon for their guidance to give an opinion as to whether lands at Penang are to be considered *real* or *personal* property; and as we could not meet in town, he has invited me to dine and sleep at his house, that we may consult and write our judgment to-morrow morning.

New Street: Friday, October 17, 1834.

. . . You will be able to think of nothing but the terrible fire which has burnt down the Houses of Lords and Commons. I received a wound on my knee—not seriously hurt—in working an engine to save Westminster Hall, which was twice in flames.

Mary and the children are gone to Abinger. I follow to-morrow for a couple of days. . . .

I am going again to look at the ruins. I saw the conflagration almost from its commencement. I returned home about eleven o'clock, having tasted nothing since breakfast. I afterwards returned. I received the wound on my knee between two and three. I am greatly delighted that the Hall was saved. The last person I conversed with was the Speaker's son, who was wandering about, having no home to go to. He was stepping into a cab to go out to dinner when the flames burst out.

In addition to my wound, I had my pocket picked of a purse with four or five pounds and a pocket-handkerchief.

Brooks's : Monday, October 20, 1834.

. . . I have been attending the Privy Council all day about the great fire. It may be satisfactory to you to know that there is the clearest evidence of its having originated from some workmen belonging to the Board of Works indiscreetly burning wooden tallies (or nick-sticks), which encumbered a room of the Exchequer, in the flues of the House of Lords.

Yet a respectable witness swore that about ten o'clock on the Thursday night at an inn in Dudley, a man entered and said he had just been informed that the House of Lords was burnt by the carelessness of some carpenters. The man is sincere, but he must have dreamed it, or it is an accidental coincidence.

Council Office : Tuesday, October 21, 1834.

. . . Here am I sitting idle while Brougham examines the witnesses. He is like Bottom in the play and likes to act all the parts himself. However I have a comfortable lounge. I sit at the head of the table as if I were President of the Council. Lord Melbourne is on my right and looks rather gloomy. I should not wonder if Brougham's 'vagaries' were the cause of this. You perceive there is now *bellum flagrans* between him and Lord Durham, and, were it not for the Chancellor's robes, there must be a duel between them. There can be no doubt that the last article in the 'Edinburgh Review' is Brougham's, and Lord Durham says that it gives a false and fraudulent representation of his conduct. The Glasgow dinner acquires importance from Brougham's imprudence. Curiosity alone will now fill the hall, however large, and draw all eyes to the scene. I confess I do not understand how any government can go on with a leading member of it acting so recklessly, and so totally setting at nought the wishes and feelings and interests of his colleagues.

There is no new *light* thrown upon the *fire*. The case was clear from the beginning, and the investigation is only continued for public satisfaction. Many have a great desire to make out a conspiracy.

Brooks's: October 24, 1834.

. . . My knee is better, but still gives me a good deal of pain when I walk.

I dined at Holland House on Wednesday with the Premier and divers members of the Cabinet. Brougham not of the party, but very freely discussed.

CHAPTER XXI.

Autobiography.

ON the 14th day of November 1834, a few minutes before ten o'clock in the morning, as I was walking down to
the Court of King's Bench, the Lord Chancellor drove past
me at a quick pace on his way to his court. Seeing me he
pulled the check-string of his carriage and beckoned to me
to approach. I ran up. *Lord Chancellor.* ' How do you do,
Sir John Campbell, Mr. Attorney no longer ! We are all out !
It was done yesterday at Brighton. Melbourne went down
Prime Minister and returned a simple individual. I am
going to give a few judgments before delivering up the Great
Seal. Good-bye, Sir John !' He did not say to me, 'The Queen
has done it all.' But the ' Times ' newspaper, which I immediately found in the robing-room, contained an article on
the subject, written by Brougham, and concluding with those
words.[1] They made Melbourne very angry and gave mortal
offence to the King, and they helped to deprive Brougham
of the Great Seal when the Whigs were restored in the
spring.

CHAP.
XXI.

A.D. 1834.

[1] ' We have no authority for the important statement which follows, but
we have every reason to believe that it is perfectly true. . . . " The King
has taken the opportunity of Lord Spencer's death to turn out the Ministry.
There is every reason to believe that the Duke of Wellington has been
sent for. The Queen has done it all." '—*Times,* November 14, 1834.

The truth was that, although Queen Adelaide was very hostile to the whole Liberal party, the King had not communicated to her his intention to change his Government, and she knew nothing of it till the arrival of the Duke of Wellington at Brighton next day. She probably, as a woman of sense, would have dissuaded the King from the preposterous attempt he was making. The removal of Lord Althorp from the House of Commons on his father's death could be no reason for dismissing a Cabinet that possessed the confidence of a large majority of the House of Commons, and of which the nation was not as yet tired, notwithstanding some murmurs against its measures. Much as the King might dislike his Ministers, he ought to have known, and would have been told by any reasonable person whom he consulted, that the season for getting rid of them had not yet arrived, and that he must 'bide his time.'

Although virtually out, I continued legally to fill the office and to do the duties of Attorney-General for a month longer, till Peel had returned from Italy, and had formed his Government.

In this interval one very disagreeable task was thrown upon me. Two men had been convicted at Chester of the most atrocious murder of a magistrate, but a dispute arose whether the sentence against them was to be carried into effect by the sheriff of the county of Chester or by the sheriffs of the city of Chester. All the functionaries refusing to act, years might elapse before this dispute could be legally determined, and till then the murderers could not be made to expiate their offence under the sentence originally pronounced against them. There was a great outcry by reason of the law being thus defeated. I boldly brought the convicts to the bar of the King's Bench, and prayed that execution should be awarded against them by the judges of that court. After a demurrer and long argument they were ordered to be executed by the Marshal of the King's Bench at *Saint Thomas a Waterings* in the borough of Southwark, aided by the sheriff of Surrey, a form of proceeding which had not been resorted to for many ages. The execution took place accordingly, amidst an immense assemblage, not only from the metropolis, but from remote parts of the kingdom.[2]

When Peel arrived, he had much difficulty in arranging his law appointments. He at first wished to make Sir James Scarlett Attorney-General. I wrote a letter (to be communicated to Peel) dissuading my father-in-law from accepting this office, and intimating that, if Lyndhurst was to be Chancellor, the least thing that could be done for *him* was to make him Chief Baron of the Exchequer with a peerage. This letter was forwarded to Peel as containing the opinion of the profession, and the suggested arrangement took place.

Nothing was done for poor Wetherell, one of the cleverest, most eccentric and most honourable men I have ever known.

Pollock was my successor in the office of Attorney-General. Pemberton, afterwards better known as Pemberton Leigh, was first named Solicitor, but he declined the office because he would not undertake to attend regularly in the House of Commons; and Follett, still wearing a stuff gown, was selected because Peel, from attending some committees where he had pleaded, had become acquainted with his extraordinary merit.

Though now only third in point of rank in the Court of King's Bench, my business was greater than ever, and from the time of Scarlett's removal till I received the Great Seal of Ireland, I was decidedly at the head of the Common Law bar.

I had soon to pay a disagreeable visit to the North. Peel, I think very injudiciously, as soon as he had formed his Government, dissolved the Parliament. It would appear that he had repented of this error from the different course which he intimated that he meant to have pursued in May 1839, when there was a prospect of his again coming into power; and little doubt can be entertained that in 1834–5 he would have had a better chance of stability if he had met the old Parliament, proposed his Bills, kept a dissolution hanging over the heads of the members of the House of

[2] *Rex v.* Garside and Mosley, 2 A. & E., 266.

Commons with doubtful seats, and at last had gone to the country, if necessary, like Pitt in 1784, with a complaint of factious opposition and a promise of popular measures. He might have foreseen that there must be a majority against him in the new House, to be elected immediately on his accession to office, and that in that case the game was up.

The Edinburgh Tories had been so well beaten in the last contest that I left London in the hope that I should be returned without opposition ; but when I arrived on a snowy morning at a place called the Press Inn, I learned that, trusting to the alleged reaction, they had actually started two candidates against Abercromby and me—my old opponent Learmonth the coachmaker, and Lord Ramsay the eldest son of the Earl of Dalhousie, a young gentleman of great promise, who had just taken a high degree at Oxford.[3]

During this contest I made a speech which was afterwards misrepresented as a declaration that in my opinion the House of Lords ought to be abolished. Lord Ramsay had pointed out boastingly the great strength of the new Government in the House of Lords. I said this reminded me of Foote's farce 'High Life Below Stairs,' where, the *Duke* trying to put down *Sir Harry* in their dispute about the respective merits of the two houses by exclaiming ' We have dignity,' Sir Harry retorts ' But what would become of your dignity if we were to withhold the supplies ? ' So I pointed out the constitutional powers of the House of Commons, exercised in the best of times, if the Crown should insist on retaining Ministers who had not the confidence of the representatives of the people. But I always scouted the notion of any organic change in the structure of the House of Lords, and never said more of reforming them than ' that their conduct should be reformed by the people returning a Liberal House of Commons, to whose opinion the Peers would defer.' I have ever felt the necessity of a Second Chamber of Parliament, and I have not been able to devise, nor have I seen pointed out by others,

---

[3] *August* 1855.—Now returning from India, *Marquess of Dalhousie*, after filling the office of Governor-General with distinguished lustre. [He died in 1860.—ED.]

one likely to contain more talent and independence, or to command more respect with the public, than the present, notwithstanding its manifold imperfections.

Lord Ramsay's conduct during the election was very unexceptionable, and he displayed a considerable portion of talent; but he exposed himself from his inexperience to a little ridicule by vaunting that he was the twenty-third in lineal descent of the noble house to which he belonged. I reminded him of what Gibbon said of the ' Faerie Queen ' and the triumphs of Marlborough as connected with the house of Spencer, and advised him to be most proud of Allan Ramsay, the barber, well known to be his cousin, and to regard ' The Gentle Shepherd ' as ' the brightest jewel in his coronet.' The coachmaker and the noble of twenty-three descents were at the bottom of the poll.

I now suggested to Abercromby the propriety of his being put in nomination for Speaker against Manners Sutton. He was at first very reluctant, but for the good of the party he afterwards consented. I never doubted the propriety of starting a Speaker of our principles on the meeting of the new Parliament, nor that Abercromby was the best man we could start.

The 20th of February, 1835, arrived; Parliament met, and the strength of parties was to be tried on the choice of Speaker. Both sides expressed equal confidence, and two or three of our friends being pledged to Manners Sutton from personal regard, the opinion rather was that he would carry the election. According to etiquette, immediately before the division he came over to our side of the House that he might vote for his rival, and he sat immediately before me. Those for him were told first, and when it was found that they amounted to 306 I congratulated him on his success, and he modestly chuckled at his victory. But what a breathless state of anxiety was the House brought to when the tellers, counting the Opposition side, sung out ' Three hundred!' and there was still a bench to be told which might or might not turn the scale. The words were at last heard : ' Three hundred and seven! Three hundred and eight!' and so on to ' Three hundred and sixteen!' A majority

of ten on a very favourable question against the new Administration !

Sir Robert himself bore the blow without any external
signs of suffering, but his colleagues and partisans could not
conceal their consternation. The painful task was to communicate the result to the King, who had hitherto been
kept in a 'fool's paradise.' When he had heard the fatal
news he exclaimed : ' But why did you deceive me ? Why
did you deceive me ? ' In truth the good old gentleman had
only to blame his own rashness. If Sir Robert Peel had been
consulted, he would have been the last man to recommend
a change of government prematurely, although he made a
very gallant effort to repair a blunder which he must always
have deplored.

Again beaten on the Address, Peel adhered to office till,
the majorities against him increasing, he saw there was no
chance of the country rallying in his favour, and that longer
to continue the struggle could only lead to the degradation
of the Royal authority, and the personal mortification of the
Sovereign.

While sitting on the Opposition bench I occasionally
joined in the nightly skirmishes which took place before the
decisive battle, brought on by Lord John Russell's motion
respecting the Irish Church. The most delightful political
position is to be a member of a powerful and united party
out of office, eagerly attacking a falling Ministry. The next
is to be in office, with the confidence of superiors, the good-
will of associates, and plenty of abuse from opponents. The
worst of all is that in which I am at present placed—seeing
a once powerful and respectable party melting away, without concert, without spirit, and without a leader.[4]

On Lord John Russell's motion, about the Irish Church,
I made a speech which I had composed in my post-chaise as
I was returning from the Cornwall assizes, where I had been
on a special retainer. My compliment to Peel was sincere—

Cum talis sis, utinam noster esses.

He ought to have belonged to our party. In his heart he is
much more of a Reformer than Lord Melbourne, and, though

[4] Written in October 1842.

not the son of a duke, I must own I think from his talents he is a fitter man to lead the House of Commons than Lord John Russell.[5]

When the resignation followed and the new Government was to be constructed, the grand difficulty was the Chancellorship.   In an interview I had with Lord Melbourne he said to me: 'Brougham is such a man that I cannot act with him.'

Brougham has told me, and I believe him, that he had the principal hand in making Melbourne Minister on the retirement of Lord Grey, and that if it had not been for a private interview he had with the King, and a public declaration he made in the Lords, 'that the Liberal Government still subsisted and was ready to go on with vigour,' the Tory party would have come into power in May 1834 ; but between that time and the change in November he played the most fantastic tricks.   The removal from the Cabinet of Lord Grey, of whom he stood in some awe, probably aggravated his rashness, capriciousness, and *faithlessness*.   He would lay important Bills on the table of the House of Lords as 'Government measures,' of which he had never dropped a hint in the Cabinet; he would promise places five or six deep which were not in his gift; he would communicate irregularly with the King upon subjects out of his department, and he was strongly suspected of writing anonymously against some of his colleagues in the newspapers,— over which, both ministerial and opposition, by a few favours and many promises he at one time had obtained a marvellous influence.

Melbourne's policy was to irritate him as little, and soothe him as much as possible.   If he was an unsafe col-

---

[a] *Hartrigge, August* 1855.—I first discovered Peel's *Liberal* propensities when serving on a Select Committee with him to inquire into the best mode of enfranchising copyholds and abolishing heriots.   While Goulburn, his Chancellor of the Exchequer, expressed great horror at the thought of any innovation on these subjects, the future Free Trader warmly supported my proposed measure, saying to me privately, 'You will easily carry it through the Commons, but it will be in great danger in the other House, the Lords being under the influence of their stewards, and not more enlightened.'

league, it was foreseen that he might be a most dangerous opponent. He was told that the King had an insuperable personable objection to him,—that a hope of this subsiding was entertained,—and that meanwhile the Great Seal should be put into commission, the Commissioners being the Master of the Rolls, the Vice-Chancellor, and a Common Law judge. In vain I urged that this was a strange plan for clearing off the heavy arrears which had accumulated in the Court of Chancery. But party expediency always carries it over the due administration of justice when they come into conflict.

When the Commission was settled I quietly resumed my office of Attorney-General.

Our great measure this session was the Municipal Reform Bill, which alone ought to make the nation gratefully remember the Whigs. Our duty and interest here fortunately coincided, for there was a general feeling that the time was come when jobbing corporations should not be permitted to pervert to individual emolument the funds intended for the public good; that self-elected little provincial oligarchies should be abolished; and that the affairs of municipal communities should be managed on a uniform system, openly and fairly, by persons representing those who were to pay and to be controlled.

I had the task imposed on me of preparing the Bill and carrying it through the Lower House. I find one of the notes preserved which were addressed to me by Lord John Russell on this subject.

April 22, 1835.

Dear Attorney,—I am obliged to you for your paper, but I wish you would write a supplement to it giving us some suggestion on the way of providing for the difficulty about magistrates. Would it do to have the aldermen elective, but not to be magistrates without the approbation of the Crown? We should likewise wish to know how it is possible to maintain the privileges of freemen which are of pecuniary value. Can they be preserved for life only? Or what can be done? Yours truly,

J. RUSSELL.

But our great difficulty was King William IV., who had been told by Queen Adelaide, and the Court ladies about him, that this was a most revolutionary scheme which would be the ruin of him and of his dynasty. Lord Melbourne, in much perplexity, addressed to me the following note and extract from the Royal remonstrance.

Downing Street : June 1, 1835.

My dear Attorney,—I send you an extract from the King's letter to me upon the Bill for regulating the Municipal Corporations. Pray write me down such remarks in answer to it as you think sufficient. . . . Yours faithfully,

MELBOURNE.

' It is impossible that the King should view or describe otherwise than as important a measure which, in principle and substance, sets out by the repeal of all acts, charters, and customs inconsistent with this Act, which revokes all *Royal* and other charters, grants and letters patent now in force relating to certain boroughs. The information afforded to the King on this head is as yet imperfect, inasmuch as the schedules to which reference is made are not annexed to the Bill transmitted, but enough has been submitted to him to show that the whole spirit of the Bill, its principle and provisions, affect most seriously the Royal prerogative, and are calculated to lessen the authority and the influence of the Crown.

' The King has no doubt that there are defects in the charters by which the bodies corporate have been constituted, and that their use and efficiency as instruments of local government have been impaired by the neglect and abuse of the privileges granted by charters, but it remains to be shown to his Majesty's satisfaction that the remedy might not have been applied by means short of *repeal*, and whether it had become necessary in every instance, or as a general principle, to substitute for the authority and prerogative hitherto exercised by the Crown, an elective power vested in the people, and tending, as his Majesty apprehends, to the production and the annual reproduction of much excitement and party agitation, from the bickerings and the squabbling which must attend the annual election of the members of the council, as well as the mayors, especially in large towns. It appears evident to the King that the ill-blood which will arise at one contest will not have subsided before the canvassing will begin in anticipation of the next ensuing election, and, in short, that these elections by all inhabitant householders whatever, of three years' standing, paying poor's rates, if registered, will be as annoying and as destructive of the peace and comfort of the boroughs in which they take place, as the election for members returned to serve in annual parliaments would be.'

I wrote a long explanation of the Bill, showing that it proceeded upon the true principles of the English Constitution, and that it would add to the stability of the throne as well as the prosperity of the people. This was laid before his Majesty, and had the effect of quieting and neutralising him, although he now looked with great suspicion on all the measures of the Whig Ministers.

The Municipal Reform was so popular that the Tories would not openly oppose it, and they were obliged to be contented with attempts to damage it as far as they could. Their chief ground was the preservation of the rights of the old freemen. I was provoked to make a very indiscreet speech against the freemen, denouncing them ' as the plague spot of the Constitution.' Of this effusion of the Whig Attorney-General, expressing, as was alleged, the sentiments of his party, above 50,000 copies were printed by our opponents to be distributed gratis in every town in England in which there were freemen possessing the elective franchise. A general storm of indignation arose, to which I was abandoned by my colleagues,—when at last Philip Howard, the member for Carlisle, came to the rescue, and amused the House by saying: ' We should remember that the honourable and learned Attorney-General once represented the borough of Stafford, and I am afraid that his recollection of the freemen there is not to be reckoned among *the pleasures of memory.*'

Most men of any note have at some time or other made use of an unlucky expression which has been permanently quoted against them. Knowing that, although the freemen are always venal and generally vote with the Tories, they are a very numerous and influential body, animated by a strong *esprit de corps*, and that in some few boroughs a majority of them were bribed by a Whig candidate, I was much to blame for pointing to them as ' the plague-spot of the Constitution.' But is it not more difficult to account for Lord Melbourne, in a speech made by him as Prime Minister to introduce a government measure, declaring in the presence of the bishops that it was ' a heavy blow and great discouragement to the Established Church of England ; '—or for Lord Lyndhurst pronouncing an anathema against the whole Irish nation as ' aliens in blood, language and religion;'—or for Lord John Russell's declaration as to the finality of the Reform Bill;— or for Lord Stanley's assertion that ' fifty millions of quarters of wheat might be imported into this country from the single province of Tamboff'?

The Municipal Reform Bill was returned to us by the Lords sadly mutilated, but most of their amendments were so outrageous that Peel could not defend them, and they were not insisted upon.

This is one of the many occasions when Peel and Lyndhurst were opposed to each other, the former always being on the Liberal side. When I urged to Lyndhurst that Peel approved of certain clauses which he had struck out in the Lords, he exclaimed: 'D—n Peel! What is Peel to me?' And this was not mere bravado or laxity of talk. About this time he and other ultra-Tories had formed a plan of deposing Peel from his lead. Stephenson lately told me that in 1835 or 1836 Lyndhurst consulted him as to whether Follett might not do to be set up as leader in Peel's place.

After a very harassing, but not formidable, opposition I carried my Bill through the Commons for abolishing imprisonment for debt and giving a more effectual remedy to creditors. This not being a party measure, I was in hopes that it would have been allowed to pass quietly through the House of Lords, but Brougham moved that it should be postponed on pretence of the lateness of the session, although when Chancellor he had professed warmly to support it; and to humour him the Government acquiesced in the proposal. I was exceedingly indignant, and I moved for a committee to search the Lords' Journals to know what had become of the Bill which 'there was reason to dread had been smothered in the dormitory of the House of Lords.' This drew down upon me the following remonstrance from the Prime Minister :—

Downing Street: September 1, 1835.

My dear Sir,—Many observations were made yesterday in the House of Lords upon what you had said in the House of Commons respecting the postponement of the Bill for abolishing imprisonment for debt. This postponement had been proposed by Brougham and acquiesced in by us. Now allow me to observe that by your strong censure you place us in the very awkward situation of condemning in the one House by the mouth of our Attorney-General a course which we have not objected to, and which therefore we must be supposed to approve in the other. This is a conduct which it is impossible to defend, and therefore when the attack is made upon this ground, we are reduced to the necessity of sitting silent and thus admitting its justice. Believe me, my dear Sir, yours faithfully,

MELBOURNE.

I good-humouredly upbraided him with his pusillanimity and want of vigour, and we were again friends.

In the following session the Bill was agreed to by both Houses, except as to imprisonment for debt after judgment, which still continues a blot upon our civil code.

I was kept in constant attendance in the House of Commons till the 10th of September, when I had to pay a visit to my constituents, and to thank them for having in the month of April, when I had vacated my seat by accepting the office of Attorney-General, again returned me to Parliament without requiring me to be present at the election.

Letters to Sir George Campbell during the years 1834 and 1835.

King's Bench : Tuesday, November 18, 1834.

. . . Whimsically enough I am now *pro tempore* Attorney-General to the Duke of Wellington, and I have been obliged to send to him for a further respite to the Chester murderers. I continue Attorney-General in point of law until my successor is appointed under the Great Seal, and shall sign the patents for the new Ministers. . . .

Scarlett is gone to the Duke of Wellington, having received a note asking him to come within the last half-hour. Copley is to have the seals in commission till Peel returns, and it is understood that he will then be Chancellor. I presume that Scarlett will have the offer of the Exchequer.

You will perceive that the ' Times ' is going to be the ally of the new Government. ' Measures, not men.' Spite against Brougham is one motive for this.

What a part he has played! He thought to please the Court by the stuff he talked about his ' gracious Master,' and there having been ' too much done last session of Parliament.' In the result he has made the King hostile to him personally, and he has almost irrecoverably ruined the character of the Whig party. ' He will still be exceedingly mischievous, and I wish he had gone over to the Tories. I am sorry to hear that from his kindness to his brother (the bright part of his character) he is involved in great pecuniary difficulties, and that with his 5,000*l.* a year he will be very ill off.

Scarlett says the King and the Duke were yesterday
loudly cheered by the mob. I am always amused by observing
how the Conservatives boast of any supposed symptoms of
popular applause, although they affect to despise it so much
when the mob are for their opponents.

King's Bench: Monday, December 1, 1834.

I am just returned from a conference with my old leader
Althorp. . . . I went chiefly to consult Lord Spencer about
the members of the late Government refusing to act any
longer. There was a strong opinion expressed at Brooks's
yesterday that we should all strike, and that we are counten-
ancing the unconstitutional state of affairs now subsisting.
However Lord Spencer says we must go on, for there is not
enough to take this case out of the common rule that, upon a
change of Ministry, those who go out are to act till their successors are appointed. We might have caused a great deal
of embarrassment to the Duke, but it seems this would be
considered factious, and disrespectful to the King.

. . . The King is to be in town to-day and was to give
audience to-morrow to Lord Spencer who was then to deliver
up his seal and his father's ribbon. But the Duke of Gloucester died yesterday evening at half-past six, and it is doubtful whether this event will not postpone the meeting.

Scarlett has been at Bagshot these two days, and is one of
the Duke's executors.

Brooks's: December 2, 1834.

. . . We had a Cabinet Council yesterday at five on the
question whether all the men retaining office ought immediately to strike. Several were very hot upon this, but Althorp's
opinion finally prevailed, and we are to remain quiet.

Brooks's: December 5, 1834.

. . . Hudson is arrived with despatches from Peel for the
Duke and the King. Peel was caught at Rome about to set
out for Naples, and is to be here on Monday or Tuesday.

King's Bench: December 8. Monday.

. . . Peel is expected every hour, and will be here to-day or
to-morrow. Till after his arrival nothing more is done. I

expect to remain Mr. Attorney till the end of the week. If Scarlett is promoted in the manner expected, I shall professionally not care much for becoming Sir John, although I am under the disagreeable apprehension of having both the new Attorney and Solicitor in King's Bench—Pollock and Follett. They are both able men, and to have them put over my head with official rank is not pleasant.

. . . All our people with one voice condemn Brougham, but they have never yet split with him or told him their opinion of him, and I know not now whether he will not be allowed to act as the head of the party. The King said yesterday to Scarlett, in reference to the manner in which the Great Seal was returned, ' I was glad to get it from him on any terms.'

Lyndhurst is very loth to give up the office of Chief Baron. He proposes to keep it till Christmas, under the pretence of clearing off arrears in the Exchequer, but really, I believe, to see how the elections go. I have however put Scarlett up to counteract this manœuvre, and I am much mistaken if Master Copley is not forthwith required to make his choice.

King's Bench : Saturday, February 14, 1835.

. . . I have just got a verdict, in a very important cause, against Scarlett—Lord Abinger. He summed up strongly against me, but the jury found in my favour. He is to dine with me to-day, and I shall crow over him excessively. It is a curious fact that, having got so many verdicts at the bar, he has lost all the verdicts since he mounted the bench—that is, that the juries have found against his direction. Nevertheless he has got great κῦδος as a judge. Even the Equity men praise him very much for his performances in Equity.

I am to have a private conference to-morrow with our new leader, Johnny Russell. I wish he could add a cubit to his stature, and were a little less puny in his bodily frame. When they were astonished in the West of England, after the passing of the Reform Bill, to find so *great* a man so *little*, Sydney Smith satisfied them by saying that ' he was wasted away in the service of his country.'

Copley has been trying to steal one of my Bills from me,

in a manner strongly to remind me of Fox Maule's expression : 'They wish to crawl into our nest to hatch our eggs.'

Brooks's : March 17, 1835.

. . . Peel himself is a much better man than any we can oppose to him. He really is exceedingly dexterous and handy, as well as eloquent and powerful. But his associates do away with the favourable impression he has made.

I play with Hally and forget politics. He is a most delightful companion.[6] He said to me this morning, while attending my toilet : 'You must go to Heaven, for you are so good a man ; but I hear people abuse you in their speeches, and I am sure they must be wrong.'

Exeter : March 25, 1835.

. . . I forget whether I told you I was going to the Cornish assizes. I am on my way to Launceston, having left London last night at ten, and arrived here this evening at seven. I am rather sorry to leave the scene of action at present, but I shall be at my post again on Monday. . . .

I never was in Devonshire before—a magnificent country ; but nothing can be more miserable than Wiltshire and Dorsetshire. I am going down to try whether the plaintiff be, or be not, entitled to receive sixteen shillings. The question was tried before (a question of tolls), when Scarlett was for the defendant and got a verdict. The Court of Exchequer granted a new trial, the judges being furiously in support of the toll. I shall have Mr. Baron Gurney very strong against me, and my only chance is with the jury.

I proceed to Launceston to-morrow morning.

House of Commons : Monday, March 30, 1835.

. . . I have lost my cause in Cornwall, as I hear within the last half-hour. I left Launceston on Friday night at eleven when the jury were locked up. I understand they continued out till ten on Saturday morning, when they found a verdict against me on a ground that is wholly untenable, and which was abandoned by the plaintiff's counsel. This is a mishap which I must bear with an equal mind.

[6] Aged five.

I have about one hundred and fifty letters a day about Imprisonment . for Debt, and many deputations, and the measure would occupy the whole of my time.

I got home at two o'clock on Sunday morning.

King's Bench: May 12, 1835.

. . . I am in a perpetual hurry, and am *hunted*, as it were, from morn till night.

All Edinburgh is now in London. I had begun a party for Saturday; but meeting Abercromby last night at the Duchess of Kent's, I was ordered to transfer myself and my guests to him. I have refused all invitations for Saturdays to keep them open for my constituents.

John Russell is to come in for Stroud.

Committee Room, Edinburgh Water Works:
Friday, May 15.

. . . I am now in the delightful situation of attending private Committees in which my constituents are interested. There are three of these to-day, for which I have cut Westminster Hall. They are likely to go on for some weeks, and I know not what is to become of me!

House of Commons: May 19, 1835.

. . . The only news is that I am going to take the Chiltern Hundreds and retire into private life. The representation of Edinburgh is too much for me. I have smashed two Bills, which my constituents disliked, after hard struggles, and my labours are only beginning. I have just been complaining to Abercromby. . . . He makes an exceedingly good Speaker.

I am to have a great Edinburgh party on Saturday—the Lord Provost, etc. etc.

Monday, May 25, 1835.

. . . My dinner on Saturday went off well. I had at table two Antiburgher ministers, who said grace before and after meat with great unction. I am to give a dinner of a very different sort on the King's birthday. I sent out eighty-five cards, and shall have sixty guests, at the Freemason's Tavern.

May 28, 1835.

I am just returned from the Drawing-room. .. . . I rallied
Melbourne about his three Chancellors, who were sticking close together to show they formed one officer. What
amused me most was an account Lord Shaftesbury gave
me of the contests between Brougham and Copley as to
which shall sit on the woolsack at the hearing of appeals.
Brougham one morning got a bishop and had prayers said
before ten o'clock, that he might be first. To keep the peace
between them Shaftesbury is to act as Speaker in the mornings for the rest of the session.

Saturday, May 30, 1835.

. . . I continue to be terribly harassed by Edinburgh
local matters and I have more upon my hands than any man
can manage.

I am better off, however, than my friend the ex-Chancellor
of Ireland. I met him at the Drawing-room on Thursday
just after I had been talking to Lyndhurst, whom I addressed
as Field Marshal on account of his splendid uniform, which
he has devised as the costume of an ex-Chancellor. I asked
Sugden why he had not the same. He told me seriously
that he had asked and obtained his Majesty's permission to
wear it, and that he was to have one immediately. I said, 'I
am glad to hear that his Majesty rewards merit. This is a
suitable return for your great services in Ireland.'

June 16, 1835.

. . . A few days ago Copley played off what he thought
a good joke on Brougham and myself. Wishing to see
Brougham while the House was sitting, I went in my gown
and full-bottom to the door by which the Chancellor enters.
Copley said : 'Walk in, and take your seat on the woolsack.
Brougham ! here he comes, here's the spectre ! ' Brougham
came out very sulky, not at all relishing the joke. I understand, while I was arguing Lady Warrender's case, Brougham
said : 'How ill he is doing it,' upon which Copley said :
' Mind what you say. He will be sitting here presently.'
This is merely to plague Brougham.

July 4, 1835.

. . . I am to have an interview to-morrow with Lord Melbourne about a notice given in the House of Commons respecting the state of business in the Court of Chancery. I presume he will be prepared to tell me what are the intentions of Government respecting the Great Seal, and I think I am authorised in requiring some explanation on this subject. They would be delighted if the Great Seal could be sunk 400 fathoms deep, and I have very little notion what they will propose. They will be very adverse to any arrangement which would take me out of the House of Commons, for there would be a great difficulty in appointing a new Attorney-General. They have no dislike to me. For example, Lord Holland is coming to dine with me on the 11th, although he has not dined out for a twelvemonth except with the King. Lord John also comes and most of the Cabinet.

July 24, 1835.

. . . Now that the courts are up and committees are over, and the House of Lords is not hearing appeals, it appears to me that I am as much hurried and overwhelmed with business as ever. But I must write you two lines. . . . Fred has come home from school and he and I have already read through the first book of the Æneid.

I am going on special retainers to Shrewsbury and Liverpool and perhaps to Chester, but I do not leave London for a fortnight.

Chester: August 23, 1835.

. . . I am engaged in the most horrid cause here that ever was tried, respecting the right to a great variety of parcels of waste land in Wales, and we have been obliged to go through the conveyances and enjoyment of them, from the year 1198 before the conquest of Wales, when they were granted by Prince Llewellyn to the monks of Conway. I made a speech yesterday to the jury of six hours. The trial will not be over for some days to come, but, thank God, I am obliged to go to-morrow evening to Liverpool. I can now be spared here pretty well, and my client has had an excellent pennyworth of me. You may believe I am very impatient to get back to London.

Liverpool : Tuesday, four o'clock.
August 25, 1835.

. . . I am just going to set off for London. In four hours
I got a verdict for the Crown—without much glory—for tech-
nicalities shut out the great question which the other side
wished to try. But we have got the verdict, and with little
trouble, which is a great thing for me now, for I really in my
mind do want repose. The Chester trial is not yet over, and
I would not engage in such another for twice my fee. I shall
be in good time for the row with the Lords. I go to Manchester by the railroad, and post on without stopping.

House of Commons :
Thursday, September 10, 1835.

. . . We are waiting for the arrival of the Speaker. The
King comes at two. I hear his Majesty yesterday in Council
made a rather extraordinary speech, *advising his Ministers*
to keep up the Militia, that constitutional force, in spite of
Irish agitation. I hope he will not throw aside to-day the
speech of the Minister, and deliver one of his own in defence
of the Irish Church.

I start at four by the Brighton coach, unless it should
continue to rain, in which case I must post, for there is no
inside place to be had. Direct to me Lewes Crescent, Kemp
Town, Brighton.

Brighton : October 4, 1835.

. . . I met the other day, as motto to a chapter in a novel,
with a stanza by my great *predecessor* Sir Thomas More,
which ought to make me thankful and cheerful in the contemplation of my large share of the good things of life.

> Some manne hath goode but children hath he none,
> Some man hath bothe, but he can get no healthe ;
> Some hath all three, but up to *Honor's throne*
> Can he not creep by no manner of stealthe.
> To some she sendeth children, riches, healthe,
> Honor, worship, and reverence all his life,
> But yet she pincheth him with a shrewd wife.
>   Be content
> With such reward as Fortune hath you sent.

I have got most of this catalogue of desirables without

being pinched with a shrewd wife, and if I can neither creep nor jump into *Honor's throne*, I shall be content.

I have had famous rides with the children here. To the great admiration of Brighton, I place Hally before me on Gloucester and canter round the Steyne.

To-morrow the Scarletts are coming to pay us a visit. If the Edinburgh and London Railway were completed to join the London and Brighton, now resolved upon, your party from Edenwood might easily come up and see our 'splendid mansion' in Kemp Town.

> King's Bench : Monday, November 23, 1835.

. . . Hally is going to school at Christmas. I shall be exceedingly sorry to part with him, but I think it time he should be removed from home, where he is rather too much petted. Fred comes to us on the 8th of December. In England, where boys go to boarding schools, if the holidays were not long there would be no opportunity for cultivating the domestic affections.

> December 19, 1835.

. . . I am amused by your ' six hours.' Hard labour, indeed! I may say sixteen. I have not tasted dinner for three days, and have worked from nine in the morning till one next morning. Trust me, it is better to go to Cupar and read the newspapers and return with a good appetite.

People suppose a leader at the bar makes a fine speech which he has prepared, and gains applause. I have, of course, as often a bad case as a good one ; and what with disagreeable and formidable opponents and imbecile judges, I lead a life worse than a convict in the treadmill. I often know my briefs very imperfectly, and am in constant apprehension that I may injure my client and my own reputation.

What is to become of me when the 5th of February arrives —Parliament and the courts of law sitting together ?

Autobiography.

Things went on very smoothly till the end of the year, when the horizon began to look black and a heavy storm was impending. As I had foretold, the arrangement in the Court of Chancery had caused much dissatisfaction. The Master of the Rolls and the Vice-Chancellor, sitting as Lords Commissioners, were obliged to neglect the business of their own courts, which fell more and more into arrear, and considerable grumbling was produced by their sitting jointly in a court of appeal from each other's judgments; for it was remarked that if a decree of one was reversed, a decree of the other was reversed soon after, so as to keep the tale of affirmances and reversals exactly equal between the two Equity Commissioners; Bosanquet, the third Commissioner, being always ready to reverse that he might show his impartiality. The appeals in the House of Lords likewise went on very badly without a Lord Chancellor—Lord Lyndhurst and Lord Brougham undertaking to hear them alternately, but at that time not by any means acting in concert in this department.

Sir Edward Sugden, ex-Lord Chancellor of Ireland, published a very spirited pamphlet upon the subject, severely condemning the system, or want of system, which prevailed, and it was clear that some new arrangement must be made before Parliament again met. It turned out that, without ever consulting me, Lord Melbourne and his Cabinet had resolved that I should be retained in the House of Commons, where my services were considered important; that Pepys should be made Chancellor, and Henry Bickersteth should have the Rolls with a peerage.

Hearing a rumour that some new arrangement was in contemplation, I wrote to Lord Melbourne and Lord John Russell begging to be informed what it was. They told me it was proposed to make Pepys Chancellor and Bickersteth Master of the Rolls. I wrote back that the Minister must be allowed to choose his own Chancellor, who was to sit in the Cabinet with him, according to his taste, but that I considered I had an unquestionable right to the Rolls, and that if this was disregarded I should certainly resign my office of Attorney-General. They strongly urged me not to resign, and to wait to see what could be done to satisfy me. Lord John Russell's letter was very frank and friendly, but my resolution to resign if Bickersteth was made Master of the Rolls remained unshaken.

I had several interviews with Lord Melbourne, and several notes passed between us in the beginning of January without any decisive declaration on either side.[7] I stated all the facts of the case and communicated all the correspondence to my colleague Abercromby, the Speaker, who thought me atrociously ill-used, and undertook to remonstrate with the leading men in the Cabinet upon the subject. He soon after informed me that he understood that Bickersteth actually was appointed. I went home, wrote a formal resignation of my office, ' which I could no longer hold with honour to myself or advantage to the public,' drove in a cab to South Street, and saw Lord Melbourne. He admitted that the King's pleasure had been taken on Bickersteth's appointment. ' There, then, is my resignation of the office of Attorney-General.' He begged me to keep it till he had made me a proposal which he thought might satisfy me. He assured me that one great object was to retain my services in the House of Commons, without which the Government would have great difficulty in carrying through the measures they had in contemplation; that when it was very desirable to keep a political man in the House of Commons and to mark the sense entertained of his public services, there were several approved precedents for making his wife a peeress; that a peerage thus conferred on my family would be very honourable to me and would effectually remove any notion of my being slighted; that, if I would consent, he trusted the King would agree to this arrangement; that my promotion was only deferred, as a Bill would be brought in to make a permanent Chief Judge in the Court of Chancery, leaving the Chancellor to hear appeals in the House of Lords and in the Privy Council; and that some consideration was

[7] The following letter from Lord Melbourne to Lord Lansdowne, dated January 10, 1836, appears in the lately published *Life of Lord Melbourne*, vol. ii. p. 172 :—' Campbell, after much discussion on the subject, which I must say, considering how deeply his interests are involved and his feelings touched, he has carried on with great fairness and good temper, has this morning sent to me his final determination, which is that he cannot submit to be passed over, and must resign if our arrangement is carried into effect.'—ED.

to be had to the credit and interest of the party. I yielded, and brought home my resignation with the seal unbroken. A messenger was immediately despatched to the King at Brighton, and next day I learned that his Majesty made no objection, and that I had only to choose a title. Pollock, and one or two others, blamed me for not resigning, and said I had lowered the office of Attorney-General; but Abercromby, Follett, and those whose opinions I most regarded, approved, and I have never since repented any part of my conduct on this occasion.

The Gazette immediately announced that his Majesty had been graciously pleased to raise to the peerage Mary Elizabeth Campbell, by the name, style and title of Baroness Stratheden of Cupar in the county of Fife. We thought this a proper mark of respect to the place of my nativity, and to the memory of my father. The creation came intermediately between that of Pepys by the title of Lord Cottenham, and that of Bickersteth by the title of Lord Langdale.

Letter from Mr. Speaker Abercromby.

January 13, 1836.

My dear Campbell,—Poulett Thomson came here yesterday with Melbourne's concurrence to tell me what had been proposed, and later in the evening I had a note from Lord Melbourne on the subject. It is the best thing that the Government could do under the circumstances, and I think you could not have hesitated. It is an answer to all observations—it is great homage to you—it secures an important object for your family, and it puts beyond all doubt the value that is attached to your services. *I* sincerely rejoice in it on all accounts, and it relieves you from an embarrassing and painful position. Now that it is over, I may say that I have never been engaged in any transaction that gave me more vexation. On the one hand I saw all the evil to the Government, and on the other no man could feel more strongly than I did the true character of the situation in which you were placed. It was not easy to steer clear of difficulties in such circumstances, but I have found that directness and plain speaking have been good protections, as both you and Lord Melbourne are satisfied with what I have done. It would not have been so if Lord Melbourne had not been a candid and just man. He possesses these qualities more than any Minister I have known. Yours very sincerely,

J. ABERCROMBY.

Letter from Viscount Melbourne.

Private.   Downing Street : January 13, 1836.

My dear Attorney,—I have just received his Majesty's entire approbation of Lady Campbell's elevation to the Peerage. It is impossible to describe the relief which this gives, and I assure you that I have felt very sensibly the good temper and fairness with which you have acted during the whole of these very painful discussions. Yours faithfully,

MELBOURNE.

Letter from The Right Honourable Edward Ellice.

Private.   Paris : Sunday, January 17, 1836.

My dear Campbell,—I must write one line to congratulate you—or rather to express my own satisfaction—that they have shown their sense of the justice of your claims, and the value of your services, and that at the same time an arrangement is made to secure your assistance to the popular party in the House of Commons. *Reste à voir* if Equity lawyers are the best Equity reformers, and have pluck and tact to fight the battle with Brougham and Lyndhurst in the Lords. Sure I am they have great odds in their favour, in their case, and with their character, and that if they fail it will say little for the judgment of those who have placed them there. I do not, however, look at the wrong side of the picture, and hope they may be as successful as I am satisfied with any arrangement which is creditable to you and keeps us all together.

I shall be over by the first of the month. We shall have a hard stand-up fight for it, but if our leaders will only do their duty and show a bold front, I can have no fear of winning cleverly. My kindest remembrances and best compliments to my Lady on her new honours. Ever sincerely yours,

EDWARD ELLICE.

CHAPTER XXII.

Proposed Judge of Appeal in the House of Lords—Opposition of Lord
Langdale—Defends Lord Melbourne in the Case of Norton *v.* Mel-
bourne—Lord Lyndhurst's Obstructive Policy in the House of Lords—
Public Dinner at Cupar—Speech at Edinburgh—Proposed as Lord
Rector of Glasgow University—Duties as Attorney-General—Church
Rates Bill—Publishes 'Letter to Lord Stanley'—Question of Parlia-
mentary Privilege—Stockdale *v.* Hansard—Death of William IV.—
The Queen's first Council—Dissolution of Parliament—Conduct of the
Tories towards the Queen—Is returned again for Edinburgh—Mr.
Speaker Abercromby—Autumn at Erlwood—The Duchess of Glouces-
ter—Dinner at Buckingham Palace.

Autobiography.

THE King's Speech on the meeting of Parliament held out the
prospect of great judicial changes. The Minister made his
Majesty say: 'The speedy and satisfactory administration of
justice is the first and most sacred duty of a Sovereign, and I
earnestly recommend you to consider whether better provisions
may not be made for this great purpose in some of the departments of the law, and more particularly in the Court of
Chancery.'

A conference was held in South Street, attended by Lord
Melbourne, Lord Cottenham, Lord Langdale, Lord Denman,
Lord John Russell, Lord Howick and myself, at which the subject was fully discussed, and it was resolved that a Bill dividing
the duties of the Lord Chancellor should be introduced, so as
to have a permanent judge presiding in the Court of Chancery,
and a judge of appeal, removable with the administration, to
preside in the House of Lords and the Privy Council. This
latter office it was understood I was to fill.

However the Bill was not brought forward till April 28,
when it was introduced in the House of Lords by the new

Chancellor, with good faith, I believe, but I can by no means
say with ability.   He had shown himself an excellent Equity
judge, but he had no faculty to address a deliberative assembly,
and his speech on this occasion was tame, confused and *dis-
suasive.*   Lord Lyndhurst made a few observations against
the Bill, 'reserving his detailed objections to it for a future
stage;' but any subsequent opposition to the Bill was rendered
unnecessary by 'the heavy blow and great discouragement'
it received from Lord Langdale, who said 'he did not think
the Bill went far enough, as it did not entirely separate the
judicial and political functions of the Lord Chancellor, and he
disapproved of some of its provisions about Chancery appeals.'

The Bill stood for a second reading on June 13, when
it received its *quietus.* On this occasion Lord Langdale
delivered a good prepared speech expounding his Bentham-
ite notions upon the judicial character, and explaining how
there ought to be a *tripartite* division of the Lord Chancellor
—one third to sit in the Court of Chancery under the ancient
title, one third to sit in the House of Lords and Privy
Council under the title of 'Lord President in matter of
Appeals and Writs of Error,' and one third to superintend the
administration and improvement of the law under the title
of ' Minister of Justice.' Such discredit was thrown upon the
Bill by Lord Langdale's opposition, that only twenty-nine
ministerial peers could be got to vote for it, and it was rejected by a majority of sixty-five. Lord Langdale himself
voted in the minority, professing an opinion that he entirely
approved of its principle, and that, with a few alterations,
which might easily be made in Committee, it would be found
to work very beneficially.

Lord Melbourne had soon occasion to express his satisfaction that I was still at the bar, an action being brought
against him for criminal conversation with the beautiful and
celebrated Mrs. Norton, the wife of the Honourable George
Norton, brother of Lord Grantley. This retainer caused me
more professional anxiety than I ever experienced. If the
action had succeeded, the Premier's private character would
have been ruined, and there would have been an end of his
Administration.

The charge turned out to be false, but I then knew not what foundation there might be for it. Although no violation of confidence and the laws of hospitality had before been imputed to the noble defendant, his morals were not supposed to be very strict, and in a former instance a similar action being brought against him under rather venial circumstances, the verdict of *Not guilty* pronounced in consequence of the witnesses not appearing raised a not improbable suspicion of compromise. The Tory newspapers now anticipated his condemnation, and asserted that letters would be read on the trial from him to the lady not only proving the case but showing that he had been guilty of the most shameless profligacy as a Minister. He wrote the following letter to me and earnestly implored me to act upon it.

South Street: June 19, 1836.

My dear Attorney,—I have been thinking over again the matter of this trial, and I know not that I have anything to add to what I have already written, and to what passed the other day at the consultation. I repeat that I wish it to be stated in the most clear, distinct, and emphatic manner that I have never committed adultery with Mrs. Norton, that I have never held with her any furtive or clandestine correspondence whatever, and that both in visiting and in writing to her I always considered myself to be acting with the full knowledge and with the entire approbation of her husband. My visits, for instance, were neither more nor less frequent when he was away than when he was at home. At the same time, I wish any evidence which may come out of this nature to be so managed as to appear to be used rather for the purpose of vindicating me than of criminating him. The first must be my principal, if not my sole, object. If I cannot persuade the jury that there has been no criminal intercourse, it will be of little advantage to my character to show that I thought I was carrying it on with the knowledge and connivance of the husband. These arrangements are supposed frequently to exist, and whilst they are only supposed, they are certainly treated with great indulgence and made the subject of jest and levity. But a different judgment is pronounced upon them when they are proved and established in a court of justice. There is great indignation against him, and a great desire to see him exposed, but we must consider what is best for ourselves. If you require any further explanation or instruction, I shall be happy to give it. Believe me, yours faithfully,

MELBOURNE.

The cause attracted the attention of all Europe, as it was supposed to involve the stability of the present Government in England; and on the day of trial there were couriers ready to start for foreign Courts with news of the result.

I had lain awake the greatest part of the night before, and at last falling into repose I had overslept myself, so that I was obliged to dress in a hurry and run off without my breakfast. On my arrival at the Court of Common Pleas I found the doors surrounded by such an immense crowd that the police could scarcely procure me admittance. The body of the court was almost entirely filled with gentlemen in wigs and gowns, who availed themselves of their professional privilege to enter before the public.

I was in a state of great tremor till Sir William Follett, counsel for the plaintiff, read the much-talked-of letters of the Prime Minister—when I could breathe, for they were ludicrously immaterial, like the parody of them by Dickens about ' chops and tomato sauce ' in the trial of Pickwick. My confidence increased when the first witness, the clergyman who performed the marriage ceremony, stated to me in cross-examination that in visiting Mrs. Norton he entered the house by the same private door which was to establish the clandestinety of the visits of Lord Melbourne, and that ' he did so without any improper views upon the wife of his friend.' Here there was a loud laugh, in which judge and jury joined, and I felt that the verdict was in my pocket. Nevertheless a large body of evidence was brought forward which, if believed, would have been fatal; and the plaintiff's case did not finish till past six in the evening.

Being somewhat exhausted, and afraid that the jury might be so too, I applied for an adjournment, which was luckily refused, for I then made a far better speech for effect than I could have made next day.

When the jury gave their verdict for the defendant there were shouts of applause in court and in Westminster Hall, which were heard in the House of Commons, then sitting, and caused a great sensation during the debate. I immediately unrobed and entered the House. As I passed from the bar to my place I was received with immense cheers from our side and a few faint ones from the other, uttered by Tories who wished to repel the imputation that the action was a party manœuvre. I cannot say with whom the action originated, but I do aver that it was taken up with great eagerness by the great bulk of the Tory party, and that they were most cruelly mortified when it failed.

Lord Melbourne sent me the following acknowledgment.

South Street: June 23, 1836.

My dear Attorney,—I write one line to return you my best thanks for your very able and successful exertion of last night, as well as for your whole conduct of the cause. Pray say the same for me to Serjeant Talfourd and Mr. Thesiger, who I am sure will excuse my writing to them separately.

I hold the obtaining a verdict to have been a most difficult achievement, considering the prejudices both general and personal which naturally prevailed upon the subject, and considering the latitude of inference in which Courts of Justice think themselves justified in indulging in these cases, and the reliance they are disposed to place upon circumstantial evidence, both of which principles of proceeding must, I feel certain, often lead to gross injustice, as they would in the present case if the verdict had been the other way. Believe me, my dear Attorney,

Yours faithfully,
MELBOURNE.

The Administration, instead of being overturned, was considerably strengthened by the result.

But in the House of Lords we were at the mercy of our opponents. The plan laid down by the Opposition this session of Parliament—systematically acted upon and not disguised—was to obstruct all our measures, however good, without any discrimination, and if they could not be decently resisted in the Commons to smother them in the Upper House. Lyndhurst avowed their object to be to turn against Lord Melbourne a sentiment of William III. which Lord Melbourne himself had once quoted with approbation, that ' while there were debates about the best form of government, some preferring monarchy, some aristocracy, some democracy, he would not pretend to decide between them, but he was sure that the worst government was that which could not carry its own measures.' So bent was Lyndhurst on illustrating this maxim that he would not even allow Bills to pass which had received Peel's express approbation. For example, there was a Bill of mine to alter the mode of revising the electoral lists, and to have ten barristers constantly employed in this work, instead of 150 for a few weeks in the year. I proposed privately to the Opposition that the ten barristers should be

named in the Bill, and that five should be appointed with the
consent of each side. This was agreed to. Sir Frederick
Pollock named the five Conservatives and I the five Liberals,
and the ten names were approved by the Commons. But
when the Bill went to the Upper House, Lyndhurst said ' he
was no party to the arrangement, and it should not pass.'
He was as good as his word, and threw it out on the second
reading.

I must say that our party was deplorably ill off for some
peer to take care of such Bills. Lord Melbourne would give
himself no trouble about them. They were left to Duncannon,
who, though a man of excellent good sense, was wholly in
competent to enter the lists with Lyndhurst, and contented
himself generally with reading the title of the Bill, moving
that it be read a second time, and when it was opposed
saying: 'Well, my Lords, if your lordships object to the
Bill, it would be vain for me to press it, and therefore I withdraw it.'[1] In this way several other unexceptionable Bills,
which I carried up to the Lords for the correction of mistakes
in the Municipal Corporations Act, and other such useful
purposes, met their fate. When I privately remonstrated
with Lyndhurst on the subject, he laughed and joked very
agreeably, but remained inexorable.

To another Bill, ' for regulating Charities,' I thought he
would be shamed out of his opposition by a public exposure.
According to his tactics, he returned this Bill to the Commons
so damaged that we could not accept it in its altered form.
We sent a message to the Lords that we·disagreed to their
amendments; and we had so many conferences with them,
in which the correspondence was by written reasons, that we
had either to drop the Bill altogether or to adopt the next procedure between the two Houses—*an open conference*—where
the debate was to be carried on *vivâ voce*. This had fallen

---

[1] It is curious enough that within a week after writing this I met
Lord Duncannon at Brooks's, and, talking of Ellenborough, Governor-
General of India, he said, 'Ellenborough is a man of extraordinary
industry. He used to read all the Bills and all the Blue Books. When we
were in office, and Government Bills came up that I knew nothing about,
I used to ask him what they meant, and he would take me into the
library and explain them to me.'

into desuetude for a century. I was in favour of the open conference, and I was appointed one of the managers for the Commons. We met the managers for the Lords, and had a long *palaver*, without any converts being made on either side. I had the honour to answer Lord Ellenborough, and with due decorum I ventured to glance at the obstructive course which their lordships were pursuing. However, they insisted on their amendments and we could do no more.

At the conclusion of the session, Lyndhurst in a declamatory speech took a review of it, showing how little had been done, comparing Melbourne to Cardinal Wolsey, and his promise at the beginning of the session with his performance in the course of it—

> His promises were, as he then was—mighty ;
> But his performance as he is now—nothing.

He likewise did me the honour to introduce my name several times, and to talk of the Radical propensities of the Whig Attorney-General.

Letters to Sir George Campbell in the year 1836.

Court of Exchequer : Saturday, April 22, 1836.

. . . I wish for promotion much more from what I should avoid than what I should gain. The bar has now become most irksome to me, and my duties are too much for any individual.

I am waiting here to my great annoyance till a cause in which I am is called, and I shall very likely be summoned to the King's Bench before it comes on. But I have a very agreeable dinner in prospect at the Royal Academy, the only pleasant public dinner during the year. You dine in the great picture room, and the *élite* of London society is present. In the evening I mean to go to the Lord Chancellor's levée.

Follett, poor fellow, is again ill, and unable to come into court.

King's Bench : May 23, 1836.

. . . I was occupied all last week (our supposed holidays) with Lord Breadalbane's appeal before the House of Lords. I had the satisfaction to please my client. He said I had

argued it for him like a friend and a clansman, and Lady
Breadalbane flattered me very agreeably in her narration of
the account she had received of my exertions. I was in a
horrid funk before I began to reply. I am at times as
nervous as when I was first called to the bar.

I suppose Melbourne's affair has reached you. The
action *is* going on, and I am to have the honour of defending
him.

King's Bench : May 28, 1836.

. . . I was at the levée yesterday and presented a petition
from Edinburgh. From the King's manner I really believe
he thought it was for the abolition of the peerage, as he
seemed much startled ; but if he read it (as I dare say he
had the curiosity to do), he would find it conceived in terms
of the most fervid loyalty, praying his Majesty to become
patron of the National Monument.

We dined yesterday at Holland House and had a very
gracious reception from 'her Majesty the Queen of Mada-
gascar.' Her Majesty was graciously pleased to order me to
take her out to dinner in presence of men of much higher
rank. Such are the topics to which I am reduced in these
quiet times, but we shall have a storm very soon.

May 31, 1836.

. . . We are going to the Duke of Devonshire's grand ball
on Friday. We have our christening on Saturday, and on
Monday we go to the Duchess of Kent's. So you see in the
midst of our troubles we are very *gay* !

June 4, 1836.

. . . Having divided this morning at three, I drove by
daylight to Devonshire House and carried the news of the
majority. Mary was impatiently expecting me, and the tide
of fashion continued to make for half an hour.

Little Cecilia is to be christened to-day, by a bishop
too—the Bishop of Durham, Maltby, who is an old private
friend of mine ; but I have some scruples, and I doubt
whether this be in the true spirit of our ancestor the Marquis
of Argyle : ' *I hate popery and prelacy and all superstition
whatsomever.*'

House of Commons : June 16, 1836.

. . . Melbourne's trial now weighs upon my mind. It presents an aspect more and more disagreeable, although I believe in the defendant's protestation of innocence. He attended a consultation on his case yesterday at my house. He proposed that his counsel should come to South Street or Downing Street; but I would make no exception in favour of the Premier to the rule that the client must come to the counsel.

House of Commons : June 23, 1836.

. . . You will rejoice very much in the verdict in favour of Melbourne. This is the most brilliant event in my career. I am almost suffocated with congratulations.

When I left the Common Pleas last night I heard the House of Commons was still sitting, and I could not avoid the temptation of showing myself. The House was crowded, and the moment I showed myself at the bar the cheering began, and I walked up to my place in the midst of the most rapturous plaudits. The Tories even affected to cheer, although the result was a deep disappointment to them.

Had the verdict been the other way, it would most probably before long have brought about a change of Government. Melbourne must have resigned, and, if he had continued in office, the stain upon his character would most essentially have weakened the Administration.

I passed a horrid day, and success is not a corresponding reward for my anxiety. I did not till the last know what sort of case was to be made against us, or how it was to be encountered. I was not at all in a good state of mind or stomach when my turn came to address the jury, and I was under the most exquisitely painful apprehension that I might not be able to do my duty.

However I got through very well, and at all events people judge by the event. I conducted the examination of the witnesses with great tact, and my speech, though irregular, was effective. To get a verdict, the way is not to consider how your speech will read when reported, but to watch the jury, and to push any advantage you may make, disregarding irregularities and repetitions.

House of Commons: June 24, 1836.

. . . I am like the Duke of Wellington after the battle of Waterloo, not knowing how great a victory had been achieved. I am absolutely overwhelmed by compliments and civilities, and everybody says (what I did not believe) that my speech was admirable. I did not expect more than that I had got off without discredit, having some *éclat* from the successful result.

After giving you many a melancholy *effusion* when I despaired of ever doing any good in my profession, I think it right to give you some account of my present palmy state. Party feeling, you may suppose, is the great cause of the excitement, and of the commendations bestowed upon me. There were the most serious apprehensions, and a deliverance from these gives a very joyous feeling. Indeed it is truly said that so much never before depended upon any civil trial in an English court.

July 3, 1836.

. . . I am rejoiced to think that our children are running about happily together. This must be exquisite weather for St. Andrews. I am just returned from Holland House, where Mary and I have been dining. Both my Lord and my Lady most extravagantly praised my efforts in the great cause. It is curious that Melbourne himself has not said a word to me on the subject since the trial. Yet last night at Holland House he spontaneously and freely spoke about the trial to Talfourd, and said the Attorney-General's speech as a forensic display was equal to anything in ancient or modern times.

July 20, 1836.

. . . It delights me very much to think of my two girls being with you at St. Andrews. They write us long and lively accounts of all their proceedings. Loo is particularly touching in her account of Cupar, where her father lived when a boy, and Cupar pulpit in which her grandfather so often preached and was so much liked.

I am going to Huntingdon to-morrow, and thence to Cambridge.

Huntingdon : July 23, 1836.

. . . I have won my cause here, which excited great local interest, being a prosecution by the Conservative association against the leader of the Reformers in this county for a conspiracy to put bad votes on the register.

I am now going to Cambridge to try whether a child is the illegitimate child of a lady who is the plaintiff, or the legitimate child of a gentleman who is the defendant. There has not been such a case since Solomon's time. I know not whether Chief Justice Tindal will follow the example of the wisest of men and order the child to be cut in two.

House of Commons : August 1, 1836.

. . . I have had a delightful trip to Erlwood, which we had all to ourselves, the Curreys being at Abinger.

Cissy, just a year old, runs after the chickens with the most intense earnestness and delight. Dudley is a giant in miniature. Fred, Hally and I shot with the bow and ran races—and I could beat them hollow in both exercises.

Liverpool : August 20, 1836.

. . . I cannot return to the South without giving you a line. I am unexpectedly released here by a juryman being taken ill during the trial. This circumstance led to a compromise.

I am exceedingly delighted to think that my labours and cares are over for this campaign. I do not much like special retainers, as they are attended with so much responsibility and anxiety. It is full time that I should be released from the wrangling of the bar, but of this there is no longer any prospect.

Autobiography.

After the prorogation, having made a tour round the Isle of Wight, passed some weeks at Hayling Island, and put my eldest son to school at Eton, I went to the North in a Dundee steamer, and paid a delightful visit to my brother at Edenwood, now become Sir George Campbell; and, what is better, living in the highest state of domestic happiness with a beautiful woman for his wife, and surrounded by five lovely children.

I here very unexpectedly received an invitation to a dinner to be given to me at Cupar by my native county, where I did not look to be at all honoured as a prophet. However this turned out to be a sort of miniature representation of the Grey Festival at Edinburgh. St. Andrews, Cupar, Kirkcaldy, Kinghorn and all the royal burghs in the county voted me the freedom of their corporation, now to be presented by deputations. They all formed a grand procession and conducted me in triumph over the bridge across the Eden, past the house where I was born, on to the Cross, and so I was placed under a canopy in the Town Hall. But when the addresses began I was so affected that I could only sob violently, and the more I tried to command my feelings I sobbed the more. The memory of my father came across me, and I thought with myself what his sensations would have been if he could have witnessed this scene. I am exceedingly uncertain as to being melted to tenderness or remaining firm. Sometimes, hearing the most painful intelligence and suffering the utmost mental agony, I do not shed a tear. At other times, when I ought hardly to be at all touched, I cry like a child. Military music makes a great impression upon my nerves, and some airs give me an almost irresistible inclination to tenderness. On this occasion the music, I believe, assisted to overcome me. However, all was ascribed to 'goodness of heart,' and no eloquence could have more ingratiated me with my fellow townsmen. After dinner I rallied, and made an appropriate speech about the banks of the Eden and the Lomond Hills. My name was coupled in some of the toasts with that of Wilkie the painter, who was born within three miles of Cupar. I was amused by a sly remark in my ear from Drinkwater Bethune, representative of the family of the Cardinal, that Stratheden appeared to have been so overcropped by producing two such great men nearly at the same time, that nothing but dullness could be expected from it for a century to come.

On my return to Edinburgh I met my constituents in the Waterloo rooms, and I paid off in full my debt to Lord

Lyndhurst. I too took a review of the last session, adding a review of his conduct. As to his reproach that we had carried none of our Bills, I said he was like a man who should murder all our innocent babes and then taunt us with being childless. I enumerated the Bills of mine that he had murdered. I mentioned one little one to which I was particularly attached, and which I went down on my knees to implore him to spare—

> —unam, minimamque relinque,
> De multis minimam posco.[2]

But the fatal arrow flew, and it was laid prostrate with its bleeding brothers. In his speech in the House of Lords he had talked of 'the prudence and discretion of Sir John Campbell,' and I concluded by expressing a hope that I had preserved my reputation in his eyes, and that he would not change his opinion on this subject as he had on every other.

He has never since attacked me or boasted of his own consistency. My speech was not only printed in all the newspapers, but it passed through several editions in the shape of a pamphlet and was copiously distributed by orders of our Secretary of the Treasury.[3]

I believe it was this speech which induced some students at Glasgow a few weeks after to put me up for the office of Lord Rector of the University. But I had a very powerful opponent,—no less a person than Sir Robert Peel,—and

[2] Ovid's *Metamorphoses*, VI. vii. 33, 34.

[3]   *Letter from Lord John Russell.*

Brocket Hall : October 27, 1836.

My dear Attorney,—I am sorry to have missed you yesterday, but I was kept till past six at the Palace. . . . I admired, with all the world, your excellent speech at Edinburgh, and I wish you would have it printed in a cheap form, for the diffusion of the useful knowledge it contains.

Yours truly,

J. RUSSELL.

Extract from a Letter to Sir George Campbell.

November 3, 1836.

. . . After some delay Lord Melbourne has ordered my speech to be published and distributed, and yesterday he sent Cowper, his private secretary, to speak about it. I should be as well pleased that it were forgotten. I have no pleasure—although not much pain—in being abused.

Conservatism was making great progress among the professors, who exerted themselves to the utmost against me. When it came to the election I had only one nation, and he had three. At his installation, however, he spoke very handsomely of me, and said ' it added to the glory of his triumph that he had been preferred to a man who was justly considered a credit to his country.' I wrote him a letter of thanks for his civility, and received a very polite reply.

While in Scotland I had been kept in a state of constant bustle and excitement; but I enjoyed an interval of tranquillity on my return to London. November term was a period of comparative relaxation, as Parliament was not sitting. No attendance in the House of Commons in the evening, no distraction from pleading in the House of Lords in the morning. I never while at the bar had anyone to answer cases for me or to assist me in getting up special arguments. When I had pupils I found I was rather embarrassed than forwarded by their attempts at help, except of course in preparing written pleadings. The official business unconnected with Parliament was not heavy. When Sir Samuel Shepherd was Attorney-General he gave up his private practice entirely, and went about to all the public offices to offer them verbal advice when he was sent for; but this had been corrected by Sir James Scarlett and other intervening law-officers. Upon departmental matters I was never consulted except by a written case regularly laid before the law-officers for their opinion.. Not unfrequently I had conferences with the Prime Minister, or the leader of the House of Commons, on general measures, and sometimes I was called in to attend meetings of the Cabinet.

My first appearance as assessor to this august conclave was in Lord Grey's time, when the question was whether there should be a prosecution for a libel written by Daniel O'Connell in an Irish newspaper. I was strong against the prosecution, but I was overruled, I suppose by the influence of Stanley. Lord Grey himself was never averse to severe measures on the other side of St. George's Channel. They all afterwards most heartily regretted that my advice had not been followed.

I must observe that there is a great inclination in all governments to prosecute the press. I know that the prosecutions for which Sir James Scarlett was so much blamed while he was Attorney-General were forced upon him by the Duke of Wellington, who of all men might have been expected to despise personal abuse. Our people never cared for that, but I have been repeatedly obliged to discountenance prosecutions for sedition and blasphemy, which I am sure would have been injurious.

On the 31st of January 1837 Parliament met, and from that time I had labours cast upon me which I could only have gone through from the combination of great strength of constitution and great temperance.

The Royal Speech contained a recommendation to the two Houses 'to consult upon such further measures as might give increased stability to the Established Church and produce concord and good will.' This was meant to introduce the measure for the abolition of Church rates, and providing for the repair of churches and the proper celebration of Divine worship from the improved management of Church lands. The forthcoming measure had been communicated to me some months before, and I highly approved of it. In truth it was only extending to England the provisions of Stanley's famous 'Irish Church Temporalities Bill.' The secret motive for introducing it was to please the English Dissenters, on whom our Government a good deal relied, and who clamoured very much about the hardship of being compelled to contribute to the expense of a worship of which they disapproved. As the measure depended much on the existing law respecting Church rates and Church property in England, I was specially ordered to be aiding and assisting in carrying it.

Unfortunately the introduction of it was left to Spring Rice, the Chancellor of the Exchequer, who could not successfully handle a subject of such magnitude. When he sat down Follett said to me, 'The Lord has delivered you into our hand;' and all England was instantly in a flame. Some zealous friends of the Church were really alarmed, and there was a furious outbreak of faction.

The regular debate came on after the interval of a fortnight, and the Tories, from the vantage-ground they had
gained, put forth all their strength.   Follett rose, and it was
arranged that he should be answered by Poulett Thomson,
then a member of the Cabinet and afterwards Lord Sydenham,
the successful Governor of Canada.   As Follett proceeded
with great force and amid much cheering, Thomson said to
me, ' I cannot answer this,' and he retreated into the library.
I was then pressed into the service, and I made a speech in
answer to Follett.   Within just bounds I was sarcastic on
Stanley, reminding him of his declaration that the fund
arising from the improvement of Church lands brought about
by the Legislature belongs to the State, and insisting
that a measure to provide for the repair of churches and the
proper celebration of Divine worship in England from such a
fund could not be very consistently resisted by the author of
the Irish Temporalities Act, which, by the very same means,
under the very same circumstances, had effected the very
same object in the sister kingdom.

On the succeeding night Stanley closed the debate in a
very clever speech in which he attacked me most furiously
and most unfairly.   I was obliged repeatedly to interrupt
him and to complain of his misrepresentations ; but when he
finished it was past three in the morning, the House was
impatient for a division, and I had no opportunity of being
heard in my vindication.   In consequence I published a
pamphlet in the shape of ' A Letter to Lord Stanley on the
Law of Church Rates,' which went through many editions
and called forth many answers.   I took great pains with it,
and had a high compliment for it from the Rev. Sydney
Smith, who said it was ' an excellent specimen of Liberal
juridical reasoning and of genuine Anglicism, neither to be
expected from a *Scot.*'

I have the satisfaction to think that the law which I there
laid down, and which was so furiously assailed in the House
of Commons, was afterwards confirmed by the unanimous
judgment of the Court of King's Bench and of the Exchequer
Chamber, and it is now universally admitted that church-
wardens cannot make a valid Church rate without the assent

of the vestry; that if the vestry refuse to make a Church rate, there is no practicable mode of compelling them; and that it is only a Church rate made by a majority of the vestry which is valid and may be lawfully enforced.

The second reading was carried, but, the outcry against the measure being so loud, it was necessarily abandoned. The consequence is that Church rates continue an inexhaustible source of litigation, animosity and confusion, and still bring an odium upon the Establishment from which I was sincerely desirous to relieve it. The attempt very much damaged our party and hastened our downfall.[4]

We had a seasonable diversion in the question of Parliamentary privilege which now sprang up, and on which Peel, to his honour, split with his party. They, rancorously hating a reformed House of Commons in which they were still a minority, would have been glad to see it degraded and disgraced. He manfully stood up for the constitutional powers and privileges of that assembly of which he was then the most distinguished member, and the determinations of which he perhaps foresaw he should ere long be able to control at his pleasure.

The grand question was 'whether an action for a libel could be maintained against the printer of the House of Commons for publishing their proceedings by their authority.'

It first arose at Nisi Prius, before Lord Denman, in an action brought by a publisher of obscene books, of the name of Stockdale, for an alleged libel in a Report of Inspectors of Prisons, ordered to be printed by the House, which stated that an obscene book published by him had been circulated among the prisoners in Newgate.

The brief for the defendant[5] in this cause was brought to me two days only before the trial, and then I heard of it for the first time. I relied upon a plea of justification that the book *was* obscene, contending at the same time that the autho-

---

[4] *September*, 1860.—Since 1855 a Bill for entirely abolishing Church rates, without any substitute, has been annually passed by the Commons and rejected by the Lords,—when, consistently with all I had said on the subject elsewhere, I voted with the majority, as such abolition without any substitute is *spoliation*.

[5] Hansard, the Parliamentary printer.—ED.

rity of the House of Commons was, at all events, a defence.
The jury found the special plea in my favour, and the judge
might easily have avoided giving any opinion upon the question of privilege, in which case it would have quietly gone off to
rest. But he chose to deliver a strong tirade against the House
of Commons for ordering to be published what might be
injurious to the character of others, and a peremptory opinion
that their authority did not amount to any defence.

I brought the matter before the House, and a Select
Committee was appointed to consider the subject, consisting
of Sir Robert Peel, Lord John Russell, Lord Howick, Lord
Stanley, Sir James Graham, Serjeant Wilde, Mr. O'Connell,
Sir William Follett and Sir Robert Inglis. With the exception of the last-named member, we all agreed in a Report,
drawn up by Serjeant Wilde, strongly asserting the privilege
of the Commons to publish what they thought fit for the
information of the people, and insisting on the immunity of
their servants acting under their orders. The House adopted
the Report by a very large majority.[6]

Pending these proceedings Mr. Stockdale, encouraged by
the Chief Justice's law, brought another action in respect of
another copy of the same Report, which he caused his son to
purchase.

What was the House to do ? Either at once to send Mr.
Stockdale to Newgate, with all who should assist him in
prosecuting his action, or to appear and plead, and trust to
the court deciding in favour of *privilege*, notwithstanding
Lord Denman's ill-considered declaration ? I was to decide.
To lessen my responsibility, as this was no party question, I
called upon Peel and asked his opinion. He was very civil
to me, but said that the matter was so important it should
be decided by the Cabinet. A Cabinet was accordingly called,
which I attended ; but they merely said they would go by
my advice. Had it been *res integra* I should not have
hesitated to proceed *brevi manu* by commitment, without
running the risk of bringing a great question of constitutional law before Lord Denman and Justices Littledale,

[6] May 30, 1837. Adoption of the Report moved by Lord Howick, the
Chairman, and carried by 126 to 36.—ED.

Patteson, Williams and Coleridge. But in the late case of
Sir Francis Burdett, who instituted an action against Speaker
Abbott, the House had desired the Attorney-General to
appear and defend ; public opinion, guided by the press, was
rather against us ; and I, *bonâ fide,* believed our case to be
so good that we must be safe in the hands of any judges.
Accordingly, on the 8th of June, after a speech of considerable
length, in which I entered into the authorities and precedents
in point, I moved a resolution that it was the opinion of the
House ' that the petitioner (the defendant) be allowed to
appear and plead to the action, and that the Attorney-
General be instructed to defend the action with a view to
the privileges of the House.' Sir Robert Peel, in rather a
Jesuitical manner, regretted that the House should not at
once vindicate its authority by stopping the action, although
he would not recommend this course after the speech of the
Attorney-General. Upon the general question he very admirably vindicated the privileges of the House. Lord John
Russell supported my motion on the part of the Government,
and it was carried without a division.

In obedience to the orders laid upon me, I prepared a
special plea to the action on the ground of privilege, and
this was demurred to by the plaintiff. The argument ought
to have come on in the King's Bench immediately, but, on
account of the great arrears of business in that court, the
case was not reached in its turn till the month of April 1839.
I employed all the leisure I could command during the
interval in preparing my argument, which was the longest, if
not the most elaborate, ever delivered in Westminster Hall.

If the reign of William IV. had been prolonged a few
months he would have enjoyed the pleasure of forming a
Tory Government without difficulty. The Whigs, a minority
in the Upper House, had not a ' working majority' in the
Lower. While the Court was strongly against them, they
were without any popular counterpoise, and their fall seemed
inevitable. But Lord Melbourne was about to see a change
which was to him most auspicious.

On the 20th of June 1837 died his Majesty King William
IV. Without education or much natural shrewdness, he had

the good qualities of sincerity and honesty, and as King he had upon the whole performed the part more reputably than had been expected by those who knew him as Duke of Clarence. This demise of the Crown had been foreseen some time, and I had settled that the new Sovereign should be proclaimed by the name of Alexandrina Victoria, the name by which she had been baptized, and by which she was called in the Regency Act, leaving it to her thereafter to determine by what name she should reign. This matter was settled in the lobby of the House of Commons between Charles Greville the Clerk of the Council, myself, and Lord Lyndhurst, whom I called in as one who might be in power when the proclamation was made, although I had a pretty significant hint that all would be right under Alexandrina, or Victoria, or Alexandrina Victoria, or Elizabeth II.—for this was the name that some were desirous she should assume.

As soon as I heard that King William had expired, I hurried to Kensington to be present at the first Council of the new Sovereign. This, I think, was the most interesting scene I have ever witnessed. Her simplicity, her dignity, her grace, made even Peel enthusiastic when he tried in the House of Commons to describe 'the something which art cannot imitate and lessons cannot teach.' Lest my children, from seeing Wilkie's picture, in which I am introduced, should suppose that I attended in a silk robe and full-bottomed wig, let me say that the costumes are all the invention of the painter. The Privy Councillors and others who were present attended in their usual morning dresses, and the Queen was in black, instead of wearing a white muslin robe, as, for artistic effect, he has represented her.

All doubts respecting her inclination in favour of Lord Melbourne's Government were soon removed, and we basked in the full glare of royal sunshine.

Letters to Sir George Campbell.

New Street : June 20, 1837.

. . . I assisted at the Council to-day, although not a Privy Councillor. I am quite in raptures with the deportment of the young Queen. Nothing could be more exquisitely proper. She looked modest, sorrowful, dejected, diffident—but at the same time she was quite cool and collected and composed and firm. Her childish appearance was gone. She was an intelligent and graceful young woman, capable of acting and thinking for herself. Considering that she was the only female in the room, and that she had no one about her with whom she was familiar, no human being was ever placed in a more trying situation.

Her first public appearance certainly gives a very favourable omen of her reign.

House of Commons: Monday, July 17, 1837.

. . . Parliament is to be dissolved to-day as well as prorogued. This step is thought wise, that the metropolitan elections may begin on Saint Monday.

I am waiting here till the Queen comes. The streets are now tremendously crowded. . . .

P.S. The ceremony has gone off very auspiciously. The young Queen read the speech most beautifully, and so articulately that, with a soft silvery tone, she was distinctly heard in every corner of the House.

Autobiography.

Parliament was soon dissolved, and I proceeded to Edinburgh to solicit a renewal of my trust from the electors. Nothing could exceed the rancour of the Tories against the Queen when they found that she cordially supported the Liberal Government which she found upon her accession to the throne. They did not venture absolutely to deny her title, but they openly (even in such a respectable publication as the 'Quarterly Review') regretted that the Salic law was not established in England as in France and Germany. In my speech from the hustings I paid off Mr. Croker, the author of this article, for some of his personal atacks upon myself. As often as I quarrelled with him while he was a member of the House of Commons, he libelled me the next Sunday in the 'John Bull' newspaper; and subsequently in

CHAP.
XXII.

A.D. 1837.

his 'Quarterly' political article he often did me the honour to
introduce me, and malignantly to misrepresent my conduct.[7]

From the beginning of the new reign till the change of
government in September 1841, there was a constant system
of personal slander of Queen Victoria in the Tory press. At
any public dinner the toast of 'the Queen Dowager' was the
signal for an outbreak of Tory spleen against the reigning
Sovereign, and the effort was to exhibit a marked contrast
between the manner in which the healths of the two Queens
were received, by the long continued and enthusiastic cheers
bestowed upon the supposed impersonation of Toryism, and
the solemn silence awarded to the supposed patroness of the
Whigs. Since the Tories have been restored to office Queen
Adelaide has been dropped and neglected, and her health
causes less sensation than that of the Lady Mayoress of
London.

Abercromby and I were again returned for Edinburgh
without opposition. I am afraid he was a good deal disappointed at not being promoted to some high efficient executive office in the new reign. He had been the confidential ad-
viser of the Duchess of Kent, and was particularly intimate with
Sir John Conroy, her equerry, who was now expected to have
unbounded influence. But there was no proposal to promote
Abercromby higher than the chair of the House of Commons,
and henceforth he complained of the sacrifice he had made
to his party in accepting it; he fulfilled its duties discon-
tentedly, and he was pettishly desirous to resign it. These
feelings were a little exasperated by the absurd imputations
which the Tories cast upon him. They had formed a scheme
to turn the majority in their favour by election petitions, with
the aid of the 'Spottiswoode gang.'[8] This utterly failed,

---

[7] *September*, 1857.—Strange to say, I afterwards was reconciled to
Croker. He flattered me as an author, and used to write to me about questions of literary history for his edition of Pope. I had an interview with
him at his apartments in Kensington Palace a few weeks before his death.
Stranger to say, although there had been a far bitterer enmity between
him and Brougham, they became sworn friends.

[8] A clique of ultra-Tories, with Mr. Spottiswoode, the Queen's printer
at their head, subscribed and collected a large sum of money for this purpose. They went by the name of the 'Spottiswoode gang.'

and it was said that the Committees were so favourable because the Speaker had packed the balloting box with the names of Liberal members. There never was such an absurd calumny. The Speaker always showed himself a man of the most inflexible integrity and the nicest sense of honour. The only instance in which I think his conduct was blamable was when he voted against his own interest, and I suspect against his opinion, lest he should be suspected of partiality. I had moved that engineers should be appointed by the Government to ascertain which would be the best line of railway between England and Scotland,—a motion in which our constituents at Edinburgh took a lively interest, and which they were very desirous to see carried. After a smart debate, upon a division, the numbers were equal. The Speaker voted in the negative and the motion was lost, although there was no technical rule upon this occasion to prevent him saying *aye* or *no* as he thought fit.

Letters to Sir George Campbell.

New Street : July 31, 1837.

. . . I did not arrive till past twelve on Saturday night (from Edinburgh). Friday was delightful, and we expected to be at Blackwall by ten on Saturday morning; but having passed Yarmouth, we encountered a very heavy gale of wind from the south-west, which did not abate till we had got to our moorings. The consequence was that at times we could make hardly any way, and we ran aboard a schooner and almost sent her to the bottom.

Edina is a nice lively baby with dark hair. Loo and Molly express great delight at having another sister. I am afraid they will be pretty nearly *tocherless* damsels; but, setting aside *penury*, which is a great evil, I do not think that happiness depends much upon wealth.

I dined at Holland House yesterday, where they were *croaking* about the elections. The Duke of Sussex said to me, ' I should like to see your father-in-law's face when the Norwich bills are brought in to him.'[9] Lord Suffield, who

---

[9] Robert Scarlett had been returned for Norwich with Lord Douro.—ED.

was on the spot taking an active part, admitted that on the Liberal side they spent above 13,000*l.*, but said that votes were higher to the Tories, and that their expense must have been much greater.

Erlwood : October 15, 1837.

. . . We leave this place at eight o'clock to-morrow morning, and proceed to Littlehampton, on the coast of Sussex. Mary and the children will remain there till December. I must return in the end of this month to London. We have had a very tranquil and happy *séjour* at Erlwood. I could write you of my rides with Fred, Loo and Polly ; and Dudley, who has rode before me on Lady Blanche to the distance of several miles from home. Cissy even has had a ride before me, to her great delight. I have played much with Edina, who delights to be taken notice of and immediately reciprocates a smile.

My great boast at Erlwood is having gained the good opinion of her Royal Highness the Duchess of Gloucester. She writes to Lady Currey, ' I am quite in love with Sir John Campbell, *notwithstanding all we have heard of his politics*,' and she is never tired of praising me in conversation ; so you see I have mistaken my line, and I ought to have been a Court page instead of a demagogue !

We dined at the Park[1] yesterday to meet the Duke of Cambridge, and to-day we all walked with the Duchess and the Duke in her beautiful gardens. Dudley had the honour to sit by her in her garden chair, and she made Cissy a present of a beautiful doll.

Are not these much better topics for a letter than divisions and elections ?

New Street :
Wednesday night, November 1837.

. . . If you look in the Court Circular of to-morrow you will probably see among those who had the honour to dine with her Majesty, ' the Attorney-General.' At ten o'clock to-day came a card of invitation for the Attorney-General and Lady Stratheden to dine with her Majesty at seven.

I was obliged to send a note to the Lord Steward with

---

[1] Bagshot Park.

my humble duty to her Majesty to explain why Lady
Stratheden could not obey the Royal mandate.

I went and found it exceedingly agreeable, although by
no means so grand as dining at Tarvet with Mrs. Rigg.[2]

The little Queen was exceedingly civil to me and said she
had heard from the Duchess of Gloucester that I had the
most beautiful children in the world. She asked me how
many we had, and when she heard *seven* seemed rather
appalled, considering this a number which she would never
be able to reach. She seems in perfect health, and is as merry
and playful as a kitten.

House of Commons : Saturday, December 23, 1837.

. . . We are all now at home and in perfect health.
Hally joined us on Thursday.

When I look at them I cannot repine at the tremendous
labour and constant anxiety to which I am subjected. Mary
and I, with two or three of the children, are going to Abinger
in the beginning of the week.

To my unspeakable annoyance, Parliament is to meet
again on the 16th of January. Parliament and the courts
together are too much, and I cannot stand my present life
much longer.

[2] The big house in Cupar parish.—ED.

CHAPTER XXIII.

New Parliament—Prisoners' Counsel Bill—His Chambers burnt down—
Autumn at Duddingstone House—Advice of his Friends to accept a
Puisne Judgeship—Illness of his Wife—Argument in the great
Privilege Case—Attempt of Sir Robert Peel to form a Government—
Penny Postage Act—The Chartists—Controversies with America—
Question of International Law—Visit to Paris—Louis Philippe at St.
Cloud—Mdlle. Rachel—Hesitates about taking a Puisne Judgeship—
Rolfe, the new Judge—Wilde, Solicitor-General—Trial of Frost and
the Chartists at Monmouth—Question of Privilege renewed—Sheriffs
taken into Custody—Question settled by Act of Parliament.

Autobiography.

CHAP.
XXIII.
———
A.D. 1837.
·

THE new Parliament met in the end of the year. When it
reassembled after Christmas I had a laborious session with the
Irish Municipal Reform Bill, and various other Bills, which
the Government expected me actively to support; but nothing
came forward in which I took part deserving of special notice,
except the Bill to allow a speech by counsel for prisoners
charged with felony. I had in former sessions supported
this measure, and I was now able materially to assist it in
passing through the House. I am glad to think that it has
worked most beneficially, and that the prophecies of its ill
consequences have turned out like such as were no doubt
uttered by the enemies of innovation respecting the Bill prohibiting torture, the Bill for abolishing the Star Chamber,
and the Bill for allowing the prisoner's witnesses to be examined on oath. These Bills would have been strenuously
opposed by Lord Eldon, Lord Redesdale, and Lord Tenterden.
I am sorry to say that twelve out of the fifteen judges strongly
condemned the Prisoners' Counsel Bill, some of them actuated
unconsciously by the apprehension of the boring speeches

they must listen to, and the additional labour which would
be cast upon them. Mr. Justice James Allan Park wrote me
a letter stating that if I allowed the Bill to pass he would
resign his office. Their lordships might have foreseen that
they would have a compensation for the multiplication of
speeches in the abridgment of cross-examinations.

Letters to Sir George Campbell.

House of Lords: Tuesday, March 6, 1838.

. . . My chambers in Paper Buildings have been burned
to the ground, and not an atom of anything belonging to me
saved—furniture, books, briefs, MSS., Attorney-General's
official documents, above all a great collection of letters from
my father and from you while in India—all consumed. I
heard of the fire this morning while in bed. I could only
thank God it was in Paper Buildings—not No. 9, New
Street, Spring Gardens. I went immediately to the Temple
and found Paper Buildings a heap of smoking ruins, the
south end only being preserved. I had no insurance on my
chambers, though I have on my house.

The fire broke out in Maule's chambers, immediately
under mine. He had gone to bed leaving a candle burning
by his bedside.

No lives were lost, but several had a very narrow escape.

House of Commons: March 6. Half-past six.

. . . I have had many condolences on my loss. It certainly is very serious, even in a pecuniary point of view.
Beyond the replacing of my library, I shall lose hundreds of
pounds from the destruction of my fee-books. There was a
cash-box, which will probably be found among the ruins.
Meanwhile my business is entirely suspended.

Mary shows me Edina and the other children all safe, and
I am comforted.

House of Lords: March 8, 1838.

. . . The House rises at two that the Chancellor may
attend a Council, and I am going once more to view the smoking ruins of Paper Buildings. I must find some other place
where I may hoist my flag. The ruins are not yet examined.

The loss of my retainer book and fee books causes the greatest confusion.   There were briefs burnt in more causes than the Queen's Bench will decide for a twelvemonth, with my notes for arguments in a great many cases.   I think I told you I had at my house the notes I had made for my argument in the case of the Privileges of the House of Commons, the fruit of last long vacation, which I would not have lost for 500*l.*

House of Commons : March 15, 1838.

. . . I am now only beginning to feel my misfortunes. Nothing was saved except the Attorney-General's seal of office, almost entire, found under a brick, and the remains of an old watch which I brought from Scotland with me, and I believe belonged to our father before the gold one given to him by Lady Betty Anstruther.[1]   The top and bottom of the cash-box were found, but the sovereigns were melted and had disappeared.   I believe I told you Wilkie's picture of our father is safe in New Street.

Queen's Bench : April 21, 1838.

. . . Follett has been telling me that there is to be a dinner given to Peel on the 12th of May, and that above three hundred Conservative M.P.'s will sit down at the table. He has been advising me to join the party.   I, on the contrary, recommend that Peel should come over to us, and that, acting on his own principles, he should avow himself a Liberal.   I have been sitting with him in a Committee about reforming the tenure of land.   He takes rather a Radical view of the subject, making Goulburn's hair stand on end, and he talks of the House of Lords in a way that would subject me to severe censure.

Queen's Bench : May 2, 1838.

. . . I met Tom Chalmers under the gallery last night.[2] He has promised to dine with me on the 12th to meet the Bishops of Durham and Norwich after the christening of Edina. ·

[1] Wife of General Robert Anstruther, of Balgarvy, near Cupar, Fife. —ED.

[2] The Rev. Dr. Chalmers, who had been his fellow-pupil at St. Andrews. —ED.

Last Saturday I drank whisky toddy at the Duke of
Sussex's.   He said this was his beverage after dinner.   I
begged leave as a true Scotsman to join his Royal Highness
in a tumbler.   Abercromby was the third.   Afterwards we
saw the experiment repeated of coining quicksilver.   The gas
is turned into a liquid by compression.   It is allowed to
evaporate, and the evaporation is so rapid that cold 150
degrees below zero of Fahrenheit is produced, part of the
liquid becoming solid.   The quicksilver is poured into a
mould.   The frozen liquid is put upon it, and with the
assistance of ether the quicksilver becomes a solid medallion
with a head upon it.   In a few minutes it again becomes
liquid.

New Street : May 5, 1838.

. . . I am going to-day to the dinner of the Royal
Academy.   I shall see myself in Wilkie's picture of The
Queen's First Council.   I met Croker to-day, who is in a great
rage that the Lord Mayor and the Attorney-General should
be introduced, although not Privy Councillors.

Autobiography.

This summer I rented the Marquess of Abercorn's house
at Duddingstone, near Edinburgh, and hastened thither immediately after the prorogation.   I gave a dinner in the
baronial hall to the Lord Provost, bailies and councillors,
and had to go through a severe course of dinners in return.
I could not boast very much of their refined manners,
although they are 'very superior to the men I met with at
Stafford and Dudley ; but though I might be obliged to mix
with them occasionally, Edinburgh is the place I shall choose
for my residence, when by hard necessity I am driven from
London.   Jeffrey, Cockburn, Murray, Rutherfurd, Lauder,
Cuninghame, and others to be met with there, are as accomplished and delightful companions as any who whose society has
charmed me in any part of the world I have visited, and I
shall always gratefully remember the genuine kindness and
elegant hospitality with which they received me.[3]

---

[3] *September* 1860.—Alas ! all; that I have here named are gone, and I,
like Job's messenger, am alone left to tell the sad tale.

In the month of September I went to attend a great gathering of the Campbells at Oban in Argyleshire. I think I was the third or fourth Sir John Campbell, and Sir Colins and Sir Donalds were there without number. I had some misgivings whether they would not look askance upon me as little better than a *Southron*; but I was hailed as a clansman, and great satisfaction was expressed that another branch of the clan was ennobled.

Having visited Staffa and Iona, I continued my tour through the great glen which intersects Scotland by Fort William and Fort Augustus to Inverness; and, after paying a visit to Edward Ellice at Invereishie, I returned home by Killiecrankie, Dunkeld, and Perth.

I then had my annual meeting with my constituents in the Waterloo rooms. The Tories did not ostensibly appear to annoy me; but they now began their policy of encouraging Chartists to disturb meetings held by the Constitutional Liberals either for a repeal of the Corn Laws or for any other purpose. On this occasion the brawlers were soon expelled, and I had a favourable hearing.

We returned to London by Carlisle and Lancaster, paying a very agreeable visit to my brother-in-law James Scarlett,[4] now become major of the 5th Dragoon Guards and M.P. for the borough of Guildford.

Letters to Sir George Campbell.

. . . Whatever part Durham may take, I see not how the Government is to get over the session. Lord Glenelg continues Colonial Secretary, and no better front is to be shown to the enemy in either House. *Rebus sic stantibus,* I do not believe that our usual supporters will come to the scratch, and I expect before long to see the Government in a minority. With such prospects I ought by this time perhaps to be Mr. Justice Campbell, a puisne judge of the Court of Common Pleas.[5] This Lord Abinger strongly

---

[4] Living at Bank Hall, near Burnley.—ED.

[5] The death of Mr. Justice Allan Park had made a vacancy.—ED.

recommends. But such a step on my part would be considered as the precursor of a general break-up. The wily Scotsman would be complimented on his prudence and discernment, but would be accused of raising the cry of *sauve qui peut*. I act deliberately upon the expectation of being suddenly turned out, and my preference is to the bar instead of being shelved. I could not now quit my post without bitterly and permanently quarrelling with the whole of the Whig party; and I could not endure the notion of being reproached with leaving them in their difficulties.

Brooks's: Christmas Day, 1838.

. . . There is nothing announced, and I believe nothing resolved, about the new judge. On Sunday I called on Baron Parke, who strove hard to persuade me to join the brotherhood. He says truly that I lead a life of great labour and anxiety, and that out of office my position at the bar may not be very agreeable. But I feel that I cannot become a judge at present without degradation, and therefore I must run all risks rather than do so.

I mean to have a little talk with Melbourne this week about the appointment of a proper man.

Autobiography.

This narrative would be an imperfect representation of what I have felt and suffered if I were not to mention an illness of my dear wife about this time. She had a dreadful cough and other symptoms, which rendered it necessary that I should call in Dr. Chambers, the fashionable physician of the day. He was to examine the state of her lungs with a stethoscope, and certainly the most painful moments of my life were passed while this process was going on. He would not by any means pronounce the case free from danger, but hoped that by being shut up in the house the whole winter she might recover. For some weeks I beheld with the deepest anxiety the daily approach of his chariot with grey horses, but at the end of that time she suddenly got quite well, and I cannot help suspecting that, as her illness was no more than an ordinary catarrh, he frightened me unnecessarily and unjustifiably. Perhaps physicians are never without a spice of quackery in looks and language, and could not carry on their profession without it. Their chief value is in freeing us from quacks more ignorant and presumptuous. Surgeons are of infinite use to mankind; but, according to the opinion expressed to me by Dr. Matthew Baillie, the most eminent physician in my time, physicians cannot claim higher praise than that which I have awarded them.

In 1839 nothing remarkable either professional or parliamentary occurred, till the argument at last came on in the great privilege case of Stockdale v. Hansard. I had spent many weeks in preparing for it during the two preceding long vacations. My great difficulty was to manage my materials, and to bring my address to the court within some reasonable limits. I had read everything that had the smallest bearing on the subject, from the earliest year book to the latest pamphlet—not confining myself to mere legal authorities, but diligently examining historians, antiquaries and general jurists, both English and foreign. Joseph Hume told the House of Commons that he grievously grudged my fee of three hundred guineas; but if I had been to be paid according to my time and labour, I ought to have received at least three thousand. I had myself read and abstracted every case which I cited. I had written and rewritten all that I had to say. But when in court, except in quoting authorities, I trusted entirely to memory. I occupied the time of the court exactly sixteen hours—four the first day, eight the second, and four the third.

I received great applause for my address, particularly from Peel, and even Sir Edward Sugden generously said in the House of Commons that, 'after all the debates upon the subject in Parliament were forgotten, this would remain to posterity as a monument of Sir John Campbell's fame.' In any future dispute about parliamentary privilege, it will certainly be referred to as a repertory of all the learning on the subject; for, not confining myself to answer what was openly urged by the counsel for the plantiff, I referred to and answered every authority and argument that could be urged against me.

The ill-considered and intemperate judgment of the court was not pronounced till the 31st of May. I went from the Queen's Bench bar straightway to the House of Commons, and in my place narrated what had happened, with the declaration of the Chief Justice that ' the courts of law have supreme jurisdiction respecting all parliamentary privilege,' and Mr. Justice Patteson's warning that the privilege to print criminatory papers being confined to the use of the members, any person on ceasing to be a member of the House must burn all his parliamentary papers in which there is any criminatory matter, or be subject to an action or indictment. The idea of this *auto da fè* set the House in a flame, and there was no resolution I could have proposed—if it had been at once to commit Lord Denman and the other judges of the Queen's Bench to the Tower—which would not have been carried by acclamation. But I advised them to set an example of forbearance and moderation and temperance to Westminster Hall—where it was rather needed—and for the present to content themselves with appointing a Select Committee to inquire into the proceedings in Stockdale *v.* Hansard, and to report their opinion thereupon to the House. The Committee was appointed.

All the lawyers of any eminence on either side of the House agreed that the judgment was quite erroneous, but there was a great difference among them as to the course now to be adopted. Some were for bringing a writ of error, which would have subjected the case to the House of Lords. Others were for committing all who should act upon the judgment—which seemed inconsistent with our course in appearing and pleading to the action. I thought the least evil was to suffer the damages to be paid in this case, but to determine ever after to act firmly on the ancient maxim that the House is the sole judge of its own privileges and, in imitation of the Court of Chancery and other courts in Westminster Hall, to stop in a summary manner any action that might in future be brought against any of our officers for acting in obedience to our orders. This view of the case

I

was adopted, and the question of privilege was got rid of for the present session of Parliament, but only to break out with fresh fury.

Letters to Sir George Campbell.

April 24, 1839.

. . . I have got through by far the most formidable job I ever was concerned in,—the argument on the Privilege case between Lord Denman and the House of Commons. I had bestowed upon it a degree of labour of which you can hardly form a conception. Two long vacations and much time in London I spent upon it. Then I had the misfortune of addressing Denman, he being vehemently against me. Out of hatred to the reformed House, the other judges, as Tories, were all strongly inclined to agree with him. Brougham and Lyndhurst, ex-Chancellors, coalescing, came in to back Denman. However I showed a bold front, and I have strong hopes that the cause of law and good sense will triumph. The reply is postponed till next term. It was a most memorable case, and will be quoted three hundred years hence, if the British Constitution last so long.

April 30, 1839.

. . . I am thicker with Brougham than I have been any time these five years. When he came into the Queen's Bench in the Privilege case, I wrote him a note saying I was glad he was to be present, as I meant furiously to attack him.

He threw me down the enclosed.[6] After my attack in the Lords, he came up to me very familiarly and told me what the judgment is to be on Thursday in the Auchterarder case. I afterwards wrote him a note asking him to vindicate me from the calumny that I had spoken irreverently of the Church of Scotland. I enclose his answer.[7]

---

[6] 'I am here stuck up in the position of poor Whitbread at St. James's Church, when Tierney lent him his pew, and told him in a P.S., "I think it right to mention that *no reply* is allowed at our church."'

[7] 'Dear Attorney,—I can and will do so very easy and naturally—for I *have to screen myself* (grandson and great-nephew of Scotch ministers) from a like charge—so I can, *when my hand is in*, take you also out of the fire. Yours truly, 'H.'

He is now going to take up the cause of the Jamaica House of Assembly and the negro drivers. What a strange, inconsistent animal he is.

House of Commons : May 2, 1859

. . . Brougham kept his word, and gallantly rescued Mr. Attorney from the imputation cast upon him of speaking irreverently of the Kirk. After boasting of his own descent from Scotch ministers, he alluded to Mr. Attorney, 'descended from a venerable clergyman of the Church of Scotland.' Our beloved father would have been much gratified could he have been conscious of what was going on.

Autobiography.

On the 6th of May, there being only a majority of five on the second reading of the Bill for suppressing the House of Assembly in the island of Jamaica, next day the whole Cabinet resigned, and Sir Robert Peel was sent for by the Queen to form a new Administration.

Letters to Sir George Campbell.

House of Commons : May 7, 1839.

I am again ' plain John Campbell.' You will address me as ' Attorney-General ' no more. Lord John has just announced the resignation of the Government. The division [8] turned out even worse than was apprehended, and has left no alternative. I entirely approve of what has been done, and we rather make a good end. A longer continuance in office would only have exposed the Administration to a lingering illness and an inglorious death.

There has been a talk of a new Liberal Government being attempted under Lord Normanby, but this is absurd. We might bring back the eleven Radicals, but' we should lose eleven Whig Conservatives, and more. The Queen must instantly send for the Duke of Wellington, who will advise her to send for Sir Robert Peel, and a Tory Government will be formed. A dissolution, I presume, will immediately follow, and I know not how soon I may be in Auld Reekie.

[8] On the Jamaica Assembly Bill.—ED.

The Cabinet met at twelve, and I believe unanimously
agreed to resign. The whole party approve. I first learnt
the fact from the Chancellor, whom I saw at half-past two.

House of Commons: Friday, May 10, 1839.

. . . What do you think? Peel has quarrelled with the
Queen, and for the present we are all in again. He insisted
on her removing all her ladies, which she peremptorily refused. Peel sent his final answer yesterday evening, which
she received at dinner, saying that, on consulting his colleagues, they could not yield, and that his commission was
at an end. She then sent for Melbourne, who had not seen
her since his resignation. At eleven a meeting of the old
Cabinet was called. To-day Melbourne has been with her,
and, Bear Ellice says, agreed to go on with the government.

Reports differ as to the exact conditions. Our people say
she was willing to give up the wives of peers. Sir George
Clerk asserts she insisted on keeping all—*inter alias*, the
Marchioness of Normanby.

There never was such excitement in London. I came
with hundreds of others to the House of Lords, which met
to-day, in the expectation that something would be said, but
all passed off in silence.

Brooks's: Saturday, May 11, 1839.

. . . The Cabinet is still sitting, and we know nothing
more to-day. . . . I was several hours at the Queen's ball
last night, a scene never to be forgotten. The Queen was in
great spirits and danced with more than usual gaiety. She
received Peel with great civility; but, after dancing with
the Russian Bear, took for her partner Lady Normanby's son.
The Tories looked inconceivably foolish. Such whimsical
groups!

Autobiography.

I had a considerable hand in the leading measure now
introduced and carried, which was said to be the price for
the promised support of the Radicals, who had deserted us
on the Jamaica Bill—I mean the Penny Postage. My constituents, who could have had their letters carried from

London by a private conveyance for less than a penny, were
very much discontented at being obliged to pay a shilling
to the Government, and all classes and parties in Edinburgh
concurred in petitions for the redress of this grievance. I
strongly agreed in their opinion, and, though in office, I
headed a deputation, consisting of Mr. O'Connell and other
leading members of the House on the Liberal side, to Lord
Melbourne and the Chancellor of the Exchequer, Spring
Rice, to urge them to agree to the grand scheme of a
uniform postage of one penny. I should be well pleased to
think that it was carried by the arguments and entreaties of
this deputation. That it would immediately increase the
revenue, I never expected, as I knew well people cannot
suddenly change their habits so that at once there should
be ten times as many letters sent by the post as before. But,
as a social improvement, I thought, and I think, its merits
cannot possibly be overstated, and I have no doubt that,
being adopted by foreign nations, it will soon facilitate the
transactions of commerce, and the reciprocation of the sentiments of affection among separated relations and friends
throughout the world. I was thereby deprived of the privilege of franking as a member of the House of Commons, and
I now lose the privilege of franking as a peer ; but I rejoiced
in the sacrifice for the general good, although the loss of
consequence from ceasing to be able to frank a letter for a
lady, or, in travelling, for the waiter at an inn, gave great
disgust to many members of both Houses, Whig as well as
Tory, and made some of them openly declare that there
was no longer any use in being in Parliament.[9]

The chief administrative difficulty of the Government
now was in keeping down the Chartists. They not only
inveighed against the Reform Bill, and disturbed all public
meetings held for the repeal of the Corn Laws, but they
intimated a resolution to carry by force the five points of

[9] The measure was particularly disrelished by the ' Conservative Whigs,'
a section of our supporters almost as injurious to us as the ' ultra-Radicals.'
They hated O'Connell and Ireland, and were among the most devoted
enemies of Free Trade. They were on the Liberal side chiefly from family
connection, not from personal inclination, and they were constantly
grumbling and sowing dissension among us.

the Charter—universal suffrage, annual parliaments, ballot, no qualification in members of Parliament, and wages to be paid to them while they serve. Not only most inflammatory and seditious language had been used by their leaders, but there had been among them repeated outbreaks of popular violence. Some politicians by way of remedy recommended the suspension of the Habeas Corpus Act, others the renewal of the Six Acts. But I warmly supported the opinion entertained by the Government, that peace might be preserved, and the law vindicated, by the vigorous administration of justice without any infraction of the Constitution. I directed a great many prosecutions; the most important of these I conducted in person at Warwick and Chester. The juries uniformly did their duty, and in the autumn tranquillity seemed completely restored throughout the country.

About this time I had thrown upon me the conduct of a controversy with the American Government, about a claim of compensation for liberated slaves, and a demand of reparation for the destruction of the 'Caroline' steamer, sent down the Falls of Niagara during the Canadian insurrection. In two instances which had occurred while slavery was permitted in our colonies, American ships going from one state to another with cargoes of slaves, being forced by stress of weather into English ports and the slaves having been liberated, I had advised compensation to be given; but slavery being once abolished, and Bermuda being the same for this purpose as Portsmouth, I advised that the demand should be refused. Stevenson, the American Minister, made a tremendous bluster, and gave in a long-winded note, which would have been unanswerable if there had been no distinction between a cargo of inanimate matter and a cargo of human beings having independent rights within our territory. In my reply I pointed out this distinction, and gave the American Government such a licking that they allowed the claim to drop, and they have not set up a similar one since.

The affair of the 'Caroline' was much more difficult. Even Lord Grey told me that he thought we were quite

wrong in what we had done. But assuming the facts that
the 'Caroline' had been engaged, and when seized by us was
still engaged, in carrying supplies and military stores from
the American side of the river to the rebels in Navy Island,
part of the British territory—that this was permitted, or
could not be prevented, by the American authorities—I was
clearly of opinion that although she lay on the American side
of the river when she was seized, we had a clear right to seize
and to destroy her, just as we might have taken a battery
erected by the rebels on the American shore, the guns of
which were fired against the Queen's troops in Navy Island.
I wrote a long justification of our Government, and this
supplied the arguments used by our Foreign Secretary till
the Ashburton Treaty hushed up the dispute.

But the question of international law upon which of all
others I took the most pains while I was Attorney-General,
was this : ' Whether if the subjects or citizens of a foreign
State with which we are at peace, without commission or
authority from their own or any other government, invade
the English territory in a hostile manner and levy war
against the Queen in her realm, we are entitled to treat them
as traitors ? ' The Canadian court held that we could not, as
they had never acknowledged even a temporary allegiance to
our Sovereign ; and of this opinion was Sir William Follett.
But, after reading all that is to be found upon the subject, I
came to the conclusion that they owed allegiance when
as private individuals they voluntarily crossed the English
frontier ; that it was no defence for them to say that they
then had arms in their hands and intended to murder the
Queen's subjects ; and that they were in the same situation as
a Frenchman would be who should land at Brighton with a
pistol in his hand and, seeing the Queen on the beach, should
instantly march up and fire at her. This man all the world
would say might be tried on the statute of King Edward III.
for imagining the death of the Sovereign. The Canadian
judges very absurdly and inconsistently held that these
' sympathisers ' might be tried for murder.[1]

---

[1] The paper which I wrote on this occasion, and which was signed by
the Queen's Advocate and the Solicitor-General, must be in the archives

Letters to Sir George Campbell.

Queen's Bench : May 24, 1839.

. . . I suppose you have by this time seen Abercromby's farewell address to his constituents.[2] Macaulay is likely to be returned without opposition. A deputation to invite him is expected in town to-day.

House of Commons : June 19, 1839.

. . . I have just been listening to Macaulay's first speech as M.P. for Edinburgh. It was good, but not equal to his former efforts, and I think will cause some disappointment. He used to be the best speaker to listen to that I ever heard.

House of Commons : June 28, 1839.

. . . I ought now to be working at Guildhall, but I may say, for the first time in my life, I have voluntarily shirked work. There is a most horrid action going on there which I strongly dissuaded. It arises out of a case you may remember at the Old Bailey about the forgery of a will ; and I feel such disgust at going over the same topics again— where the innocence of parties honourably acquitted is voluntarily put in jeopardy by themselves—that I have not stomach for it. I opened the plaintiff's case in a speech of an hour and a half at Guildhall, I then drove off to the House of Lords and addressed their lordships in a peerage case, I then concluded my reply in the great case of Lady Hewley's Charity—and I mean to be idle for the rest of the day. I am engaged to dinner at Lord Abinger's, to meet— whom ? Lord Lyndhurst and Lord Brougham !

House of Commons : July 12, 1839.

. . . The most whimsical event that has lately happened to me was dining on Wednesday with Lord Brougham, after his recent furious attack on me in the Lords about the Canadian prisoners—in revenge for what I had said of him

of the Foreign Office. I never kept a copy of any opinion I wrote,— private or official.

 [2] Abercromby, M.P. for Edinburgh, had been created Lord Dunfermline. —ED.

in the Queen's Bench in the Privilege case. I met Webster, the great American lawyer, and a very agreeable party.

I am going down to Brighton on Monday to attend a compensation case, and I have two or three special retainers in the wind. But I have had a great deal too much of forensic wrangling, and I do not think I can carry on the war much longer. During the last six months I have been in more important cases than have occurred in the same space of time for a vast many years—the Canadian Prisoners case; Auchterarder case; Lady Hewley's case; Privilege case; case of Scotch *antenati* succeeding to English estates, &c. I now wish very much for repose.

July 27, 1839.

. . . The disturbed state of the country keeps me in great trouble. I have been employed for the last eight hours in reading 'precognitions' and libellous newspapers. I am at last going to file my first *ex officio* information after having been more than five years Attorney-General—against Feargus O'Connor, for his incentives to insurrection and spoliation.

Warwick: August 2, 1839.

. . . I have to-day convicted the first batch of the Chartists. The town is uncommonly tranquil—although we had one outbreak of Chartism in court.

Liverpool : August 26, 1839.

. . . My cause here, which I apprehended might have lasted a week, is over, and I have got a verdict, subject to some frivolous points of law, which are sure to be decided in my favour. The question was about the validity of the charters of incorporation to Manchester and the new boroughs—which formed one of the subjects of Lyndhurst's review—and great party importance is attached to it.

They say 'I have chained Victory to my chariot wheel.' I should be delighted never to have another special retainer. The anxiety is greater than ever, and I have but very slender pleasure in success.

I return to London by this evening's train.

Autobiography.

This autumn I paid a visit to Paris, not having been upon the Continent for thirteen years. I was accompanied by my wife and my two eldest daughters, now old enough to take an interest in new scenes and manners. The pleasure of beholding a foreign country for the first time is renewed and increased by showing it to one's children. We crossed over from Brighton to Dieppe and, spending a day or two at Rouen, travelled up the Seine to Paris. The white flag, which I had seen floating on the Tuileries when I was last in Paris, was now replaced by the tricolor, which I had seen there in 1802. But 'the monarchy surrounded by republican institutions,' produced by the barricades and the three days of July, was quietly settling into a more absolute government than had subsisted in France under the exiled branch of the Bourbons at any time since the Restoration. In the reigns of Louis XVIII. and Charles X. I used to see caricatures on the boulevards successfully turning them into ridicule : now no caricature was permitted. The press, which brought about the Revolution, was now awed by packed juries and the arbitrary decisions of the House of Peers. All the symptoms of a military government were apparent. But these things gave no uneasiness to the French nation, who were eager for the humiliation of England and of Germany, but perfectly indifferent as to their own internal freedom. They certainly have a passion for the law requiring the equal partibility of property among all the children, which they consider necessary to prevent the recurrence of what they formerly suffered from, the exclusive privileges of the *noblesse*; but they would care little if the Chambers were abolished, and the new fortifications of Paris were occupied by an army of a hundred thousand men commanded by a warlike Sovereign.

There being no general reception at Court during our stay, I intimated in the proper quarter that ' Madame la Baronne mon épouse ' and I wished to have the honour of paying our respects to their Majesties, and we were invited to drink tea with them at St. Cloud. Louis Philippe was very polite to me, and even jocular. When I was presented he said, speaking English like a native, ' I find *the Campbells are coming,* and I am very glad to see them.' The Queen and the Princesses were exceedingly courteous to Miladi, seated her at the tea-table along with them, and kept her in conversation till, according to the etiquette of the Court, they all withdrew.

A gloom was cast over Paris by the dangerous illness of Mademoiselle Rachel, the tragic actress, till exceeding joy was occasioned by a bulletin announcing her convalescence, though there was no hope of her again acting for weeks to come. I have since seen her in London. Though I cannot deny her to be very clever, her *physique* must ever prevent her from being truly great, and in force and majesty I must place her far below Madame Duchesnoy, and a great deal farther below Mrs. Siddons and Miss O'Neil.

We admired at Versailles the efforts of Louis Philippe to tickle the vanity of the nation by his historical statues and pictures; and the Bourse, the triumphal arch at the Barrière de l'Etoile, and the Madeleine, all lately finished, pleased us much; but there was nothing by which I was so much struck as the increased cleanliness and comfort which seemed to me to be discoverable in almost every quarter of the city of Paris, showing that under the most defective political institutions improvement will go on if there is tolerable protection for property, and a decent regard for personal liberty.

We returned by Beauvais, Abbeville and Boulogne to London. In the provinces things remain nearly stationary; but if the population of France has increased, as represented, agriculture must be making rapid advances. Although it is said that the peasant has not a fowl in his pot as often as in the time of Henri IV., and that less butcher's meat is now consumed in France than fifty years ago, I presume there can be no doubt that the mass of the inhabitants are better fed, as well as better clothed and lodged, than they were when subject to the *taille* and the *corvées.*

While in Paris I heard of the death of Mr. Justice Vaughan, one of the judges of the Court of Common Pleas, and I wrote to Lord Melbourne begging that the office might not be filled up till I had had time to consider whether I would not accept it.   To this letter I received the following reply :—

Windsor Castle : October 11, 1839.

My dear Attorney,—I have received your letter of the 1st inst. and have communicated it, as you desired, to the Lord Chancellor and to Lord John Russell. Of course we can do no otherwise than comply with your wish, but it had perhaps better not be mentioned until your return to England.

We shall be most sorry to lose your services as Attorney-General, which have been so efficient and authoritative, and which have conferred upon the Administration so much both of character and strength.

With respect to your unwillingness to terminate your career by accepting the office of a puisne judge, that is a matter for your own consideration. If it should be repugnant to your own feelings or those of your friends, I shall be sorry; at the same time, for my own part, I do not partake of those feelings. I do not think so much of superiority, pre-eminence, title, and position as others are inclined to do. When the Abbé Siéyès, in the early part of the Revolution, went ambassador to Berlin, he was upon some public occasion, either designedly or accidentally, placed in a seat below the dignity of the country which he represented. He sate down in it without remonstrance, observing, ' The first place in this apartment is that which the Ambassador of the French Republic occupies.' I know not whether this anecdote be true—few anecdotes are so—but I have always admired it ; and depend upon it, wheresoever you may be placed, you will soon make the seat which you fill equal, if not superior, to the first in the court. Believe me, my dear Attorney,   Yours ever faithfully,

MELBOURNE.

However, Lord John Russell, my House of Commons *chef*, wrote me a very kind and friendly letter,[a] and I agreed to run all risks with the Government, notwithstanding its then ' staggering state.' The consequence is that I am at this time without office, profession or pension. Yet I cannot regret the resolution I then formed. I was partly actuated by the bitter sarcasm of Brougham upon Sir Vicary Gibbs, in his

[a]
' Buckhurst: October 20, 1839.

' My dear Attorney,—You were quite right to write to Lord Melbourne, who constantly communicates with me. But I was sincerely sorry to find that you thought of taking a puisne judgeship. . . . I earnestly hope we may be able to keep you ; but I cannot control events, or ask you to remain if you think your reputation does not require your refusing this judgeship.   ' Yours truly,

' J. RUSSELL.'

' Sketches of British Statesmen,' when he relates that, the Prime Minister being supposed to be tottering, ' the Attorney-General in a fit of terror sunk into a puisne judge.'

Rolfe had made up his mind to accept the place if I declined it. His situation at the bar would not have been very comfortable had he lost his official rank, and his seat in Parliament, by no means a secure one, required certain compliances which the Reform Bill was for ever to do away with. He turned out a very good judge, and he is respected by the public as much as he is beloved by his friends in private life. There never lived a better man than Rolfe.

I supported Wilde as the new Solicitor-General. He had immense business in the Common Pleas, and was no doubt the most laborious man who ever entered our profession, his daily habit being to go to chambers at six o'clock in the morning summer and winter, to remain there till he went into court, and, only going home to dinner for a few minutes, to return to chambers and to remain there till between two and three in the morning. If hard pushed he did not mind sitting up all night.

I found Wilde a very honest, good-tempered and comfortable coadjutor, although I was obliged to answer many more of the Government cases than before; and, with the exception of the Privilege case, on some parts of which we differed, we always went on together most harmoniously.

Letters to Sir George Campbell.

Brooks's : October 28, 1839.

. . . I have no news. Lord Holland having called yesterday, wishing to see me, I went to-day to Holland House. He was gone to Windsor, but my Lady received me. When I told her I was not to be the judge, she said, ' Je respire.' She had been alarmed by strong reports that I wished it, and was to withdraw in disgust. She observed that Lord Holland wished very much to have me in the House of Lords, and she thought Plunket would withdraw. But upon this occasion she has not been called into council, and she knows nothing about the matter. Mary and I are to dine at Holland House to-morrow and may hear something more.

New Street: December 5, 1839.

. . . I have great pleasure in sending you a letter from Stanley Clarke, which amounts to an absolute appointment of my nephew George as a writer to Bengal. This consoles me very much amidst the vexations and mortifications to which I am exposed.

Autobiography.

In the beginning of November, to the great delight of the Tories, there was a Chartist insurrection, or rather rebellion, in Monmouthshire; Frost, at the head of above 10,000 men armed and disciplined, having attempted to storm the town of Newport, and having been repulsed by a military force. At a meeting of my constituents a few weeks before, upon my return from France, I had boasted of our having entirely put down Chartism by legal and constitutional means. While I was sitting in the Queen's Bench, Sir William Follett with great glee laid before me the second edition of a newspaper containing an account of the battle of Newport. There was much jocularity in the press on ' the second-sight of Sir John Campbell,' and H. B., the popular caricaturist, honoured me with a well-imagined print representing me addressing the electors of Edinburgh, with an extract of my speech coming out of my mouth, and, in the distance, Frost leading on his army to the assault on Newport.

I was soon deeply involved in the law of high treason, and preparing for the special commission before which the traitors were to be tried at Monmouth.

The trials at Monmouth, which began the first day of the new year, excited deep interest throughout the country. Frost was defended by Sir Frederick Pollock, the late Attorney-General, and Mr. Kelly,[4] one of the most acute and powerful advocates at the bar. I had the able assistance of the new Solicitor-General. We obtained convictions in all the cases tried, subject to the opinion of the fifteen judges on a question reserved as to the effect of the Solicitor to the Treasury having given the prisoners the copy of the indictment sooner than was necessary.

' Sir Fitzroy Kelly, Lord Chief Baron from the year 1866 till he died, September 1880, aged 84.—ED.

Letter to Sir George Campbell.

Monmouth : January 8, 1840.

. . . I must send you one more frank, which will be my last; but the prepaying can be no impediment to our correspondence. Before this reaches you, you will have heard of Frost's conviction. I have passed a very anxious day, as if I had been myself on trial. To my utter astonishment and dismay, Tindal summed up for an acquittal. What he meant, the Lord only knows. No human being doubted the guilt of the prisoners, and we had proved it by the clearest evidence. It was of the last importance to the public tranquillity that there should be a verdict of guilty. Chief Justice Tindal is a very honourable man, and had no assignable reason for deviating from the right course. Yet from the beginning to the end of his charge, he laboured for an acquittal. Before he concluded I had not the faintest notion that the jury could act otherwise than according to the view he gave them. When they retired, I called a consultation of all the Crown counsel at my lodgings to consider what was to be done upon the acquittal, and we agreed that there was no use in prosecuting the others for treason. While we were still in deliberation, a messenger announced the verdict of guilty. . . .

Autobiography.

A great share of public attention was now attracted to the question of *Privilege,* which had assumed a very formidable shape. Stockdale had brought a third action during the vacation against the printer of the House of Commons for the alleged libel in the Report on Prisons. There being no appearance entered, there had been judgment by default, the jury had assessed heavy damages, and a writ of execution had been issued to the Sheriffs of Middlesex. If the damages had been levied and paid over to the party before the meeting of Parliament, the privileges of the House would have been for ever gone by such a precedent. This would have been the result had Parliament not met till the usual time in the beginning of February. I made a representation on the subject, and a Cabinet was called, which I attended.

Some were swayed by the inconvenience of facing a trouble-some assembly prematurely, but Lord John Russell, ever eager for the dignity of the House of Commons, and regardless of personal labour, took my side, and the meeting of the two Houses was fixed for the 16th of January.

The last trial at Monmouth finished in the evening before Parliament was to meet. I travelled all night and stepped out of my carriage at the House of Commons as the debate was beginning. Privilege had superseded the Address; and the grand consideration was, what steps were to be taken to prevent Stockdale from obtaining the fruits of his judgment. Peel was steadfast, but the great bulk of his party were against him, and the Tory lawyers, as if they thought he was insincere, exerted their utmost ingenuity and zeal to thwart the measures taken for the protection of the House.

Before I set off for the State trials at Monmouth, I had received the following letter from Lord John Russell.

Bowood: December 23, 1839.

My dear Attorney,—I have asked Lord Melbourne to write to you respecting the Bills concerning Prince Albert. They will require your supervision, and it will be desirable to give directions before you leave town.

I hope you will arrange with Wilde our first steps about Privilege. It seems to me we must commit the sheriff, at all events,—he has robbed our servant of 600*l.*

For my own part I should not dislike a declaratory Act, but I doubt whether we ought to propose any such thing.

Pray let me know what you think, and I will inform the Speaker. If you can see Sir William Follett, so much the better. Yours truly,

J. RUSSELL.

I had accordingly arranged our plan of operations, though greatly disturbed by Wilde, who was always for pushing Privilege to a mad extreme. He was quite sincere, and not, as some supposed, aiming at popularity and trying to throw into the shade the Attorney-General, who was for more moderate and prudent counsels, but less relished by a majority of the House.

We first committed Mr. Stockdale to Newgate, and then made an order on the sheriffs that they should restore to

Hansard the printer the amount of the damages which he had deposited with them in order to prevent the sale of his goods.   The sheriffs refusing to obey this order, we committed them to the custody of the Serjeant-at-Arms.

Next came a proceeding which placed me in a most difficult position, and the public never knew the danger which then existed of a convulsion unexampled in our history.   The sheriffs sued out a writ of Habeas Corpus directed to the Serjeant-at-Arms, commanding him to produce before the Court of Queen's Bench the Sheriffs of Middlesex, alleged to be illegally in custody, with the cause of their detention.   Wilde, the Solicitor-General, was strong for refusing to make any return to the writ, and for setting the Court of Queen's Bench at defiance.   Had I concurred in this opinion, it certainly would have been acted upon.   The consequences would have been that the Serjeant-at-Arms, even with the mace in his hand, would have been sent to Newgate by the Court of Queen's Bench.   The House must have retaliated by committing the judges.   The Crown would then have had to determine on which side the army should be employed, and for a time we must have lived under a military government. I was of opinion that both law and expediency required that the writ of Habeas Corpus should be obeyed ; that, notwithstanding one or two irregular precedents in bad times, the superior courts in Westminster Hall had jurisdiction to direct such a writ even to an officer of either House, although the moment the judges ascertained that there had been a commitment by either House for contempt, their jurisdiction was gone, and they could only remand the prisoner ; that we were still to expect from the judges a performance of their duty ; and that, if we must come to a rupture with them, we should take care to select a point on which we were sure we were right, and on which we could rally public opinion in our favour.   The only opportunity I had of consulting a member of the Cabinet was in a short conference I had with Lord John Russell behind the Speaker's chair.   He agreed with me ; and the writ was to be obeyed.   To obviate a threat of Lord Denman that if upon the return to a writ of Habeas Corpus it appeared that the commitment was by a House of

Parliament for a cause which the court thought insufficient, they would discharge the prisoner, I framed a general return, merely stating that the sheriffs were committed for a breach of the privileges of the House, and, to refresh the memory of the judges, I made a speech in the House of Commons, citing various authorities to prove that such a general return must be held sufficient.

This return was accordingly made; the sheriffs were produced at the bar of the Queen's Bench by the Serjeant-at-Arms, and a motion was made for their discharge. But Lord Denman, after strong observations upon the impropriety of concealing from the court the real cause of the commitment, and a little bravado as to what he would have done had it appeared to be for obeying the process of the court, confessed that they had no power to inquire into it by affidavit, and remanded the prisoners into the custody of the Serjeant-at-Arms, who brought them back to 'Little Ease.' There they lived some time very luxuriously, having every morning a levée of Tory members, who congratulated them on their patriotism, and exhorted them to persevere. Every evening we had motions for their discharge, and at last one of them was set at liberty on the score of ill health, which he said in his petition arose from confinement, but which Mr. Wakley, the member for Finsbury, a medical man and coroner for Middlesex, alleged was caused by high living, and might be cured by abstinence.

We were further obliged to commit a Mr. Howard, an attorney, who had brought still another action, at the suit of Mr. Stockdale, for the alleged libel; and also two clerks, who carried it on while Mr. Howard was in Newgate.

No one could foresee the termination of the controversy. The Tory party were still more annoyed by it than we were, for it divided them from their leader, and till it was settled there was hardly a possibility of their coming into office. The great obstacle to a settlement was the Duke of Wellington. He highly disapproved of Peel's conduct, and he had taken up an inveterate notion that the sale of libels must of necessity be unlawful. Various attempts were made to instil into him the distinction between the publication of criminatory matter by proper authority for a proper object, and a gratuitous calumny, but it was all to no purpose. The matter being of such consequence to the Tory party, Lord Lyndhurst, Lord Aberdeen and Lord Ellenborough tried, in vain, to soothe him. At last the settlement of the question by Act of Parliament was suggested to him. To this he at first strongly objected, but when he was told that it would not reverse the judgment of the Court of Queen's Bench, he very reluctantly gave his consent.

I confess I was at first as hostile to a Bill as the Duke himself, but I consented to it on condition that it contained in the preamble a recital that ' the power of the House to publish whatever it thought necessary for public information was essential to the due exercise of its legislative and its inquisitorial powers.' The negation of this proposition was the foundation of the judgment of the Court of Queen's Bench, and the assertion of it in an Act of Parliament was virtually a legislative reversal of the judgment.

The Bill was introduced by Lord J. Russell, and was passed by a great majority.[5] I cannot regret the course I adopted. The Bill for ever secured to the two Houses of Parliament the right to publish what they please without the control of any court of law, and it affirmed in the most unqualified terms the broad principle for which we had been contending.

[5] Leave to bring in the Bill was carried by 203 to 54, March 5, 1840. —ED.

CHAPTER XXIV.

MARCH 1840—JUNE 1841.

Spring Assizes—Leeds Rioters—Feargus O'Connor—Trial of Oxford—Will
Cause at Liverpool—Ashtead, Surrey—Death of Lord Holland—Trial
of Lord Cardigan—Appointed Lord Chancellor of Ireland, and raised
to the Peerage—Takes his place in the Privy Council—Letters of
Congratulation.

Autobiography.

AT the Spring assizes I went to York to prosecute some
persons who had been engaged in proceedings at Leeds
which might well have been construed into high treason; but
I was contented to convict them of misdemeanour, although
they had had a plan for murdering the magistrates and
getting possession of the town, and they were beginning to
carry it into execution, when they were overpowered and
taken prisoners.

I likewise here conducted the trial of the only criminal
information I ever filed for a libel,—having held the office
of Attorney-General longer than any one since the time of
Sir Dudley Ryder, except Lord Thurlow who exceeded me by
a few months. The person against whom I pointed my
artillery was Feargus O'Connor, the editor of the ' Northern
Star,' a nephew of the great Arthur. He thought he was
perfectly safe by never being present at any Chartist riot, and
only *instigating* insurrection and plunder. He defended
himself on this occasion with great address, and thought to
awake the sympathies of a Tory jury by assuring them that
he hated the Whigs and loved the Corn Laws. But I
counteracted his eloquence by pointing out in my reply the
passages in which he recommended that there should be a
redistribution of landed property, and that the people should

seize and divide among themselves the soil of which they
were now unjustly deprived by the squirearchy. I begged
'that they would acquit him unless they believed that, by
the publications complained of, he deliberately intended to
incite to insurrection and plunder.' The jury convicted him,
and he was sentenced by the Court of Queen's Bench to
eighteen months' imprisonment.

Yet there were petitions to the House of Commons for a
free pardon to him, to Frost, and to the Leeds rioters, on the
ground that they had only been guilty of ' political offences.'
To throw odium upon the Government, the subordinate
members of the Tory party asserted that they and the whole
body of the Chartists had been persecuted. When Goulburn, once a Welsh judge, brother of the Chancellor of
the Exchequer, stood for the city of Carlisle, he denounced
the prosecutions of the present Attorney-General as tyran-
nical and oppressive, and pledged himself that, if returned, his
first act should be to present a petition to the Crown for the
immediate liberation of that much injured man Feargus
O'Connor.[1]

The next *cause célèbre* in which I was concerned was the
prosecution, for high treason, of Oxford, who shot at the
Queen.[2] The jury first found that ' there was no evidence of
the pistol being loaded with ball,' and then, that ' the prisoner
was in a state of insanity when he did the act.' There ought
to have been a simple verdict of *guilty*, but no blame was
imputable to me. It was said that the Attorney-General
kept back clear evidence which had been furnished to him
of the pistol having been loaded. For more than a week the
most diligent search had been made in vain for a ball. At
the end of that time an Irish labourer brought a pistol bullet
to the Home Office, saying that he had picked it up near the
brick wall opposite to which Oxford stood when he fired.
In this wall a hole had been discovered, which might have
been made by a bullet. But, unfortunately, the bullet pro-

---

[1] Serjeant Goulburn personally is a singularly good-humoured and
agreeable gentleman. We have since been excellent friends, and have had
many a good laugh at his Carlisle speech.

[2] The offence was committed Wednesday, June 10, 1840. The trial
took place July 9 and 10.—ED.

duced was entirely spherical, without any dint or flattening. I myself made experiments in the Tothill Fields prison-yard, by firing bullets against a brick wall at various distances, and I uniformly found that they were rendered nearly as flat as little pancakes. Some persons about the Queen wished me to call this man as a witness, and to produce the bullet as the very one which had been fired from Oxford's pistol. But I positively refused to do so, being convinced that the story was false. On the second day of Oxford's trial, which took place at the Central Criminal Court, I had the honour to dine with the Sheriffs of Middlesex, and, all our animosities being forgotten, we merrily talked over their adventures while at my instance they were prisoners at ' Little Ease.'

In the summer, I went to the Liverpool assizes in a great will cause, with a fee of five hundred guineas, and made a speech which lasted a day and a half; but much of the time was occupied in reading letters written by the testator to prove his sanity, which I further corroborated by the evidence of Sir Frederick Pollock, who had visited him, and whom I examined as a witness. I caused some diversion by pitying the sufferings of my brother barrister while he listened to me, and by quoting a passage from Quevedo, the Spanish poet, intimating that the punishment of wicked fiddlers in a future state will be, being condemned to hear fiddling in which they are not permitted to join. Wilde, on the other side, was obliged to surrender.[3]

Letters to Sir George Campbell in the year 1840.

New Street: March 21, 1840.

. . . After being tossed about for some months on a stormy sea amidst breakers, I am all at once in smooth water. The State trials are all over, and the Privilege Bill has passed the Commons. . . . My campaign against the Chartists was

---

[3] My greatest fee while at the bar was for arguing the case before the Privy Council on the will of James Wood, of Gloucester—one thousand guineas, with very large refreshers ! Since I left the bar, my client, who succeeded, has made me a present of a candelabrum worth as much. The stake for which we contended was above a million.

very successful and not without glory. To file an *ex-officio* information against Feargus O'Connor, and to face him in person, required some courage and energy. To have convicted him is very creditable to the Government. I do not remember any event of the same sort which has caused such general satisfaction. When I entered the House of Commons on Thursday I was warmly congratulated on all sides, including Tories and Radicals.

There is a rumour that Lord Melbourne is going to retire, which is a little countenanced by a conversation I lately heard him engaged in at Holland House about Sylla, Diocletian and Charles V.; but I cannot believe, although he croaks so much about his health, that he will actually abdicate. On this occasion I witnessed a burst of feeling from him for which I was not prepared. He was talking of the Queen having said to him, among the first things she uttered after her accession, that her father's debts must be paid. In repeating this declaration he shed tears and was much affected.

House of Commons: June 12, 1840.

. . . I was engaged the greater part of yesterday in examining the witnesses against Oxford. All flattery apart, the Queen certainly is a very extraordinary young woman. She told Lord John Russell, who told me, that when she heard the first shot, she did not know she had been fired at, but she immediately saw the assassin aiming the second pistol at her, and then she stooped down to avoid the ball, and, finding herself safe, she gave orders to drive to her mother's. She was quite calm, even amidst the enthusiastic cheers of the multitude on her return to the Palace.

House of Commons: July 22, 1840.

. . . The most distinguished event of my life has been that on Tuesday morning I was strongly urged by the Lord Chamberlain to dance a Scotch reel before the Queen. We have taken for a year the house at Ashtead, near Epsom, which Lord North inhabited when Prime Minister.

New Street: August 11, 1840.

. . . We may be in a fool's paradise, but we close the session in great spirits, and certainly the Tories are in a state of dismay. At our fish dinner on Saturday we duly commemorated the services of Sir John Yarde Buller, who by his vote of want of confidence certainly was of signal service in getting us through the session. We drank health and long life to him with three times three.

Ashtead: August 21, 1840.

. . . Summer has returned to us in full splendour. To-day there is not a cloud in the firmament. I hope you are equally fortunate and that you will soon have fine crops in your stack-yard.

We continue to enjoy Ashtead very much. We all dine together at three, and have nice walks, rides, and drives in the evening. The day for my trial at Liverpool is not yet fixed. I do not allow my repose to be disturbed by the apprehension of a French war, but I fear that M. Thiers may find it inevitable. Successive French Governments have planned the obtaining of an ascendency in Egypt and Syria, as a counterpoise to our Eastern Empire, by making Mehemet Ali a French *préfet*, and no Minister can well stand in France who abandons this policy.

But I ought rather to tell you of our cows, pigs and poultry. I have the establishment of a country squire—ten men servants to pay and feed. The Edenwood ponies are come home, much grown and improved. Hally rode the chestnut to Abinger and back, and Molly is mounted on the grey. A donkey forms part of the establishment, for which we have a Spanish saddle with panniers to hold Dudley, Cissy and Ena.

New Street:
Friday night, September 18, 1840.

. . . Mary and I have been in town some days. We came to carry Hally to school, and I have been detained by some official business. We return to Ashtead to-morrow morning.

I dined to-day at Holland House. On my way thither I

stopped at Brooks's and was shown for the first time a paragraph in the newspapers stating that Plunket is certainly to resign immediately and to be succeeded by Mr. Moore, the Irish Solicitor-General. I mentioned this to Lord Holland, who said he had heard nothing of it, and did not believe it. If such an appointment were so made, I should consider it a deliberate insult, and should send in my resignation. I desired Lord Holland to intimate as much to Lord Melbourne. He was very friendly upon the occasion, and said that, however much my withdrawal from the House of Commons was to be regretted, this consideration ought not to weigh in the filling up of an office which I am qualified for, and am willing to accept. He has been long very desirous to have me in the House of Lords to keep Brougham in check; but this is now considered of less importance since Brougham's hostility, or activity, has subsided. Lord Holland told me a saying of his grandfather to show that it is not so difficult a thing to be Chancellor. Someone having asked Fox what the Government would do for a Chancellor if Lord Hardwicke should resign. *Fox.* 'Give the Great Seal to John my coachman.'

Ashtead: October 1, 1840.

. . . I continue to enjoy Ashtead as much as ever. You ask me how my Equity studies come on. Alas! I can tell you of nothing but *novels*. I have been *privately* reading ' Clarissa Harlowe.' I cannot say that it uniformly delighted me so much as in my young days, and I was obliged to skip over whole letters as tedious; but the pathetic scenes still touched me to tears, and the last day I spent twelve hours over it, sorry when it was done. In the evening I read Miss Austen's novels to Mary and the girls; and I must admit that, with almost equal genius, she displays much better taste than Richardson, and that her writings are much better adapted to the youthful mind.

I will tell you however a book which has delighted me beyond all measure, and which, if you have not read, I strongly recommend to you, 'Letters from the Mountains,' by Mrs. Grant of Laggan, a Highland minister's wife. I prefer them to those of Madame de Sévigné or Lady Mary

Wortley Montagu. They are particularly interesting to me, from their allusions to the society and modes of life in which I was reared. I know not which to admire most—her pictures of natural scenery or her delineations of human passions, feelings and manners.

I have not been altogether idle. Besides answering official and private cases sent down to me here, I have spent upon an average two or three hours a day upon the practice of the Court of Chancery and Equity pleading. I hear nothing more of the Irish Chancellorship, and I take it for granted that the rumour of Plunket's resignation is unfounded.

The Irish Chancellorship would not be by any means a desirable destiny for me, but it is better than anything else that is open. I would not by any means accept an Equity judgeship unless I were convinced I could adequately discharge its duties; but the truth is, I am so thoroughly founded in the Common Law, and have been so much in the Privy Council, the House of Lords and the Court of Chancery itself, that I am not by any means appalled by the mystery which Equity draughtsmen would make of their craft.

I am glad you have got the Life of Sir Samuel Romilly. Look in the last number of the 'Quarterly,' where you will find it reviewed. The evidence of Dumont on the inquest there given no one can read with a dry eye. In all history and fiction I know nothing more truly tragic.

We continue to have nice rides on the downs, and in the romantic lanes in this country. Diamond chose to kick off Loo the other day on Mickleham downs. She behaved very gallantly, however, sprang up, caught him, and galloped away in a few minutes. Jack the donkey is the most important member of our stud. We have a Spanish saddle for him, on which sit Cissy and Ena. Dudley, who rejoices in being a donkey boy, leads him across the common so loaded, and Mary and I follow behind.

All this must soon be exchanged for the bickerings of the bar. But I believe my repose will be undisturbed till term comes round. Mr. Andrew Millar informs me that my presence in Edinburgh may for the present be dispensed with.

Ashtead : October 18, 1840.

. . . I am going to town on Tuesday to see about the trial of Lord Cardigan before the Peers, but I hope to return on Wednesday and to have another week of dear Ashtead. Loo, Molly and I still ride out daily, exploring the green lanes and discovering fresh beauties in this delightful country.

New Street : November 1, 1840.

. . . I have not yet got over the death of Lord Holland. I was engaged to dine at Holland House the day he was taken ill. When I entered the drawing-room I was surprised to find it empty. Dr. Holland by and by came in, saying he had been sent for, and that Lord Holland was dangerously ill. I came back to town in Lady Holland's carriage, sent to bring Dr. Chambers. When I sent to inquire next morning, the answer was that Lord Holland had died at six o'clock ! I had received more personal kindness from him than from any other public man. I had a letter from him about Fred (in whom he took a lively interest) the very day before he was taken ill, and probably the last letter he ever wrote.

Autobiography.

The session of 1841 began with the trial of the Earl of Cardigan at the bar of the House of Lords for fighting a duel. The result of this was very discreditable to the administration of justice, the noble prisoner having been acquitted because the witnesses did not prove that his antagonist, Captain Tuckett, was known by each of the names Harvey Gurnett Phipps Tuckett, by which he was described in the indictment, although there was no question as to his identity. I could take no blame to myself, as I had pointed out the necessity of such evidence, and I was told it would be given. Although Lord Cardigan was by no means a popular man, there was the strongest wish among all his judges that he should escape on some ground or other.

I was censured for speaking so lightly on this occasion of the moral guilt of duelling ; but my observations were confined to the case where a man, without being at all to

blame himself, is so circumstanced that to preserve himself
from infamy and ruin he is compelled to send or to accept a
challenge ; and I confess I do not see how such a man in going
into the field of honour violates the law of God more than by
firing against a public enemy on the field of battle. If he is
the offending party and kills his antagonist, he is a murderer.
It is delightful to think that from increased refinement of
manners the practice of duelling disappears, and that, instead
of conferring distinction, a duel is at present considered a
misfortune and a discredit to a man as long as he lives.

The Melbourne Administration was now tottering to its
fall. The Tories skilfully brought forward an Irish question
on which the Government might be weakened by the unpopularity of O'Connell. The English nation hated him as
an Irishman and a Roman Catholic ; they justly condemned
the coarseness of invective in which he indulged, and they
very unfairly forgot the zealous and effective services he had
rendered to Ireland. The Government was most absurdly
blamed by many moderate and many liberal men for accepting
his support, without proof or charge that to please him any improper measures had ever been brought forward or supported.

Lord Stanley's Bill to regulate the registration of voters
in Ireland was represented as so imperatively required to put
down fraud and perjury, that all legislation must be suspended
till it passed. The object of its promoters being gained, it is
now thrown like a worthless weed away.

Ought the Whig Ministers to have resigned as soon as
they found the House of Commons against them ? Or were
they justified in bringing forward their Budget and appealing
to the people ? I was strongly for the latter course, and the
result has in no degree altered my opinion. We did well both
for the sake of the nation and for the sake of the party. The
Free Trade Budget laid the foundation for Peel's Tariff and
for the relaxation and speedy destruction of ' the sliding scale,'
and we are now in the proud situation of seeing our measures
carried into effect by our successors. Upon the dissolution
the elections went dreadfully against us, but the result would
have been worse if the Tories had been allowed to take the
government in the month of April. It would have been said

that we had resigned to please O'Connell, and because we saw that Stanley's Registration Bill was to *cut off the tail* of the Liberator. Peel would have strictly concealed his intentions with respect to Irish Registration, the Poor Law, the Corn Laws and the Tariff for the rest of the session and, dissolving the Parliament in the first flush of victory, the Liberals would hardly have had the courage to contest a single seat. Thus his majority would have been much more overpowering. Besides we must ever remember that it is not fair to judge entirely by the event; there was a chance that the people might then have seen their true interest with regard to Free Trade and the other measures we proposed, and might have enabled us to carry them.

As soon as the dissolution was resolved on, Lord John Russell and Lord Melbourne spontaneously intimated to me that they wished me to hold the Great Seal of Ireland as successor to Lord Plunket, and to take my place in the Upper House, which would create no permanent addition to the Peerage. I accepted the offer. The arrangement was the best that they had it in their power to make for me, and I had no doubt that by caution and assiduity I should be able creditably to discharge the duties of my new office. About the same time Wilde had an intimation that he was to be Attorney-General, and Erle had the offer of being Solicitor-General.

I imagined that Lord Plunket's consent had been obtained, and I was not aware that I had anything to apprehend except uncertainty of tenure, till one evening at the very close of the session I received a letter from Lord Melbourne stating that Lord Plunket refused to resign. I made a great stir at first, but I was calmed down, and I agreed to remain Attorney-General and again to stand for Edinburgh.[4]

[4] *Letter to Lord Melbourne.*

New Street, Spring Gardens: June 12, 1841.

Dear Lord Melbourne,—I am satisfied. From William Gibson Craig's refusal to come forward as a candidate at Edinburgh, the field is clear for me, and I believe I shall be returned without opposition. Yours faithfully,

J. CAMPBELL.

Letter from Lord Melbourne.

My dear Attorney,—I am much relieved and gratified by your letter. It was a blundering thing to open this matter before the preliminary step

A different turn was suddenly given to the affair by Lord
Fortescue, the Lord Lieutenant. He had been absent from
Dublin, on account of the illness of his father in Devonshire,
when Lord Melbourne's letter to Lord Plunket had arrived
asking for the resignation; and when, on his return, he heard
of the refusal, he wrote to Lord Plunket strongly urging the
resignation.[5]

Lord Plunket wrote back that such favours had been conferred upon him and his family by the Government, that he
could no longer refuse to do what they so earnestly wished.
But on the day of his last appearance in court he declared
to the bar that the resignation was forced upon him to make
way for Sir John Campbell; that he was no party to the
arrangement; that he highly disapproved of it; that though

was fully arranged, but I thought I had reason to believe that it would be
so without difficulty. It is also another proof of your devotion to your
principles and party, and an addition to the many and great services which
you have already rendered. Believe me, my dear Attorney,

Yours faithfully,

MELBOURNE.

[5] *Letters from Judge Ball.*

Dublin: June 13.

My dear Attorney-General,—Lord Ebrington arrived at two o'clock
this morning from Devonshire, and he has already written to Plunket,
requesting to see him as soon as possible. It is Lord Ebrington's intention
to represent to Plunket in the most determined manner and terms that he
cannot without disgrace refuse to give effect to the engagement he gave
in writing last year to retire whenever required.

June 16.—Lord Ebrington and Plunket had a very stormy meeting,
and Plunket put his refusal distinctly on the ground of his apprehension
of being compromised in public opinion if he should be instrumental to
your getting a retiring salary after a few weeks' or months' service—in the
event of the Government being obliged to go out on the meeting of the
new Parliament.

June 17.—This morning Lord Ebrington wrote a letter to Plunket,
urging the matter in such terms that the latter came to him at two
o'clock, and announced his resignation. Lord Ebrington has told Plunket
that he takes upon himself the entire responsibility of the arrangement, so
that Plunket will not have to encounter the obloquy he so much dreaded.

June 20.—I must now tell you that Lord Ebrington has written by this
post to Lord Melbourne to announce that he resigns unless your appointment takes place, and he has requested me to say that he is exceedingly
desirous that you should come over here to assume your office *with the least
possible delay.*

personally and politically he had a great respect for Sir John Campbell, he thought the office of Chancellor ought to be filled by a member of the Irish bar—a bar so renowned for honour and independence and so rich in learning and genius.

This speech of course set the Four Courts on fire. A meeting of the bar was immediately called, and strong resolutions were passed against the threatened intrusion.

Lord Fortescue remained firm and wrote to Lord Melbourne that if I was not appointed Chancellor he would immediately resign his office of Lord Lieutenant.

I proposed that I should be appointed without the pension in case of removal from office, to which in the usual course I should have been entitled. My suggestion was adopted, and it was announced in the ' Morning Chronicle ' that Sir John Campbell was to hold the Great Seal of Ireland without any retiring pension. But the Tory papers all asserted that the appointment was a job to procure me a pension, and that a pension I was to have notwithstanding the denial of the fact. To this day many believe that I am in the receipt of 4,000l. a year for having held the Great Seal of Ireland six weeks.[6]

I rejoice that I am poor and pensionless. The pension would have been very convenient for me and my family, and the services I am now gratuitously rendering to the public

[6] *Letter from Earl Fortescue.*

Phœnix Park : June 22, 1841.

My dear Sir John,—Though I begged our friend Ball to write to you yesterday, I add a line myself to say how glad I shall be to see you here with Lady Stratheden and any of your family whom you may wish to bring over with you before you have made arrangements for fixing your own residence. I am going to Devonshire to-day for the performance of a melancholy duty, but I propose being back on Saturday, and I shall be ready, if it suits you, to receive you on that day.

You know, of course, what a strong prejudice has been raised against your appointment. Your waiver of the pension in case of our being turned out by the result of the elections has, however, removed the only reasonable ground of objection to it, and though storms are easily raised among the excitable spirits of this country, they seldom stand long against reason and justice when backed by calm and firm determination. Believe me always, my dear Sir John,   Yours very faithfully,

FORTESCUE.

as a judge in the Privy Council and in the House of Lords would not be adequately compensated by the amount of the pension of an Irish ex-Chancellor ; but it would have exposed the Government to obloquy, and would have been a subject of very painful recollections to myself.

No one can charge me with having 'lived upon the taxes.' When in office I received no emolument except for business done. In 1831 the Whigs (I think rather capriciously) cut off the salary of the Attorney- and Solicitor-General, together with the wages of 40l. a year formerly allowed to the King's counsel. I was even compelled to pay land-tax upon my salary as Attorney-General which I never received, and threatened with proceedings against me in the Exchequer if I refused, although no one could tell me in whose name the proceedings were to be instituted. Such was the economy of the Whig Government that they would not even give the Attorney-General the usual stationery, nor any allowance for it, so that he was obliged gratuitously to draw public Acts of Parliament on his own paper, and with his own pens and ink. Had this been known to Joseph Hume it would have softened his harangues against ministerial extravagance.

I had now only to choose my title ; and, never having done anything to make me ashamed of my name, and that name sounding well and being distinguished, I became ' John Lord Campbell, Baron Campbell of St. Andrews in the county of Fife.' Time was when I should have considered it a mighty affair to be a lord, but in reality I rather felt lowered by the elevation.

The Council at which I was sworn in a Privy Councillor was a very dismal scene. Her Majesty sate at the head of the board, with Prince Albert on her right hand. Lord Lansdowne, who officiated as Lord President, was very ill and had his arm in a sling. Lord Melbourne himself had a fit of the gout, and could hardly walk between his chair and the Queen's, when he wished to instruct her in the ceremonial of receiving wands and giving them away. This was the day when Lord Surrey resigned his office, and several other alterations were made in the Household.

Her Majesty gave me her hand to kiss very graciously,

but said nothing. After a melancholy shake of the hand
from my brother Councillors, I took my place at the board.
Lord Marcus Hill was sworn in after me, and the gloom was
for a moment relieved by a suppressed laugh from the ludi-
crous circumstance of there being no chair for him at the
' board,' and his being obliged to sit down at a side-table.

[I add three out of the many congratulatory letters which
my father received on this occasion.—ED.]

Letter from Sir William Gibson Craig.

Edinburgh : June 20, 1841.

My dear Sir John,—I congratulate you most sincerely upon your new
appointment, the right to which no man could have more honourably
earned. I must admit however that the intelligence was on other grounds
far from welcome. I regret that Edinburgh has lost the best and most
efficient representative she ever has had, or for a long time at least is
likely to have.

As it seems really impossible to find any other candidate who would be
acceptable to the constituency, I have consented to come forward in your
place. This appears to give satisfaction, and it is believed that there will
be no opposition. It is the last place in Great Britain I should have wished
to sit for ; but resolutely as I had determined never to become a candidate
while there was a chance of another Liberal being found, I never could
have allowed from mere personal feelings so important a representation
being lost to the party.

I remain, my dear Sir John,
Yours very truly,
W. GIBSON CRAIG.

Letter from Lord Dunfermline.

Colinton : June 27, 1841.

Dear Campbell,—I hear from Lord Cuninghame that you are to be in
Dublin this week. I cannot resist my desire to say a few words to you on
your retirement from an office which you have so long filled. According
to my observation there is no situation in the law which tries more or
indeed *so* severely the knowledge, judgment and, above all, the sterling
qualities of the understanding, than the office of Attorney-General. I
think so, because it appears to me that there have been in my time lawyers
who stood justly high as judges, whose legal reputation was impaired by
the recollection of their mistakes and failures while holding the office of
Attorney-General. I have often said that I did not think that any Attorney-
General had, within my recollection, passed through the trials of the office
with the same success that has marked your long course. It is presumptuous in me to offer an opinion on a matter of which I am necessarily

a most imperfect judge ; but it is what I think, and it is a pleasure to me to express it to an old colleague and friend.

You know what my opinion was when the office of Master of the Rolls was given to Lord Langdale. My opinion has undergone no change, but I should hope that you think, as it appears to me that you very reasonably may do, that your present position is in various respects more satisfactory and advantageous to you, than if you had then been placed on the bench.

I can tell you little about the elections here. . . .

Believe me to be,
Yours very truly,
DUNFERMLINE.

Letter from T. B. Macaulay.

London : July 7, 1841.

Dear Lord Campbell,—I am delighted to hear that you have triumphed over the senseless opposition of a part of the Irish bar. I am greatly concerned at the part which Plunket has acted.

At Edinburgh everything went well. Your name was never mentioned except with respect and good-will. We drank your health with great enthusiasm at the dinner of the conveners of committees.

Our course I take to be clear. We must meet the new Parliament. I suppose that we shall be beaten on the choice of a Speaker. If so, I think that we ought to resign directly. Such a vote could be considered only as a declaration of want of confidence. If they let us keep Lefevre, we shall be beaten on the Address; and of course then we go.

I have no doubt that we shall muster three hundred at least. Ever yours truly,

T. B. MACAULAY.

CHAPTER XXV.

Autobiography.

In a few days I took my departure for Ireland, accompanied
by my wife and my eldest daughter Louise. I had written
a respectful letter to Plunket announcing my approach. On
landing at Kingstown I received a civil answer from him
delivered by his secretary. The Lord Lieutenant's carriage
was waiting to conduct us to the Viceregal Lodge in the
Phœnix Park. The same day a Council was held at the
Castle; Plunket resigned the Great Seal; it was handed
over to me, and I was sworn in an Irish Privy Councillor.

Lord Fortescue magnanimously invited Plunket to
dinner; we drank wine together, and I afterwards visited
him at Old Connaught, his country seat.

I only sate in court as Chancellor a few days, the circuits
having begun and the time having arrived when, according to
the custom in Ireland, the Court of Chancery adjourns for the
long vacation. I was dreadfully nervous in taking my seat
on the bench, but the second day I became cool and collected.
The bar behaved to me most respectfully and courteously.
Short as my experience was, I saw enough to persuade me
that I should have been complete master of the court, and

CHAP.
XXV.

A.D. 1841.

that I should have given general satisfaction. But fate had decreed a very speedy termination to my career in Ireland.

The news of the elections in England soon arrived and became daily more disastrous. I had been in treaty for a fine house on Stephen's Green when I heard of Lord Morpeth's defeat for the West Riding of Yorkshire, and I immediately broke off the negotiation.

I did not then foresee the utter prostration, I may say *extinction*, of our party which has since taken place, and, in the hope of a lively opposition to the new Government and speedy restoration to power, I spent my time very gaily. I gave only one dinner—this was at my hotel, to the officers of my court and the Attorney and Solicitor-General; but I had constant invitations from the Whig judges and the leaders of our party in Dublin. In spite of my being an alien, they treated me with very great kindness. At Howth and Malahide we were entertained by the descendants of the companions of Strongbow, in castles erected in the reign of Henry II.

I met Daniel O'Connell only once, at the table of Fitz-symonds his son-in-law. We were very cordial. I must say he behaved exceedingly well to me. Although the Orange-men often taunted him with my appointment, and inveighed against it as a mark of Irish degradation—and, in his contest for the city of Dublin, West, his opponent, accused him of supporting a Government which had conferred a pension of 4,000*l.* a year on Sir John Campbell for doing nothing—he never joined in the popular cry nor, either publicly or privately, did anything to annoy me. Certainly it would have been considerable treachery if he had yielded to the temptation. When Peel's negotiation for a Ministry in 1837 broke off, O'Connell said to me, 'Now do you set off for Ireland as soon as possible.' And Lord Duncannon having sounded him whether my appointment would be objected to by the Catholic body, he had expressed his entire approbation of it. He hated Plunket, and as no Catholic could hold the Great Seal he would rather have seen it in the hands of a foreigner than of an Irish Protestant. Besides he had personal good-will for me, as I had always, as far as I could, supported Catholic Emancipation and the cause of Ireland.

Our touring was confined to the Vale of Avoca and the beauties of the county of Wicklow, which are certainly very striking.

A few days before our departure for England, Norman Macdonald, the Under Secretary, entertained us sumptuously at his charming official residence in the Phœnix Park. As he showed us his grounds, his gardens, and his conservatory, which he was so soon to leave, I said to him, ' Norman, these are the things which make death dreadful.'

Our last piece of gaiety was a grand ball given by Lord Morpeth at the Rotunda to all the pretty women in and near Dublin, whether Tory or Whig, Conservative or Liberal, Orange or Green. I never saw anything so handsomely and tastefully done, and I could no longer wonder that he was the most beloved of Irish Secretaries.

At the close of the Chancery sittings, when the event of the elections might be considered doubtful, I delivered an address to the Irish bar on Equity Reform, which was well received. On the eve of my departure I again sate in court to call within the bar a new batch of Queen's counsel. We parted with good feeling on both sides. I might have been jestingly complimented in an address declaring that while I held the Great Seal of Ireland I had never given offence to anyone, and that none of my decisions would ever be reversed. But it was not an occasion for banter, and there were no serious topics for a public valediction.

Having dined in Dublin, we were attended to Kingstown by kind friends who bade us a tender adieu, and expressed a sincere but vain wish for our speedy return. At seven o'clock next evening we dined in New Street, Spring Gardens.

Thus was I of office, pension and practice at once bereft. With decent resignation I put on my scarlet robes as a peer, was introduced by the Earl Marshal and two Barons, had my patent read at the table, took the oaths, and, after making the requisite number of bows, was placed upon the Barons' bench.

Once more I appeared as Lord Chancellor of Ireland. In that capacity I was invited to a grand official dinner, given by Lord Melbourne as Premier, the day before the opening of Parliament, to read the Royal Speech. I had heard Pitt perform the same duty at the Cockpit, Whitehall, where, according to ancient usage, the Royal Speech was always read by him whose speech constitutionally it was, in the evening before the day when it was to be delivered from the throne. For the eight preceding years I had heard the Speech read before dinner by the leader of the House of Commons. On this extraordinary occasion a copy of the Speech was sent to the Duke of Wellington.

After dinner Melbourne read his 'last speech, confession and dying words' very gracefully, and till we left him he acted his part with gaiety of heart. But I am sorry to say he failed most miserably in the House of Lords next day. Here was an opportunity for a grand vindication of his Government, for a defence of himself, and an attack upon his opponents. He knew that he was addressing the Peers, as Minister, for the last time. He had filled the office above six years, during which, peace being preserved, the glory of the country had been raised in the eyes of foreign nations; our territory had been extended; our manufactures and commerce had flourished, and many measures of much value had been passed for the internal improvement of the country. He was supplanted by men whose only chance of retaining power was to adopt his policy. Yet his defence was short, jejune, in a tone of bad pleasantry, and every way unworthy of the occasion. Brougham followed, and lashed him in a manner almost to satiate the deepest vengeance for having been excluded from office and made an outcast. I was very indignant that the debate was allowed to close without any attempt at a reply; but if members of the Cabinet who were present chose to submit to the imputations cast upon them, it was not for me to interfere. The provoking circumstance was that Brougham's speech, though very impressive, was full of misrepresentation, and the greatest part of it might have been triumphantly answered.[1]

---

[1] Among other unfounded charges he accused the falling Ministers of having illegally misapplied the funds of the savings banks to conceal the deficiency in the revenue. Melbourne in much distress came to Spring Rice (Lord Monteagle), who was sitting by me, for an explanation, which was given to him; but he allowed the calumny to go forth without refutation or notice.

At the same time I feel great satisfaction and pride in CHAP. the thought that I was so long connected in office with men XXV. who, I sincerely believe, did more to improve our institu- A.D. 1841. tions and to promote our prosperity than any who ever governed this country. Lord Grey with all his faults will go down to posterity with a reputation little inferior to that of Lord Somers, for having brought about a bloodless revolution by which the Constitution was adapted to the altered circumstances of the age and, alarming perils being warded off, freedom and prosperity are secured to the nation. Lord Melbourne as Minister certainly had not displayed proper activity and energy, but he conferred strength and dignity on the Administration by his skilful management of the Queen, by his singular felicity of manner to friends and foes, and by the spirit and animation with which, when roused, he could occasionally repel and retaliate the fiercest assaults of his opponents.

Lord John Russell made a very gallant defence in the debate on the Address in the Commons. If he had only Lord Melbourne's manner, what a leader he would be! Though often giving offence, and causing much grumbling among his friends, he was the life of the late Government; and if the Whigs are ever restored, he must be at the head of affairs.

Here I will briefly state the causes which in my opinion reduced us to our present melancholy condition. After the result of the first general election under the Reform Bill was known, the exclamation resounded throughout the land : 'The Tory party is annihilated!' The Whigs believed that they were firmly established in power for half a century, and their opponents, although they talked of 'reaction,' had no serious hopes of rallying during the present generation. When the first reformed Parliament met, there was not nearly room for the Liberal members on the ministerial side of the House of Commons, and Peel's small band of adherents seemed so insignificant that even their possession of the front Opposition bench was disputed by ultra-Radicals. How happened it that in seven years the same Peel was at the head of a large majority in both Houses of Legislature, and that the authors of the Reform Bill were turned out of office not only with the concurrence of the landed aristocracy and the clergy, but likewise of the moneyed interest, and to the general satisfaction of the nation? Over some of the causes of this wonderful change the Whigs had no control; others, by their imprudence, they originated or wantonly aggravated.

I begin with the extravagant expectations which the masses fostered of the benefits to be derived from the Reform Bill. For these I cannot say that its supporters in Parliament were answerable, as they had only pointed out the specific abuses in the representative system which it was calculated to rectify; but the general notion was that the Reform Bill would cure all political and social evils, and introduce prosperity and happiness into every class of the community. Deep disappointment was felt, much discontent was created, when the effects were still seen of bad passions which cannot be eradicated, and when calamities were felt by which nations ever will be visited. The Reform Bill was blamed, and its framers fell in public estimation, if there was an instance of an elector being bribed or intimidated, if there was manufacturing distress in any district from over-production, or if, from bad seasons, provisions were scarce or dear.

More serious mischief arose from the absurd conduct of the ultra-Radicals in the House of Commons. This is a party to which I acknowledge that I have a particular antipathy, and I think not without fair grounds. Not content with what had been accomplished, feeling no gratitude to Lord Grey and his colleagues, showing no consideration, forbearance or tenderness for the Whig leaders, still aiming at what was impracticable or mischievous—they would not give the Reform Bill any fair chance of retaining popularity; they made the lovers of rational freedom dread that organic changes were still to go on, and that all our time-honoured institutions were to be swept away. Perpetual motions were brought forward for vote by ballot, for the extension of the suffrage, for shortening the duration of Parliaments, for doing away with the qualification of members, and for altering the composition of the House of Lords. Some of these propositions are in themselves very fit for discussion, and one or two of them might possibly have been advantageously embraced in the Reform Bill; but I think all reasonable men are now agreed that after the Reform Bill had passed it ought to have been taken *for better for worse*, and that 'a revolution every year' was hardly consistent with regular government or the purposes for which government is framed. The people out of doors were thus taught to believe that very little had been done for them, and (what was worse) the Ministers in the House of Commons had the invidious task cast upon them of resisting popular measures, and sometimes naturally used language which was liable to be misconstrued, as Lord Russell's declaration respecting '*finality*.' By this ultra-Radical policy a double mischief was done to the Whigs, for one section of their former supporters deserted them from the fear of further innovation, and another because the Whigs were charged with having ceased to be reformers. A serious detriment to them likewise arose from Sir Robert Peel's moderation, and his giving a new name to his party. Had he threatened to repeal the Reform Bill, or had he still professed to be the leader of the 'Tories,' he would have prolonged the popularity of the Reform Ministry, and alarmist or disappointed Whigs could not easily have joined his standard. But his acquiescence in the new representative system being recorded, there was no longer any occasion to rally round its champions for its preservation, and many who would have been ashamed to be called Tories gloried in the new appellation of Conservatives.

However, in spite of all the difficulties which the Whigs had to encounter, they might long have retained power if, as partisans, they had acted skilfully. They certainly did introduce most excellent practical measures—such as the abolition of Slavery, the opening of the trade to India and China, the Reform of Municipal Corporations, the Poor Law Bill, the Dissenters' Marriages Bill, the Irish Church Temporalities Bill, and the uniform Penny Postage; but they had not any grand principle of action, they wavered between the two extremes of their supporters, by turns disgusting both; and they committed several palpable blunders by which their influence was rapidly undermined.

I must begin with their first act in the first reformed House of Commons—the appointment of Manners Sutton as Speaker. The Premier was abundantly strong enough to select Abercromby or Shaw Lefevre, or some other adherent who would have been agreeable to his own party, and who would have commanded the respect of the House. The preference of a bitter Tory, who had been prepared to give his casting vote against the Reform Bill, shocked all good Reformers. The argument that he alone, from his experience and authority, could preserve order in such a tumultuary assembly, justly called forth the remark that Lord Grey, like Frankenstein, was himself afraid of the monster he had created.

A much more serious error was the famous ' Coercion Bill.' Ireland certainly was in a dreadful state, the proximate cause being the general refusal to pay tithes. But a better remedy might have been expected from the champions of liberty than the suspension of the Constitution, and trial by court-martial as a substitute. One fatal effect of the measure was to cause a split in the Liberal party which could never be effectually repaired. Mr. O'Connell, who had cordially supported the Reform Bill, and indeed may be said to have furnished the means of carrying it against a majority of English members, now denounced 'the base and bloody Whigs,' and he was joined in opposing the measure with the utmost violence not only by the numerous band of Irish members returned through his personal influence (who were called ' his tail '), but by the bulk of English Radicals then high in reputation. Even that ' good old Whig ' Abercromby voted against the clause empowering a court-martial to try felonies and to pass sentence of transportation. Had the system of conciliation been then adopted which operated so beneficially two or three years later, it would have been happy for Ireland and for the Whig party. But force was then thought the only instrument by which that country could be governed ; no confidence was placed in the Roman Catholic body, and Orangemen were delighted, in the hope that their rule was to be prolonged.[2]

[2] From a letter of Lord Wellesley written in August 1834, it appears that he recommended the making of Roman Catholic judges and Privy·

I must next mention as a fertile source of odium to the Government, their palliation of the abuses of the Pension List. It was understood that there had been a sort of compact upon this subject with William IV., and that, to please him, the grants of his predecessors out of the public revenue to unworthy favourites and to poor relations of rich peers were protected. Daniel Whittle Harvey's motion on this subject caused nearly as great an excitement as the Reform Bill, and our whipper-in found the greatest difficulty in mustering our men to vote against it.

Through these means, so early as the spring of 1834, the Whig leaders, who had lately been so idolized, were by a large portion of their worshippers considered little better than apostates. I myself had a mortifying proof of the unpopularity into which the Government had fallen, for it was then that, vacating my seat on being appointed Attorney-General, I was disgracefully beaten at Dudley. The same fate was experienced by several of my colleagues from other constituencies.[3]

Then followed the disputes in the Cabinet respecting ' the Appropriation Clause.' I fully justify those who were for applying the surplus revenue of the Irish Protestant Church to the purpose of general education, and I can only regret that they did not express their opinion more boldly, and adhere to it more resolutely. When Stanley and Graham were got rid of in May, 1834, the ship righted, and with proper pilotage might have prosperously pursued her voyage; but she was soon wantonly cast among breakers. Lord Grey's resignation, which followed, was most unnecessary and unjustifiable. With due energy Brougham might have been kept in order, and the efforts of the Court, become decidedly hostile, as well as the recklessness of the ultra-Radicals, might have been set at de-

Councillors, but that down to that time no such policy had been adopted. Lord Wellesley's letter was read by Lord Brougham in the House of Lords, and I suppose will be found in his *Life*. It is a very curious document, and by no means creditable to Lord Grey's Irish policy.

[3] *Inter alios* Sir John Hobhouse, on being appointed Irish Secretary, was thrown out for Westminster, upon which there came out a very popular caricature by H. B., entitled 'The Two Sir Johns,' representing us meeting in St. James's Street, and condoling with each other.

fiance. As yet Peel's party in the House of Commons in point of numbers was contemptible.

Brougham displayed great vigour in preventing the government from immediately falling into the hands of the Tories, and a better selection could not have been made of a successor to Lord Grey than Lord Melbourne. The chief danger now was from the restlessness and irregularities of the Chancellor, who, thinking that he had made the Minister, wished to be ' viceroy over him,' and both in the Cabinet and in the House of Lords was nearly unmanageable. There were no means of getting rid of him without an entire disruption of the Government, although when he set off for Scotland after the prorogation, Lord Melbourne complained to me that 'he was actually out of his mind.' If William IV. had had patience till Parliament again met, I think the vagaries of the keeper of his conscience would soon have given him the opportunity of dismissing the Whigs constitutionally and creditably; but by his *escapade* in November he kept them in power during his own lifetime, and for some years of the succeeding reign.

I have nothing to object to the conduct of the Whigs during 'the hundred days.' Their opposition to Sir Robert Peel was vigorous and skilful, and they thereby recovered a considerable share of their former popularity.

The reconciliation of the Whigs with O'Connell, called 'the Lichfield House compact,' was perfectly legitimate, as it amounted to no more than an understanding that in consideration of a Liberal policy towards Ireland he was to support them ; and, notwithstanding the complaints of Conservative Whigs, I am not aware of any bad measure or bad appointment that can be ascribed to it. Little right had the Tories to taunt us with trying to please O'Connell, as they were eager at all times to co-operate not only with the ultra-Radicals but with the Chartists.

Nor can I blame the exclusion of Brougham on the formation of the new Ministry. The last necessity only could justify so harsh a step, considering his great abilities and his great services to the Liberal cause. But he was likely to be more dangerous as a colleague than as an opponent, and the public safety was to be preferred to private feeling.

Lord Melbourne made a good fight against an adverse
Court while William continued on the throne, and any faults
which he showed appeared in an aggravated form when he
had become the petted Prime Minister of Queen Victoria. I
will therefore proceed to consider in what respect his conduct
is to be blamed in the new reign.

First, I think he displayed too great a disposition to cultivate the Duke of Wellington. His own inclinations were
in favour of Conservative principles, and he spoke, I believe,
very sincerely when he lamented 'the heavy blow and great
discouragement' he was to give to the Church, and declared
that 'to do away with the Corn Laws would be nothing short
of absolute madness.' By the tone he assumed, the Duke
himself was for some time considerably softened,⁴ but it did
not in the slightest degree relax the efforts of the Tory party,
who were impatient again to be in office, and the Liberals
became alarmed and scandalised.

A more fatal fault was our Premier's listlessness. He gave
himself very little trouble with respect to anything his colleagues were doing, and there was now 'a government of
departments' without unity or pervading plan.

The feeble fight which ministerialists generally made in
the House of Lords, I think, led mainly to Melbourne's overthrow. He was sure to be outnumbered if a division were
called, but wherever he had public opinion strongly in his
favour, his opponents were afraid to employ their brute
strength against him. Under the auspices of Lord Lyndhurst, seconded by Lord Brougham, the 'obstructive' policy
was now pursued, that is to say, to throw out all Whig Bills
the rejection of which should not excite much outcry, and
then to assert that the Whigs ought not to remain in office,
as they could not carry the measures which they deemed
essentially necessary for the public good. Various important
Bills which the Tories had not ventured to oppose in the
House of Commons, and for which a decisive expression of

⁴ I know from Lord Wellesley that the Duke said he had so much disliked being under Peel during the hundred days, that if Lord Melbourne
would only behave tolerably well he would sooner support him than return
to office as a subordinate.

popular applause might easily have been obtained, were allowed silently to sink into oblivion.

I will only add to the causes of our downfall the delay and seeming reluctance with which popular measures were brought forward—such as the uniform Penny Postage and Free Trade in Corn—which caused serious doubts as to the sincerity of Ministers, and gave rise to the noted saying that they were of 'squeezable materials.'

For these or other reasons the Whigs, notwithstanding the many admirable measures they had carried, and many others which they had introduced, and which, through the factious efforts of their opponents, were defeated, had now certainly lost the public confidence, and when they put themselves upon the country by a dissolution of Parliament, the verdict was decidedly against them. Setting aside the unscrupulous manner in which many 'Conservatives' carried their elections by abusing the new Poor Law, sympathising with the Chartists, calumniating Queen Victoria, and pledging themselves for ever to stand by 'Protection,' there never was a more legitimate or constitutional change of administration than that by which Lord Melbourne was at last supplanted by Sir Robert Peel.

I had not to go through any form of resigning to the Queen. I was virtually out of office on the day of Lord Melbourne's resignation, though I continued legally Irish Chancellor for several weeks till Sir Edward Sugden went over to Ireland and took possession of the Great Seal.

Letters to Sir George Campbell.

New Street: September 1, 1841.

. . . Perhaps you may have some curiosity to know, what the newspapers cannot tell you, how *the Party* bear this change :—stunned, in a state of stupor, with a feeling of annihilation, quite unlike Milton's devils awakening in Hell, who were animated by revenge and meditated schemes again to *get in*. Peel bestrides the world like a Colossus, and we are only looking out for dishonourable graves. At Brooks's 'Hope ne'er comes that comes to all.' 'Voi che entrate lasciate ogni speranza.' The universal opinion is that the game is irrecoverably up, and that the Tory party will be in power for fifty years to come. Most of our men are gone to Scotland to shoot, or are flying abroad. The few who remain in London say there is no use in attending either House.

I called on Melbourne this morning, between twelve and one. I found him shaving. This was his levée. I said I came to offer my congratulations on his release from the cares of office, and that I hoped he was happy. 'Oh, very happy.' He smiled, but 'in such sort—'

In truth he will feel it more than any of us. He not only loses the occupation and excitement of office, but his whole existence is changed. With him it is as if a man were to have his wife and children, with whom he had lived affectionately and happily, torn from him when he falls from power. He consorted constantly with the Queen on the most easy and delightful footing, and he is necessarily banished from her presence.

He seems to think that it would have been better to have resigned without a dissolution; but I told him sincerely that in my opinion there is no cause for regret, and that both for the party and the measures proposed we stand better after an unsuccessful appeal to the people.

I know not what is to become of him. The shade of the trees at Brocket will be very funereal. Johnny Russell will get on much better, for he not only has his young wife to amuse him, but he will soon mix in the proceedings of the House of Commons as leader of a party once formidable. I do not believe that Melbourne will come near the Lords, or that he will make any exertion when he comes.

This is rather a trying time for myself. As yet I have indulged in miscellaneous reading, but I must engage in some definite pursuit to fill up my mornings, and to prevent me from going to sleep on the sofa in the evening.

I had a call from Denman yesterday, who professed great satisfaction that I was now in the Lords, where he says I shall be able to render such services to the public.

We have had great enjoyment in Ashtead, which we surrender to-day. I would have kept it on, but that there are too many trees about it, and after this time of year, when the leaves begin to fall, it is not very wholesome.

We were all very happy together yesterday. With such a family, and the means of decently supporting them, I should meet with, and I should deserve, little sympathy if I were so absurd and so ungrateful to Providence as to complain of my lot.

Brooks's : Friday, September 3, 1841.

. . . I have just seen here several of our friends returned from Claremont. Both parties met there at one. They were shown into separate rooms. The Queen sate in her closet, no one being present but Prince Albert. The *exeunters* were called in one by one, and gave up the seals or wands of their offices and retired.

The change is very constitutional and legitimate. The worst feature is that the House of Commons assumes the choice of Ministers without asserting any principle whatever. The Whigs are cashiered without any condemnation of any one of their measures, and the Tories who succeed are at liberty to follow all the policy of their predecessors. Nor is it for any want of administrative powers that we are dismissed. The British name never stood higher in the world, and the United Kingdom never was more tranquil.

The Orange lords over the way at White's are already abusing Peel most scurrilously, but in my opinion he may set them at defiance. Our friends are as desponding or despairing as ever. They feel as if the end of the world had come. The only cheerful Whig I have seen is the Duchess of Sutherland, with whom I dined at Lady Holland's the day she ceased to be Mistress of the Robes.

The new men by mistake went to Claremont all in their Court costume, whereas the Queen at Windsor and Claremont receives her Ministers in their usual morning dress.

Normanby says taking leave of the Queen was very affecting.

New Street : September 10, 1841.

. . . All the official men who vacated their seats are to be re-elected without opposition, and I sincerely and potently believe that the public are pleased with the change.

Change is always amusing and agreeable to those who do not actually suffer by it, and the numerous class who are depressed in their circumstances and are struggling with difficulties have all a latent hope that the new Government may do something to help them. For example, I hear that the Westminster shopkeepers voted for Rous in the expectation that they will have more custom when the Tories are in office.

I yesterday met Melbourne at dinner at Lady Holland's. He was very gay, and I begin to think that he will carry it off the best of us all.

New Street : November 13, 1841.

. . . The feeling still continues very strong that the present Government is likely to last many years, and this is strengthened for the moment by the joy and contentment of the vulgar on the birth of the Prince of Wales, which is considered a proof of the blessings we may expect from the Tory rule.

I see Lord Melbourne almost daily at Brooks's, but have no conversation with him on the prospects of the party. He sets an excellent example to all ex-officials. Instead of languishing, as I expected he would, he is as merry as a grig. Without affectation, he really seems cheerful and happy. He talks very copiously on the weather, the forged Exchequer bills, the illness of the Queen Dowager, and the newspaper topics of the day. I expect him to dine with me on Tuesday to meet Lady Holland.

I have never once met Lord John since I returned from Ireland. Rolfe told me yesterday it was reported he had said the existence of the present Government is to be calculated by months, not by years. I cannot believe he has said anything so absurd. The worst symptom is the discontent of our own partisans. All those who were disappointed in their expectations of preferment are loud against the manner in which the Whigs disposed of their patronage, and those who have lost their seats in the House of Commons complain bitterly of the Corn question being brought forward, and of the dissolution before resignation. Till the Tories have been in office some ten years, and wear themselves out in the same manner, I see no chance of a change. The English nation is determinately Tory. Not only the Peerage, the Church and the land are Tory, but commercial and professional men think it more genteel and fashionable to take the Tory side, and to such an immense body of property and influence there is no counterbalance. The Dissenters are completely cowed, and though merchants and manufacturers privately disapprove of the Corn Laws, they quietly submit to the present system of monopoly, by which we not only eat dear bread, but, what is worse, our monetary operations are subject to constant derangement.

New Street : December 29, 1841.

. . . On Friday we are all going to Abinger. I have resolved upon a grand work to be called 'The Lives of the Chancellors.' I mean to give an account of all the Chancellors from the time of William the Conqueror to Lord Chancellor Lyndhurst. This may be made an intensely interesting book. It will be a sketch of the history of England on a new plan,—the Chancellor for many ages having been the King's Prime Minister. I can introduce views of general history just when it suits me. But the careers and characters of the Chancellors, the intrigues by which they got and lost the Great Seal, and a comparison with their rivals, might be made as entertaining as a romance.

The undertaking will be one of great labour and must take a good long time. The beauty of the plan is that I shall be working in my vocation ; for it will be my duty to inquire what Chancellors did, what alterations they introduced into the administration of Equity, and what are the leading characteristics of their decisions.

Autobiography.

During the short session which followed the appointment of Sir Robert Peel as Prime Minister I took no part in any of the discussions in the House of Lords, except by introducing into a Bill which was passing for other purposes a clause to authorise the appointment of Irish barristers to judicial offices in England. I thought this a just compliment to the Irish bar from an Irish ex-Chancellor, and Lord Lyndhurst and

Lord Brougham, after a strenuous attempt, found that they could not decently further resist it.

The utmost seeming good-humour however has always prevailed between us. The first day I met Brougham in the House he said : ' How do you do, *my Lord*, Jack no longer ? ' I asked him not to remind me of my misfortunes. *Brougham*. ' Well there is one consolation for you here—that you may speak when you please, and as often as you please, and on what subjects you please, and you may say what you please.' *Campbell*. ' I suppose you lay down the rule of the House from your own practice, but it will only suit *you*. None but yourself can be your parallel.'

Lyndhurst, once more on the woolsack, resumed his gay disclaimer of love or enmity in politics, whereby he disarms resentment, and has the benefit of standing well with the world.

I now employed my leisure in revising some of my speeches at the bar and in the House of Commons, which I soon after published. I rejoiced in the opportunity of marking my affection and regard to my dear brother by a dedication to him which does not exaggerate the tender friendship which has subsisted between us since our earliest years.

While Chancellor of Ireland I was appointed by the Queen a member of the Judicial Committee of the Privy Council, the supreme tribunal of appeal in all causes from the Ecclesiastical Courts, the Court of Admiralty, and all colonial courts. The Judicial Committee sitting several weeks before Christmas, I took my place as a member, and I have regularly attended all its meetings down to the present time, my associates being Lord Brougham, Baron Parke, Justice Erskine, Lushington the Judge of the Admiralty Court, and Jenner the Dean of the Arches. I have found the occupation very agreeable, and I have reason to think that I have been of some service to the public, although voluntary and gratuitous service is not likely to be much appreciated.

Parliament met in the beginning of February 1842. Nothing could be more unsatisfactory than our position in the House of Lords. The Government bench was exceedingly feeble, and might have been assailed with certain effect. The Duke of Wellington, the nominal leader, never a good spokesman or a powerful reasoner, was so enfeebled by age and disease, that when he rose to address the House painful apprehensions that he would discredit himself were excited in the breasts both of his friends and opponents.[5]   The Earl of Ripon's extreme weakness excited astonishment that he should ever have risen on the death of Canning to the post of Prime Minister.   The Earl of Aberdeen, a very able and right-headed man, always remained silent unless when he was reluctantly compelled to give an answer to some question about our diplomatic relations with foreign countries.   It would have been well for the Government if Lords Hadding-ton, Wharncliffe, and Fitzgerald had been mute after his example.

But all this weakness availed us nothing, by reason of the extreme listlessness of our own friends.   Lord Melbourne lounged down to the House generally about five o'clock, and remained till it rose, or it was time to go to dress for dinner; but he seemed to feel as if he had been sitting at Brooks's, and that he had nothing to talk or think of beyond the gossip of the day.   He would not have taken the trouble to repress activity in any of his party, but he had no desire to see activity in any of them, and he would have made little objection to a general resolution that all Bills proposed during the session should pass—the House to adjourn till the day of prorogation.

The Marquess of Lansdowne came out now and then with a string of magniloquent sentences, but displayed no zeal or effective talent.   Lord Minto, the late First Lord of the Admiralty, once said something in defence of his dock-yard appointments, and was heard no more.   The Marquess of Normanby was more disposed to be adventurous.   He twice brought forward a charge against the Lord Chancellor, but each time rashly, indiscreetly, and without any concert,

---

[5] *October* 1846.—About this time the Duke of Wellington had several fits, from which he seemed to suffer much both in body and mind.   But he afterwards rallied wonderfully, and I have since known him speak and act with great vigour and success.

and got severely beaten, although he had justice on his side, and with good management might have gained a triumph. Lord Clarendon was both able and inclined to take a stirring part in opposition, but, meeting with no encouragement, he did nothing.

Under such circumstances for me to attempt anything in the political line was wholly out of the question. When the Bill to abolish (as I thought very unnecessarily) the House of Assembly of Newfoundland came up from the Commons, I said to Lord Melbourne, 'Is this Bill to pass without opposition?' He answered in the hearing of several Tory peers who were passing by, 'I can only say that I for one highly approve of it. I wish all colonial legislatures were abolished. The worst thing these gentlemen ever did to us was stopping our Jamaica Bill.'

The House was at all times more like a club chatting upon the news of the day than a deliberative assembly met to make laws for a mighty empire. There was no occasion for the standing order passed in more pugnacious times against ' hot and taxing expressions,' for all the members of both parties were reciprocally ' noble friends,' and anything approaching to keen debate would have been considered a breach of good manners. A noble lord did not rise to speak after seven o'clock without an apology. ' My Lords, at this *late hour of the evening* I hope your lordships will believe that I mean to occupy your attention only for a very few moments.' Very different this from the House of Commons, where I remember rising to move for leave to bring in a most important Bill a little before two in the morning, making a long statement which was attentively listened to.[6]

I was necessarily confined to measures connected with the law. I brought forward Bills for transferring all appeals from the Privy Council to the House of Lords, and for having a permanent judge in the Court of Chancery, the Chancellor to preside in hearing all appeals in the last resort, and the House of Lords to sit for the hearing of appeals during the whole judicial year. There were debates on the first and on

[6] The Bill to abolish imprisonment for debt.

the second reading of the Bills—when I had not only the
Lord Chancellor but Lord Cottenham and Lord Brougham
down upon me. I had to fight them single-handed, and no
doubt appeared worsted, although I dealt some stout blows
even when beaten down to the ground.[7]

The only other considerable effort I made during the
session was in moving for a standing order 'that no member
of the House of Commons shall be heard as counsel for or
against a Bill depending in the House of Lords.' This
motion was first suggested to me by Lord Shaftesbury,
Lord Redesdale and other Tory lords, and would have been
carried if Lord Brougham had not very vigorously interfered
in order to patronise Mr. Roebuck, who would have lost a
brief by the standing order. The Commons had passed a
Bill to disfranchise the borough of Sudbury for bribery, and
the honourable and learned member for Bath, who had voted
for it as a legislator, was retained to support it at the bar of
the House of Lords as a paid advocate. Lord Brougham so
earnestly canvassed the Lord Chancellor, after my notice of
motion was given, that the Government declared against it;
the two noble and learned lords spoke strongly against it;
as usual I stood without assistance, and I was obliged to
content myself with a smart reply, without venturing on a
division.[8]

In the judicial business of the House I went on very
harmoniously with the Chancellor and Lords Brougham and
Cottenham. The Chancellor sate three days of the week
when Lord Brougham and I assisted him. We three sate
another day without the Chancellor, taking the woolsack by
turns. We never differed except in one or two cases, and then
with great mildness of manner as well as sincerity of sentiment. Fortunately we all agreed in the great Auchterarder
case respecting the Church of Scotland. I took great pains
with my written judgment upon it. The appeal business of
the House of Lords never was done so satisfactorily as during
this session of Parliament. I do not presume to put myself
on a level with any of the other three, all most able and

---

[7] Hansard, vol. lx. pp. 1243–1246; vol. lxii. pp. 175, 195, 198.

[8] Hansard, vol. lxv. p. 730.

distinguished men ; [9] but I humbly contributed to the result, and I was always able to support my part decently and creditably. I could now take my seat in the Court of Chancery in Ireland or in England without dismay.

Letters to Sir George Campbell in the year 1842.

New Street : January 10, 1842.

. . . We had a very pleasant visit to Abinger. I came to town for a day or two and we all returned on Friday. On Saturday I sat in the Privy Council and met Brougham. I asked him to dine with me, undertaking to invite Lady Charlotte Lindsay and a small party of his private friends. He began to weep bitterly—said he could not now go into society—that on his brother's death he had felt a disinclination to this—that his daughter had prevailed upon him to do so, to amuse her with an account of what he had seen— but that since her death he had been wholly unfit to dine out, although he was able to have small dinner parties at home. The tears ran down his cheeks and he sobbed violently. He was quite sincere, and at the moment believed he had, for the reason assigned, never dined out since his daughter's death. The truth is, he has been very much depressed and has gone very little into society—but I believe chiefly from an apprehension of meeting some of his old friends whom he wished to shun. I understood he has dined out occasionally and been the life and spirit of the company. However, to show he felt no unkindness to me, he asked me that very day to dine with him to meet Lady Charlotte Lindsay, Denman, and the Polish Count Zamoiski. I went, and found him very entertaining and agreeable. I am to dine with him again soon, to be shown a collection of letters written by George III. to Lord North while he was Minister.

[9] I do not agree in the truth, though I cannot object to the point, of the remark on Brougham when he was Chancellor,—'It is a pity he has not a little law, for then he would have a smattering of everything.' He has a very good head for law, and can be made to understand perfectly any point of law, however difficult and abstruse,—though I must confess I should not like to have a great cause of mine to come before him sitting alone if I were entitled to succeed.

The originals were given to Brougham by Lady Charlotte, Lord North's daughter. George IV. borrowed them from Brougham and never returned them. A copy was fortunately kept. This, William IV. on his accession expressed a wish to see. Brougham expressed some hesitation, lamenting the loss of the originals. 'Oh,' said King William, 'I know what you mean, but *I* am an honest man and always return what I borrow.' *Brougham.* 'Oh, Sir! your Majesty cannot suppose I had any apprehension of that sort.' *King William IV.* '*I* understand you—*I* understand you. Send them to me; they shall be safe and I will return them.' So his Majesty had them, and by returning them showed he was an honest man.

New Street: February 1, 1842.

. . . On Sunday I dined with Brougham to hear read George III.'s letters to Lord North. No one else present but Sir Benjamin Brodie. We had a very pleasant evening. Brougham talked in the most unreserved manner of all his intercourse with William IV., and told us how he made Melbourne Prime Minister when Lord Grey resigned in June 1834.

Private Room, House of Lords: July 2, 1842.

. . . I trust that George [1] was in good time for the Dundee steamer on Wednesday, although he was obliged to run it very close. This visit to you will rapidly pass away, and you must not allow its enjoyment to be dashed by the prospect of its termination; for really, from the quick and regular intercourse with India, it is not much more for a Scotsman now to go to Calcutta than it was a hundred years since to go to London. I remember hearing old Dempster of St. Andrews once say that he was above six weeks in sailing in a Leith trader from the Firth of Forth to the river Thames. The Indian mails now arrive as punctually as the coaches from York or Exeter.

I am now sitting in my private room. Such an accommodation was only given to the Chancellor till about two months ago, when private rooms were assigned likewise to the Law Lords, Brougham, Cottenham, and Campbell. This

[1] Now Sir George Campbell, M.P.

will be very convenient for me when I go to my new
residence, which is nearly two miles from here, as I can not
only keep my papers and write my letters in my private
room, but have a mutton chop, or dress when I dine out.
However, I shall sadly miss Spring Gardens. I now run
out between the judicial and political business, have a little
dinner with Mary or some of the children, and return. I
avoid the almost universal custom of the peers, to sit down
to a great dinner every day at eight o'clock. I have tea at
the same hour, and this gives me a cool evening and a quiet
night. When I dine out or receive company at home, of
course I must conform to usage.

Autobiography.

The session being over, I forgot all mortifications in a
delightful tour with my wife and two eldest daughters. We
crossed over to Antwerp, and proceeded by Liège and Aix la
Chapelle to Cologne. The rapture of the girls when they
first beheld the broad and rapid Rhine, of which they had read
and heard so much, and the sweet kisses they bestowed on
me for showing them such delightful scenery, gave me more
true pleasure than I could have derived from official station
however eminent. We visited Coblence, Ems, Schwalbach,
Schlangenbad, Wiesbaden, Frankfort, Heidelberg, and Baden-
Baden. We then sailed down the Rhine to Cologne and,
after a short stay at Brussels, returned to London. My
passion for travelling remains unabated, and in such company
the pleasure I experience from it is undiminished.

On my return I paid a short visit to my brother in
Scotland, looked at some estates with a view to 'locating'
my family,[2] rejoiced in the society of Lord Jeffrey—gay,
festive, and sociable as ever, and passed a night at the
château of my old colleague Abercromby, now become Lord
Dunfermline. We returned to London in the middle of
October, and a few days afterwards I began this memoir.

---

[2] *October* 1846.—I then for the first time saw Stewartfield (or Hartrigge)
in Roxburghshire, where I am now revising this memoir, and where I
hope by the blessing of God my descendants may long flourish.

I am now employed in preparing to leave a residence where I have passed many happy years, with the view of taking possession of another,[3] which I expect to occupy till I am summoned to that mansion 'where the weary are at rest.'

Whatever may betide me in this life, I ought to be, and am, grateful to Almighty God for the many blessings which He has showered upon me, and which I still continue to enjoy—health; competence; if no brilliancy of fame, a fair character with the world; friends who are kind to me; a beloved wife, the model to her children of every grace and every virtue; sons promising by their talents and assiduity to acquire distinction; daughters who, imitating the filial piety which distinguished their mother, make my happiness the great study of their lives. I humbly and devoutly pray that I may ever entertain a just sense of the goodness which Providence has vouchsafed to me, and that I may adequately perform the duties cast upon me, and fitly prepare for that awful day when I must render to an omniscient God a strict account of all my actions and all my thoughts.

I began this sketch on the 27th of October last, and I finish it on the 27th of November. I have written it entirely from memory, with a few references to parliamentary debates. Notwithstanding some inaccuracies which may probably be found in it, I believe that it is substantially correct, and I am sure that my great object has been to adhere to the truth, nothing extenuating, and setting down naught in malice. If my life were worth studying, it would best be found in my letters to my father, to my brother, and to my wife. Since I first left home down to the present time I have been in the constant habit of unbosoming myself in succession to one or other of these dear relatives, disclosing all that befell me, and all that I hoped or feared.

No. 9 New Street, Spring Gardens:
November 27, 1842.

[3] Stratheden House, Knightsbridge.

CHAPTER XXVI.

Autobiography.

[In the autumn of the year 1847 my father resumed his Autobiography, continuing from the point where it had stopped in November 1842.—ED.]

CHAP.
XXVI.

A.D. 1842.

I took possession of my new house a few days before Christmas, and found it most convenient. The famous Lady Holland said there were three great pieces of good luck which had befallen me: the first was marrying my wife, whose grace and sweetness she justly prized; the second was the selection of my subject for a literary work, ' The Lives of the Chancellors;' and the third, purchasing Stratheden House.[1] I looked into Hyde Park, I was near

---

[1] The house had been called Dunstanville House, having belonged to Lord de Dunstanville, from whose daughter, Baroness Basset, I bought it. I changed its name out of compliment to my dear Mary, and dated the preface to my *Chancellors* from it, thus bringing together in one view my three pieces of good luck.

Kensington Gardens, I breathed as pure air as any in England, and I was only twenty minutes' walk from St. James's Street. Above all, I was pleased with the noble room I had for my library, in which all my law, classical and miscellaneous books could be ranged.

Here I now in good earnest began my biographical labours. I had been at work some months in collecting materials, and I lost much time in discovering where my materials were to be found. I looked into all the old English historians, beginning with the Venerable Bede, whose talent for narration and whose familiarity with the Latin classics greatly astonished me. My early heroes being all ecclesiastics, I was obliged to trace them in the annals of different dioceses, and to try to discover something of their career before and after they had held the Great Seal. A catalogue of Chancellors I had found in the works of Dugdale and other antiquaries, but it was long before I had any hope of being able to furnish a connected account of them. I was likewise alarmed by hearing that two other gentlemen—Mr. Hardy, the Keeper of the Records in the Tower, and Mr. Foss, editor of ' The Grandeur of the Law '—were engaged in a similar undertaking; and I suspended my researches till I had an assurance from them that I should not clash with anything they had on hand. I met with little encouragement from anyone to whom I mentioned my project, and those best acquainted with the book trade told me that, although something might perhaps be made of recent Chancellors, no publisher would have anything to do, except at my sole expense and risk, with those who flourished before the Revolution of 1688. I still thought the series of early Chancellors a good vehicle for sketches of the history and manners of the times in which they lived, and I persevered in my plan of presenting them in succession from the foundation of the monarchy.

I first broke ground by translating, from Fitzstephen, the striking. passages of his life of Thomas à Becket with which I have enlivened my account of this extraordinary man. Postponing my introductory discourse respecting the nature and functions of the office of Chancellor, I then began with

Turketel, and during the session of 1843 I had got, with CHAP.
blanks to be filled up, through the Chancellors to about the XXVI.
middle of the reign of Henry III.; but there I stuck fast, A.D. 1843.
and before I went to Paris in the autumn of that year I had
thrown aside the work in despair.

My position in the House of Lords was rendered very
embarrasing by the illness of Lord Melbourne, who had a
paralytic seizure in the autumn of 1842. He was prevented
for some months from appearing in public, and when he again
occupied his seat in the House of Lords, though his features
were little altered, and he could walk supported by his staff,
slightly dragging one leg, there was no speculation in his
eye; sometimes when he spoke his voice was broken as if he
had been going to burst into tears, and it was evident that
his mental faculties had been seriously affected. His friends
knew not whether they should do more than salute him,
being afraid, on the one hand, of his suspecting that they
treated him with neglect, and on the other of distressing
him by conversation to which he was unequal. We soon
found that we could not consult him as our leader ; and, both
with respect to Ireland and other subjects, his sentiments
appeared to have become Conservative.

Lord Lansdowne under these circumstances was naturally
to be looked up to, but, out of delicacy, he both ostensibly
and privately declined to act as our leader in the Lords. He
would not even give the usual dinner on the day before
the commencement of the session. This we had once at
Kensington Palace from his Royal Highness the Duke of
Sussex, and after his death at Brooks's club-house.

As to the course I should take in the House of Lords, I
was thus left to the freedom of my own will. When I stated
my situation to Lord John Russell, he advised me actively to
assail the enemy on every favourable opportunity, but he
never interfered specifically with regard to any of our proceedings.

There was, generally speaking, much languor on both
sides. The ministerialists were almost as much without a
leader as ourselves. They were earnestly disposed to show
deference to the Duke of Wellington, and were afraid of

appearing to encroach upon his supremacy; but he was neither disposed nor able to come forward on ordinary occasions as the organ of the Government, and we were often prevented only by our respect for his services and his character from successfully assailing him.

The House was occasionally amused by skirmishes between Brougham and myself. He had expected that I should succumb to him like other Whig peers. Great was his astonishment when, early in the session of 1842, I was bold enough to controvert and to refute what he had laid down for law, and to contrast his career in the House of Commons with the course which he was now pursuing. During the session of 1843 our conflicts were more frequent and severe. Although the eager partisan of the Tory Administration, he continued to sit on our benches, and he appropriated to himself a seat next to the one I had selected, the gangway only dividing us. This was exceedingly unfair, for he not only attacked us with more effect pretending to be our friend, but he actually overheard our conversation and our consultations as to the conduct of business. Though this was considered his 'place,' and he rose from it to speak, he could never rest in it above a quarter of an hour continuously; he wandered about, much like a perturbed spirit, conversing with peers on both sides of the House, and with strangers under the bar and on the steps of the throne. The greatest part of the evening he sat on the woolsack, seeming to hold divided empire with Lord Chancellor Lyndhurst. He never took a note, and he showed a most marvellous power of memory by being able to quote with perfect accuracy (although he often wilfully misrepresented) all the arguments of his opponents.

The members of the Government were very civil to him, for, though he had little or no influence out of doors, he conduced considerably to their leading a quiet life in the House of Lords. I am afraid likewise that the great Duke was pleased with the gross and fulsome flattery which Brougham offered to him. The victor of Waterloo did not care much for being put above Hannibal and Napoleon as a general, but he evidently showed a radiant glow of complacency, and became dearer to himself, when told that he was a consummate orator, and that he had equalled the finest bursts of Lord Chatham and Mr. Burke.

.   .   .   .

Peel was now in the zenith of his power and popularity. He had carried his Tariff, reformed the sliding scale, and restored our financial credit.   The apprehensions at first entertained of a ruinous importation of cattle had passed away, the price of corn was moderate and steady, and the new income tax, which I had thought must inevitably render the proposer of it odious, was rapturously applauded by all who had incomes under 150*l.* a year; and was very patiently borne by those of greater wealth, even including those who lived by a precarious profession.

The Prime Minister, having as yet given no intelligible intimation that he meant to depart further from the Protectionist principles which he had professed when assailing the late Government, continued to possess the confidence of the great bulk of the Conservative party, and was even enjoying Court favour.   The Queen had parted very reluctantly with Lord Melbourne, but she has ever proved herself to be the most constitutional of sovereigns.   From the beginning she gave the new Minister her public confidence, and by degrees she became quite reconciled to his manners, although they were sadly wanting in ease and grace.

The Whigs seemed for ever prostrate.   In the House of Commons they made a slender show of opposition, but in the House of Lords as a party they neither proposed nor resisted any measure whatever.

The longest speech I made this session was on the Ashburton Treaty, for settling the north-eastern boundary between Canada and the United States, resisting Brougham's motion for a vote of thanks to our negotiator.[2]

Letter to Sir George Campbell.

Stratheden House : April 10, 1843.

My dear Brother, . . . Though so much dissatisfied with my speech on Friday night on the Ashburton Treaty, I find

[2] Hansard, vol. lxviii. p. 653.

that it has considerably raised me with our party. Both
Lord and Lady Palmerston almost overwhelmed me with
acknowledgments. The Duchess of Inverness told Mary
his Royal Highness[3] was quite delighted with it. On the
strength of this I called on him yesterday, and he strongly
advised me to print it. The Duke abusing Peel very much,
I observed, 'But if your Royal Highness had been on the
throne, you must, as a constitutional monarch, have submitted
to employ him as your Minister.' *Duke.* 'But I should have
said, as my father did when he had a Whig Minister forced on
him, "I take you against my will, and mind I shall get rid of
you as soon as possible."' This is certainly the principle on
which George the Third acted, but I never before heard that
he was so openly sincere.

Autobiography.

I made a vigorous effort to prevent the disruption of the
Church of Scotland, and I should have succeeded if the
manner in which it was opposed had not given the non-
intrusion party reason to believe that the Government was
about to espouse their cause, and at once to legalise the
Veto Act, and to throw all power into their hands. I moved
a string of resolutions highly lauding the Church of Scotland,
but denying the power of the General Assembly to abolish
patronage, which had been established by Act of Parliament,
and maintaining that the Church courts had not any exclusive
and absolute jurisdiction on any question of civil rights. After
alluding to my early connection with the Church of Scotland,
and expressing my veneration and my affection for it, I gave
a sketch of its recent pretensions, showing that they were
more extravagant than any ever set up by the Church of
Rome, and wholly incompatible not only with established
law, but with the existence of civil government.[4]

Lord Aberdeen, without trying to refute my reasoning,
shilly-shallied in such a way as to induce the Presbyterian
popes to believe that the Government was afraid of their

---

[3] The Duke of Sussex.
[4] Hansard, vol. lxviii. pp. 37, 218.

anathemas, and at the last moment would succumb. They
accordingly entered into an engagement, from which they
could not *resile* without deep disgrace, to leave the Church if
their demands were not complied with; and the disruption,
which might easily have been prevented, was in a few weeks
consummated, to the great surprise and mortification of a large
majority of those who were concerned in it.

The establishment of the *Free Church* was a very great
calamity to Scotland, and Sir Robert Peel has not been blamed
for it as he deserves to be. Not only has the schism materially weakened the old Presbyterian Church which had conferred such benefits on the country, but it has been very
unfavourable to true religion. From the fanatical rivalry
which it has generated, dissension has been introduced into
the bosoms of thousands of families.

Letter to Sir George Campbell.

Stratheden House: March 18, 1843.

My dear Brother, . . . I was obliged to postpone my
motion about the Kirk, as there is to be another Cabinet
to-day, when Government will determine whether they will
support my resolutions. I was amused with Brougham's
sudden conversion into an ally the moment I told him that
Aberdeen approved of my motion. There has come out a
very good caricature by H. B., representing Brougham as
a pasteboard marionette, which the Duke of Wellington
holds in his hand, and makes to caper by drawing a string.
But he pretends to move the Duke by secret springs.
He told me yesterday that on Thursday evening he introduced the Duke to a very pretty woman in the House
of Lords, and that the Duke expressing great admiration
of her beauty, Brougham said, 'She is coming again on
Monday and wishes exceedingly to hear you speak, and you
will have an opportunity, as Campbell's motion about the
Church of Scotland is coming on.' 'Well,' said the Duke,
'to please her I will say a few words.' Upon such things
depends the fate of the Church!

Autobiography.

My next undertaking concerned the law of defamation
and libel, which was in a most unsatisfactory state in England. The periodical press was neither properly deterred
from calumny, nor protected from vexatious and oppressive
litigation. There were newspapers that lived by extorting
money under the threat of attacking private character, and
the established doctrine that truth could in no case be
pleaded or given in evidence by the defendant in a criminal
prosecution for libel, with other anomalies and absurdities,
exposed the proprietors of the most respectable journals to
be fined and imprisoned like the worst of criminals. This
state of the law was a principal reason why the profession of
a 'journalist' had been discreditable in England, although
it is liberal and honourable in itself, and the public good
evidently requires that it should be held in respect.

I began with moving for a Select Committee upon the
subject, introducing my motion with a long speech, in which
I gave the history of the English law of defamation and
libel from the Star Chamber downwards, and pointed out
all its defects and ill consequences. Before the Committee,
which sat day by day for some weeks, I examined lawyers not
only from England, Ireland, and Scotland, but from most of
the Continental States, and from America. We had likewise
the editors and printers of all the principal London newspapers, and of many published in the country. I framed
a Report concluding with a great number of resolutions,
meant as the heads of a Bill. I drew the Bill with the
assistance of Mr. Starkey, author of the 'Treatise on the
Law of Libel.'

This was a far more important measure than 'Fox's
Libel Bill,' but I carried it through the House of Lords
without difficulty.[5] It was mutilated a little in the Commons,
but, after showing how in recent times our branch of the
Legislature, as far as Law Reform was concerned, was in
advance of the other, I advised their lordships to acquiesce
in the supposed 'amendments' lest the whole measure should

[5] Hansard, vol. lxx. pp. 1252, 1356 ; vol. lxxi. p. 987.

be lost. So 'Lord Campbell's Libel Bill' received the Royal assent.

This was my most popular legislative exertion, as the public had paid little attention to the Real Property Bills which I had introduced in the House of Commons. The respectable journals of all parties acknowledged that I had conferred an essential obligation on the press, and several expositions of the new law by professional men were published—with dedications to me in very flattering terms. It certainly has operated most beneficially. There are no longer such newspapers as the 'Satirist,' which traded in slander; actions are no longer brought against newspapers by pettifogging attorneys with a view to costs; and, an opportunity being given in criminal prosecutions to prove the truth of the charge, and to show that the defendant was not actuated by any malicious motive, indictments are no longer preferred by swindlers in the hope of recovering their character, or being revenged upon those who have exposed them.

Letter to Sir George Campbell.

Stratheden House: September 16, 1843.

My dear Brother, . . . I enclose you a letter from O'Connell. Keep it, as it may one day have an historical interest. If there is to be separation or civil war, it may be stated that at one time Dan, in the midst of apparent fury, was very peaceably inclined, and would have been glad of a pretext for relaxing from Repeal agitation. I had merely sent a copy of my opinion to O'Connell under a blank cover.

Merrion Square, Dublin: September 9, 1843.

My Lord,—I beg you will accept my best thanks for your kindness in sending me the opinion you pronounced in the case of the Queen against Mills. I read it with sincere admiration. Nay, I am *tradesman* enough to have read it with great delight. It is really a model for a law argument. I remember Curran said of an eminent Irish lawyer that 'his mind floated in a legal atmosphere.' The figure may not be a very brilliant one, but it conveys, I think, an accurate idea of the impression that your argument has made upon me, as to your power of *thinking* law. Your judgment is certainly quite conclusive against the totally untenable opinions *huddled* together by the twelve judges.

N 2

I avail myself of this occasion to return to you, my Lord, my most sincere and cordial thanks for the friendly, and at the same time manly, part which you have taken during the last session of Parliament on all subjects connected with Ireland: You really are the only efficient friend the Irish have had in the House of Lords during that session.

You of course blame my *prejudice* in wishing never to see a *Saxon* Lord Chancellor in Ireland,—yet I do not hesitate to say that the opinion is universal amongst the popular party here, that if we are to have a British Chancellor, your appointment would be more satisfactory than that of any other *stranger*—and you have certainly deserved this sentiment.

Allow me to say (*par parenthèse*)—and I consent that you shall totally forget what I say in that parenthesis—that the Whig leaders do not behave well towards their supporters. Our Irish movement has at least this merit, that it has roused the English nation from slumber. There can be no more dreams about Ireland. Our grievances are beginning to be admitted by all parties, and by the press of all political opinions, to be afflicting and not easily endured. I ask—of course without expecting an answer—why the Whig leaders are not up to the level of the times they live in; why do they not propose a definite plan for redressing these grievances? Peel, while in opposition, used to enliven the recess by his state epistles, declaratory of his opinions and determination. Why does not Lord John treat us to a magniloquent epistle declaratory of his determination to abate the Church nuisance in Ireland, to augment our popular franchises, to vivify our new corporations: to mitigate the statute law as between landlord and tenant; to strike off a few more rotten boroughs in England, and give the representatives to our great counties; in short, why does he not prove himself a high-minded, high-gifted statesman, capable of leading his friends into all the advantages to be derived from conciliating the Irish nation, and strengthening the British Empire?

It will be quite plain to your lordship that I do not expect any manner of reply to this letter. I merely seek the gratification of being permitted to think aloud in your presence. And if there be anything displeasing to you in this indulgence, I entreat your forgiveness upon this score—of its being the farthest thing in the world from my intention to say anything which I thought *should* displease you. I have the honour to be, respectfully, my Lord,   Your faithful servant,

To Lord Campbell, &c., &c.   DANIEL O'CONNELL.

Autobiography.

In the autumn I had a charming trip to Paris with my wife and daughters. We crossed over from Southampton to Havre and proceeded by a steamer to Rouen. I rejoice exceedingly in the scenery of the Seine, which, if not very grand or picturesque, has to me a more *riant* aspect than that of almost any other river.

To an Englishman, Normandy is the most interesting country beyond the seas, not only presenting to him the scenes of so many historical events, but being intimately connected with our existing laws and institutions. In visiting Rouen I am almost as much excited by an old copy of the 'Coustumier,' to which Littleton's 'Tenures' may be traced, as by viewing the spot where the Maid of Orleans, for saving her country, was burnt as a witch.

In former days I used to be two days in posting from Rouen to Paris. Now we were transported by the railroad in little more than two hours; but I regretted the night at the 'Cheval Blanc' at Mantes, wishing again to see the brick floors, and to listen to the crack of the postilion's whip.

At Paris we found Mlle. Rachel now in full force, and we saw and admired her in her principal parts.

After a few weeks we went to Fontainebleau, my favourite retreat, and spent ten days there most delightfully. I have a peculiarly agreeable recollection of a walk which we had through the mazes of the forest to Thomery, the place where the famous Fontainebleau grapes are produced, and wandering among the vineyards, then loaded with the most delicious fruit in the world. Our landlord told us that in the opening of spring Fontainebleau is a still more delightful place of residence, and I do not despair of spending my Easter holidays there, seeing the buds burst and breathing the sweet odours of the thyme and the violets.

In the beginning of November we returned from Paris to London by the same route, after encountering a little peril by being stranded on a sand-bank in descending the Seine.

Settled at Stratheden House for the winter, I felt rather desolate. Parliament was not to sit till February, and Michaelmas Term was going on briskly in Westminster Hall; but, a poor peer, I was debarred from taking a brief. In my dreams, unconscious of my disqualification, I used to imagine that I was still at the bar, and that all my business had left me. I could not fill up my time with miscellaneous reading directed to no object.

My only resource was to resume the 'Lives of the Chancellors.' I did so with an energy and perseverance for which I am grateful to Heaven. In one year and ten months from that time my first three volumes, down to 1689, were

actually printed and ready for publication. Assuming it to
be a 'standard work,' as it is at present denominated, I doubt
whether any other of the same bulk was ever finished off
more rapidly.

What I had previously written would not have amounted
to more than one hundred printed pages, and I rewrote all
the early lives down to Henry III., where I had stuck. By
a violent effort I extricated myself and bridged the chasm.
Resorting to further antiquarian research, and calling in the
assistance of Mr. Foss, who had long been digging in the
same mine, I got material facts respecting almost every
Chancellor to be recorded; and, mixing up my heroes with
the historical events of their day, I composed a continuous,
flowing narrative, which, even in the darkest periods, I hoped
might be read with interest and instruction.

I was more and more amazed at the extreme jejuneness
of the historians, especially of Hume, who often does not
even mention the names of those men whose counsels directed
the events which he commemorates.

How delighted was I with discoveries which I knew must
enliven my work and amaze my readers—as that Queen
Eleanor had been 'Lady Keeper of the Great Seal,' and that
Richard de Bury, the first and greatest of English biblio-
maniacs, was a Lord Chancellor.

I thought my perplexities were over when in the reign
of Edward III. I got to Sir Robert Parnynge and the lay
Chancellors praised by Lord Coke; but I had a dreary task in
travelling through the wars of the Roses, during which our
records are far more defective than in the times of the
earliest Plantagenets, and a Chancellor occurs of whose origin,
rise, death, or armorial bearings no trace can be found,
although he held the Great Seal in two reigns and took a
leading part in important historical events.[6]

At last I got to Cardinal Morton under Henry VII., when
I found myself in the steady light of authentic history, and,
arriving in the next reign at Cardinal Wolsey, I was perplexed
by the multiplicity of materials heaped around me. 'Inopem
me copia fecit.' Now however I took extreme interest in my

---

[6] John Searle, *temp.* Richard II. and Henry IV.

labours, and I really wrote *con amore.* I was sure that by a proper selection and arrangement of facts and documents, with some appropriate observations, all the great men whose lives I had to narrate might be made more interesting than they had appeared in any former biography.

Of all my heroes I was most attached to Sir Thomas More. I bestowed most care on Bacon.[7] I took particular interest in the Keepers of the Great Seal during the Commonwealth, of whom little was before known, and this part of my work gives a new and, I think, curious explanation of Cromwell's Parliament and his administration of justice. But the life of Whitelocke, of which I had formed high expectations, attracted little notice.

Working very hard, I was approaching the Restoration of Charles II., when, in the end of September, Parliament was prorogued, and I went with my family to Boulogne.

But I must take some notice of the events of the preceding session.

[Before the session began he gave a dinner to the leading Whigs, and wrote the following letter to his brother.—ED.]

Stratheden House : January 31, 1844.

. . . I promised you some account of my dinner. *Socially* it went off very well—*politically* in a manner to lead to despair.

Lord John, who had promised to come, was kept away by the illness of his little boy. We had Melbourne, Normanby, Duncannon, Howick, Palmerston, Methuen, Labouchere, Sir

---

[7] *September* 1860.—I was bitterly assailed by some writers who laboured under the monomaniacal delusion that Bacon was an immaculate character, and was to be loudly praised for every action of his life and for all his writings. Therefore, because I ventured to intimate my opinion that Bacon had disgraced himself in Elizabeth's time by blackening the fair fame of his patron and friend the Earl of Essex, and had taken bribes when Chancellor to James I., and that his *History of Henry VII.* and his jest-books were inferior literary productions, criticisms were written upon me in newspapers and reviews abusing me as if I had attacked the character of the sacred Founder of our religion, and had vilipended the Holy Scriptures. My belief, however, is that my readers will have a higher notion of the genius and good qualities of Bacon than can be impressed by indiscriminate adulation.

George Grey, C. Buller, Wilde, Stephenson, Tufnell, Le-
Marchant, Easthope, Fonblanque, Lord Ponsonby, Lord Monteagle.   We were very merry, and all were well pleased with
their entertainment.   But as for making any arrangement for
opening the session, it was a deplorable failure.   Melbourne
was very flat at first, but revived with a little wine and
talked a great deal.   His tone, however, was not at all
satisfactory.   You know he affects always to be a mocker.
He rather defended the sliding scale and the general conduct
of the present Government.   All others in the company were
impatient for war, but lamentably divided as to the manner
in which it should be carried on.   Some were for moving
an amendment; some, without an amendment, for strongly
condemning Peel's Irish policy, particularly the manner in
which the prosecution against O'Connell has been conducted.
Some thought this would be very inexpedient, and that it
would be much better entirely to reserve our Irish fire till the
trials are over.   We parted without anything being determined.

Our party never was in a more dilapidated or ruinous
condition.   And what is more, I see no hope for the country.
England will have Peel and a Tory government.   With Peel
and a Tory government Ireland never will be reconciled, and
cannot long be kept in subjection.

I have a great mind to retire to some remote corner and
devote myself to my Chancellors.

Autobiography.

Peel's chief difficulty now was Ireland.   He had acted
very indiscreetly with respect to the monster meetings for
Repeal.   He would not declare them to be illegal, or take
any steps to suppress them, while in a most inconsistent and
irritating manner he cashiered all magistrates who attended
them.

At last O'Connell, who had been allowed to hold these
meetings without check for above a twelvemonth, was suddenly prosecuted under a monster indictment, containing an
infinite number of counts, which charged him with an infinite

variety of offences, and sought to make him personally answerable for all that had been done, written, or spoken respecting Repeal for a long period of time in every part of Ireland.

This course was most unfair and most unwise. The mode in which the prosecution was conducted was still more reprehensible. A packed jury was impanelled from which all Roman Catholics were excluded, and the Chief Justice, Pennefather, for the purpose of obtaining a conviction, was guilty of such gross partiality that the counsel for the Crown and the Ministers in England were scandalised, and could not say a word in his defence. Upon several of the most important counts the jury found a verdict in words which the court in Dublin thought amounted to *Guilty*, but which were clearly an insufficient finding. On all the other counts, several of which afterwards turned out to be bad in point of law, they found a general verdict of *Guilty*, and upon the whole record the court, ' for the offences aforesaid,' passed a heavy sentence of fine and imprisonment.

Soon after the meeting of Parliament, the Marquis of Normanby brought the subject before the House of Lords by a motion on the state of Ireland. . . . The next proceeding connected with O'Connell's case was a Bill I introduced to allow bail in error in cases of misdemeanour. I pointed out the monstrous injustice of hearing the merits of a conviction after the sentence had been carried into execution, introducing the well-known quotation :—

> Gnossius hic Rhadamanthus habet durissima regna
> Castigatque, auditque dolos.

(He first inflicts the punishment, and then he hears the writ of error.)

But Lyndhurst made a strong speech against the Bill and it was thrown out. In the following session he highly praised it, and it passed.

When the writ of error came to be argued—O'Connell lying in prison in Dublin—the most intense interest was excited, and the eyes of all Europe were upon us.

The main question was whether, there being in the indictment good counts on which there was a regular verdict of *Guilty*, the judgment sentencing the defendant to a discretionary fine and imprisonment could be supported, there being bad counts in the indictment, and good counts without a regular verdict of *Guilty* upon them, the sentence purporting to be pronounced in respect of all the offences mentioned in the indictment. There was likewise a serious objection to the formation of the jury, which was raised by a plea in abatement.

The Crown lawyers contended that we must presume that the Irish judges knew which *counts* were good as well as which *findings* were good and which defective, so that the whole punishment awarded must be taken to be for the offences in the good counts on which there was a regular verdict of *Guilty*. This certainly would have been a presumption of law entirely against *truth*, for the Irish judges thought all the counts in the indictment good, and particularly relied upon several which all the English judges thought bad; and the Irish judges had denied that there was any insufficiency in the findings of the jury. In truth the supposed presumption was contrary to all principle, and was unsupported by any authority; the saying that 'it is enough if there be one good count in an indictment' applying to a motion in arrest of judgment before sentence, and not to a writ of error after sentence.

All the English judges, however, except two, were for overruling all the objections. The two dissentients (Parke and Coltman) thought that the judgment ought to be reversed, as credit must be given to the averment in the record that the punishment was awarded for *all* the supposed offences enumerated in the indictment, whereas some of these were not indictable, and of others the defendant had not been lawfully found guilty.

Of the law lords in the House two were now Tories, Lyndhurst and Brougham; and three were steady Whigs, Denman, Cottenham, and Campbell. It did so happen by some strange chance that the two were for affirming the judgment, and the three were for reversing it. We delivered written opinions. I took immense pains with mine, which may be seen in Clark and Finelly's Reports, vol. ii. p. 155.

Were the lay lords to vote, although they had not been present at the argument of the case, and were incapable of understanding it? There were present a large number of ministerialists who, when the question was put 'that the judgment be reversed,' hallooed out 'Not content,' and who if they had divided would have constituted a large majority for *affirming*. But the Government was afraid of the effect to be produced in Ireland by an affirmance so obtained; and Lord Wharncliffe, the President of the Council, strongly advised that the lay lords should not vote. I said that the Constitution knew no distinction between lay lords and law lords, but that there was in reason a distinction between lords who had heard the case argued and those who had not, and that if any of the latter class should vote, the decision would bring great disgrace upon the administration of justice in that House. The lay lords then all withdrew, and the question being again put, we five law lords alone being in the House, Denman, Cottenham, and Campbell said *Content*, and Lyndhurst and Brougham said *Not content*, when, without a division, Lyndhurst said 'The contents have it.' So the judgment was reversed, and O'Connell was liberated.

Brougham immediately came up to me and said, 'Well, you have made Tindal a peer. The Government will not endure a majority of Radical law lords in the House.' Nevertheless poor Tindal died a commoner.

I never gave a more conscientious vote. There was an awkwardness in going against a large majority of the English judges in a political case, but our judgment was generally approved of in Westminster Hall.

In the debates which arose during this session upon the practice of opening letters at the Post Office under a warrant from the Secretary of State, I contended that it was neither authorised by common law nor statute, although the Secretary of State, like any other magistrate, or indeed any private individual, may seize and detain documents which constitute evidence of the commission of a crime. Various instances were adduced from a remote time of the Secretary of State, out of mere suspicion or curiosity, having opened letters at the Post Office which he resealed and forwarded to their destination; but this is like the practice of granting general warrants to arrest the author of a libel, which prevailed till it was adjudged to be illegal. Of all Secretaries of State, Mr. Fox, during his short tenure of office, appeared to have carried the practice to the greatest excess, and both parties were pleased to have the matter hushed up by the appointment of a Select Committee.

On two measures very creditable to Sir Robert Peel I strongly supported the Government. The first of these, the Dissenters' Marriages Bill (Ireland), became necessary by what I considered an erroneous decision of the House of Lords on the question whether at common law there might not be a valid marriage by consent and cohabitation without the intervention of a priest episcopally ordained. A majority of the Irish judges had held a marriage by a Presbyterian minister to be invalid unless in the particular case where it was authorised by Act of Parliament. The English judges were unanimously of the same opinion. The law lords were equally divided—Lord Lyndhurst, Lord Abinger and Lord Cottenham being against the validity of the marriage, and Lord Brougham, Lord Denman and Lord Campbell in favour of it. According to the rules of the House, the question was put 'that the judgment be reversed,' and the rule being *semper præsumitur pro negante*, the judgment was affirmed. A Bill was therefore brought in generally to recognise and regulate such marriages for the future. The measure was strongly opposed by the Irish Primate and several of the ordinary supporters of the Government, but was carried by our assistance.

The next measure, called the Dissenters' Chapels Bill, was still bolder, and if it had been proposed by a Whig Government would have set all England in a flame. The object of it was to protect the Unitarians in the enjoyment of chapels which had been endowed by orthodox Presbyterians when there was a penal law against all who denied the doctrine of the Trinity, but of which congregations had long been in undisputed possession after they had gradually become Unitarians. Although patronised by Sir Robert Peel, still considered the head of the Conservative party, the measure caused a cry that the *Church was in danger*, and it was very distasteful to Evangelical Dissenters as well as to High Churchmen. But the judges have determined that there is now no difference as to legal capacity and right between Unitarians and other classes of Christians dissenting from the Church of England, and upon the principles of *prescription* the possession of the Unitarians was to be protected. I supported the Bill in a speech for which Lyndhurst expressed much gratitude, and it passed with great applause from all lovers of religious liberty.

[In the early part of this session the death of his father-in-law, Lord Abinger, had occurred, to which the following letters refer.—ED.]

Stratheden House:
Wednesday, April 3, 1844.

My dear Brother, . . . Lord Abinger has had a very dangerous paralytic attack on the circuit at Bury St. Edmunds, and I should not be surprised any minute to hear an account of his death. The news of his illness came yesterday morning when Lady Abinger, Robert and Peter immediately set off for Bury. The accounts this morning are very alarming. You may suppose that Mary, the most pious of daughters, is in a state of great anxiety and distress, though she still hopes the best.

This is a very sudden reverse; for on Monday we were all thrown into a state of great joy by Lord Aberdeen having appointed Peter secretary of legation at Florence.

Stratheden House:
Monday, April 8, 1844.

. . . You will be prepared for the bad news I have to communicate. Lord Abinger expired yesterday at two o'clock. You may believe that Mary is in the deepest affliction, and that my great occupation now is to support and comfort her. . . .

At present I can only think of the good qualities of the deceased, which made all his children most tenderly attached to him. He was likewise kind and generous to all depending upon him, and very steady in his early friendships.

Stratheden House: April 13, 1844.

. . . The funeral is to be to-morrow morning, and Fred
and I go down to Abinger to-night.

Autobiography.

Parliament was not prorogued till the 5th of September.
Soon after, I went with my family to Boulogne and stayed
there two months. Here I sat down resolutely to my Chancellors, and I never wrote so much in the same space of
time. I had a daily airing on the pier, or the fortifications
of the Haute Ville, and, except when at my short meals, I
shut myself up in a little octagonal closet sequestered from
the rest of the house. *Clarendon* was the result, with a
good deal of work to some other lives.

Two great men passed through Boulogne while I so-
journed there. The first was Lord Brougham, on his way to
Cannes. . . . A few weeks afterwards I saw Louis Philippe
walk down the Grande Rue on his return from his visit to
Queen Victoria. Now was the *entente cordiale* at its height,
and we Englishmen cheered him loudly, his own subjects receiving him rather coldly from knowing him better. Even
then I detested his Spanish policy, and thought that, instead
of seeking the glory of being the first magistrate of a free
State, he was aiming at absolute power and family aggran-
disement; but I was little aware of the detestable artifices
and meannesses to which he would resort to gain his object.

On my return to London by the railway from Folkestone
I was thrown into a terrible *quandary* by the loss of the
box which contained the MS. of my 'Lives.' The recovery
of it was very doubtful, and I should have been wholly
incapable of trying to rewrite it, or even engaging in any
other literary undertaking. But in the course of the night
the box, which had been sent by mistake to Dover, arrived
safely at Stratheden House.

I was the more eager to be in print that I might protect
myself against such accidents. My labours were a little interrupted by the sittings of the Judicial Committee of the
Privy Council, but I so well employed every interval of

leisure that I could see to the termination of the first series, which was to finish in 1689 with Jeffreys. Shaftesbury now gave me much delight. I was particularly pleased, from respect for my craft as a lawyer, with showing that, being unimbued with professional knowledge, he in truth was a wretchedly bad judge, and that Dryden's praise of him was *purchased*. Nottingham I found very dull, but I was consoled by thinking what variety of characters I had to pourtray, and by anticipating the effect to be expected from the contrast between them. It rejoiced me when I could gratify the malignity I had long cherished against that sneaking fellow Lord Keeper Guilford, although I had some remorse when I recollected that my friend the charming Lady Charlotte Lindsay was his lineal descendant. The last in the series was morally the worst, but dramatically the best, of the whole. Macaulay has said that it is allowable to exaggerate for effect—a licence I have never acknowledged; but it was fortunate for my conscience in this instance that I could not possibly overcharge the profligacy and cruelty of my hero, and I could not help anticipating with complacency the interest which a narrative of his adventures would excite.

Meanwhile Parliament met on the 4th of February. I still regularly attended the judicial business of the House of Lords four days every week, and after the morning work I was always again in my place from five o'clock till the motion for adjournment was made and carried.

[The gravity of the judicial business was enlivened by jokes among the law lords, as the following letters show.—ED.]

House of Lords : Friday, July 19, 1844.

My dear Brother, . . . I am writing to you with a pen *ex dono Domini Cancellarii*. I admiring his steel pen, he offered me a present of a paper of them. *Campbell.* But this must be without prejudice to my right to oppose your Government. *Brougham.* You are a lucky fellow, for you oppose his Government and are rewarded, while I support him and get nothing.

Brougham's love of vengeance is insatiable and will keep

him the enemy of the Whigs for the rest of his days. The Tories certainly give him nothing beyond fair words. There are three things he wished to have had during the present session: the Lord Lieutenancy of Westmoreland, the Garter, and the Presidency of the Judicial Committee. It is a great pity that he is so utterly void of faith and principle, for he is not only pleasant but good-natured, and as a companion he is infinitely to be preferred to Cottenham. I asked him to-day how he supposed Cottenham now spends his time. *Brougham.* I understand that he stays at home and knits stockings, like the Aberdeen sailors mentioned by Adam Smith, and that he sells them for threepence a pair, which he is able to do, his time being of so little value to him.

Stratheden House: May 26, 1845.

. . . To prepare you for the following jest, I must tell you that last session Lyndhurst carried a job through Parliament whereby he appointed his two secretaries, very foolish fellows, Commissioners of Lunatics. I showed Lyndhurst and Brougham a proof-sheet giving an account of Cardinal Wolsey's fool being made a present of to the King, with this note: ' A fool was so necessary to the establishment of a Chancellor that we shall find one in the household of Sir Thomas More. It is very doubtful when Chancellors ceased to have any such character about them.' I afterwards privately suggested to Brougham that Lyndhurst knew better how to provide for his fools than making a present of them to the Queen and Prince Albert, but that this was so near the truth that I did not venture to compliment him upon it. *Brougham.* ' Oh, a great man ought always to hear the truth.' He then runs up to Lyndhurst and tells him how Campbell had been complimenting him. Lyndhurst laughed good-humouredly. . . .

Autobiography.

Peel's Government was now all-powerful, and a general opinion prevailed that it might last as long as Sir Robert Walpole's. No one gifted with second sight would have gained credit to a vaticination that before the year closed it would receive its death-wound, and that the great Conservative party was about to be dissolved.

Having renewed the income tax, and repealed the glass duty and other imposts weighing heavily on industry, Peel triumphantly put an end to the session, and was worshipped, I might almost say, by all parties as a Heaven-born Minister. But a *blight*, or a little *insect*, was already invisibly at work to hurl him from power.

We spent the autumn at Abinger Hall, which was lent to us by my brother-in-law. I had given up all thought of political changes, and had become reconciled to my banishment from office for the rest of my days. I first heard a gossiping old lady say that the *potatoes were all rotting*, and she added that they were turned to poison, and that hundreds of people were dying from eating them. I disbelieved the whole of her story, but the first part of it soon turned out to be too true.

By the time we returned to London, which was early in November, there was a general alarm of famine, and rumours were propagated that Ministers were about to open the ports for the free importation of corn. Then came Lord John Russell's letter from Edinburgh, requiring a total abolition of the Corn Laws, and even denouncing the fixed duty which he had once proposed as a compromise. The day on which this letter appeared in the London journals I met Lord Palmerston riding in Hyde Park, and he very freely censured ' John's temerity in writing and publishing this letter without the sanction of his party,' complaining that it might be the means of preventing our return to power.

Soon came the astounding intelligence that Sir Robert Peel proposing to repeal the Corn Laws and being overruled by his colleagues, had resigned, and that Lord John Russell was sent for to form a new Administration.

I expected to be in Dublin in a week. What then was my surprise when Lord John Russell sent for me, and told me that he meant to act on the principle of ' Ireland for the Irish,' and that he was resolved for the public good not only to have an Irishman for Lord Lieutenant, but an Irishman for Chancellor. Personally he was abundantly civil to me, and said that some other arrangement should be made for me.

Luckily for us all, in a few hours the whole concern was blown to atoms. I was not on this occasion summoned to the meetings in Chesham Place, but I knew all that passed from Lord Auckland. Lord Grey was certainly much to be blamed for abruptly declaring, when everything had been settled, that he would not sit in the Cabinet, Palmerston being Foreign Minister; but his *brusquerie* saved the country, and certainly saved our party. If Lord John Russell had then taken the Government, he would have had no chance of carrying the abolition of the Corn Laws; not twenty Conservatives would have supported him in the House of Commons, and a vast majority of peers would have been against him. At all events the Whigs must have been turned out the moment the measure was carried, as there would have been no permanent quarrel between Peel and the Conservatives.

Peel was greatly delighted when he had patched up his Cabinet, inducing all whom he really liked to remain with him. He was not sorry to get rid of Stanley, with whom he had never been cordial, and he confidently expected to have all the glory of establishing free trade in corn *and likewise to retain his office.* He knew that his Corn Law measure would be strongly opposed by a large section of the Tories, but he confidently believed that, when the storm had blown over, they would again rally round him for the purpose of keeping out the Whigs. His colleagues who stuck by him believed the same. Most of them would have seen him at the Devil rather than support free trade in corn as they did (contrary to their own opinion and their wishes), had they not expected that thereby they secured to themselves their continuance in office.

His and their speculations were plausible enough, and had Lord George Bentinck and Benjamin Disraeli not been members of the House of Commons, my notion is that their speculations would have turned out to be well founded. These two men, and these two alone, carried on the war *usque ad internecionem.* Their great object was (in which they fully succeeded), to make Peel personally odious to the Tory party, to provoke him to retaliate upon them, and to render a reconciliation with him utterly impossible. It is owing to them that Peel eulogised Richard Cobden, whom he had once charged with a premeditated purpose of assassination.

In May 1845, the composition of my first series being finished, I had entered into a negotiation with Mr. John Murray, of Albemarle Street, for publishing it, and he agreed to print an edition of 1250 copies, we dividing the profits. By the beginning of September the three thick octavos were ready, but it was deemed not advisable to publish them till December. I was still very doubtful of their success, as those best acquainted with book-making had pronounced so strong an opinion against the project. No one except the printer had read a line of it till the printing was finished.[9]

My first comfort was from Senior, the Master in Chancery, to whom I sent a copy that he might consider of reviewing it for the ' Edinburgh.' He wrote me ' that it was as entertaining as a novel, and that Mrs. Senior, who out of curiosity had looked into it, could not leave it off till she had read the whole.' Next Murray told me that Lockhart had written an article upon it for the ' Quarterly,' which alone was enough to sell an edition. Several copies which I distributed among private friends brought compliments more than the promptings of mere civility.

At last Mr. Murray's trade sale came (I think the 15th of December), which was the day of publication, and a rumour having got abroad that the book was lively, the chief part of the edition was ' subscribed for,' that is, taken by the retail booksellers. In a few days the ' Quarterly Review' appeared with warm commendation of the work, and the same strain was adopted by other periodicals—daily, weekly, monthly and quarterly. I can safely say that no new work of solid information had caused such an excitement for many years. In a very little time it was ' out of print,' and a new edition was called for.

---

[9] I now recollect that the proofs of one or two short lives had been shown to Lady Holland; but the manuscript was not even seen by my own wife or children.

Letters to Sir George Campbell.

Stratheden House : January 16, 1846.

My dear Brother, . . . The success of the ' Chancellors'
is greater and greater. Compliments and congratulations
pour in from all quarters. Murray has requested me to prepare a second edition. I have made great progress with the
fourth and fifth volumes, which come down to Thurlow. Him
I once saw with my own eyes.

House of Lords : January 22, 1846.

. . . I am going to press as soon as I can with my second
edition. The most extraordinary panegyric is from my old
enemy Croker. He told Murray that the 'Quarterly Review' did not praise it sufficiently, and he is going to get
me some MSS. for the second series. . . .

Stratheden House: Friday, January 23, 1846.

. . . As I am afraid I have often annoyed you by my
despondence, I will try to amuse you for once by my vanity.

When I had finished my note to you yesterday I went
down from my private room to the House, and if I had been
made an Earl I should not have been received with such distinction. First began the Duke of Richmond, and spoke of my
book in such terms that I said, ' Really you almost persuade
me to become a Protectionist.' Lyndhurst, having praised it
extravagantly, said, ' You throw out some reflections in a sly
manner on living Chancellors. I take none of them myself :
you could not mean me. But I hear that Brougham is much
offended by your saying that Lord Ellesmere did not waste
his time on the bench by writing notes and preparing
speeches in Parliament.' *Campbell.* ' I had in my mind only
the bad practices of Turketel and Saint Swithun.'

I was quite alarmed when Lord Melbourne addressed me,
sitting at a little distance from him—for he raised his voice,
and, from his infirmity, it was broken as if he had been going to
burst into tears. He then contrived to say, ' Campbell, your
book is excellent. I know not whether it is more entertaining
or instructive.' *Lord Ducie.* ' Campbell, you have saved my

life. I was in bed three weeks, and if it had not been for
the entertainment you afforded me, I never should have
recovered.' Lord Lansdowne, Lord Wilton, and other peers,
were equally complimentary. . . .

CHAP.
XXVI.

A.D. 1846.

Stratheden House : January 29, 1846.

My dear Brother, . . . You greatly overrate the importance of the work, but our success is not to be despised.
Brougham has exploded in the ' Morning Herald,' the journal
in which he now lauds himself and vituperates his friends.
Last Saturday appeared there an editorial article—violently
abusing me rather than my ' Lives,' which are denominated
' ponderous trifles,' but calling me ' plain John,' and alluding
to my peerages and my son Dudley, etc.—so evidently from
Brougham's pen that everybody immediately recognised the
author. When he first met my eye on Monday he did for a
moment look a little embarrassed, but when he had sat down
near me I relieved him by saying that I had received a long
letter from Jeffrey highly complimenting me on my ' ponderous trifles.' He turned off the conversation by talking of
Jeffrey's health. Soon after he said to me, ' How far down
do you come in your Lives of the Chancellors—to the reign of
Henry the Eighth or the Revolution ? Someone was talking
to me of your life of Lord Somers—but there are no materials
for such a life. I have not yet been able to look at your
book.' I only laughed in his face without giving him any
answer. He is the strangest of mankind, for, writing in his own
laudation or against others, he seems to be at no pains to
conceal himself, and afterwards, when the composition has
been published, he talks as if no one could suspect him.

House of Lords : Friday, February 13, 1846.

. . . I find that Stanley is about to head the Protectionists.
He said to me yesterday evening, ' You laid down very sound
doctrine in presenting the Birmingham petition.' *Campbell.*
'I always do.' *Stanley.* 'But why should the duties on
copper ore and all raw materials be repealed ?' *Campbell.*
' That we may have a cheap manufactured article.' *Stanley.*
' To protect native industry. This is *Protection.* I had a

great mind to tell you so at the time—but I shall bring it up
against you.' With all his cleverness he does not know the
first principles of political economy. But his leadership will
give great vigour to the Protectionists. If he had remained
in the House of Commons, I think they would have won the
day.

House of Lords: March 3, 1846.

. . . Having blamed me much for never mentioning my
book to you, I fear you will now think that I perpetually bore
you with the subject, but you must still a little humour
the vanity of an author. I continue to receive many compliments by word of mouth and by letter. On Sunday I met
Peel in the Park, and rode with him for some time. At
parting, he begged permission to express the great delight
he had had in reading my Lives of the Chancellors, and he
extolled the value of the work most extravagantly. Yesterday evening, when the House was breaking up, Lord Strang-
ford said to a pretty girl on his arm, ' Here, Mary, thank
Lord Campbell for the entertainment he has given you.'
Miss Smythe. ' Yes, indeed, Lord Campbell's is the most
charming book I ever read.' But I will spare you from
further *blarney*, although I might go on for an hour.

House of Lords : June 11, 1846.

. . . Yesterday I had the honour to dine at Lincoln's Inn
with our brother bencher, Prince Albert. He shook me
cordially by the hand, and entered into a long conversation
with me about my book. He began this by saying: 'I have
been reading your ·Lives of the Chancellors, Lord Campbell,
with the Queen, and we have received from you much
amusement and instruction.' He evidently showed that he
had read and understood the book. He asked me about the
continuation, and was much tickled by some anecdotes I told
him of George I. When I mentioned a paper written by
Lord Cowper to inform that sovereign, on his arrival in this
country, of the state of parties, he observed : ' I think it
would puzzle any man to write a paper giving an account of
the state of parties now—who and what are Whigs; and who
and what are Tories ! '

I apologised in the best way I could for not sending a copy of my book to her Majesty and his Royal Highness— and I must send them a copy of the second series.

Autobiography.

I did not take any very prominent part in the business of the session of 1846. Lord Howick, on the decease of his illustrious sire transferred to our House, had taken Brougham off my hands. This stout Earl by no means imitated the timid Whigs who treated the *renegade* with cowardly courtesy. Brougham called him 'my noble friend,' but could never get any appellation in return but 'the noble and learned lord.'

As the Irish Coercion Bill, on which Peel was turned out, was passing through the Lords, it was warmly supported by some of our party, and countenanced by almost all the rest. But, although I did not venture to divide the House upon it, I kept up an incessant fire upon it in all its stages, and, damaging it in public opinion, prepared the opposition which was fatal to it in the other House. I now succeeded in getting through both Houses my Bills for the abolition of deodands, and for giving a compensation by action to the families of those who are killed by the negligence of others.

The session of 1846 was by far the most important since the Reform Bill. The great measure was the abolition of the Corn Laws, and upon this I thought it more becoming to give a silent vote. But I watched its progress with intense interest. Sitting near Prince Albert, who countenanced it, I heard Peel's speech introducing it, and I heard Lord George Bentinck when he first fell foul of its author, and showed that, if it was carried, the Conservative party would be annihilated. But the treat was to listen to the invectives of Benjamin Disraeli against Peel. So great was the *prestige* attached to Peel's name, that he would have continued Minister had his conduct not been thus assailed in a manner tending to make him appear both odious and ridiculous.

The question was 'What will the Lords do?' The conduct of the Duke of Wellington was most extraordinary. He canvassed for the Bill and, when any objection to it was made, he said, 'That is nothing; you can't have a worse opinion of it than I have; but to support the Queen's Government we must carry it through.' The Duke very well saw that the Government could not stand after the Bill was carried, and he was indifferent about the change, for his subjection to Peel had become very irksome to him. But the situation of those peers who, disliking the measure, had agreed to support it in the hope of keeping their places, was such as to excite the pity of their opponents. When the Bill came to the Upper House, they were still bound to support it, and they felt that as soon as it was carried they must inevitably be turned out. I never saw such lugubrious faces as they exhibited. It was excellent fun for us Whigs to divide with them and, as we went in great strength below the bar, to congratulate them on the triumph of the Government.

The new Irish Coercion Bill meanwhile was pending in the Commons and, Whigs and Protectionists combining against it, Peel was undone.

I heard his farewell speech upon his resignation. It fully verified old Eldon's prophecy, ' The time will come when Mr. Peel will place himself at the head of the democracy of England '—although the last part of the prophecy I hope will be falsified—' and overthrow the Church.'

Lord John Russell was now certainly to form an administration. Lord Bessborough, who was going Lord Lieutenant to Ireland, having expressed a clear opinion that the Irish Chancellor should be taken from the English bar, and having always stood strenuously by me, I expected that, notwithstanding what had passed in the preceding month of November, my former office would be restored to me.[1] But

[1] The following is Lord Bessborough's letter:—

' Bessborough: December 23, 1846.

' My dear Campbell,—As far as my own opinion goes, I have always thought that the Chancellor of Ireland should be an English lawyer, and have expressed that opinion both to Lord Grey and to Lord Melbourne. On your appointment I communicated with O'Connell, and he entirely approved; but he is so capricious a person, and depends so much on the impulse of the moment, that I don't know what he may say at present. I should, however, persevere in my own opinion, that for very many reasons an English lawyer should preside in Ireland. I have never found a

Lord John stated to me that from the representations made to him from Ireland the necessity for giving the Great Seal to an Irishman continued; that he had been strongly urged to appoint an Irishman likewise to be Chief Secretary; that this arrangement he thought inadmissible, but that the public good required him to sacrifice private feeling with respect to the Great Seal. He therefore offered me the Duchy of Lancaster, which, as he observed, had been held by Dunning,'—with a seat in the Cabinet.

In point of profit I was a great loser by the substitution, but I was in a more dignified as well as a more agreeable situation.

I was glad likewise to think that I should be able to finish my ' Lives of the Chancellors.' Having published a second edition of 2,000 of the first series, I was vigorously employed on the second series, from the Revolution in 1688 to the death of Lord Thurlow in 1806. This must have been suspended, and, in the intervals of leisure snatched from an office having such heavy political as well as judicial duties belonging to it, the third series never could have been begun.

The transfer of the ministerial offices took place at Buckingham Palace on the 6th of July. I ought to have been satisfied, for I received *two* seals—one for the Duchy of Lancaster, and one for the County Palatine of Lancaster. My ignorance of the double honour which awaited me caused an awkward accident; for when the Queen put two velvet bags into my hand, I grasped one only, and the other with its heavy weight fell down on the floor and might have bruised the Royal toes, but Prince Albert good-naturedly picked it up and restored it to me.

The same day I was invited to a grand entertainment

difference of opinion, except from interested persons, that great improvements have been made in the Irish Courts since Sugden was there, and there are so many yet to be made that I should be very sorry to see an Irishman, with Irish ideas of justice, equity, property, lunacy, and many other things, however excellent a person he may be (and there are many such), appointed to that situation. Believe me, faithfully yours,

' BESSBOROUGH.'

² John Dunning, Lord Ashburton, was Chancellor of the Duchy of Lancaster in Lord Rockingham's Administration, A.D. 1782.—ED.

given by the benchers of the Inner Temple. After the rising of the House of Lords, Lyndhurst, who had just surrendered the Great Seal, Brougham and I went there together in Lyndhurst's carriage. We had a very jolly evening. It had been agreed that there should be no speaking, but poor Charley Wetherell was there (being the last time he ever appeared in public, for he was killed by an accident shortly after), and we could not resist the temptation of forcing him up. He was richer than I had ever known him at the bar or in the House of Commons. He repeatedly called me his 'noble and biographical friend,' and warned me how I was to write the lives of Lyndhurst and Brougham, he courteously but most grotesquely pointing out their supposed good qualities. They were obliged to speak in reply, and both of them performed exceedingly well. When it came to me, I expressed a wish that Wetherell might still live to be Chancellor, in which case he would eclipse the fame of the most distinguished of his predecessors, and if I should have the misfortune to survive him I might have the melancholy consolation of celebrating his genius and his virtues.[3]

During the revelry above described we little thought that an old and valued friend with whom we had often jested and laughed was actually in the last agony. I heard of Tindal's death next morning.

When going to see Lord John Russell on business connected with the Duchy, his private secretary put into my hand a letter from him to me, excusing his not appointing me to the vacant office of Chief Justice of the Common Pleas, and announcing that it was to be given to Serjeant Wilde. I could not complain of this as a grievance, for I had made no condition about judicial promotion. He mentioned to me a *dictum* of Sir Edward Coke, that 'the cushion of the Common Pleas belongs to the Attorney-General to repose upon,' and said that an arrangement would be made with the new law officers whereby, if a vacancy should occur in the office of Chief Justice of the Queen's Bench, and my appointment should be deemed advisable, it might take place.

---

[3] He had resigned the office of Attorney-General in 1829 rather than agree to the Roman Catholic Emancipation Bill.—ED.

CHAPTER XXVII.

The New Cabinet—Comparison of Lord Grey, Lord Melbourne, and Lord John Russell as Prime Ministers—Lord Cottenham—Lord Lansdowne—Lord Palmerston—Lord Grey—Sir George Grey—Sir Charles Wood — Lord Auckland — Labouchere — Lord Morpeth—Macaulay — Lord Clarendon—First Questions before the Cabinet—Prorogation—First Summer at Hartrigge—Meetings of the Cabinet in October and November—Publication of the Second Series of the ' Lives of the Chancellors '—Christmas in Scotland—Hudson, the Railway King—Session of 1847—The Queen pricking a Sheriff—New Councillors of the Duchy of Lancaster—Lord Stanley's Opposition—Dinner to him and the Councillors—Dinner at Buckingham Palace—The New House of Lords—Meeting with Miss Strickland—Dissolution of Parliament —Cambridge Election—Last Series of the ' Lives of the Chancellors ' printed—Vacation in Scotland—Cabinets in October—Visit to Lord Melbourne at Brocket—Proposal to suspend the Bank Act—End of Autobiography.

Autobiography.

My narrative might now be expected to become much more interesting, but I am afraid that disappointment will follow. In my opinion it would be highly unjustifiable at any period, however distant, to publish to the world all that passes in a Cabinet. Under the apprehension of such a disclosure, the members would not freely and boldly do their duty. But when times and characters have become historical, there are deliberations of the Cabinet which may fairly be made matter of history, and which those who took part in them would not wish to be concealed. A few such deliberations I shall introduce as occasion arises, trusting to the discretion of those who are to come after me that no improper use will ever be made of any of my statements.

I begin with a slight sketch from nature of the members of our Cabinet, not aiming at anything like regular or artistic

CHAP. XXVII.
A.D. 1846.

portraits, but trying to bring out a likeness by a few hasty strokes ;—and first for Lord John. He is the third Premier under whom I have served. First came the high-mannered and high-minded, but somewhat stiff and stately Grey. It was pleasant enough to communicate with him on business, for he had a clear understanding, he was desirous of being instructed, and he could easily be made to comprehend any question of municipal or international law on which the measures of government might depend. But I could soon discover that he had the old Whig love of prosecuting for libel, and the old Whig dislike of any liberal concession to the Irish. His Reform Bill ought to place him in a temple of British worthies by the side of Lord Somers, for it wisely remodelled the Constitution, and it is hardly less important than the Bill of Rights.

Of all the public men I have ever known, Lord Melbourne was approached with the greatest pleasure and satisfaction. He cannot be said to have speedily put people at their ease, which indicates to a certain degree a protecting, patronising, condescending tone. From the first instant of meeting, all who came into his presence felt themselves on a footing of perfect equality with him. The impression made by his elegant figure and handsome countenance was every moment confirmed by his manners. He seemed to have no reserves, and to make everyone his confidant. Yet without any duplicity or deceit he was exceedingly prudent, and to those only whom he knew that he could perfectly trust did he say anything that he wished not to be repeated. Then he had singular rectitude of judgment and much vigour in cases of emergency, his courage always rising with the danger. Although by no means a finished rhetorician, he spoke very impressively, and, when properly roused, he could make Brougham and Lyndhurst quail. His great defect was that he had no fixed system of policy. In his heart he was inclined to Conservatism. He was negligent in superintending the general affairs of the State, leaving everything to the heads of departments, and in conducting the government business in the House of Lords he sometimes showed the most unaccountable apathy, quietly submitting to defeat when he might at all events have made a glorious resistance. Imitating the gods of Epicurus, he was contented with indolence and luxury, and cared little about the active exercise of power.

How different in all respects is Lord John! His thin, diminutive figure and shrivelled countenance so much astonished the people of the West of England when he went among them after passing the Reform Bill, that Sydney Smith was obliged to say to them, 'Oh, if you had but seen him a twelvemonth ago! Now he is worn down to a threadpaper by working in the cause of the people.' What is worse, his manners are cold, and he not only takes no pains to please, but, by neglect of the courtesy which good breeding as well as policy would require, he sometimes has an air of *hauteur* and superciliousness which, although quite foreign to his nature, gives cause of offence. But in truth he is a very amiable as well as a very great man. His benevolent and intellectual smile indicates the high qualities of which he is possessed. Not only is he most exemplary in all the relations of domestic life, but he is warm and steady in his friendships, and he not only breaks no promise, but disappoints no reasonable expectation of favour. His talents are of a high, although I cannot say of the highest, order. In authorship he did not gain much distinction. His prose works, though neat and clear, are wanting in energy: 'Don Carlos,' his only poetical effort of which I am aware, is flat and frigid. Serjeant Talfourd used to say that Lord John opposed the Bill for prolonging the period of copyright because his own writings had already fallen into oblivion.[1] Nor can I celebrate him as a first-rate orator. His information is copious, his reasoning is sound, and his sentiments are noble, but he is wanting in rapidity of thought and of utterance. His vehemence does not rouse, nor can he excite sympathy by any touch of tenderness. I would much sooner read his speeches than hear them. Yet he is listened to in the House of Commons with uniform respect, and he often elicits the loud cheers of his party. They feel that there is no one nearly so well qualified to be their leader. It was perhaps lucky for them

---

[1] The best specimen of his composition is his Preface to the *Letters of John Duke of Bedford*.

that Lord Stanley became a Tory, for he would perpetually have got them into difficulties. Lord John to great boldness adds consummate discretion.[2] The effect of his talents is enhanced by his noble birth, but still more by the honesty of his character and the uniform consistency of his career. Lord Grey's aristocratic tendencies had led him to combine with the Duke of Wellington against the Liberal Administration of Canning; and Lord Melbourne was a sudden convert from the Conservatives. Lord John has ever acted as a sound constitutional Whig—attached to limited monarchy as the form of government best calculated for rational liberty, and never forgetting that the end of all government is the good of the people. He has had the felicity to bring forward in the House of Commons the great measures which have rendered the system of civil and religious liberty in this country as nearly approaching to perfection as is compatible with human institu tions,—the repeal of the Test Act, the Reform Bill, the Municipal Corporations Bill, and the Bills respecting marriage and the registration of births and deaths which have left the Dissenters without the shadow of a grievance. He has always risen with the occasion, and now very worthily fills the office of Prime Minister. His deportment to the Queen is most respectful, but he always remembers that as *she* can do no wrong, *he* is responsible for all the measures of her government. He is enough at Court to show that he enjoys the constitutional confidence of the Sovereign, without being domiciled there as a *favourite*. He is indefatigable in business, and without any vexatious interference is aware of what is going on in every department. Although acting, as he ought, upon his own judgment with respect to the great measures of his Administration, he is always ready to listen to his colleagues, and to give due weight to their suggestions. As far as *they* are concerned, his manners, instead of being repulsive, are rather winning. Upon the whole, I am highly contented to serve under such a chief.

I must next take in hand my noble and learned friend

---

[2] *September* 1860.—I will not alter this, but I cannot now by any means concur in it. He has since 1850 on several critical occasions acted most rashly and indiscreetly.

Lord Cottenham. He is a most excellent Equity judge, but not a great jurist, being not at all familiar with the Roman Civil Law, and being profoundly ignorant of the codes of all foreign nations. Even of Equity he knows little before the time of Lord Nottingham, and his skill in deciding cases arises from a very vigorous understanding, unwearied industry in professional plodding, and a complete mastery over all the existing practice and all the existing doctrines of the Court of Chancery. He considers the system which he has to administer as the perfection of human wisdom. Phlegmatic in everything else, here he shows a considerable degree of enthusiasm. In seeking to extend the jurisdiction of the Court of Chancery, he reminds me of Hildebrand and the other Popes who subjected Europe to the tyranny of the See of Rome. In the Cabinet he is silent unless some point of law is expressly put to him. Nevertheless he is a great credit to the Government from the satisfaction he gives as a magistrate, and he is personally much more acceptable to the Minister than if his accomplishments were more varied and his powers were more brilliant.

Next in rank is our President of the Council. Lord Lansdowne has risen considerably in my estimation since he has been the Government leader in the House of Lords. I used to consider him only a maker of frothy sentences. I must still admit that he is too uniformly magniloquent, and that he never says anything very new or memorable; but he displays considerable energy as well as discretion in managing the Peers, and his loss would be severely felt by our party. He continues a very *moderate* Whig, as when he was induced to hold office under Canning and Lord Goderich, but he is not at all obstinate in Council, and he very sincerely and earnestly tries to carry through measures which he does not entirely relish. He is by far the most experienced among us, having been a Cabinet Minister in four reigns—in 1806 under George III., in 1827 under George IV., in 1830 under William IV., and again in 1841 under Queen Victoria. On questions of precedent and etiquette he is supreme. I ought likewise to mention the credit he brings to the party by presiding in Lansdowne House. Political characters of all hues are received there, as well as literary and scientific men of our country, and all distinguished foreigners; but still it is a Whig establishment, and I have heard Tories bitterly lament that they have nothing to countervail it.

The chief prop of our Administration I take to be Palmerston, the Foreign Secretary. I have the highest opinion of his talents and of his services. Instead of being warlike, I am persuaded that continued peace in Europe is very much to be attributed to him. But for him the French would have committed some insolent outrage which would have rendered submission and accommodation impossible. He is a very useful member of the Cabinet, showing great promptitude and tact as often as he expresses an opinion. In the House of Commons he is a powerful and dexterous debater. But he labours under the misfortune of having belonged to various Tory administrations; and although since 1830 he has been an unflinching Liberal, ready to go still further than John Russell, doubts arise as to his principles, and if he were to try for the Premiership he would find a great obstacle in the suspicion that he is more able than steady.

I should not be at all surprised if his enemy, Lord Grey, were yet to turn out a very eminent statesman, and to add new lustre to the name he bears. He is intrepid, vigorous, disinterested, and sincere. He certainly *was* very ill-tempered and wrong-headed. I had myself several unavoidable quarrels with him in the House of Commons when he was Under Secretary of State and I was Attorney-General. Since July 1846 I must say that he has conducted himself in the Cabinet with uniform moderation and courtesy. He has occasionally expressed his own opinion with vivacity, but without giving just cause of offence, and without offending anyone.

His cousin Sir George, the Home Secretary, is a man of fine intellect, and from a boy has been well-tempered and unassuming. I knew him well when he was at the Bar, and I augured favourably of his progress. I thought he acted very imprudently in renouncing his profession for the office of Judge Advocate, and so thought he between 1841 and

1846, when the Whigs were in a state of banishment *sine spe redeundi*. During this dreary interval his practice in the Court of Chancery might have brought him in many thousands a year. At present I suppose he is pleased with his destiny, but it is still doubtfu whether he was wise in preferring politics to law. He is a most agreeable colleague and a very efficient member of the Administration. I believe he does the business of the office very satisfactorily, and in the House of Commons he is not only a lively debater but generally loved and respected.

I will finish off the Grey section of the Cabinet by taking Charles Wood, our Chancellor of the Exchequer. He is an excellent fellow and I have a great regard for him. He has considerable acuteness and grasp of intellect, and is pretty well versed in his own *métier* of finance. I believe that he has done exceedingly well since he came into his present office, although he has had difficulties of unexampled magnitude to deal with. He fought the Irish famine; the recent and, I am sorry to say, still existing monetary crisis [3] has tried him more severely. He has gone through it with courage, and I believe that more could not have been done to alleviate mercantile distress. His *brusquerie* of manner, which we do not at all mind in the Cabinet, has unintentionally offended various deputations who had waited upon him, but I know no one of our party who could fill the office better.

Of Lord Auckland, the First Lord of the Admiralty, I am disposed to say everything that is kind, for there hardly ever was a man so earnestly and devotedly anxious to do his duty. He toils day and night throughout the year, he has an excellent head for business, and I believe that his department is exceedingly well conducted, but if I were forming an administration, I am afraid I should not name him for a high political office. Although, like his father, he would have done well for diplomacy, he is of no use in Parliament, and not only cannot he take a part in general debate, but he cannot on any provocation put two sentences decently together when questioned respecting his own official conduct. I must add that I cannot forget the disasters

[3] October 28, 1847.

of Afghanistan. His invasion of that country was clearly
impolitic, and the armies which perished there might have
been saved by the forecast of a Governor-General. I am
not sure whether I would not sooner employ Ellenborough.
In the hour of danger, if the plans of the latter were not
the wiser ones, he would inspire more spirit into those employed to carry them into effect.

What shall I say of the meek Labouchere? How pleased
he must be again to find himself safely moored in his old
berth of the Board of Trade. He was found singularly unfit
to enter into a contest with Irish Repealers, Irish priests, and
Irishmen of all descriptions, who were sure to bully and deceive him. His appointment as Chief Secretary in Ireland
was the least felicitous which Lord John made. But he will
now do very well. He is familiarly acquainted with commercial affairs, he is a very pretty speaker, and he is such a perfect gentleman that in the House of Commons he is heard
with peculiar favour.

I am sorry that Lord Morpeth, our First Commissioner of
Woods and Forests, one of the most amiable and excellent of
men, has rather gone down in the world lately. He had a
brilliant reputation at the conclusion of Lord Melbourne's
Government, and I remember the Duke of Sussex prophe-
sying to me that Morpeth would one day be Prime Minister.
Losing his election for the West Riding of Yorkshire in
1841, he was too long out of Parliament. His travels in
the United States of America rather cooled his zeal in the
popular cause. But he has been most damaged by his
sanitary measures, which he brought forward with pomp, and
was obliged with disgrace to abandon. He may rally again, but
I would not give much for his chance of the Premiership.

I pass over Lord Minto, Lord Privy Seal; Sir John Hobhouse, Head of the India Board; Lord Clanricarde, Postmaster
General, and come to Macaulay, our Paymaster General. He
will have a far greater name with posterity than any other
public man of the present generation. I cannot say that he displays much tact in debate, and he could not well manage such
a noisy popular assembly as the House of Commons. Nevertheless he is an infinitely more agreeable speaker to listen to

than Lord John Russell or Sir Robert Peel, and, when nothing is remembered of them except that they were engaged in party squabbles, everything that they ever wrote or said being forgotten, his 'Essays' and his 'Lays' will continue to be read and admired. If his forthcoming 'History of England' should answer public expectation, it will raise him still higher above vulgar politicians, although they may have governed empires. He likewise is now out of Parliament, my old Edinburgh constituents having eternally disgraced themselves by rejecting him on the plea that he is not civil to them. Tom's manners I cannot defend. To him it is a matter of utter indifference who the company may be,—ladies, bishops, lawyers, officers of the army, princes of the blood, or distinguished foreigners, whom the guests are invited to meet,— off he goes at score with hardly a gleam of silence, without any adaptation to his auditory of the topics he discusses, and without any remorse or any consciousness of his having acted at all improperly when they have left him in disgust. But such defects are a very poor palliation of the misconduct of the citizens of Edinburgh (calling themselves 'Athenians') for rejecting a man who conferred such high honour upon them by being their representative. I hope most earnestly for the sake of our party that Macaulay will be speedily restored to the House of Commons, as he is a great credit to us, and in a weighty debate a set speech from him, if it does smell too much of the lamp, is of essential service. For his own sake I doubt whether it would not be better that he should retire from politics and devote himself to literature. He will never be celebrated as a practical statesman, and I do not know that he is likely to advance much higher his reputation as an orator, while his political occupations not only waste his time but divert his thoughts from higher objects.[4]

[4] *September* 25, 1857.—I think the result shows that I had taken a just estimate of the character of Macaulay. It was a lucky thing for him that he lost his seat in Parliament and was obliged to resign his office. By devoting himself in retirement to his History, he has acquired a greater name than if he had been a successful Prime Minister. But I highly approve of his acceptance of a peerage, for this will not interfere with his literary pursuits; and by occasional speeches in the House of Lords, when

I have now only Lord Clarendon, although last not least—indeed the fittest man of our party, after John Russell, to be Prime Minister, and not unlikely to be his successor. He had the unspeakable advantage of being, till he succeeded to the earldom, plain George Villiers, and having to fight his way in the world. He was exceedingly well pleased to accept the office of Commissioner of Excise in Ireland, the country which he is now governing with such lustre as Viceroy. Having been transferred to Spain as our Ambassador, he gave earnest of those talents for public life which will place him in the first rank of English politicians. His manners are perfect, being simple, dignified and engaging. He has great acuteness and comprehensiveness of view and he is intimately acquainted with political science. Never having been a member of the House of Commons, he is not a bold and ready debater ; but he speaks in a gentlemanlike, scholarlike and statesmanlike strain, and when he is roused he is eloquent. At the formation of the present Government he was placed in a post which he did not like, at the head of the Board of Trade, and he did not take kindly to railways and tariffs. For a time he relished his present situation as Lord Lieutenant still less, and he only accepted it from a sense of what every citizen owes to the State. He is now reconciled to it. In the midst of difficulties and dangers he is performing its duties most admirably, and he will save Ireland if Ireland can be saved.

I must now come back to our Cabinet deliberations in July 1846, at the formation of the Government. The first question was whether we should agree to Lord Powis's Bill about the bishoprics of Bangor and St. Asaph. . . . The determination was mildly to oppose the Bill, though we should be beaten in the Lords, and not to let it pass the Commons, but to intimate privately that some satisfactory

inclined to come forward again as an orator, he may add to his fame, and be of service to his country.

September 1860.—Alas ! without his having once spoken in the House of Lords, in December last I was a pall-bearer in his funeral procession to Poets' Corner. He once came down fully prepared to make a great speech on Education in India in opposition to Lord Ellenborough, who, afraid of him, withdrew the motion and never renewed it.

arrangement to preserve both bishoprics would be made
before another session of Parliament. This was wise policy,
for we have had the bishops with us, and nothing has been
done to please them of which the Dissenters can have the
slightest cause to complain.

Next came the consideration of an admirable measure
(almost as important as the abolition of the Corn Laws), the
importation of foreign sugar at a reduced duty, without
attempting to keep up the delusive distinction between
slave-grown and free-grown. It was said that we were to be
ejected upon this, and many of our friends out of doors
advised that it should be postponed for another year, when
the Government might be expected to be stronger. Peel, in
his farewell speech, by some ambiguous words had reserved
to himself the power of opposing such a modification of the
sugar duties, and it was said he would now league with the
Protectionists to defeat it. However, the members of the
Cabinet were unanimous for immediately bringing it forward,
as, if we could not encounter such a peril, the sooner we met
our end the better. Peel behaved handsomely, and we had
a large majority also in the House of Peers, notwithstanding
the violent opposition of Lord Brougham, Lord Denman and
the Bishop of Oxford.

The only other important point then decided was whether
Parliament, which had sat only five years, should be immediately dissolved, or should be allowed to sit another
session. Some were of opinion that, as we really were in a
minority in the House of Commons, it would be impossible
to get through another session without a dissolution, and
that we should forthwith take the chance of gaining a
majority, the Government being at present more popular
than it was likely to be a twelvemonth hence. Lord John
alluded to a sentiment of Peel's in his late valedictory
harangue, 'that it was highly improper to dissolve Parliament with a view to strengthen a party' (which, by the bye,
Peel himself did in the winter 1834–5), adding that the
Queen had applauded this sentiment, and that, although
she might probably be induced to agree to a dissolution
if pressed, it would be better to go on with the present

Parliament, there being no certainty that we should by instantly dissolving gain a majority. The dissolution was therefore wisely negatived, although we were not insensible of the inconveniences necessarily to be experienced in a session which must be the last of a Parliament.

I had the honour to act as one of the five Lords Commissioners representing her Majesty to prorogue the two Houses, and to express her Majesty's satisfaction in giving the Royal assent to the Bills for facilitating the importation of corn *and sugar*. We had then leave of absence till the 20th of October, when the Cabinet was to reassemble.

I followed my family to Hartrigge, in Roxburghshire, an estate which I had lately purchased, and which, with God's blessing, I hope my descendants may long possess. It is situate in a beautiful country, near the junction of the Jed with the Teviot; it is finely timbered, and it has in it several most romantic glens. The architecture of the house I cannot commend, but from its windows you see the venerable ruins of the ancient abbey of Jedburgh, a great expanse of orchards and cornfields, and the range of the lofty hills running into Liddesdale which form the boundary between England and Scotland. By walking to an eminence on the estate not two miles off, I can see the Eildon Hills and the Lammermuirs on the one side, and the range of the Cheviots on the other, with the whole course of the Teviot till it falls into the Tweed at Kelso.

The house, garden, and pleasure grounds were in a sad state of neglect, the former laird having been in embarrassed circumstances, and having let them to a succession of bad tenants. I began with some zeal to repair and improve. I am a decided lover of London life, admiring the saying of the old Duke of Queensberry, who still sticking to his house in Piccadilly in the month of September, and being asked whether the town was not now rather empty, replied, 'Yes, but the country is much emptier.' Nevertheless I am by no means insensible to the beauties of nature, and although I could not write a treatise *De Utilitate Stercorandi*, and most of the rural occupations enumerated by Cicero in his *De Senectute* are much above me, I have great delight in gardening. I have even a little farm in my own hands, and my heart swells within me when my turnips are praised as the most luxuriant, and my *stooks* are declared to be the most crowded to be seen in Teviotdale.

My great pleasure from the place however is in observing how it pleases my wife and children. They were delighted with it at first sight, and they have constantly become more and more attached to it. What a spectacle for me when the little girls cantered in the park on their ponies, or scrambled like goats along the steep banks of the Tower Burn! Then I had such walks with Mylady, and such rides with my two eldest daughters. Fred is not yet inoculated with the love of rural sports; but Hally and Dudley think that shooting and fishing are the only objects worth living for. I had likewise the satisfaction of receiving under my roof my brother and my sisters, who were proud in seeing me become a Scotch laird, and rejoiced to view the spot where they hope that the Lords Stratheden and Campbell may long be settled. I myself took particular interest in examining the cemetery in the ancient abbey of Jedburgh where our mortal remains are to repose.[5]

I was summoned to attend a meeting of the Cabinet on the 20th of October, and I went to London, leaving my wife and children behind me at Hartrigge. The defective harvest in England, and the failure of the potato crop in Ireland, had caused great alarm, but as yet the full amount of impending calamity was by no means ascertained or dreaded.

Lord John Russell has been severely blamed for not having immediately made an Order in Council to open the ports for the introduction of corn *duty free.* He actually proposed this measure, but was overruled, his colleagues being almost unanimously against him. In our then state of knowledge, I still think we were right not to tamper with the law as it had been recently settled, particularly as an Order in Council of this nature would have induced a necessity

---

[5] *September* 27; 1857.—I have now rebuilt and refurnished the house and reformed the pleasure-grounds at an expense of near 10,000*l.*; but the money is well spent, as it has been the cause of so much amusement and pleasure to the family.

for the immediate meeting of Parliament, which, on account
of the state of Ireland, was universally deprecated. The course
we adopted was applauded, till the accounts of Irish destitution became daily more appalling.

We employed ourselves in considering the Bills which
were to be brought forward at the meeting of Parliament,
and committees of the Cabinet were appointed to prepare
them. Cabinet dinners were given once a week, and we
were still in good spirits, hoping that the scarcity of this
winter would not be more severe than that of the preceding.

My second series of the 'Lives of the Chancellors' was
now published, 'from the Revolution in 1688 till the death
of Lord Thurlow.' Its success was not at all inferior to that
of the first. I printed 3,000 copies, and 2,050 were sold the
first day. To lessen my vanity I was told that at the same
time 3,000 copies were sold of a new cookery book, and 5,000
of a new knitting book. These, however, cost only half-a-
crown, while my two volumes cost thirty shillings.

After bringing out a second edition of my first series, I
had worked very hard at the second, and had been furnished
with most valuable new materials, particularly for Lord
Cowper, Lord Camden, Charles Yorke, and Lord Thurlow.
I took most pains with Lord Somers, but my life of
Thurlow was the most popular, and it was pronounced
to be as good reading as Boswell's 'Life of Johnson.'
Higher praise could not be bestowed. I was most pleased
with the praise bestowed upon this series, in all com-
panies, by Lord Melbourne, which was too warm for me to
repeat.

At Christmas I went down to Scotland and, crossing the
Cheviots, was nearly lost in a snow-storm. After spending a
fortnight most agreeably at Hartrigge, I brought my family
to London. At York I had the honour to be presented to
Hudson, the Railway King. There is nothing so disgraceful
to the present age as the manner in which this vulgar dog
is flattered by all ranks. His elevation has greatly contributed to the gambling mania from which we are now
suffering, and nothing would so much tend to reconcile men

to the sober pursuits of industry as if he were to appear in the 'Gazette' as a bankrupt.[6]

The session of 1847 for me was very dull, and I often wished that I were again on the Opposition side, sparring with 'my noble and learned friend' Lord Brougham.

Letter to Sir George Campbell.

Stratheden House: Saturday, February 6, 1847.

My dear Brother, . . . I now lead a quiet and a rather dull life. My chief business is to act as a Lord Commissioner in giving the Royal assent to Bills and making three bows to the Speaker of the House of Commons when he enters and withdraws.

On Thursday, indeed, I went to Windsor and shook hands with Prince Albert, the Prince of Wales, and their Royal Highnesses the Princess Royal and the Princess Alice. By the bye, there was rather an amusing scene in the Queen's closet. I had an audience that her Majesty might prick a sheriff for the county of Lancaster, which she did in proper style with the bodkin I put into her hand. I then took her pleasure about some Duchy livings and withdrew—forgetting to make her sign the parchment roll. I obtained a second audience and explained the mistake. While she was signing, Prince Albert said to me: 'Pray, my Lord, when did this ceremony of pricking begin?' *Campbell.* 'In ancient times, Sir, when sovereigns did not know how to write their names.' *Queen* (as she returned me the roll with her signature). 'But we now show that we have been to school.'

---

[6] *September* 30, 1849.—When this was written his Majesty the Railway King was in the zenith of his power and splendour, and was really a man of more note and consequence than any duke in England, except the Duke of Wellington. I travelled in the same carriage with him from York to London, and found his head quite turned by the flattery administered to him. Amongst other things he said to me: 'The old nobility, sir, are all paupers. What a sad state my neighbours at Castle Howard are in. I am going to-morrow to Clumber, where a large party of nobles is invited to meet me, but I could buy them all.' My wish is now realised. The Railway King is dethroned like Louis Philippe and other crowned heads, and he is more to be pitied than any of them. I blame chiefly those who worshipped him, and now spit upon their idol.

Autobiography.

I had now to parry an attack made by Lord Stanley respecting the new Council for the Duchy of Lancaster. With a view to the better management of the revenues of the Duchy, John Russell had, rather indiscreetly, agreed to a proposal, that some new Councillors should be appointed, without any view to party, who should continue permanently to serve. There was no constitutional objection, and I agreed. Accordingly, Lord Lincoln, Lord Hardwicke, Lord Spencer, Lord Portman, and Sir James Graham were sworn in. I made out a tolerably good case, rather treating the matter with levity. Brougham of course supported Stanley, but the discussion went off very well for me.

Letters to Sir George Campbell.

House of Lords: March 2, 1847.

My dear Brother, . . . The Duchy of Lancaster affair went off on Friday evening with good humour. When it was over, I stepped across the House and invited Stanley to dine with me on the 13th, to meet the Councillors, new and old—and he readily agreed. The party will be a very miscellaneous and whimsical one. Brougham, Lyndhurst, and John Russell are to assist. So we shall have all the parties in the State represented—Lord Lincoln and Sir James Graham having the Peelites for their constituents.

Stratheden House: Tuesday night, March 9.

. . . This day I have been to Osborne attending a Council. Had it not been so bitterly cold I should have enjoyed it. I had a private audience of her Majesty, and when my business was over she said, 'How you were attacked in the House of Lords the other night, Lord Campbell—most abominably.' I gave a courtierlike answer, without telling her Majesty of the dinner I am to give on Saturday to Lord Stanley and Lord Brougham, for she was excessively angry with them; and she would not understand the levity with which such matters are treated among politicians of opposite parties.

Stratheden House : March 14, 1847.

. . . I would willingly give you an account of my Duchy dinner; but, though it went off well, it was too noisy and riotous to allow much to be said of the intellectual part of it. Besides myself and Lord Stanley there were present—Lord John Russell, Prime Minister; Lord Lyndhurst and Lord Brougham, ex-Chancellors of Great Britain ; Earl of Lincoln, Earl of Hardwicke, and Sir James Graham, Councillors of the Duchy; Mr. Twiss, Vice-Chancellor of the Duchy; General Fox, Receiver-General of the Duchy ; Mr. Lockhart, Auditor of the Duchy; Mr. Danvers, Clerk of the Council; Earl Granville, Lessee of the Duchy; and Earl of Clarendon, ex-Chancellor of the Duchy.

I doubt whether I can recollect any of the conversation. Brougham and Lyndhurst came together, and were the first. They were very hot upon a controversy I have got into with Lord Grey, on the question whether his father joined the Tories in opposing Canning in 1827, and they strongly supported me. There was no awkwardness even before dinner, although several of those present, having been *associated*, had been *dissociated* pretty considerably. Brougham shook hands with the Premier, and called him ' John.' Stanley said to Sir James Graham, ' Graham, how are you?' We kept up the old fashion, and all drank wine with each other. Lord Lincoln, as a duke's eldest son, was on my right hand, Brougham on my left, and we kept up good-humoured badinage during the evening. I first attacked Brougham about his ' *chasse* ' in his forest at Cannes, of which there had been an account in the ' Times ' as well as in ' Punch.' He related a supposed speech of Sir Charles Wetherell, complaining that death is now attended with a fresh terror from Campbell writing the life of the deceased as soon as the breath was out of his body. We then considered what his biographer would say of him. He declared that he had much improved in oratory since he came into the House of Lords. *Lyndhurst.* ' Then you don't agree in the general opinion that Henry Brougham was a greater man than Lord Brougham.' *Brougham.* ' Most decidedly not.' *Campbell.* ' I am afraid this is like Milton, preferring

'Paradise Regained' to 'Paradise Lost.' . . . Lord Hardwicke said he was sending a portrait of his ancestor to
Lincoln's Inn. *Campbell.* 'And I hope another to Stratheden House, for I wish it to be known that I expect portraits
of all the Chancellors whose lives I have written from their
representatives—and there you behold Fortescue and Nottingham.' I called upon Hardwicke to explain to Stanley
the functions of his new office, but he could only say: ' In
certior multò sum quam dudum.' I gave the health of the
' Duchess of Lancaster'—but you must have enough of it, as
nothing very piquant was said. We sat at table till near
eleven. . . . As Lyndhurst was getting into his carriage he
was overheard to say to Lord Brougham, 'I wish we had
such a council as this once a month.'

House of Lords: March 22, 1847.

. . . You will see by the ' Court Circular' that Mary and
Loo and I dined at the Palace on Saturday. The invitation
only came on Friday, and we were engaged to dine with
Sir John Hobhouse. There is not much to tell to gratify
your curiosity. On our arrival, a little before eight, we were
shown into the picture gallery, where the company assembled.
Bowes, who acted as Master of the Ceremonies, arranged
what gentleman should take what lady. He said, ' Dinner
is ordered to be on the table at ten minutes past eight; but
I bet you the Queen will not be here till twenty or twenty-
five minutes after. She always thinks she can dress in
ten minutes, but she takes about double the time.' True
enough, it was nearly twenty-five minutes after eight before
she appeared. She shook hands with the ladies, bowed to
the gentlemen, and proceeded to the *salle à manger.* I
had to take in Lady Emily de Burgh, and was third on her
Majesty's right—Prince Edward of Saxe-Weimar and my
partner being between us.

The greatest delicacy we had was some very nice oat-
cake. There was a Highland piper standing behind her
Majesty's chair, but he did not play as at ' State dinners.'
We had likewise some Edinburgh ale.

The Queen and the ladies withdrawing, Prince Albert

came over to her side of the table, and we remained behind about a quarter of an hour; but we rose within the hour from the time of our sitting down. A snuff-box was twice carried round and offered to all the gentlemen : Prince Albert, to my surprise, took a pinch.

On returning to the gallery we had tea and coffee. The Queen then came up and talked to me. . . . She does the honours of her palace with infinite sweetness and grace—and, considering what she is, both in public and domestic life, I do not think she is sufficiently loved and respected. Prince Albert took me to task for my impatience to get into the new House of Lords, but I think I pacified him, complimenting his taste. A dance followed. The Queen chiefly delighted in a romping sort of country dance called the *Tempête*. She withdrew a little before twelve, and we went to Lady Palmerston's.

Brougham, now sitting by me, has just said, ' That portrait of your father, by Raeburn, is the finest of his works that I have ever seen.' I would not shock him by telling him it is only a *copy*.[7]

Autobiography.

We continued to hold Cabinets once or twice every week, but these chiefly turned upon the Bills pending in Parliament, to which no permanent interest belonged. I may observe that our deliberations were conducted with great cordiality and with entire unanimity at times when it was asserted in the newspapers that there were violent quarrels among us. I never saw any symptom of our being actually divided into sections, and Lord Grey and Lord Palmerston went on together as if they had ever entertained the highest opinion of each other's good temper and discretion.

The greatest *coup* we had was suddenly determining on the ' Protocol ' for putting down the civil war in Portugal. This threatened at first to upset the Administration, but turned out eventually very much to our credit. The con-

[7] The original belonged to Sir George Campbell, and was at Edenwood. An excellent copy hung at Stratheden House.—ED.

test which had begun, if it had been allowed to go on, might have embroiled us with France, and brought on a general war all over Europe.

The death of Lord Bessborough was a heavy blow to us. A most excellent choice was made in his successor. I was extremely sorry to lose Lord Clarendon from the House of Lords and from the Cabinet; but he was likely to do, and he has done, special service to the country in his new capacity as Viceroy of Ireland.

Letters to Sir George Campbell.

House of Lords : Monday, April 26, 1847.

My dear Brother, . . . Our new House [8] is very splendid, and I think will turn out commodious, when the buzz of the crowd of strangers has subsided. There was a pleasant story which amused the town at the opening of the new House. Many bets were laid that Brougham would be the first peer to speak in it. In point of fact he was hurrying down for that purpose when the wheel of his carriage flew off, and he was delayed a quarter of an hour. In the meantime Lord Campbell took advantage of his absence and opened the ball. So far is true. But to improve the humour, it is invented that Lord Campbell, to gain an advantage over Lord Brougham on this great occasion, bribed a man to take out the linch-pin of Lord Brougham's carriage. . . .

Stratheden House : May 16, 1847.

. . . My exploit in the House of Lords last night was introducing myself to Miss Strickland, authoress of the ' Lives of the Queens of England,' who has been writing a violent letter against me in the newspapers. After I had conversed with her for a quarter of an hour she exclaimed, ' Well, Lord Campbell, I do declare you are the most amiable man I ever met with.' I thought Brougham would have died with envy when I told him the result of my interview, and Ellenborough, who was sitting by, rubbed his hands in admiration.

[8] The new House of Lords.—ED.

Brougham had thrown me a note across the table saying, 'Do you know that your friend Miss Strickland is come to hear you?' . . .

Autobiography.

When July approached, our Bills were getting on very slowly, and it was of importance that the dissolution should not be much longer delayed. I had been member of a committee of the Cabinet to superintend the elections with the Secretary to the Treasury, and we all thought there could not be a more favourable time for immediately going to the country. Accordingly the Railway Bill, the Health of Towns Bill, the Irish Encumbered Estates Bill, and divers others were abandoned, the less evil being to be accused of doing nothing than to have an adverse return of members to the House of Commons. It was even suggested that, to expedite the election by a day, the Queen should dissolve the Parliament in person from the throne. I found one precedent for this since the Revolution, in Lord Eldon's time; but I pointed out a better expedient—that the Queen should prorogue as usual, and that, holding a Council immediately after, she should there sign the Proclamation for the dissolution and the calling of a new Parliament, the writs going out by the post the same evening. This course was successfully adopted.

It was some comfort to me that I could not lose my seat in Parliament from the corruption or caprice of constituents, but I was very anxious about one election—for the borough of Cambridge, where my eldest son was a candidate. He had commenced operations there entirely out of his own head, and he conducted them to a prosperous issue, without any assistance from the Government, or from any friends except those which he himself had made upon the spot. On the day of the poll I had constant telegraphic despatches till I knew that he certainly was returned. This was a most joyous event, which reconciled me to any disappointments I might have suffered from.

I remained at Stratheden House for a few weeks to complete the printing of the last series (vols. vi. and vii.) of my

Lives of the Chancellors, coming down to the death of Lord
Eldon in 1838, and comprehending all the English Chancellors who have paid the debt of nature. The printing of
the whole was finished within one year from the day that I
wrote the first line of the life of Lord Loughborough. I had
worked very hard, and I should not have done it better if
I had taken a longer time. What · reception these two
volumes are to have, still remains to be seen, for Mr.
Murray has advised that the publication of them should be
delayed till the month of December. My own opinion is
that they are more interesting than any of their predecessors. The new materials with which I have been
furnished for the life of Loughborough are of great historical importance, and many parts of his career are as extraordinary as if they had been purely fictitious. Erskine's life
was to me a labour of love. His vicissitudes of fortune,
his speeches, his jokes, his virtues, and his follies, blended
together, make (if I mistake not) reading fit for a boarding-
school girl or for a philosopher. Eldon's hypocrisy, his
canting and his bigotry, are brought out in high relief with
the aid of seeming candour and generosity. In writing his
life I received very material assistance from Sir Robert
Peel. He laid before me the whole of their correspondence.
From this I made extracts for insertion, which I submitted
to him for his sanction. The latter part of this life is the
first attempt at a history of George IV. and William IV.
Nevertheless the world may be sick of legal biography,
and my 'Third Series' may fall still-born from the press,
unpraised and uncensured. Mr. Murray has prepared me
for a very slow sale, on account of the badness of the times.
He says that books are the first luxury abandoned; for if a
man puts down his carriage, or leaves off champagne at his
dinners, all the world discovers his poverty; but unobserved
he can borrow a publication he wishes to look at from a
circulating library, or be content with the extracts from it
which he sees in the newspapers.

When I went to Scotland I found myself for the first
time for many years completely *désœuvré*. As yet I have
not suffered for want of an exciting object. I read Thiers'

'Le Consulat et l'Empire;' and, wishing to have, by way of contrast, specimens of what history ought to be, I read a good deal of Livy and Tacitus. Living amid the scenes so graphically portrayed by Walter Scott, I once more went through his 'Lay of the Last Minstrel,' and most of his other Border poems.

I then visited my brother in Fife, and saw with great interest the scenes of my childhood. I was particularly struck with a small footbridge across the Swilkin burn at St. Andrews, which stands exactly as I had left it about half a century ago. I remembered every stone of this little arch as well as I did the ruins of the Cathedral, or St. Regulus's Tower.

I afterwards had a delightful excursion with my wife and two eldest daughters to Loch Katrine and Loch Lomond, after which we returned to Hartrigge. Alas! on Monday the 11th of October I was forced to bid them farewell, for next day at two there was to be a Cabinet in Downing Street. From that day till this present day (the 1st of November), when I am now writing, Ministers have been surrounded by the most appalling difficulties, there being an apprehension that the dividends may not be paid, and that the Bank of England may stop, and that there may be a pecuniary crash, public and private.

[During this interval he accepted an invitation to pay Lord Melbourne a visit at Brocket, of which he gives the following account.—ED.]

Letter to Lady Stratheden and Campbell.

Stratheden House:
Sunday night, October 24, 1847.

My dearest Mary,—You will be surprised to receive this letter from Stratheden House. The mystery is that, as I was stepping into my carriage yesterday at half-past three, a summons was put into my hand requiring me to attend a meeting of the Cabinet on Sunday at three o'clock. This was a damper, for I was in hopes that things would go so smoothly that we might dispense with Cabinets for a long while to come.   As Panizzi[9] was waiting for me at the British Museum, I thought that I was bound to go.   We had a very wet drive, but he rattled away agreeably, and made me forget the Cabinet and all my cares.   We were little more than two hours and a quarter in driving down in a hack chaise.   Alas! Lord Melbourne was confined to his room by a fit of the gout.   We were received by Lord Palmerston and Lord de Mauley, who had arrived a little before us.   Soon after Lady Beauvale came in.   I admire her very much.   She not only speaks English perfectly, but she has a pure English accent, and looks and converses and demeans herself like an Englishwoman.   Lady Palmerston soon followed, still quite juvenile.   She was exceedingly gracious and talked of our rencontre with her daughter Fanny on Loch Lomond.   Lord Palmerston said that the Queen was greatly delighted with the Highlands, in spite. of the bad weather, and that she was accustomed to sally forth for a walk in the midst of a heavy rain, putting a great hood over her bonnet, and showing nothing of her features but her eyes.   The Prince's invariable return to luncheon at two o'clock, in spite of grouse shooting and deer stalking, is explained by his voluntary desire to please the Queen, and by the intense hunger which always assails him at this hour, when he likes in the German fashion to make his dinner.

We then went to dress.   We sat down to dinner at eight. There was no one else except Lord Beauvale, who is very good-natured and entertaining, dealing pretty much in persiflage like Lord Melbourne.

We went to Lord Melbourne's room to take tea and coffee. He was lying on his back on a sofa, but in his mind better than I have seen him for a long while.   He talked of books and men with all his wonted vivacity.   At ten we returned to the drawing-room, and chatted till past twelve, when we retired for the night.

The morning was brilliant and lovely.   At eight I sallied forth to view the grounds, which are exquisitely beautiful. The river Lea flows by the house, and there is a very fine

[9] Sir Antonio Panizzi, Principal Librarian of the British Museum. He died A.D. 1879.—ED.

piece of water made by damming it up, with a grand water-fall. Then the trees are such as we have no notion of in any part of Scotland—oaks under which Queen Elizabeth sat, and all the new shrubs and pines from the Himalaya mountains. I ferried myself across the lake, in a boat which is moored by ingenious machinery. On the other side I met Panizzi, and we rambled about till ten, said to be the hour for break-fast. When we returned there was no one visible; but Lord Palmerston at last appeared, and we three sat down by our-selves. Lady Palmerston followed. Lady Beauvale always breakfasts in her own room.

It was agreed that Palmerston was to take me with him to London, and I was strongly pressed to return with him after the Council, but I declined. We were to start at half-past twelve. Panizzi, Lord de Mauley and I visited the gardens, which are superb. I then paid a short visit to Lord Melbourne, who was very kind to me, and invited me to come to Brocket again soon. He has invited you, and who says that we may not some Saturday run down together?

Palmerston was very conversible on the journey, and we settled together all the affairs of Europe, and discussed the interests and prospects of the Whigs.

As we drove into Downing Street we met Lord John Russell entering the Chancellor of the Exchequer's, where the Council was to be held. Here of course I must stop. I may without breach of privilege tell you however that, after our business was over, I walked home and found two charming letters. . . .

Autobiography.

On Sunday, the 24th of October, I was summoned to attend a Cabinet—there having been no Cabinet on a Sunday for more than ten years. It was then proposed to suspend the restriction on Bank issues created by the Act of 1844. I regretted the concession to public clamour, although it was not for me to express dissent on such a subject. I have since been convinced that Lord John Russell was right on this occasion, for you must regard, in legislation and government, the alarms and the prejudices and the wishes and the fears of mankind—without considering what would be for their advantage if they were always to think and act like reasonable beings. The responsibility of further resistance would have been too great for any shoulders. Peel's Bill is condemned, but I do not believe that the amount of paper circulation can be fixed by any inflexible rule. Convertibility into specie is the grand recipe against over-issue of paper. Private banks, if allowed to issue paper at all, may be limited according to the bullion they possess; but the Bank of England, under the control of the Government, must be allowed to issue paper according to the exigencies of commerce. Its credit may be high while its bullion is low, and when the metallic currency is reduced is not the time for reducing the paper currency also.

To amuse my solitude since I returned to London, I have resumed my Autobiography, and brought it down to the present time, when Parliament is about to assemble and great events may arise.

If anything hereafter occurs to me worth noticing, I shall record it in the form of a journal. My daily actions and thoughts are much too insignificant to interest anyone, however tenderly attached to me; but it is possible that I may still be mixed up with events which may touch my own fortunes, and show the form and pressure of the time.

I finish my Autobiography for the present, Monday, the 1st of November, 1847, at half-past eleven at night.

CHAPTER XXVIII.

NOVEMBER 1847—AUGUST 1849.

Considers of a New Subject for Biography—Meets Sir Edward Sugden at Lincoln's Inn—Question of Marriage with a Deceased Wife's Sister—Measures for Ireland—Cabinet at Lord John Russell's Private House —Publication of vols. vi. and vii. of the 'Chancellors'—Judgment in the Hampden Case—Revolutions on the Continent—Alarm in England —Feargus O'Connor and the Chartists—The Duke of Wellington's Arrangements—The 10th of April—Irish Sedition Bill—Prince of Prussia—Royal Christening—End of the Session of 1848—Threatened Irish Rebellion—Visit to Lord Brougham—State of Political Parties —Peel—Lord George Bentinck—Disraeli—Lord Stanley—During the Vacation writes the Life of Lord Mansfield—Cabinet Council in October—Sittings of the Judicial Committee—Pemberton Leigh—Christmas at Hartrigge—Macaulay's 'History'—Death of Lord Auckland—Negotiation for bringing in Sir James Graham—Opening of the Session of 1849—Journey to Windsor—Correspondence of Lord Melbourne—Joseph Hume—Lord Hardinge—Navigation Bill—Completion of the 'Lives of the Chief Justices'—Passing of the Navigation Bill —Illness of the Lord Chancellor—Parting with his Second Son—End of the Session of 1849—Political Leaders—Illness of Lord Denman—Prorogation of Parliament.

Journal.

Stratheden House : November 8, 1847.

I BEGIN my 'Journal' because I have nothing else to do. I already feel severely the want of my 'Chancellors.'

I had intended to take up the Irish Chancellors ; but although some of them might be made interesting, I am afraid as a body they would appear very dull; and, unless during the struggle for independence in 1782 and the Union in 1800, the public events with which they were connected would not rouse the sympathies of Englishmen. A good deal might be made of Lord Clare ; and if Lord Plunket were dead, his life would be a fine vehicle for the history of Ireland during the last half century. I, therefore do not abandon this subject, but I am inclined first to go on with the 'Lives of the Chief Justices.' As a Common lawyer I owe something to the memory of the sages who have gained distinction in my own department of the profession. Fixing public attention with Lord Chief Justice Tresilian, who was hanged, drawn, and quartered, I think I could make an entertaining and instructive book by a selection of his successors, down to Lord Mansfield, who has as yet received no justice from any biographer.

My ambition, however, is to produce a specimen of just historical composition. I shrink from the task of writing the *annals* of any country. I would not for the world be condemned to notice all memorable public events for a given period of time. An author who professes to do so must either be flimsy like Hume, or tiresome like Henry. I have great doubt whether Macaulay himself can be both faithful and lively. What I should like would be a separate independent subject, like 'Catiline's Conspiracy,' or the 'Wars of the Fronde.' I have thoughts of attempting the 'History of the Long Parliament.' The reign of Charles I. has been recommended to me, but his 'life' would be better, as I could thus give an air of novelty to his times, and I should have a greater choice of the public events which I might wish to interweave with my narrative.

Before I have fixed upon a subject the session of Parliament will have commenced. What a new interest for me in my son, now a member of the House of Commons! If he succeeds I shall be indifferent about everything which personally concerns myself. In the present awful gloom arising from commercial and financial distress, and from the utterly demoralised condition of Ireland, I find some difficulty in supporting my spirits, and preparing to perform the duties which may be cast upon me; but I hope that by God's blessing I may live to see happier times.

November 12.—I went to Lincoln's Inn library to-day to consult some rare books. While there, Sir Edward Sugden, ex-Lord Chancellor of Ireland, came up to me. We shook hands and were very cordial, agreeing to stay and dine together in the hall. He had been examining MSS. for his new

work, 'A Review of the Decisions of the House of Lords on
Questions of Real Property for the last twenty-five Years,' in
which he is cruelly to cut up chancellors and law lords. We
had a very jolly dinner, and, all rivalry being at an end or suspended, we talked to each other without reserve. I thanked
him for not reversing any of my numerous decrees, and I
anticipated my reputation with posterity when it shall be
recorded that no decree of mine ever was reversed, either on
a rehearing by my successor, or on appeal by the House of
Lords. I told him (what he had not heard before) Baron
Alderson's joke—that the collection of his decisions during
his first chancellorship, which was not much longer than
mine, instead of 'Reports *tempore* Sugden,' should be
'Reports *momento* Sugden.' I at last asked him if there
was any truth in the story which O'Connell had told of him
to this effect:—Sir Edward Sugden, holding the Great Seal
of Ireland, as guardian of lunatics was in the habit, very
laudably, of visiting the lunatic asylums in the neighbourhood of Dublin, accompanied by Sir Philip Crampton the
surgeon, who was the official inspector of these places of confinement. It happened that on one occasion Sir Philip forgot
his engagement, and the Lord Chancellor went alone. At the
first asylum to which he drove the keeper knew him, and
he was very respectfully treated; but when he came to the
second they took him for a lunatic who had made his escape,
and were going to lay hold of him, when he exclaimed, 'Do
you know who I am? I am the Lord High Chancellor.'
'We are highly honoured by the presence of your lordship;
we have got a court here for your lordship to preside in, and
I shall have the honour of conducting your lordship to the
bench.' Two underkeepers then seized him, whereupon, he
becoming furious, they put a strait-waistcoat upon him, and
carried him to a cell in which they locked him up. There he
lay till Sir Philip Crampton arrived and asked whether Lord
Chancellor Sugden was there, expressing regret that he had
been prevented from joining his lordship in Dublin at the
appointed hour to accompany him in his round.

Sugden asserted positively that there was no further
foundation for the story than that he and Sir Philip Cramp-

ton had visited the lunatic asylums in the neighbourhood of Dublin together, but that he had always been duly recognised, and that he received civil and respectful treatment whenever he appeared. He said he suspected the hint of the story had been given to O'Connell by Sir Philip Crampton, famous for waggery as well as for surgery.

November 17.—Sat all day in the Court of Queen's Bench, where I had not been, except to take the oaths, since I had left the bar. My object was to hear the question argued, ' Whether it be lawful for a man to marry the sister of his deceased wife,' upon which I had several times in debate in the House of Lords expressed a strong opinion in the negative, with a view of checking an agitation got up in favour of marriages which I believed to be forbidden by law, and which I considered inconsistent with the peace and purity of domestic life. The judges and the bar behaved to me very courteously, and I was gratified by finding my opinion confirmed by the unanimous decision of the court. I rather regretted that I had not continued to practise as an advocate. I make little doubt that I should have retained my business, and I certainly should have led a more stirring as well as a more *profitable* life.

November 22.—There have been frequent Cabinets of late, chiefly on the subject of Ireland. I have strongly combated *coercion,* for which there is a call from all quarters. I preach up a more vigorous exercise of the existing powers of law to prevent, to detect, and to punish crime. Lord John's views are very constitutional and enlightened. But I fear that some new measure must be resorted to in disturbed districts against the conspiracy to commit murder and systematically violate the rights of property. This, I trust, will rather be in the nature of a police measure than a violation of the Constitution. *We* should ask for ' coercion ' with a very bad grace, having come into power upon a division for refusing it to Sir Robert Peel.

December 10.—Lord Cottenham's illness assumes a serious aspect. It is now three weeks since he burst a blood-vessel, and as yet he is confined to his room, is fed on brown bread and ice, and is not allowed to speak to anyone. Several

times there has been a return, though slight, of the effusion
of blood, with inflammatory symptoms, and I have been told
that his medical attendants are doubtful about his recovery.
He has not at all interfered in government matters since his
first seizure.

. . . Our Irish Coercion Bill is very popular; and all
that we have to do is to defend ourselves from the charge of
not making it sufficiently stringent.

I am a member of the Select Committee on the question
of Peel's Bill of 1844—and have attended two meetings;
but, having ordered all manner of returns to give us necessary information, we have adjourned till after the Christmas
recess.

December 11.—Lord John being laid up with the in-
fluenza, we had a Cabinet to-day in his house in Chesham
Place. I may mention, as an illustration of ministerial
manners in the nineteenth century, that when we meet at
the Foreign Office, our usual place of assembling, where
there is a room fitted up for the Cabinet, there are no
salutations of any sort except after the autumn recess; but
that when, on account of the indisposition of a member of
the Cabinet, we assemble at his house, he shakes hands with
each of his colleagues, and they severally hope that he is
better.

December 16.—Yesterday my third series was published
at Murray's trade sale, where 2,200 copies were disposed of.
I had a malicious pleasure in showing Brougham, as we
sat in the Judicial Committee, a note from Murray commu-
nicating the intelligence. He said, people were obliged to
make up their sets, having bought the former volumes.

December 18.—There have been frequent Cabinets respecting measures for Ireland and diplomatic intercourse
with the Pope. Lord John has desired me to take in hand
the Encumbered Estates Bill, which was under the special
superintendence of the Lord Chancellor.

December 21.—I have received very flattering compliments on Loughborough, Erskine and Eldon, and volumes
vi. and vii. promise to be fully as popular as any of their
predecessors. W. E. Surtees, author of 'Sketches of the

Lives of Lords Eldon and Stowell,' and a nephew of Lady Eldon, has written me a letter warmly commending the impartiality with which I have discussed the character and conduct of his kinsman. Critiques on the new volumes appear in all the newspapers—not withholding praise, but generally in a flippant, envious strain. I am not much excited now by puffing or vituperation.

February 1, 1848.—I have been filling up my leisure by revising my first three volumes for a new edition. I began with inserting in the proper places the additional materials and the corrections which had been supplied to me; and then I read through the whole, improving the style here and there by varying a phrase which appeared too frequently, or removing an ambiguity arising from the collocation of relative and antecedent. The question now is, in what shape the third edition is to come out, upon which I must be guided by my publisher.

We have had divers Cabinets to prepare measures for Ireland. There is great reason to rejoice that we did not adopt the advice pressed upon us by our opponents and by some of our friends, to suspend the Habeas Corpus Act there, and to establish courts-martial. Under the special commission in the disturbed districts, jurymen and witnesses are doing their duty most nobly, and, after many convictions, tranquillity is restored and the law is again respected.

I went to-day to the Court of Queen's Bench to hear the judgment in the great case of the mandamus to the Archbishop of Canterbury to receive and decide objections to the orthodoxy of Dr. Hampden. It was a very amusing exhibition, the judges being equally divided, and all differing from one another. Denman deserves great credit for his firmness in refusing the mandamus—which would have upset the Church and endangered the State.

April 12.—Since I last made an entry in my Journal, the face of the world is completely changed, and events have happened to fill many volumes of history. King Louis Philippe is an exile at Claremont, and Guizot, his Prime Minister, is my near neighbour, living with his family in a little lodging at Brompton. There have been revolutions not only in Paris, but at Berlin, Vienna, Munich, Naples, Rome, Turin, Milan, Venice, and various other places 'too numerous to mention.'

A few days ago we had considerable reason to dread that London and Dublin would be added to the number. But, thank Heaven, we now breathe freely, and we may look forward to the continued enjoyment of repose and liberty. For some time past Cabinets have been held almost daily, and we have had most anxious deliberations on the proper line of policy to be adopted, and the proper dispositions to be made.

Letters to Sir George Campbell.

Stratheden House:
Friday night, April 7, 1848.

My dear Brother, . . . The public alarm increases every hour, and many believe that by Monday evening we shall be under a Provisional Government.

'The National Convention,' as the delegates of the Chartists formally style themselves, have sent us a proud defiance, and you will see that Feargus O'Connor has declared that he will head the procession.

Yesterday evening the Duke of Wellington beckoned to me to cross over to him, and he said to me: 'Lord Cammel, we shall be as quiet on Monday as we are at this hour, and it will end to the credit of the Government and the country.' But he was never famous for knowing the state of the public mind.

There is no real danger beyond a riot not to be quelled without bloodshed, but this danger does exist to a serious degree. It is nothing however to what would have existed if 50,000 men had been allowed, in the present state of the public mind and with the views which many of them have, to parade the principal streets of the metropolis and surround the Houses of Parliament.

I hope you will approve of our measure for converting *high treason* into *felony*, punishable by transportation, to catch the Irish 'Confederates.' I am answerable for it.

We are to have another Council to-morrow, but I shall have nothing more to tell you till Monday night.

I suppose we shall all fly to Hartrigge,—if I can escape in disguise !

Stratheden House:
Sunday night, April 9, 1848.

My dear Brother, . . . This may be the last time I write to you before the Republic is established. I have no serious fears of revolution, but there may very likely be bloodshed.

I have had some recompense for my anxiety in a scene I witnessed yesterday. Of this I can give you some notion without disclosing State secrets, but I would not have the matter mentioned by you to anyone. We were considering in the Cabinet how the Chartists should be dealt with, and when it was determined that the procession should be stopped after it had moved, we agreed that the particular place where it should be stopped was purely a military question. The Duke of Wellington was requested to come to us, which he did very readily. We had then a regular Council of War, as upon the eve of a great battle. We examined maps and returns and information of the movements of the enemy. After long deliberation, plans of attack and defence were formed to meet every contingency. The quickness, intelligence, and decision which the Duke displayed were very striking, and he inspired us all with perfect confidence by the dispositions which he prescribed.

There are now above 7,000 regular troops in London, besides a train of artillery. The special constables, as you will see, are countless.

We are most afraid of disturbances after the procession is dispersed, and of the town being set fire to in the night. There are in London a number of foreigners of the most desperate character.

It was not I alone who was struck with the consultation yesterday. Macaulay said to me that he considered it the most interesting spectacle he had ever witnessed, and that he should remember it to his dying day.

. . . The Duke's prophecy uttered on Thursday will turn out to be true. Cottenham and I resolved to meet our fate like the ancient senators of Rome from the barbarians, and we assembled to-day at the usual hour to hear Scotch appeals. Walking from Stratheden House, I found all the gates of Hyde Park closed, and the metropolis in a state of great excitement. We proceeded very calmly to business, although we heard of large bodies marching to Kennington, and that by twelve o'clock there were above 50,000 assembled there.

The Attorney-General told me that the Chartist leaders had been with Sir George Grey early in the morning, offering to abandon the procession to Westminster if they were allowed to march across Blackfriars Bridge to Islington, where they were to disperse, and that he had very properly intimated that none of them would be permitted to return from Kennington in procession across the Thames. I therefore thought that a conflict at the bridges was inevitable. But the next news was that the Chartists were all dispersing; and our librarian, who had been on the ground as a scout, arrived after hearing and seeing Feargus O'Connor implore them to abandon the procession, which they had agreed to do.

For the last half-hour Westminster Bridge has been open to them, and they have been peaceably crossing in small numbers at a time. Feargus is to present the petition at five o'clock, attended by ten persons.

This result is certainly a great relief to my mind, as a frightful shedding of blood might have been necessary to restore tranquillity.

From the beginning, and before I heard any military opinion, I was clear that the Chartists ought not to be allowed to march through Westminster as they proposed, but that it would be dangerous to attempt to prevent them from assembling on Kennington Common or beginning the procession, and that they should be stopped *coûte que coûte* at any bridge which they might attempt to force.

. The arrangements of the Government are excellent. George Grey has all the merit of them. It is very lucky

that at such a time the office of Home Secretary is filled by
so able a man.

But we must not halloo till we are out of the wood.
There is still great danger of disturbances both in London
and the provinces. We know by the electric telegraph, of
which the Government has assumed the exclusive use, that
the Chartists have met to-day in immense numbers at Manchester, armed and ready to act upon receiving news that
London was in possession of O'Connor.

I do not remember whether I told you yesterday that the
object of taking the direction of the electric telegraph was to
prevent false intelligence being sent to the great towns in
England and to Ireland.

In Ireland the stopping of the procession must have a
very good effect, and the notion, pretty prevalent on the
Continent, that we were on the eve of revolution, will be
checked, to the great mortification of those who hoped that
we should be involved in the general ruin.

Brougham arrived last night in Grafton Street, but has
not yet appeared in the House. I expect that he will make
a great splash at five o'clock.

House of Lords : Tuesday, April 11, 1848.

My dear Brother, . . . We are in a state of the most
perfect tranquillity to-day, and the Chartists are so cowed and
disheartened that we shall be quiet for some time.

The fine thing yesterday was when the Duke came to the
House of Lords. I went up to him and said, 'Well, Duke,
it has all turned out as you foretold.' *Duke.* 'Oh, yes, I
was sure of it, and I never showed a soldier or a musket.
But I was ready. I could have stopped them wherever you
liked, and if they had been armed it would have been all
the same.' *Campbell.* 'They say they are to meet next on
the north side of the town and avoid the bridges.' *Duke.*
'Every street can be made a bridge : I can stop them any-
where.' *Campbell.* 'If your Grace had commanded Paris on
the 25th of February, Louis Philippe would still have been
on the throne.' *Duke.* 'It would have been an easy matter.
I should have made the Tuileries secure, and have kept my

communications open.' Then, *more suo*, laying hold of my arm and speaking very loud, and pointing with his finger, he added, ' Always keep your communications open and you need have nothing to fear.'

This reminds me of the striking speech he made on the Afghan disasters, which he entirely ascribed to our General not *keeping his communications open.*

Various other peers afterwards offered the Duke their congratulations, and he looked so much delighted that I really believe he was not more pleased the day after the battle of Waterloo. No one was more rejoiced that the affair went off without bloodshed.

Lord Lansdowne told me he had yesterday seen Guizot, who was lost in admiration at the manner in which the inhabitants of London had conducted themselves. There must be deep disappointment to-day in Paris. I am just going to a Cabinet. We shall be more light-hearted than when we assembled at Lord John's on Sunday evening.

Journal.

April 12, 1848.—. . . Still we shall have formidable work with the Chartists in England, and still more with the Repealers and Confederates in Ireland. I suggested and drew the Bill now passing through the House of Commons for reducing the offences created by the Act of 1796 from treason to felony, and extending the same law to Ireland, where at present there is no punishment for any revolutionary movement, except treating it as a misdemeanour or as high treason under 25 Edw. III. Something must be done to put down the open preaching of *separation* and the avowed preparation for *armed rebellion.*

We have been very dull in the House of Lords, for Lord Brougham has been detained by illness at Cannes, and only reappeared two days ago.

In February and March I attended in the Judicial Committee of the Privy Council almost daily, and, since, I have been assisting in hearing appeals in the House of Lords. The Chancellor continues robust. He comes to the Cabinet as little as possible ; but he continues to do his judicial business with nearly the same vigour and ability as before.

I go on steadily with my 'Lives of the Chief Justices,' and to-day I have finished off Sir Edward Coke.

April 21.—The Sedition Bill has now passed, and we have reached the Easter holidays. It is something for me to have originated a measure which will have a lasting influence upon the law against political offences in this country. I do not believe that *high treason*, which has sounded in the ears of Englishmen for so many centuries, will be much more heard of. I prophesy that it will be long before we have another trial for high treason ; and Frost's, which I conducted, may remain the last, unless there should be (which is very improbable) an actual attempt upon the life of the Sovereign. 'Constructive treason' is gone for ever, there being now a plain, easy, popular mode of proceeding substituted, by which *incipient traitors* may be prosecuted as *felons*, and transported beyond the seas.

The Bill has already produced a good effect in Ireland. Disaffection is there as rife as ever, but the open preaching of rebellion is checked, and the fear of an outbreak has subsided.　　　　　　　•

Letters to Sir George Campbell.

Stratheden House : May 1848.

My dear Brother, . . . I think I ought to tell you the compliment paid to me by the Prince of Prussia,[1] whom we met at dinner on Wednesday at Bunsen's. He said he had heard much of my great biographical work. I answered that it was only for the English. 'Pardon me,' he replied, ' it has a high reputation and is read all over Europe.' I was more tickled by his observing to me that my daughter spoke German beautifully.

House of Lords : May 15, 1848.

My dear Brother, . . . I wish I could find something in the Royal christening to amuse you—but it was dull.

Sitting near the Duke of Wellington in the chapel, he said he was to have his Waterloo dinner this year on the

---

[1] The present German Emperor.—ED.

19th of June, as the 18th is a Sunday. *Campbell.* ' Your Grace did not mind fighting the battle on a Sunday.' *Duke.* ' It was a work of necessity.' I told him, which he did not seem to be aware of, that the battle of Edgehill was fought by the Puritans against Charles I. on a Sunday. In the evening he introduced me to the Prince of Wales. The little boy running up to him when I was standing by, he said to him, ' Do you know Lord Cammel ? You should know Lord Cammel.' So I shook hands with his Royal Highness.

All danger in Ireland has blown over for the present, but looking towards France the sky is very black. If we could only remain at peace with honour, we should do very well. The danger is that the new republic may do something so outrageous as to drive us to war.

Journal.

July 28.—The session of Parliament draws to a close, and the Whigs are still in office. We have been in great jeopardy, particularly on the question respecting relief to be given to the West Indians. In three days I thought we must be irrecoverably gone. For the first time there was in the House of Commons a coalition of Peelites and Protectionists against us. Peel himself stood by the Government ; but his subordinates, Lincoln, Goulburn, Gladstone, and Cardwell, were very eager for our defeat, in the hope that they might have come in. Yet I have no notion of the grounds of their calculation, for their party is not numerous in the House of Commons, and in the House of Lords it has hardly the shadow of an existence. There Stanley gains strength as head of the *Protectionists*, but I hardly know a peer who would acknowledge Peel as chief.

Lord Lansdowne has performed admirably as leader in our House. I had rather a mean opinion of him when he was in opposition, and I thought his style of speaking turgid and vapid. As organ of the Government he has not only shown sound discretion and tact, but on several occasions he has spoken most admirably, and, upon the whole, I am proud to

serve under him. He has, at all events, a great advantage
over our Premier in manners. Lord John is constantly giving
offence by coldness and indifference, which induce a belief
that he is proud and insolent. To us who know him this
defect is of small importance ; but country gentlemen, merchants, and lawyers who are well affected to the party, he
drives into the Opposition lobby by withholding from them a
nod or a smile. Lansdowne makes every man who approaches
him dearer to himself (*sibi cariorem*), and at the same time
is a model of a high-bred gentleman.

Between Brougham and me there is at present an *entente
cordiale*. We not only do not spar, but we compliment each
other. He has lent me the MS. of his History of Henry V.,
written on the principles of historical composition for which
he contends in his Life of Robertson. It is not badly done,
but I do not think it will add much to his literary fame.

By great trouble, patience, and management, I have
carried through the House of Lords the Bill for abolishing
Scotch Entails, the Bill for establishing in Scotland a Register
of Births, Marriages and Deaths, the Bill for amending the
Law of Marriage in Scotland, the Public Health Bill, and a
number of minor Bills for improving the administration of
justice. I may say that I do the Chancellor's work in the
House of Lords as well as in the Cabinet. He thinks of nothing
but his business in the Court of Chancery. He very often
does not come to the Cabinet, and he might just as well stay
away altogether.

I have had several interesting conversations lately with
the Duke of Wellington, and this very day he was good-
natured enough to explain to me the military dispositions he
had made in Ireland : one army to be stationed near Clonmel
and another near Dublin ; showing me the base of their operations, and how they could put down every move of the rebels ;
thus concluding : ' And now, not a cat can jump in Ireland
without my permission.'

What dreary work we have had with this threatened Irish
rebellion ! Yesterday all London was thrown into a state of
consternation from a hoax practised on the directors of the
electric telegraph in Liverpool, who transmitted a message

to all the newspapers 'that there had been dreadful fighting in the South of Ireland, that the troops were disaffected and were beaten, and that the railways were in the power of the insurgents.' A Cabinet was called. John Russell tried to look firm, but was evidently much appalled, and we were all in deep dismay. The Duke of Wellington was sent for, and orders were issued for pouring in reinforcements of infantry, cavalry, artillery, and ships of war from all quarters.

These orders are by no means thrown away, for rebellion is imminent, and nothing but force can restrain it.

I have been still more alarmed by the reports of the re-appearance of the *potato plague*. This would be a greater calamity than rebellion and cholera put together. I look forward to it with the greatest horror. After England has been drained of her resources to feed the destitute Irish, they now accuse us of having brought famine and pestilence upon them. The Poor Law, which was rendered necessary by the utter failure of the food of the people, is one great cause of the disaffection prevailing among the higher classes of Irishmen, who are absurdly disposed to impute all their sufferings to English connection. One shocking circumstance attending a new famine in Ireland at present would be that the Irish, I fear, would be allowed to perish without any assistance from England. The people here are so exasperated and disgusted by the ingratitude and the folly of the Irish, that all Christian charity towards them is extinguished.

I suppose that party struggles are now over for this session, and that we must remain in till Parliament meets again. Our safety lies in the division of our opponents, not in our own strength. . . . We have sustained a heavy loss of credit by the retirement of Macaulay. He certainly was of no use in the Cabinet, and he has no administrative powers; but from his literary and rhetorical reputation he was an ornament to the Administration, and he could occasionally make a speech in the House of Commons which was of considerable service to us.

Lord John having in 1846 offered to take Lincoln, Sidney Herbert, and Dalhousie into his Cabinet, I wonder that he has not since formed a coalition with the Peelites,. for in political opinions there is really no difference between him and them. But on neither side does any such notion seem to be entertained at present. I wish we were strengthened, although I should not like to give up the Duchy to a Peelite recruit, and I do not know who might be called upon to retire for the public good!

Having finished the life of Lord Hale, I have been amusing myself with sketches of the early Chief Justiciars, and in ordinary times I think I could have made a good deal of Odo Bishop of Bayeux, Glanville, &c. ; but I do not believe that in future there will be more interest in past history than that excited by the fossil skeleton of a mammoth. The fact is that all reading is suspended except that of newspapers. A number of the 'Times' is almost occupation for a whole day, and the events of absorbing importance which it narrates make all other reading wholly vapid.

[The session being over he went north, paying a visit to Lord Brougham on his way to Scotland.—ED.]

Hartrigge : Sunday, September 11, 1848.

My dear Brother, . . . Our visit to Brougham went off exceedingly well. The place itself is very beautiful and very interesting, and we met with a very hospitable reception. My noble and learned friend is chargeable rather with *inconstancy* than *duplicity*. Some people smile in your face at the moment when they would be delighted to plant a dagger in your heart, but Brougham in acting a part (like other great performers) believes himself to be what he appears, and his benevolent feelings, if transitory, are real. Should he next week write a malignant article against me in the 'Morning Herald,' I should not at all say that he had been insincere while I was his guest.

Having so much justly to be proud of, there is nothing that he cares to talk about connected with himself except the antiquity and greatness of his race. In the church of Brougham there was the grave of an Edwardus de Broham, who accompanied Richard I. to the Holy Land, and fought many stout battles against the Saracens. My noble and learned friend lately opened his coffin, brought away his skull, framed it and placed it in his baronial hall, under the purse which contained the Great Seal of England. Being called upon to admire the grinning Crusader, I could only say that ' I was much struck by the family likeness between him and his illustrious descendant—particularly in the *lengthiness* of the *jaw*.'

The hall in which Sir Edward appears is hung round with coats of mail and old armour, and here you dine in baronial splendour. The whole house is fitted up in the same taste, and externally has the aspect of a feudal castle. But, with these follies, the master of the mansion treated us with cordial hospitality, and in my honour produced wine from his cellar which Sir Edward might have brought home from Palestine, having received it as a present from Saladin.

We had a grand ball to celebrate the birthday of William Brougham's eldest son, who, in derogation of the right of blood which is in John's eldest son, is to be called to the throne.

On Friday we had a delightful drive by Carlisle across the Border. The Esk and the rivers running to the west were swollen and came down as red as blood, but we found hardly any water in the Teviot or the Jed, and heard the farmers say that the harvest was going on most prosperously.

Journal.

Hartrigge: September 13, 1848.—My Journal has been long neglected. This proceeds very much from my reluctance to say anything in it of the deliberations of the Cabinet, although what I write cannot be seen by anyone till a time when disclosure could not be prejudicial to the public, and could not be considered a breach of my oath as a Privy Councillor.

I suppose there is no harm in saying that we have gone on very cordially, notwithstanding differences of opinion, and that as yet there has been nothing approaching to a *split*.

During the late session we have been damaged in the House

of Commons by 'financial blunders;' but, upon the whole, we stand well in public opinion by having suppressed the Chartist movement, crushed the Irish rebellion, and preserved peace with foreign nations. Fortunately, no progress has been made in forming any party which can be formidable to us. There was a danger, if the difficulties of the nation had increased, of a general call for the restoration of Peel, under whose last administration there had been much seeming prosperity. Now, however, he is not only most odious to the Protectionists, but the *prestige* of his name among commercial men is rather passing away, and he has incurred obloquy, when he deserved the highest credit, from his policy respecting the *currency*. We are infinitely indebted to him for establishing a metallic circulation, for securing the convertibility of bank-notes, and for repressing the abuses of paper issues.

Lord George Bentinck has proved himself utterly incapable of being the head of a party, and, though he may annoy the Government, he not only cannot himself be formidable, but he is serviceable in preventing a better qualified opponent from coming forward. Disraeli must be satisfied with the *éclat* of making brilliant speeches. He might get over the recollection of his being a Jew and an adventurer; but a sad mischance compels him at present to advocate principles which can never be again adopted by any Government in this country.

Lord Stanley has exhibited admirable powers as a debater, and the old Tory aristocracy are much inclined to gather round him; but he is not regarded as a safe man, and he has not only no following in the House of Commons, but even in the House of Lords, where during the governments of Lords Grey and Melbourne the Whigs had no chance whenever it was deemed expedient to throw out their measures, *he* has been defeated as often as he has ventured to muster his strength and to hazard a division.

Hartrigge: October 23, 1848.—I am now setting off to attend a Cabinet Council in Downing Street to-morrow, after having spent six weeks here in the profoundest tranquillity. I have known nothing of politics except from the 'Times' newspaper. I had a letter from Lord John Russell while he was at Balmoral with the Queen, and all the intelligence it conveyed was that her Majesty, and the Prince, and the Royal children were in perfect health.

Forgetting and forgot as I seem to be during the vacation, I have been most happy. My spare moments when my children were engaged and I could not ride or walk with them, or practise archery, or play at bowls or backgammon with them, or read to them, or hear them repeat their *vers de société*, I have employed upon the life of Lord Mansfield, of which I have now written 158 MS. quarto pages, to the end of the review of his judicial decisions. If the world should ever again be quiet, and men have curiosity to look back upon the past, I have rather good hopes of my Lives of the Chief Justices. But as yet no one can read anything except the newspapers, and if Macaulay's long expected 'History of England' were to come out, it would cause little sensation. We seem to have arrived at an entirely new era in the annals of the human race. The religious movement at the time of the Reformation was nothing to the political movement which we now behold. The cement which held society together is suddenly dissolved, and it seems about to become a confused heap of ruins. I should not mind seeing kings and nobles swept away, if anything better were to come in their place; but the tyranny of Communists and Socialists may be more galling; and, desiring only what is most for the general happiness, I see nothing to hope.

Stratheden House: October 24.—I am again in London, and we have had our Cabinet, his Excellency the Lord Lieutenant of Ireland having been present. Ireland was of course the subject of our deliberation. I can say no more at present than that I am appointed one of a committee of seven, to consider a plan by which Ireland may be tranquillised and the empire may be saved. God send us a good deliverance!

January 11, 1849.—I continued in London all alone till the 20th of December, attending the sittings of the Judicial Committee. In Brougham's absence we went on very quietly, and much to the satisfaction of the public; my colleagues being Lord Langdale, Baron Parke, and Pemberton Leigh.

The first is a very poor hand, although exceedingly painstaking and anxious to do what is right. Parke is not only the senior but the soundest Common Law judge. Pemberton Leigh is to be Peel's Lord Chancellor, and a very good one he will make, although it will not answer for him to live in retirement as a country gentleman much longer, if he is to play a part in public life.[2]

I have spent three weeks most happily at Hartrigge in the bosom of my family. A gloom was occasioned by the cholera raging in Jedburgh. But I was under no serious apprehension for my own safety, and, to keep up the spirits of the people, I went into the town daily. My leisure moments I amused with the Chief Justices, and I have now done them all from the Conquest to the Commonwealth, with Hale, Holt and Mansfield, so that I may finish off the whole work in a few months.

The first two volumes of Macaulay's History have had a most brilliant success, but I cannot help thinking that the work has meretricious attractions which may pall upon the public taste. There can be no doubt that, to produce a startling effect, the author does exaggerate very much, if he may be defended from positive misrepresenting. I rejoice that such good principles as those which he inculcates should be found in such a popular work. The party of Young Englanders who denounced the Revolution of 1688 as a crime are demolished, and (which is of more consequence) a severe blow is given to the Chartists and the ultra-Radicals.

I arrived here yesterday to attend a Cabinet called in consequence of the death of Lord Auckland. I very much lament this event. I have never known any man so earnestly

---

[2] *August* 1855.—When Mr. Pemberton he declined the offer of becoming Solicitor-General. He afterwards succeeded to a very large landed estate, retired from the bar, changed his name to Leigh, became a country squire, and kept fox-hounds. But he accepted the titular appointment of Chancellor of the Duchy of Cornwall, and he has continued ever since to attend the Judicial Committee, much to the advantage of the public, for he makes an admirable judge, and his law seems as fresh as if he were still in full practice as a barrister. I have recommended that he should be made a peer, to assist in the Appeal business of the House of Lords, which has got into a sad state. [He became Lord Kingsdown in 1858, and died in 1867.—ED.]

and steadily bent upon doing his duty to the State. He was
a very poor hand at speaking, and I do not think he was a
man safely to originate great measures, but as an administra-
tor he was unequalled.

Are we to have Sir James Graham as his successor? I
entirely approve of the offer being made to him. He would
considerably strengthen the Government, and he would fill
the office advantageously for the public. Lord Lincoln and
the Peel clique will be against his joining us, but Peel himself cannot dissuade him without making an immediate
attempt to resume power.

January 13.—The negotiation for bringing in Sir James
Graham is at an end. He seemed at first inclined to accept
the offer, and expressed himself satisfied with Lord John's
explanations respecting the policy of the Government; but
afterwards said that our financial difficulties, our foreign
policy, and our African squadron frightened him, and that he
felt he could not join us without damaging his character.
He missed seeing Sir Robert Peel, whom he meant to have
consulted, and he professed to act entirely for himself. I presume he thinks that the present Administration, even with his
assistance, could not last, or that he himself has a chance to
have the formation of another if Peel should decline coming
into office.

February 6.—Parliament met on the 1st, and we have
made a much better start than I expected. Stanley in the
House of Lords boldly unfurled the banner of Protection, and
intimated that he was to take a division on the restoration of
the Corn Laws. To my astonishment, Lyndhurst paired off
for him.

Although Stanley ran us very close, he offended the
Peelite peers so much that they can never coalesce with
him, and a Government of pure Protectionists is impossible.

In the Commons Disraeli was installed as leader, but, notwithstanding his clever speeches, he cannot be a very formidable opponent. Palmerston made a capital defence of his
foreign policy, and turned the House quite in his favour.

Letters to Sir George Campbell.

House of Lords: Monday, February 12, 1849.

My dear Brother, . . . I am here again at the old dull work, hearing a Scotch appeal.

I was obliged to make an excursion to Windsor on Saturday and, having an audience before Prince Albert's return to lunch, I was with the Queen in her closet *solus cum solá.* But I should first tell you my difficulty about getting from the station at Slough to the Castle. When we go down for a Council we have a special train and carriages provided for us. I consulted Morpeth, who answered, 'I can only tell you how I went last—on the top of an omnibus. But the Queen was a little shocked.' I asked how she found it out. He said that he had told her himself to amuse her,—but that I should be quite *en règle* by driving up in a cab or fly. So I drove up in my one-horse conveyance, and the lord-in-waiting announced my arrival to her Majesty. I was shown into the Royal closet, a very small room with one window, and soon she entered by another door all alone. My business was the appointment of sheriff for the County Palatine, which we soon despatched. She then talked of the state of the finances of the Duchy . . . and I ventured to offer her my felicitations on the return of this auspicious day—her wedding-day.

I lunched with the maids of honour, and got back in time to take a part in very important deliberations in the Cabinet.

I saw Brougham this morning at the Judicial Committee. He is now mad about the supposed optical discovery on which he has been corresponding with Brewster. He says that 'Newton had very nearly hit upon it.'

House of Lords: February 19, 1849.

My dear Brother, . . . Brougham has been giving me an amusing account of his executorship as representative of Lord Melbourne. He says he sealed up, without reading, all the correspondence during the time when he and Melbourne were at enmity. I said to him, 'I am glad of it, for God knows what letters you might have found to him from Jack Campbell.' I expect him to dine with me to-morrow, and at present we are sworn friends.

The law lords are' very much amused by a book which Sugden has just published, abusing all the decisions of the House of Lords for the last twenty years. I come in for a share of his satire, but in good company.

February 27, 1849.

My dear Brother, . . . I hope you are not much shocked by Joseph Hume denouncing me as a sinecurist. As far as the Duchy is concerned, he is not far from the truth ; but I do not think that the country has a bad bargain in paying me 2,000l. a year for what I do in the Cabinet, in the House of Lords, in the Judicial Committee, and as a Lord of Trade and Plantations.

Stratheden House: March 19, 1849.

My dear Brother, . . . I dined yesterday at the London Tavern and sat between Hardinge and Hobhouse, so that we had a very full and confidential discussion of Punjab affairs. Hardinge fought all his battles over again, and explained to us how he managed Gough, who was for fighting very indiscreetly. He once more entered into a defence of his policy, and pointed out the serious difficulties in the way of annexation. He insists upon it, however, that he did annex one half, and the best half, of the Sikh possessions to our Indian Empire. We became very thick, and he brought me from Bishopsgate Street to Lady Palmerston's.

Journal.

Stratheden House: May 14.—We have gone through a ministerial crisis. The Navigation Bill being necessarily brought forward, it passed the Commons by a considerable majority, but there was a great doubt whether it would not be rejected by the Lords. We resolved to stake our existence upon it, and I heartily concurred in this resolution, which was finally taken at a Cabinet dinner which I gave in this house. It seems strange *primâ facie* to allow the Lords to subvert the Government against the will of the Commons, but we were so circumstanced that we could not have held office with any dignity or advantage after the loss of this measure, and we should have been so discredited that we must soon have been kicked out on some ignoble occasion.

Had we not formed and announced this resolution, the measure would certainly have been lost; the dread of a change of Ministry and of a dissolution of Parliament, has carried us over the second reading. The battle is to be renewed in the Committee on the 21st, but I think that we shall be victorious. The breach between the Peelites and the Protectionists, on which we rely for safety, is wider than ever.

Our chief prop is the Duke of Wellington. The Queen and Prince Albert are both genuine Free Traders, and hostile to a Protectionist Ministry. Prince Albert therefore wrote to the Duke of Wellington and begged him to consider not only the merits of the Navigation Bill, but the consequences of its rejection, and received a favourable answer.

Meanwhile I have finished the composition of my ' Lives of the Chief Justices,' and the work is in the press. I am printing it that it may be safe whatever may happen to me, but it is not to be published till the beginning of December. I am flattered by finding that I have considerable Transatlantic fame, for my ' Lives of the Chancellors ' have been reprinted in Philadelphia, and an American bookseller has agreed to buy 500 copies of my ' Lives of the Chief Justices.'

The convulsed state of the whole continent of Europe is still very unfavourable to any literary undertaking, except writing in a newspaper. Daily there are events to be read in the 'Times' far more interesting than can be found in old histories, and I am mortified and alarmed when I consider how trifling in comparison are the facts which I have to relate.

May 25.—The Navigation Bill is now quite secure. On the second reading, of peers present there was a majority of fourteen against us, and we made out our majority of ten by calling proxies. Stanley's plan was to crush the Bill in the Committee, where proxies are not reckoned.

At the meeting of the House on Monday the 21st we were in despair, for · three Irish peers on whom we counted were ill in bed, and we had met with other casualties. However, the Lord Lieutenant of Ireland and the Ministers from Paris and Vienna appeared, and as the debate proceeded the return of our whipper-in was more favourable. The first real assurance of victory came from Lord Eglinton, the Protectionist whipper-in, who told us we should have a majority of thirteen. And so it turned out. Protection is smashed for this session. Stanley made a wretched figure in Committee, having attempted to show that his destructive amendments harmonised with the principle of the Bill. They were not only inconsistent with it, but distasteful to his adherents, and after having for a week or two really counted on a triumphal entry into Downing Street, he lies prostrate.

The Government is now quite safe till the beginning of another session, although the destitution of Ireland continues a dreadful source of annoyance; the continent of Europe is in a more disturbed state than ever; and (worst of all) the revenue is falling off.

The Chancellor is suddenly taken seriously ill. He has again ruptured a blood-vessel, and has been in bed three or four days. This is a return of the malady which he had about a year and a half ago. I have been elected Speaker of the House of Lords the last three days, and have presided on the woolsack.

June 2.—The Chancellor is said to be better, but he is still kept in bed in a dark room, fed on iced whey, and not allowed to talk to anyone. By Lord Lansdowne's directions, when the House meets on Monday I am to take charge of any Bills which the Chancellor ought to carry through the House on the part of the Government. In the meantime, the judicial business of the House, as well as of the Court of Chancery, is suspended.

June 22.—I have entirely forgotten the Chancellor in my concern at the departure of my dear boy Hally for the East Indies. This is a very sad separation, as there is a very strong probability that I shall never see his face again. Last

Sunday morning at prayers, my wife and seven children knelt
down along with me for the last time, and there is almost a
certainty that we shall never all again meet in this world.
But we must submit to the law of our nature and the will of
God. I accompanied him to Portsmouth, saw him on board
the vessel which is to convey him to Calcutta, and gave him
my blessing.

I am roused from my melancholy by the exertions I am
obliged to make on account of Lord Cottenham's illness.
The Irish Encumbered Estates Bill and the other Irish
measures passing through the House of Lords have all fallen
upon me, and I have been dreadfully bothered by them, but
I have got through them very successfully. Lord John
Russell told me to-day that, although Lord Cottenham
was expected to recover there is no chance of his being
able to return to business for some weeks to come, and
that the plan is, to get through the session without his
attendance and to give him the long vacation to regain his
strength.

July 25.—The session ends very creditably for the Government. Every move in either House of Parliament, either by
Protectionists or any other hostile section of politicians, has
ended in their own discomfiture. It was thought that the
attack on Palmerston's foreign policy led on by Brougham
would certainly succeed, but by the assistance of proxies we
had a majority of twelve, although not a single Peelite voted
with us. The enmity between Protectionists and Peelites in
the House of Commons is greater than ever, but the Peelite
peers, headed by Aberdeen, now seem very much inclined to
enlist under Stanley.

Peel, I believe, has no longer the slightest wish to return
to office. Disraeli, the Tories now reluctantly and shame-
facedly acknowledge for their chief in the House of Commons.
He has an admirable talent for speaking, and in vituperation
he is unrivalled, but he is ignorant of political economy,
without which no one now can pretend to be a statesman,
and when he gets among statistics he is dull and inconsequent.
Setting aside all the prejudices against him from his origin
and his history, I do not think he can ever be the government

leader in the House of Commons.   Heaven only knows what time may produce.

Lord John has got on better this session than he did the last, when he seemed to have lost all control over the proceedings of the House ; he has both quickness and tact, and he performs his part very decently.

Lord Lansdowne, our leader in the Lords, I prize more and more highly.   He not only manages the government business with admirable propriety, but he occasionally makes most excellent speeches, distinguished both for depth of thought and felicity of language.   I cannot say much for my other noble colleagues.   We sadly want an increase of debating power on our side.   I do not see how another session can be attempted without some change.

In the meantime, I may employ my time better by noticing some of our opponents.   Brougham is now regularly enlisted in the Protectionist ranks, but he will not long submit to act a subordinate part, so that Stanley and he will soon quarrel.

Lord Aberdeen is quite mad from envy and hatred of Palmerston.   He is a very able man, but he is carried away by a foolish partiality in favour of Austria, because Austria has stood out for arbitrary principles of government.

Stanley is a host in himself.   He has marvellous acuteness of intellect and consummate power in debate.   There is no subject which he cannot thoroughly master and lucidly explain.   His voice and manner are so good that no one can hear him without listening to him.   He is powerful both in attack and defence.   But he is neither a great statesman nor the discreet leader of a party.   Although he inspirits his followers, he does not fill them with confidence.   I do not think that he is likely soon to be Prime Minister, or that he would long retain the post if by any chance he should once get possession of it.

There is no other Protectionist peer worth noticing. The Duke of Richmond has one short declamation against Free Trade which he constantly repeats, and he is not much better than Lord Stanhope or Lord Winchilsea.

July 27.—It turns out that Denman's attack certainly was

paralytic, and that he has had a return of it.   Lyndhurst says
to me, 'Well! you will have your choice to be a Chancellor
or a Chief Justice.'   This is all very annoying for me, and if
I had any certain cure for the Chancellor and the Chief
Justice, I should be delighted to send it to both.

August 2.—The session closed yesterday, when I had the
honour to be one of five Lords Commissioners to give the Royal
assent to sixty-seven Bills, to address the two Houses in her
Majesty's name, and to prorogue Parliament till the 9th of
October.   The Chancellor did not attend, but he made his
appearance at a Cabinet held in Downing Street immediately
after.   Although he looked very well, his hoarseness continues.
I had a little chat with him before Lord John arrived, and I
found his mental faculties quite unimpaired and unchanged.

Brougham and I heard a number of appeals, and disposed of all that were ready for hearing.   We had here no
difference, for my noble and learned friend was very docile,
and, without difficulty, took the view which I suggested of
all the cases we had to consider.   Indeed he paid very little
attention to them, and on several occasions fell into absurd
blunders in giving his opinion.   Nothing shows more
strikingly that he is a very extraordinary man than that,
after getting into scrapes of this sort which would ruin
anyone else, he soon rallies, and all is forgotten.

CHAPTER XXIX.

AUGUST 1849–MARCH 1850.

Six Weeks in Scotland—Summoned to a Cabinet—Quarrel between Russia and Turkey—Letters from Lord Brougham—Offer of the Chief Justiceship from Lord John Russell—Begins afresh to study Law—Coke upon Littleton—Motto for Rings—Letter from Baron Rolfe—Burke's Letters—Breakfast at Macaulay's—Visit to Baron Rolfe—Opening of the Coal Exchange—Legal Studies—The Gorham Case—Controversy about the Resignation of Lord Denman—Lord Brougham's Account of his Interview with Lord Denman—Opening of the Session of 1850—Cabinet Dinner—Reads Novels—Attacked in the Newspapers—Resignation of Lord Denman—Takes leave of the Cabinet—Sworn in as Chief Justice.

Journal.

Hartrigge: October 1.—After spending six weeks very quietly in Scotland, and not expecting a summons to London for a month to come, I have just received a letter ordering me to attend a meeting of the Cabinet in Downing Street to-morrow at one o'clock, and I must be off by five o'clock this evening for Sprouston, where I shall meet a train which will convey me to Tweedmouth, from which I shall soon be whirled on to London. I must make a little memorandum of my proceedings in the North. My first fortnight I spent most deliciously without stirring from home. The weather was so fine that I sat in the open air reading *sub tegmine fagi*. I had particular pleasure in watching the progress of my young plantations, and in seeing the draining and other improvements. At the expense of my private revenue, I certainly am a public benefactor, for double the quantity of grass grows on the meadows, and I have planted 200,000 trees where nothing before was produced except heather and whins.

CHAP. XXIX.

A.D. 1849.

I then accomplished a visit to Fife, to see my poor dear brother, who had suffered from a long and severe illness. I was greatly rejoiced to find him better, and I hope we may yet spend happy days together. In passing through Edinburgh, going and coming, I saw Lord Jeffrey at Craigcrook, and was tickled by his praises of the ' Chief Justices,' the whole of which he had read in the copy sent to Empson as editor of the ' Blue and Buff.' He likewise gratified me with a favourable account of the book which he had received from Macaulay. I am therefore in hopes that my reputation may not suffer from this new effort. Since I returned I have been occupied with the perusal of a chestful of letters written by me to my brother since the year 1798, which he had carefully preserved, and which he handed over to me. I had never before seen one of them since I wrote them, and I might almost say that I never read one of them before, as my constant habit was to fold up and seal my letters to my brother without ever reading a line of them. . . .

Stratheden House: October 3.—Having dined at Hartrigge, I arrived here to breakfast next morning. I formed many conjectures respecting the subject of this Cabinet, which was called by Palmerston ; John Russell having said to me a few days before that he hoped not to call a Cabinet before the 15th of November. I was afraid there was some point on which he had differed with his colleagues who were in London. *En route* I got the ' Times,' published only a few hours, giving an account of the quarrel between Russia and the Porte about the extradition of the refugees from Hungary, and I conjectured that we were assembled to sanction the offer of support to the oppressed against the oppressor. This turned out to be the case, and we were unanimous in approving the course Palmerston proposed. The demand by the Emperor Nicholas of the extradition of the refugees, contrary to the treaty which he signed, is a flagrant violation of the law of nations, and, if acquiesced in, would be followed up by the entire subjugation of the Turkish Empire. Our honour and our interest therefore require us to interfere. I am afraid however that the matter is very grave, for the Emperor of Russia would scarcely have acted in such a peremptory manner unless he had been determined to enforce his claim at every risk.

We are to have several more Cabinets. I remain at Stratheden House all alone, and without seeing much of my colleagues unless when we are met together to deliberate, for they all have villas near London where they are sojourning.

October 9.—We have now had four Cabinets, and we have adjourned till November. It is something to have assisted at such important deliberations, upon which peace or war depends, and to have had a voice upon the question whether the English squadron should not proceed to the Dardanelles, and be in readiness to defend Constantinople against the Russians. I am in hopes that Nicholas may have come to a better mind, and that it may not be necessary to resort to the *ultima ratio regum.* This blunder which he has committed is marvellous luck for Palmerston, by giving England an opportunity of interfering against the absolutists, with the unanimous sympathy and applause of all the rest of the world.

We have likewise discussed in the Cabinet various other matters of less importance, and shadowed out the measures for the next session of Parliament.

To-morrow I am to sit, as a Lord of Trade and Plantations, to deliberate upon the question ' whether a representative government should be granted to the Cape of Good Hope;' Lord Stanley when Colonial Secretary having refused it, and Lord Grey, the present Colonial Secretary, being strongly inclined to grant it. The subject is no less difficult than it is important, and I reserve my opinion till I know the facts and reasonings more fully.

Last Wednesday, the 3rd of October, I was to have given a grand dinner at Hartrigge to the judges of assize and the bar, and I wrote to Brougham inviting him to meet them. He sent me a civil refusal, on the ground that he had company in his house, and, although I had not mentioned Lord Denman's name to him, he added a P.S.: 'I expect Brodie's report of Denman, and I shall send it to you.'

On my arrival in town I received another letter from

him, enclosing one to him from Sir Benjamin Brodie. This stated that Lord Denman himself hoped before the beginning of Michaelmas Term to recover the faculty of writing and to be able to resume his judicial duties, but that it *was impossible he should be able to do so*, and that some communication should be made to him to prepare him for the shock which must be occasioned by finding his true situation. Brougham said, 'My plan is to propose retirement till Christmas, and then I shall be back to insist on total retirement. I *know* he means to listen to me. This is for yourself and J. Russell. Lay your heads together, with my love to John, and leave the Turk to his women and Stratford Canning.' At the breaking up of the Cabinet on Friday I put this letter and the enclosure into Lord John's hand, as Brougham wished him to see them and had sent him his ' love.'

October 12.—I have received the following letter :—

Downing Street : October 11, 1849.

My dear Campbell,—I agree with you that Brougham's advice is intended to postpone a resignation which I am sure Denman, in his uprightness, would at once give in, if he were informed by Brodie that he could never again expect efficiently to perform his duties on the bench.

Seeing the probable result of the attack in July, I rode over to the Chancellor's at Copse Hill and obtained his opinion that you would be the fit successor.

The Queen would, I am sure, sanction the appointment with satisfaction, as one calculated to promote the administration of justice, and give weight to the decisions of the Court of Queen's Bench. I remain,

Yours very truly,

J. RUSSELL.

So there is every probability of my name being added to the list of 'Chief Justices of England.' I can only fervently pray to Almighty God that if I am placed in this situation I may be enabled to perform the important and sacred duties cast upon me. The prospect is agreeable to me, but causes no exultation or exhilaration. Indeed I am sitting here all alone, and I have no one to rejoice with. I found Lord John's letter on my table when I came home, near midnight.

I am sure the appointment would be for the good of my family, and for their sakes I would accept it if I disliked the

labour—which I do not. But I confess I most of all rejoice
in the thought of being able to give a place to my old clerk.[1]
I have great pleasure likewise in thinking that I may do
something for my butler, who has long served me, and been
much attached to me.[2] I need not add that the thought of
being able to serve my country in a high station, and the hope
of acquiring the reputation of a great magistrate please me,
although attended with anxiety and misgivings.

My reply to Lord John :—

Stratheden House: October 12, 1849.

Dear Lord John,—Your kindness will afford an additional stimulus to
my efforts that you may not be censured for the appointment which you
propose to recommend.

Of course nothing more can be done till a spontaneous resignation shall
come in. Yours very truly,
CAMPBELL.

October 14.—I am more and more pleased with my prospect. If I really am appointed Chief Justice of the Queen's
Bench, I shall be, and I shall be allowed to be, so completely
master of my work that I shall have much less anxiety and
more enjoyment than if I had been Chancellor. The tempting
thing in this last situation is the glory to be acquired by the
introduction of reforms.

My principal difficulty at present is to get up the
Common Law decisions of the last eight years. But I must
make myself acquainted with the newest fashions of Westminster Hall. For this purpose I have written to my old
colleague and friend Baron Rolfe, that he may tell me what
Reports I must travel through, and what new treatise and
books of practice ought to be studied or referred to.

Meanwhile I have again taken to my old favourite
Co. Litt. It certainly is very pleasant reading. I am more
than ever struck by its unmethodical and rambling character,
but one must admire the author's stupendous familiarity
with all parts of the law of England; he is uniformly per-
spicuous, he gives amusing glimpses of history and manners,
and his etymologies and other quaint absurdities are as good
for a laugh as Joe Miller or Punch.

[1] Mr. Cooper, who became his clerk in 1809.—ED.
[2] Thomas Reed, who had been in his service for twenty years —ED.

Littleton's book by itself is a most exquisite production.
Its plan is perfect for giving a systematic outline of the law
of Real Property in this kingdom in the reign of Edward IV.
and all its details are most masterly. But Lord Coke's example ruined juridical composition in England. Blackstone
even has not been able to correct our taste, and the repertory
of Common Law learning at present most frequently referred
to is the trebly annotated edition of Saunders's Reports,
by Serjeant Williams, Mr. Justice Patteson, and Vaughan
Williams. In law books we are not only greatly excelled by
the French and by the Scotch, but even by the Americans.

October 15.—Have been trying to find a motto for my
rings when I am called Serjeant. Nothing better turns up
than 'Justitiæ tenax' (Juv. *Sat.* viii. 25).

I shall be the first peer ever made a serjeant, as hitherto
all peers who have worn the coif had put it on before they
were ennobled; but I suppose there is no objection to the
order being reversed. It is said that a peer cannot practise
at the bar, but I conceive that this is a matter of etiquette,
not of law. He may be disqualified to plead as an advocate
before the House of Lords, although it be usual for barristers
in the commission at the assizes to practise before brother
commissioners. The circumstance of his having a right to sit
in the House of Lords can offer no ground for preventing
him from practising before the Court of Queen's Bench.

Letter from Baron Rolfe.

Wyvel's Court: October 15, 1849.

My dear Campbell,—Nothing, I assure you, could have given me more
pleasure than the information communicated to me in your secret sheet,
which, according to your desire, I have committed to the flames. I am
very sure that we shall all welcome you as our chief with very great satisfaction. From what I had heard of Lord D. I thought it was very unlikely he should appear this next term, and I am sure he ought to resign
immediately. Lord Mansfield, indeed, held on for a year or two without
appearing in court, but that would not do now. Besides, the feebleness
of age presents no such decided line marking the boundary between fitness
and unfitness as is traced by an attack of paralysis. Even if Lord D.
were to make what should be considered as another rally, he never could
be really competent to the discharge of his duties.

With respect to the questions you put to me, I will begin by saying I
feel *quite sure* you will find no difficulty at all after the first few weeks.

I know of no book on the subject of the new rules but Jervis's, which answers every purpose. In the notes you will find references to all the cases decided up to the time of the publication of the book. There is not (at least, I believe there is not) any very recent edition, but indeed there are very few cases of any importance arising out of the new rules. If you would bring down with you a copy of Jervis's book, I think I could in a very short conversation with you point out the sort of questions which arise out of them in court, and you will see they are not such as present any difficulty. As to books of practice, I always use Chitty's Archbold, of which there is a very recent edition, and I think it is now the book most referred to. It of course contains all the changes of *practice* introduced by the new rules, and these, I think, come under discussion much oftener than the rules as to pleading. You can hardly fail to have forgotten some of the mere practice. But this, I am sure, need not trouble you. When I first came on the bench I was entirely ignorant of it, but somehow one picks it up, and no real difficulties occur. There is not, I believe, any book relating merely to the alterations of pleading effected by the new rules, but all is explained in the latest editions of Chitty; and, in truth, the new rules for the most part explain themselves clearly enough. If I were in your place I should get the 'Law Journal' of this, and perhaps also of the last, year. The reports there are for the most part very well given, and I am persuaded that, by making yourself master of a few cases there, you will see the sort of questions which arise, and which have grown up since your time. They are very few indeed.

I wish that the house we are in was larger, and then I would have said 'Come over at once,' but we have not elbow-room to do so. But on Monday we shall be delighted to see you and your son, and I have told Lady Rolfe that I shall have a great deal to say to you, so that it will excite no surprise if we are alone together. Dundas, as I told you, comes on Tuesday, but if you come in the morning, or middle of the day, on Monday we shall have that morning and all Tuesday morning alone, and I am very sure I shall have poured out all I know before that time is over.

I cannot conclude without again saying how glad I shall be to see you as our Coryphæus. I thought when you took your peerage that you were doing quite right, and I have never ceased to think so. But you made a fearful sacrifice of income, and I sincerely rejoice to think there is a prospect of your being again in a high post, for which without any flattery everyone feels you so well qualified, and which will give you some solid advantage as well as high honour. Very truly yours,

R. M. ROLFE.

October 16.—According to Baron Rolfe's advice I have dismissed Co. Litt., which I must confess at the present day is more curious than useful, and I have provided myself with ʻ Jervis on the New Rules,' ʻArchbold's Practice by Chitty,' and several volumes of the ʻ Law Journal.' With such an object before me I shall attack them with considerable appetite.

To refresh me I am reading Edmund Burke's Letters,

which are exceedingly interesting. Hastings' trial, on which he wasted his strength so many years, is now tiresome, but his views of the French Revolution from its commencement will continue to be read with delight to the end of the world. Every arrival from the Continent more fully confirms his reasoning as to the utter impossibility of suddenly framing a new constitution after sweeping away all that has gained respect from habit and prescription. Yet he carried his hostility to an extravagant and mischievous extreme by insisting that the Church, the *noblesse*, and the parliaments should be restored to all their ancient property, power, immunities and privileges. He would not even devise any expedient for breaking down the barrier between the *noblesse* and the *roturiers*. I consider this as the great and insufferable grievance of the ancient *régime*. The oppression which it produced to the great bulk of the nation is the true reason why 'equality' is now so passionately clamoured for, while much indifference is exhibited respecting political 'liberty.' The dread of the recurrence of these evils makes the law requiring an equal partition of property among all the children of every family still very popular, notwithstanding the inconvenient consequences which this *morcellement* has produced.

October 18.—Breakfasted this morning with Macaulay in his chambers in the Albany, where I met Lord Carlisle (Morpeth), Sheil, and other wits. Luckily Hallam was not there, so that Macaulay had the talk almost exclusively to himself, and we had no rivalry for a display of reading and erudition. In my passage through this world I have never met anything so wonderful as Macaulay's talk during the two hours we were with him. There was no department of literature in which he did not quote largely and appropriately—from the Greek and Latin Fathers, to the last numbers of ' Punch ' and the ' Times.'

October 27.—I have passed several days most agreeably with Baron Rolfe at his house near Reading. In our rides and walks to Strathfieldsaye, Heckfield, Silchester, &c., we had much talk about Westminster Hall, and he again assured me that I should find no difficulty in discharging the duties of Chief Justice of the Queen's Bench. I do humbly hope that if I am placed in that situation I shall not ·disgrace myself, or injure the public. By a pair of slightly magnifying spectacles my vision is made perfect, and by God's blessing my hearing and other senses are wholly unimpaired, my mental faculties being in full vigour, and I feel the same steady desire to do my best ($a\grave{\iota}\grave{\epsilon}\nu$ $\acute{a}\rho\iota\sigma\tau\epsilon\acute{v}\epsilon\iota\nu$) which has been my moving power through life.

As yet I learn nothing more of Denman's intentions. It is said to be the earnest desire of all his family that he should immediately retire from public life, and all who take an interest in his reputation would give him the same advice. He is justly and much beloved, and he is to be treated with the greatest tenderness.

October 30.—I have had a very agreeable *divertissement* to-day by assisting at a grand festivity in the City—the inauguration of the new Coal Exchange. The Queen was kept away by the chicken-pox, but Prince Albert attended, with the Prince of Wales and the Princess Royal. The day was brilliant and the river presented the most splendid pageant that I ever witnessed. The whole *corps diploma-·tique* were assembled, and I was introduced to Mr. Abbott Lawrence, the new American minister, who told me that he knew me the moment I entered the hall from the many prints of me he had seen in America, and that my works were read from the Rocky Mountains to the St. Lawrence. He added that the 'Lives' were quite as interesting to Americans as to Englishmen, 'for,' said he, 'till 1776 we have everything in common.' Notwithstanding the reputation he brings with him of being a great Protectionist, he spoke to me very sensibly about *Free Trade*, and, although he pretended that the United States were not yet sufficiently advanced to enter in all departments into competition with England, he professed a readiness to reciprocate in the repeal of the Navigation Laws, and expressed a warm wish for the continuance of good understanding between the two great branches of the Anglo-Saxon race.

November 3.—I proceed prosperously with my legal studies. I have gone through the Reports of the three superior Courts of Common Law, from 1842 to 1849, and no very important decision could be started upon me by surprise. I could take my seat to-morrow with considerable confidence. But I should struggle above all things to gain favour by mildness, courtesy, and discretion.

Now would be the time for me to try to rival Lord Hale, by laying down the rules by which I mean to be governed when I am a judge; but I can only say that, with the blessing of God, I shall earnestly strive to do my duty.

Hartrigge: December 21.—. . . The Judicial Committee has been occupied with the hearing of the great case of *Gorham v. the Bishop of Exeter,* which went on many days. I found myself a member of a tribunal to decide a question of dogmatic divinity, having for assessors the Archbishops of York and Canterbury and the Bishop of London. The great question was, whether the Church of England teaches that there is absolutely spiritual regeneration by the act of infant baptism, or whether she does not tolerate the doctrine that the regeneration depends upon the condition of *prevenient grace.*

On the last day we sat evening as well as morning, and we had an elegant repast provided for us in the Council chamber at the public expense. We afterwards held a conference and ' broke ' the question, when I was rejoiced to find that, with one dissentient, we were all inclined to the opinion, so desirable for the peace of the Church, 'That neither Liturgy nor Articles can be said exactly to define the mode by which regeneration is operated, and that the point on which the parties differ may be considered an open question.' We adjourned to January 15, 1850.

I have now joined my family in Scotland, from whom I have been separated near three months.

Stratheden House: January 12, 1850.—While at Hartrigge I read paragraphs in the newspapers positively asserting that Lord Campbell was appointed Chief Justice, and would take his seat the first day of next term; and I received congratulations by letter from Lord Dunfermline, and many other friends, on my promotion. Next came contradictions in the newspapers from Lord Denman's family, with a statement that his health was greatly improved, and that he had no thoughts of resigning

I arrived in town on the 9th of January and found that during my absence a controversy had been raging in the press respecting the resignation, boisterous beyond what I had any notion of. The 'Times' had first begun this by a leading article, written with great force and delicacy, recommending Lord Denman to retire with his well-earned glory. The 'Standard' and the 'Morning Chronicle' violently took the other side, maliciously pretending, however, to compliment me. When the court met yesterday (the first day of Hilary Term), Denman did not appear, but Mr. Justice Patteson announced 'that he was detained in Derbyshire, *only* by the illness of Lady Denman, and that, she being better, he would shortly return to London and take his seat.'

The tantalising suspense under which I have been kept for the last two months has been very annoying, and has depressed me very much. But to-day my spirits are quite roused by charming letters from my boy Hally, who seems to be going on as well as possible at Calcutta.

Tuesday night, January 29.—The plot thickens. I certainly have very disagreeable scenes before me, and the piece is likely to end unhappily.

While I was sitting in my library to-day, about three o'clock, a servant opened the door and, to my utter astonishment, announced *Lord Brougham*. Quickly he appeared and, with a few interjections on my part, he spoke as follows, standing on his legs all the time and gesticulating very violently :—

'I arrived from Paris yesterday evening and immediately saw Sir Benjamin Brodie. He told me that Denman had made up his mind to resign, and was much easier since he formed this resolution, but that he still hesitated as to the time of his resignation, and that I must see him as soon as possible. I went to him after breakfast this morning. I found his body sadly shattered, for he has almost entirely lost the use of one side, and he cannot move his fingers to write, and how he expected that he was to get on in court I do not understand, although his mind seemed active and he could talk well enough. I applauded his resolution to resign, and expressed a hope that the step would be taken immediately. He said: " Campbell is the obstacle. Do you know how he has insulted me in his life of Holt ? " He alluded to the passage in which you no doubt mean to shadow him out in describing how Chief Justices have on some points not fulfilled the expectations that had been entertained of them. Now I think you are quite wrong in disagreeing with Denman and me on the Privilege question, but it is a question on which men may form, and strongly maintain, opposite opinions, and there is no pretence for saying that in the passage he complains of you insult him, for you say that " he retained the noble aspirations of his youth," and that he was " still actuated by good intentions." [3] Indeed his observations show how his understanding is weakened, if indeed he does not seek for some reason to delay his resignation, although he says he has resolved upon it. He said to me, " I hear you favour Campbell." I answered, " Yes, I think Jack is much fitter than Jem Parke, or anyone else that can be named." He replied, " Campbell would behave ill to my puisnes. I must protect my puisnes." I asked why it should be supposed that you would behave ill to the puisnes, as you were a man of sense, and it was clearly for your advantage to avail yourself of their learning and experience. He remarked that Lord Mansfield had held the office seven terms after ceasing to sit in court. I answered, " That is the greatest reproach to Lord Mansfield's memory, and I tell you that if you delay your resignation with a view to the appointment of your successor, you not only will be blamed by your contemporaries, but in all time to come." I was afraid he would have gone off in a fit. The danger is that he may have another attack depriving him of his reason and disqualifying him to resign, and then we should be driven by necessity to bring in an Act of Parliament, as in Henley Eden's case, with a " Whereas Thomas Lord Denman,

---

[3] 'He who retains the highmindedness and noble aspirations which distinguished his early career may, with the best intentions, be led astray into dangerous courses, and may bring about a collision between different authorities of the State which had moved harmoniously, by indiscreetly attempting new modes of redressing grievances, and by an uncalled-for display of heroism.'—*Lives of Chief Justices*, vol. ii. p. 134.

by the visitation of Providence, is deprived of his reason, be it enacted," &c.'

I protested that I had ever felt the highest regard for Denman, although I had differed with him so much on the Privilege question, and that in other parts of my writings I had spoken of him very respectfully.

A message now came up from Lady Brougham, who had been left below in the carriage, that she was tired of waiting and wished my Lord to come to her instantly. He asked me to pick out some passages in which I had spoken respectfully of Denman and to send them to him, to be shown to Brodie, who was to see Denman in the evening. He then took leave, begging me not to think unkindly of Denman for what had passed, 'as he really is no longer himself.'

. I receive very abusive letters, and my merits and defects are likely for some time to be openly discussed in the newspapers. All this is very distressing.

To-morrow I go to Windsor to assist in holding a Council, and Parliament is to be opened the following day, so that I shall have no time for *ennui*.

February 6.—The session has begun very auspiciously, and our great majorities in both Houses against the Protectionist amendment make *Free Trade* quite secure. Lord John's manœuvre in getting Charles Villiers to move the address in the Commons was very masterly, and the language of the speech compelled the Protectionists either disgracefully to decline the combat, or to fight on unequal terms. Our Government is now identified with the *Free Trade* cause, and any combination of the Protectionists with the Radicals to turn us out is rendered very difficult.

Denman talks of going the Midland circuit. Lord John Russell, as an old friend, wrote to him advising him for his own sake, as well as for the sake of the public, to resign, but he has received no answer.

I was ordered to give a Cabinet dinner to-morrow (the second of the season), because it was supposed that I never should be present at another.

I am to be consoled by being appointed ' Deputy Speaker

of the House of Lords,' Lord Shaftesbury having declared that
he finds himself unfit for the labours of this office.

February 7.—Yesterday I gave my Cabinet dinner,
at which it was expected that I was to take leave of my
colleagues.

I now employ myself in reading novels. I had got up
the decisions of the courts since the time when I left the bar,
with the 'practice' recently introduced, and I shall think
no more of law till I take my seat on the bench, if that day
should ever arrive. I had continued my life of Ellenborough down to the commencement of Hastings's trial, when
I was stopped short for want of materials. Strange to say,
there is not in print any readable account of this proceeding,
so celebrated in our juridical annals, and I must refer to
shorthand writers' notes and the newspapers of the day. For
such researches I have at present no energy. Having read
'Pendennis' and 'Copperfield,' now publishing in numbers, by
Thackeray and Dickens, I have resorted to my old favourites
Fielding and Smollett, who are much superior in humour
and delineation of character, although their coarseness is
much greater than from my recollection of it I could have
imagined. Squire Western's conversation in the presence
of Sophia was such as to render it impossible that the mind
of the young lady should have been very delicate or even
modest.

February 10.—The controversy about the Chief Justiceship becomes more and more painful. My personal enemies
and the opponents of the Government are working the subject with industry and malignity in the press. The 'Spectator'
to-day has an article entitled 'Campbell *v.* Denman,' which
says that there are various sorts of *assassination*—some by
the sword, and some by poison—and that Lord Campbell is
seeking to assassinate Lord Denman by paragraphs in the
ministerial newspapers stating that he ought to resign from
ill health, whereas there is nothing the matter with him.
Other newspapers have similar statements, with invectives
against me and arguments upon the impropriety of my promotion on the ground of my advanced age.

I confess this seems rather hard upon me, as I have

not had the remotest connection or privity with anything inserted in any newspaper upon the subject, and in truth Lord Denman has been treated with great forbearance and delicacy, as nothing has been said about his *paralysis*, and the degree to which he is incapacitated has been cautiously concealed. Again, I should have thought that my political consistency might have deserved another designation than 'servility to a faction.' From my amendments of the law and from my literary labours I might have been treated with decency; but without the slightest provocation on my part, I am assailed by a storm of flippancy, scurrility, and falsehood.

I might now truly say that I am almost quite indifferent about the office. It has already lost all its charms. And indeed I do not think I could do its duties nearly as well as if I had been appointed six months ago. The personal squabble supposed now to exist is extremely degrading to me, and is most injurious both to my health and to my mental faculties.

> I have lived long enough; my way of life
> Is fallen into the sere, the yellow leaf,
> And that which should accompany old age,
> As honour, love, obedience, troops of friends,
> I must not look to have.

February 26.—There has been some danger of an immediate change of government. The division on Thursday night, leaving Lord John with a majority of twenty-one, caused great surprise and dismay; and on the Australian Bill, which was to have come on yesterday, he was likely to be left in a minority. But this measure is prudently postponed for a fortnight, and Disraeli last night, by his extreme imprudence in six times dividing the House for the purpose of obstructing the Irish Franchise Bill, which is very popular, has entirely kicked down the credit which he had acquired.

March 7.—At four P.M. on Friday, March 1st, 1850, in the presence of the Lord Chancellor, Lord Denman actually signed and sealed his resignation, and delivered it as his act and deed. Soon after, the Chancellor saw Mr. Justice Coleridge, who spoke in the name of his brethren and expressed the greatest respect for me and readiness to serve under me.

A Cabinet was summoned for half-past two on Saturday, March the 2nd. Entering the room of our meeting at the Foreign Office, I found Lord John Russell there. He informed me that he had just left the Queen, that he had taken her pleasure, and that all was quite right. He then said to the members of the Cabinet who were assembled, 'My lords and gentlemen, let me present you to the Chief Justice of England.' I shook hands with them all, thanked them for their kindness while I had been their colleague, wished them all manner of prosperity, and immediately withdrew.

We had a very merry evening at home and forgot all our anxiety. On Sunday we all went to church together and took the Holy Communion, praying that I might be enabled to perform the new duties to devolve upon me.

In the House of Lords on Monday I did not make any formal announcement of having left the Cabinet, but I published my promotion by eschewing the ministerial bench, and showing in various ways that I was no longer a member of the Government. I received the warmest congratulations from the peers on all sides, with many flattering speeches that my modesty forbids me to repeat.

Lord Ellenborough, shaking hands with me, said that he felt particular satisfaction, from the interest which he took in the office of Chief Justice, and he made an offer, which I gladly accepted, of the use of the collar oi SS which had been worn by Lord Mansfield, and through Lord Kenyon had come down to his father. This I was to have copied, and to wear till my own was ready.

Wednesday, the 6th of March, I had an audience of the Queen, when I delivered up the seals of the Duchy and kissed hands on my new appointment.

I am dreadfully harassed and perplexed about the appointment of my officers, and I almost wish already that I again enjoyed the obscure quiet of the Duchy.

The preparations for the circuit likewise keep me in a bustle. On Saturday morning I start by rail for Lincoln. What a plunge I am to make! The change is greater than ever happened to any judge before; for during nine long years I have neither been at the bar nor on the bench.

Letters to Sir George Campbell.

Stratheden House:
Sunday night, March 3, 1850.

My dear Brother, . . . I have very little more to tell you. I am overpowered by congratulations, some of which are sincere and hearty. I am most touched by the regret at losing me from the Cabinet (I believe truly) expressed by my colleagues. I certainly there acted upon our motto 'Audacter et aperte.' Prudently holding my tongue when subjects were discussed of which I knew nothing, I spoke out, and with advantage to the State, when constitutional or international questions came up.

Parke has undertaken to do all the work in Northampton-shire and Rutland. On Saturday I go down to Lincoln, and there preside on the Civil side. At the next place, Notting-ham, I am on the Crown side, and unluckily I have to begin with three horrid murders.

I have received an extremely kind letter from Coleridge, which I will send to you that you may see the hallucination under which Denman laboured in supposing that the puisnes would not co-operate with me.

I am in a terrible whirl amidst rings, mottoes, robes of all hues, wigs—full-bottom and tie, &c. &c. The leave-taking ceremony will be on Tuesday or Wednesday.

The newspapers have become very civil to me, and only object to me on the ground of my being a Cabinet Minister. Taking care, with God's help, to do my duty, I shall care very little for what they say of me for the rest of my days.

Stratheden House:
Tuesday night, March 5, 1850.

My dear Brother, . . . I assure you that your letter, so full of heart and love, which we received this evening, has made us all doubly enjoy our promotion.

The event is certain now, and nothing can deprive me of the office but death, or the two Houses of Parliament con-curring in an address against me for misconduct—

Not Fate itself can o'er the past have power ;
For what has been has been, and I have had my hour.

This morning began with 'ringing me out' at Lincoln's Inn. The prospect of the ceremony made me rather uncomfortable from the time when I knew that Brougham was to preside at it, for there was no saying what line he would take, or what topics he would touch upon—so that preparation or premeditation could not be resorted to. In the event he confined himself to an eulogium upon Lord Denman, in which I had only to acquiesce, and the whole affair was over in a few minutes. I presume that some account of it will appear in the public journals, although previous notice of it had not been communicated to the reporters. Brougham tried to play me a dog's trick by running away with my fee of ten guineas as a retainer to plead, when become a serjeant, for the Society of Lincoln's Inn. I made him disgorge the money at the House of Lords by threatening to sentence him to the gallows as a thief, and so commencing my judicial career with a notorious culprit.

I was sworn in before the Chancellor at four o'clock—Coleridge and Wightman, the only puisnes in town, attending, along with the officers of the court. First I was made a serjeant, and then my patent writ as Chief Justice was handed to me, and, having taken many strange oaths, my title to hang, draw, and quarter was complete. I continue still Chancellor of the Duchy, but deliver up the seals to the Queen to-morrow at one o'clock.

I enclose Coleridge's note. He and Wightman have behaved to me most kindly ; Erle is one of my best friends, and we shall all go on very harmoniously. I really am singularly lucky in my puisnes.

CHAPTER XXX.

MARCH 1850—DECEMBER 1851.

First Circuit as Chief Justice—Judgments during Term—Serjeants' Inn—
Sittings at Nisi Prius—Resignation of Lord Cottenham—The Great
Seal transferred to Lords Commissioners—Lord Palmerston and Don
Pacifico—Death of Sir Robert Peel—Appeals in the House of Lords—
Oxford Circuit—Lord Truro Chancellor—Tour to the Hebrides and
the Highlands—Dinner at Mr Justice Patteson's—Work in Term-
time—Writes the 'Life of Lord Tenterden'—Perilous State of the
Whig Government—Disraeli the Rising Man—Papal Aggression—
Lord John Russell's Scheme for Chancery Reform—Home Circuit—
Death of Lord Cottenham and Lord Langdale—The Great Exhibition
—Queen's Fancy Ball—His Daily Life—Sir James Graham—Lord
Truro's Opposition to the Registration of Deeds Bill—Evidence Bill
—Fusion of Law and Equity—Western Circuit—Meeting with Lord
Denman—Chief Justice's Salary—Letter from Rome—Interview with
the Pope—Working of the new Evidence Act.

Journal.

April 9.—I am returned from the circuit, having made
my *début* as a judge. I stood the fatigue well, did not get
into any scrape, and I believe I have the good word of the
Midland men. The novelty of the scenes and circumstances
through which I passed excited and amused me. The most
magnificent spectacle was the procession from the great West
door of the Cathedral at Lincoln to the choir, attended by
the Bishop and the clergy, the Chief Justice ermined, with
his collar of SS, in 'peacock state.' The most arduous duty
on the circuit was entertaining the magistrates at dinner, a
duty we had to perform at every assize town. My colleague
was Parke, who was very friendly to me. He is a very
learned and very able lawyer.

I suffered from nothing except wearing a full-bottom wig
after having been disencumbered of it for nine years. My
head ached and my faculties were cramped by the pressure

CHAP.
XXX.

A.D. 1850

T 2

of it, but I hope that use will again reconcile me to this barbarous encumbrance, although I wish that it were reserved exclusively for the purpose of making an African warrior look more formidable to his enemies in the field of battle.[1] Once I was obliged to put on the black cap, and pass sentence of death. This I did with tolerable composure, as I knew that the sentence was not to be carried into effect. After a little more practice I expect to be pretty much at my ease, sitting either at Nisi Prius or in the Crown court. That of which I am most afraid at present is the term business, till I get my hand in. Cause is to be shown against rules of which I know nothing, special demurrers are to be argued depending on the *New Rules* with which I am by no means familiar, and the *session cases* turn upon the construction of statutes which have passed since I left the bar. But silence and discretion will do much to conceal my ignorance on these points. With the great principles of jurisprudence perhaps I am as conversant as my colleagues.

May 21.—I have got on as Chief Justice much better than I expected. The first motion made before me was for a Prohibition to the Archbishop of Canterbury against carrying the sentence in favour of Gorham into execution. My brethren agreed with me that we should take time to consider whether the rule to show cause ought to be granted. Patteson at first doubted, but came round to the opinion of the rest that the rule should be refused. I wrote the judgment, which was at first much admired. My reputation, however, was considerably tarnished in about a week after, when, the motion being renewed in the Common Pleas, a mistake I had made was exposed about the times of the passing of two Acts of Parliament— 24 Hen. VIII. c. 12, and 25 Hen. VIII. c. 19. I had followed preceding writers, who had been misled by not attending to the change of style, and by forgetting that 'February 1532' came after 'May 1532.' Although immaterial to the argument, it gave a triumph to the Bishop of Exeter and his party.[2]

---

[1] For this purpose was Erskine's full-bottom purchased and exported to the coast of Guinea when he ceased to be Lord Chancellor.

[2] My judgment was affirmed in the Common Pleas and afterwards in

My brother judges have been very kind to me, and I have   CHAP.
gone on with them most harmoniously. I was often in a   XXX.
frightful mist when a counsel began to show cause against a A.D. 1850.
rule of which I knew nothing, or when, on a motion for a
new trial, the report of the judge was gabbled over, without
my having the most distant notion of the points to be discussed.   But a little daylight gradually peered in, and when
the opinion of the court was to be given, I could lead off with
some confidence.

The only memorable judgment which I pronounced during
this term was very interesting to the profession, as it discussed the question ' whether a barrister may hold a brief in
a civil suit without the intervention of an attorney?' I
traced the history of advocacy in England, introducing—

> The Serjeant of the law wary and wise,
> That often had y-ben at the Parvise.

During the term we decided off-hand all the cases which
came before us except seven. To settle these we had a
Cabinet dinner, after term, at this house, and we made up
our minds upon all. I have already written the judgments
in two of them, and I trust there never will be arrears to
complain of *tempore* Campbell.

I have dined twice at Serjeants Inn, my admission to
which cost me near 700*l.* My brethren of the bench are a
most respectable set, and I believe superior to their predecessors who filled their places fifty years ago. But I can
make no impression on them as a body, in inducing them
actively to co-operate in legal reform, although there are
individuals among them who might be made most efficient
in this department. The Serjeants are a very degenerate
race, and, their exclusive audience in the Common Pleas
being gone, it is full time that the order should be utterly
abolished.

After term I sat six days at Nisi Prius in Westminster and
London, and found it rather irksome work. There are no
longer any decided leaders at the bar, and the business is not

the Exchequer, and the Bishop of Exeter was driven to declare that the
Common Law judges were all equally wrong.

nearly so well done as I remember it to have been in the hands of Erskine and Law. It is dreadful drudgery to take down the evidence of a long string of witnesses proving the same facts over and over again. I must establish my character for *patience* before I can venture to discipline the bar, as I remember Ellenborough doing.

May 27.—Lord Cottenham has actually resigned. It was announced that he would certainly take his place to-day on the woolsack, and indeed he himself wrote a letter to this effect to Lord Lansdowne. But on entering the House I discovered that he was not there, and I was obliged again to sit Speaker myself. The news of his resignation seemed to give general satisfaction, as he is now wholly unfit to do the duties of his office.

June 16.—The Great Seal is to be transferred to Lords Commissioners Langdale, Shadwell, and Rolfe. Lord John sent to me to announce the forthcoming Commission, and to consult me about the three Commissioners he proposed to select. I told him truly that he could not well do better. He then mentioned to me his plan of having a Permanent Chief in the Court of Chancery, and a Supreme Judge of Appeal to preside in the House of Lords and the Judicial Committee.

Letter to Sir George Campbell.

Woolsack : Monday evening, June 10, 1850.

My dear Brother, . . . I am here sitting Speaker, I hope for the last time, for it is a great bore. Tuesday was once fixed for the transfer of the Great Seal to the Lords Commissioners, but the ceremony is now postponed till Thursday. Brougham is in a great rage about Cottenham's earldom.

John Russell is in a terrible fix about the bisection of the office of Lord Chancellor. There will be almost an impossibility to find a fit person to sit here and to try the appeals. Upon this very much depend the dignity and efficiency and constitutional position of this House. I have the *suave mari magno* feeling. I really prefer sitting in Queen's Bench to sitting here. The discussions there are more intellectual—to say nothing of the fact that there I have it all my own way, and here I am a member of a party in constant danger of being in a minority. This very night the Government made me oppose a Bill which they found they of themselves were too weak to throw out.

The weather has become most exquisitely genial, and I hope that you have full enjoyment of it. My health continues excellent. I have a pleasant ride every morning to Westminster Hall, and generally another home at five o'clock. It is lucky that the transit is all the way through the Royal parks. The accounts from Hartrigge are very satisfactory. You will be pleased to see our improvements. I shall delight in the garden, and I have a childish hankering after pepper-boxes for the corners of the house. We shall then exclaim, as in the novel of ' Marriage,' ' Hoose d'ye ca' it—I ca' it the Castell.'

Journal.

June 16.—To-morrow comes off at last Lord Stanley's motion in the Lords about Greece and Don Pacifico. Palmerston has had very bad luck in this affair, but I am sorry to say that he is by no means free from blame. In the first place he sent instructions to our minister and our admiral at Athens to resort to force, without ever having brought the matter before the Cabinet, although we were all in town, and the measure was more important than sending the fleet to the Dardanelles, about which we were all summoned from the remotest part of the kingdom to meet on the 1st of October last. The only reason stated to the Cabinet for Sir William Parker's visit to the Piræus was that he might try to enforce payment of the arrears of the Greek loan. Now I quite agree that the Foreign Minister must carry on the ordinary business of the office *proprio marte*, or consulting with the Prime Minister only, but where a step is to be taken which is sure to excite a great sensation in Europe, and which may lead to a European war, the Cabinet most undoubtedly ought to be consulted about it.

Without entering into the merits of this particular dispute, I should like to take a part in the debate, and to expound the law of nations on the subject. But, circumstanced as I am, I shall confine myself to my duties as Speaker. I have refused to act in this capacity any longer, and I presume that Lord Langdale will now be appointed Speaker, with a commission to me to sit in his absence.

Letter to Sir George Campbell.

Woolsack: Monday night, half-past eleven.
June 17, 1850.

My dear Brother, . . . Here I am Speaker once more. The debate on Stanley's motion is going on, and there is great reason to fear that about three in the morning I shall have to say, 'The Contents have it.' This grieves me, being still a stout party man, and moreover feeling that the stability of the present Government is for the general good. I do not believe that a resignation will follow, but the Whigs will receive a heavy blow. The debate has been a very indifferent one. Stanley was too minute, Lord Lansdowne very inefficient, Aberdeen very spiteful. I could myself lay down the law of Reprisals better than it has yet been explained, and apply it to the facts of the Greek question. The refusals and delays to do us justice have hardly been hinted at.

I hear that we are to be beaten by ten, although Lady Palmerston has been in the House all night and has been very active. Getting Langdale to sit for me half-an-hour, I went into the refreshment room and drank tea with her. She affects to be in good spirits, but she is evidently in a great tremor. Palmerston himself has been on the steps of the throne. It is very hard upon him that he cannot be heard, in the French fashion, here as well as in the Commons.

Lord Langdale is henceforth to be Speaker, and I shall be relieved from my labours. I shall leave room to give you the division :—

Contents—Present, 113; Proxies, 56 =169. Not Contents—Present, 77; Proxies, 55 =132. Poor Palm!

Journal.

June 19.—My anticipation was too true.   As Speaker of the Lords I had to say, 'So the Contents have it,' and the majority was so great that many think there must be an immediate resignation and change of government.

June 29.—Lord John stuck to the helm, and his resolution is justified by the large majority of the House of Commons in favour of Palmerston on Roebuck's motion to undo the vote of the Lords.

July 7.—We are still appalled by the sudden death of Sir Robert Peel.   There has been a wonderful inclination to do honour to his memory, and I should not wonder if he were thought a greater man by posterity than by his contemporaries.   His apparent inconsistencies may be considered his principal merit, as showing how he got over the prejudices of education and the ties of party, in the pursuit of what he considered and believed to be the truth.   His death is a very heavy blow to the Whigs.

Our Premier has made an ominous confession in admitting that he must abandon for the present the abolition of the Irish Viceroyalty, and the long promised arrangement for the bisection of the Great Seal.   When is he likely to be stronger on such questions?

The great reproach now is the administration of Equity, and the hearing of appeals in the House of Lords.   The Lords Commissioners of the Great Seal are in sad disrepute. Rolfe is much respected, but his colleagues are altogether incompetent.   Langdale is without vigour and has not a judicial mind.   I believe he might have been Lord Keeper or Lord Chancellor if he had liked, but he has an utter horror of the *mêlée* of debate, and he tells me he would on no account become a member of the Cabinet.   Shadwell is physically disqualified; ever since his appointment he has been confined to his bed.   Therefore nothing but the routine business of the Great Seal is done, and the long arrear of appeals arising from Lord Cottenham's absence remains untouched.   Most portentous of all, Lord Brougham sits alone, deciding cases in the House of Lords!   I pre-

vented him from summoning the judges, but he has been
hearing several writs of error and appeals without any
assistance.   This is a mere mockery, and must bring the
appellate jurisdiction of the House of Lords into sad discredit.   There has been a deputation from the Chancery
counsel, complaining to the Home Secretary of the inade-
quate judicial force now employed, and a petition on the
subject to the House of Commons is to be presented in a
few days.   Brougham says truly that he is as good as when
he was Chancellor, but then he made very indifferent work
of it.

I am now about to proceed on the Oxford circuit, which
I joined forty years ago, a barrister without a brief and without a friend.

August 17.—My circuit passed off very pleasantly.   I
had for my colleague my old pupil Vaughan Williams, whom
I made a judge in 1846.   I found him not only a good lawyer,
but a very agreeable companion.   We had a delightful row
upon the Thames between Abingdon and Oxford, and nice
walks together at every circuit town.   I had only once to
pass sentence of death, and this gave me little anxiety, as it
was for an atrocious murder, proved by the clearest evidence.

My chief amusement was, like Haroun al Raschid,
wandering about the town at night *incog.* and observing the
manners of the people.   At Stafford I was recognised by my
old constituents, but they did nothing to annoy me.   I
heard one tipsy man exclaim, ' I plumped for him before,
and I would plump for him again.'   The corporation presented an address to me, to which I made a suitable reply.

It is very irksome to write down the evidence in a long
cause,—witness after witness being examined to the same
immaterial facts ; but every man is doomed to spend a
considerable portion of his life in employments unpleasant
and unintellectual.   I trust that I was patient as well as
energetic in both courts.

Returning to London on Monday the 12th of August, I
went forthwith to the House of Lords, and there I saw the
woolsack occupied by Lord Truro.[3]   I was happy to find

_____
[3] Sir Thomas Wilde, appointed Lord Chancellor July 1850.—ED.

that, after a session marked by mortifications and defeats, my old friends the Ministers were able to make a tolerable appearance in the Queen's Speech. If they suffer humiliation, their opponents have no real triumphs. 'Protection' will be the ruin of the Tories as long as they adhere to it. If Lord Stanley could honestly get rid of it, he would soon be Prime Minister. With the three per cents touching par, an increasing revenue and diminishing poor rates, Free Trade is for ever established, and the Government on which it is supposed to depend is safe.

Stratheden House: October 25.—After spending about a fortnight at Hartrigge, I went with my daughter Mary on a tour to the Hebrides and the Highlands, and visited regions more distant from Westminster Hall than ever did any of my predecessors, at least since the times of the old Chief Justiciars, who made tours to Gascony and to the Holy Land. We were most hospitably entertained by Mr. and Mrs. Matheson at Stornoway Castle in the Isle of Lewis. We went next by Loch Hourn to Glenquoich in Inverness-shire, and spent five days with the famous 'Bear Ellice,' who has seen more of political leaders and political intrigue than any man in Europe. He was the mainspring of Lord Grey's Government, and had more to do with carrying the Reform Bill than Lord John Russell or Lord Althorp. Having passed through Inverness, Elgin, Aberdeen and Perth, we concluded our round of visits at Taymouth, the most magnificent and beautiful country seat in the whole world.

On my return home I had the honour to be admitted to the freedom of the borough of Jedburgh. But I may perhaps not revisit this region as, on account of my being there a few weeks of the year, I have been assessed to the poor not only on my property within the parish (all right enough), but on my salary as Chief Justice of the Queen's Bench, which is iniquitous and absurd. I decline entering into any litigation on the subject, but shall cease to be an 'inhabitant,' even for a night, till this pretension is abandoned.

I have hastened up to London before the beginning of term to superintend the projected reform of practice and special pleading in the Courts of Common Law. A very

difficult task is before me. My brother judges are disinclined
to any material change in our procedure, whereas many
foolish people are crying out for a total abolition of it, and
think that every dispute may be summarily decided on hearing a verbal altercation (or logomachy) between the parties.
The times are gone by when a Chief Justice could regulate everything by his own simple authority.   Nevertheless I hope, by discretion and tact in the management of
the judges and of the Commissioners appointed by the
Crown, to introduce some very important improvements in
procedure.

Letters to Sir George Campbell.

Stratheden House :
Sunday night, November 17, 1850.

My dear Brother, . . . I have nothing to tell you beyond
what you may learn from the ' Times,' that I am sitting
from day to day, and all day long, in the Court of Queen's
Bench.   I find the work not very burthensome or disagreeable.

I dined yesterday with my brother Patteson, to celebrate
his entrance into the twenty-first year of his judgeship.   He
was appointed when I declined Lyndhurst's offer in 1830.
We had a very jolly day, Lyndhurst himself being present
with six other judges whom he had made, and all excellent
ones.   I told him that his appointment of good judges would
cover the multitude of his sins.   He said he had some
thoughts of dying a Whig, that I might deal mercifully with
him ; and, asking me to drink wine with him, he declared that
all enmities between us down to that moment were to be
considered as buried and forgotten in the champagne.   He
has recovered his sight, and though he touches eighty he is
as brisk as a bee.

Stratheden House :
Sunday night, November 24, 1850.

My dear Brother, . . . I assure you that I should have
as much pleasure as ever in writing, and should write to you
as often as ever, if I had my former leisure for this purpose.
What I say is no commonplace excuse, but is literally and

strictly true. It is as much as I can do to dress, have prayers, and breakfast before I set off for court. From the moment I take my place on the bench till we adjourn, my mind is painfully on the stretch attending to the business in hand, in constant apprehension of getting into a scrape. I have not written one note in court since I became a judge. Change indeed from my lounging days, when hearing appeals in the House of Lords! I then walk home, and, as soon as I have swallowed a mutton chop, I sit down to prepare for the morrow. This is the life I have led during the whole term, refusing all invitations (except to the Lord Mayor's dinner, which I was told I could not shirk) and sending none. I ought to have said that my own puisnes have dined with me, but only to deliberate on judgments, and I have invited all the judges to dine with me next Saturday.

As I get warm in my seat I shall be more at liberty to relax.

Stratheden House:
Wednesday, November 27, 1850.

My dear Brother, . . . I got through all my causes this morning by ten o'clock, and I have a holiday.

I am rather disturbed and darkened by the erection of the Crystal Palace, but it will afford you some amusement when you come up in May.

Of myself I can tell you nothing more memorable than a joke which I very successfully fired off on Monday, the last day of term. You must know that there is an ancient saying in Westminster Hall that there should be nothing but what is *short* the last day of term, and that we have a proceeding called an *audīta querēla*. On this occasion a barrister of the name of C——, an uneducated man, was arguing that a writ of error would not lie, and he said ' My lords, I maintain that the proper course would have been an *audīta querēla*. (A laugh from the bar). In spite of that laugh, my lords, I do again assert that the proper course would have been an *audīta querēla*.' (Redoubled laughter.) *Campbell, C.J.* ' Mr. C. remembers the rule *that everything is to be* short *the last day of term*.' (Prodigious applause.) There has always been a great disposition to laugh at the jests of the Chief Justice. I have several times sneered at this in my ' Lives,' but I have now the benefit of it !

Journal.

November 27.—I have been working exceedingly hard, and have written two judgments (*Walton v. Holt*, and *Doe v. Challis* [*]) on questions of real property, which my brethren entirely approve of. I had serious misgivings with respect to my performance when I should have such cases to deal with, but I find that, by sitting doggedly to work, I can master them as if they only raised points about bills of exchange or policies of insurance. I have gained the most credit by my judgment in *Humphries v. Brogden*, touching the obligation of the owner of minerals to leave a support for the superincumbent surface. This I flatter myself will become a ' leading case.'

I now sit at Nisi Prius till Christmas, and, having no more judgments to write, I mean to amuse my evenings with the life of Lord Tenterden, the only deceased Chief Justice I have not portrayed.

January 10, 1851.—I have finished my life of Tenterden. If it sees the light, the old barber of Canterbury must be a great relief to the reader tired of aristocratic genealogies, and the quiet character of this Chief Justice forms a striking contrast with the turbulence of his immediate predecessor. His devotion to the composition of Latin verses gives a beautiful close to his career, and if the day was rather dull, we have a radiant sunset.

Term begins to-morrow, and I shall be in a constant bustle till the conclusion of the spring circuit.

At present no one can tell how any other government is to be formed, as Lord Stanley cannot yet shake off ' Protection,' but Lord John Russell has such storms to encounter in the approaching session that he will probably founder in one of them. Popish Aggression—Abolition of

---

[*] *September* 1860.—This latter judgment was unanimously reversed by the Court of Exchequer Chamber, and unanimously affirmed by the House of Lords in the last session of Parliament.

the Irish Viceroyalty—Division of the office of Chancellor—
Renewal of the Income Tax—Repeal of the Malt Tax, and
of all other taxes *seriatim*: these are subjects which must
come forward, and there is not one of them on which he may
not be beaten. Sensible people ought to stand by him, for
under his auspices the country is most prosperous; but there
is no enthusiasm and little coherence among his supporters.

February 17.—The session is a fortnight old, and the
Whig Government still subsists, but it is in a perilous state.

I sat by Lord Stanley last night in the gallery of the House
of Commons while Charles Wood was opening his Budget, and
we had a good deal of *badinage* together. We have long
made up our quarrel in the House of Commons about Church
Rates, and are quite cordial again. I do believe that he
wishes and expects to be Prime Minister very speedily. He
has splendid talents, and has a head for business as well as
an admirable faculty of speaking. But he does not inspire
confidence, and I greatly doubt his discretion.

Disraeli is the rising man. A few years ago he was an
attorney's clerk. Now he is the leader of the landed interest,
and, for anything I know, the Jew boy may cut out the heir
of the Stanleys, and one day be Prime Minister himself, on
high Tory and Protectionist principles, after having been a
violent Radical and boxed the political compass round and
round. He is the pleasantest speaker to listen to now living,
and he becomes rather a favourite with the House.

April 9.—A few days after the last entry in my journal
came the resignation of Lord John Russell. The Budget
proved to be the most unpopular ever proposed, and after
the defeat of Locke King's Bill by a majority of two to one,
produced by the absence of the Tories and the combined
presence of Radicals and Roman Catholics, the Whig Government was extinguished.

Lord John did well when he resigned, and he would have
done better if he had resolutely refused to return to office.
His subsequent career has been a continued series of blunders,
mortifications, and disgraces. How the negotiation failed
between him and Graham and the Peelites I do not understand. The difference on Papal Aggression could have been

no serious obstacle, if they had cordially wished to coalesce. John Russell, to retain the premiership, must have wished to have the leading Peelites for colleagues; but I suspect they had a notion that, strengthened by the Radicals, they might soon be able to form a government of their own, with Graham at the head of it. They strangely miscalculated the feelings of the English nation. By making a defence of the Pope their pretence, they have ruined their popularity, and, if a dissolution of Parliament were now to take place, most of them would lose their seats. Lord Stanley, as soon as he can get rid of the millstone of *Protection*, will swim into office. The Whigs, I am grieved to say, excite the contempt of their friends and the compassion of their opponents. Poor Lord John, after his blustering letter to the Bishop of Durham and bragging speech respecting what he would do against Pius IX., has given an immedicable wound to his reputation by his miserable Ecclesiastical Titles Bill.

He has hurt himself still more with all who understand the subject by the scheme he has propounded in the House of Commons for reforming the Court of Chancery. This has been more universally and deeply condemned than any measure I have ever known brought forward by any Government. It ruins the office of Chancellor, damages that of Master of the Rolls, and would greatly obstruct the progress of business both in the Court of Chancery and in the House of Lords. No one knows who is the author of the Bill. I never was consulted about it, nor will anyone else acknowledge any acquaintance with it. Here lies a great defect in Lord John Russell's character as a statesman, which has got him, and will get him, into many scrapes. He acts in important matters with which he is imperfectly acquainted without consulting anyone, although he has valuable and friendly information and advice within his reach.

His only hope now is to please the Radicals by promising a new Reform Bill for next session of Parliament. I am greatly mistaken if this succeeds. He must again pass through Opposition before he can recover *prestige* as a Prime Minister.

I have finished a very laborious circuit, and having been

above a year in office, I may be considered fully initiated as
Chief Justice. I had to try two murderers in Essex, who have been since executed. Their guilt was clear, and I had no uneasy thoughts about them from the time when they were sentenced, but I felt much anxiety during the trials; and when I put on the black cap my nerves were by no means firm.

I went the Home circuit as Chief Justice exactly forty-three years after having joined it as a junior barrister. Alas! the whole generation of barristers I had left upon it had long been swept away. I cannot say that I found superior genius, learning, or eloquence among their successors. The present leaders are great bores. But I got on with them tolerably well and, without any quarrel with them, considerably improved their style of doing business.

Wonderful revolution! I went to and returned from every place by railroad, except that, when all was over, I rode home on horseback from Kingston through Richmond Park. I again had Baron Parke for my colleague.

I expect to hear little else talked of for the next five months but the *Exhibition*. Unfortunately, the Crystal Palace stands before my windows, and the neighbourhood is already infested by mobs, day and night.

May 8.—News arrived to-day of the death of Lord Cottenham near Lucca. About a fortnight before him died Lord Langdale, who, if not a great judge, was a most amiable and excellent man, and a most sincere and zealous law-reformer.

It is rather a melancholy reflection to me, that of the three peers made together in January 1836, I alone survive. Of the evanescence of the portion of my career which yet remains I am frequently reminded by the rapid dropping off of my contemporaries and juniors. I can only pray to heaven to enable me to perform usefully and respectably the duties of my station while life and strength are vouchsafed to me, and to fit me for the awful change into another state of existence which must at no great distance await me.

May 23.—I have been all day in the Crystal Palace, the Great Exhibition of 1851. The wonderful success of this

project has made us forget Papal Aggression, Lord John
Russell's defeats, and all the topics which have successively
agitated the public mind during the last six months. I was
at first a strong anti-exhibitionist, and made myself very obnoxious by denouncing in the House of Lords the proposed
desecration of Hyde Park. But there is no denying that the
Exhibition has turned out one of the wonders of the world.
Since the dispersion of mankind at Babel there never has
been such a *réunion*, and we have the produce of nature
and of art from every part of the planet which we inhabit.
It really will form an era in the history of our species.

We are invited to the Queen's fancy ball on the 13th of
June, when we are all to appear in the characters or costume
of the reign of Charles II. I am to go as Sir Matthew Hale,
Chief Justice; and I am now much occupied in considering
my dress; that is to say, which robes I should wear—
scarlet, purple or black? The only new articles I shall have
to order are my black velvet coif, a beard with moustaches,
and a pair of shoes with red heels and red rosettes.

This slight deviation from the politico-professional high
road may cause some regret to my grandchildren that I do
not wander more into the byways of private life. I may now
mention some of ' grandpapa's ' habits. I never rise in the
morning to study, but get up to read the newspaper. By
half-past eight we have prayers, and all breakfast together.
Next I mount my horse to ride down to Westminster through
Kensington Gardens, Hyde Park, Constitution Hill, the Mall,
or Birdcage Walk, my dear daughter Mary generally accompanying me. I am the first in the judges' robing-room. In
drop my lagging puisnes, and, after a little friendly gossip,
we take our places on the bench. Here we sit from a few
minutes past ten till about half-past four. I go to the
House of Lords when it sits, continuing there till between
six and seven, when their lordships generally adjourn. I
walk or ride home, and have a mutton chop or some such
repast ready for me, never taking above two glasses of wine.
About eight the whole family meet at tea, a most delightful
meal. I hate great dinners, although I am obliged to submit to them sometimes, both at home and abroad. In the

evening I write judgments or look into the Crown or Special papers for the following day, going to bed about one.

During the Nisi Prius sittings, I am obliged to start half an hour earlier,[5] and I am sometimes kept in court to a late hour, but there is less extra-curial drudgery. Upon the circuit the duty is often very severe, but I always contrive to have a little walk before breakfast, and if I feast one day, I fast the next. I have great reason to bless God that my life upon the whole is a very agreeable one.

I regret that I have now very little leisure for miscellaneous reading, and I fear my literary labours are at an end. Nevertheless, I have finished the lives of Kenyon, Ellenborough and Tenterden, which I shall keep by me in MS.

June 1.—Had a long conversation yesterday in the Crystal Palace with Sir James Graham. He began with congratulating me on my ' brilliant success ' as Chief Justice, which he extolled rather extravagantly. I lamented that he was not serving his country as a Minister of the Crown. He attempted an explanation of his conduct, which was not quite satisfactory. I cannot account for the part he is playing, either on the principles of patriotism or selfishness. Although he said he should be willing to serve under Lord John if they could agree, I suspect that he looks forward to the premiership. Meanwhile he pleases no party, and is a mere isolated individual. He praises the excellent good sense of the people, which he says renders the form of government in this country of less importance, while he admits that the present extreme weakness of the Ministry endangers the throne.

The most amusing topic about town now is the Lord Chancellor's opposition to a Government Bill which, at the request of the Prime Minister, I had introduced into the House of Lords, for the registration of deeds. There has been nothing like this since Thurlow opposed Pitt's Bill for a sinking fund to pay off the National Debt. We are to

---

[5] Nisi Prius sittings then began at half-past nine, but I was soon after obliged to postpone them till ten. The courts at Westminster used to sit at seven in the morning and rise at twelve. In another generation I suppose they will sit at twelve and rise at seven.

have another tussle on Tuesday evening, and much sport is expected.   Our present Chancellor is almost as great an anti-reformer as Lord Eldon.

June 19.—Yesterday was the last day of Trinity Term, and my court sat till past ten at night; the most arduous duty I have ever had to perform, my mind being continuously and intensely at work above twelve hours.   During this time we disposed of as many cases as would occupy some courts for a twelvemonth.   The state of business is very satisfactory, as we have cleared off the Crown paper and the Special paper and the new trials and all the rules which were pending.   No complaints reach me of any want of patience.   The great thing is to find out the real question to be considered, and to keep the counsel close up to it.   The fact being known and felt that I can make it disagreeable for counsel to speak nonsense, much less nonsense is spoken. In Banco there is very little time wasted, and the practice at Nisi Prius has been much improved, although it still wants improvement.

I have carried through the Lords two very important Bills respecting the Criminal law.   The Registration Bill, notwithstanding the obstruction of the Lord Chancellor, is likely to pass, and ought to immortalise me.[6]

The great controversy now is upon the Evidence Bill, allowing the parties to be examined against and for themselves.   Brougham introduced the Bill.   It is opposed, as might be expected, by the Lord Chancellor.   If it passes, it will create a new era in the administration of justice in this country.   I support it, and I think it will be carried, although all the Common Law judges, with one exception, are hostile to it.

July 1.—Having presided to-day in the Court of Queen's Bench at Guildhall, and solemnly sentenced a man convicted before me for obtaining money by false pretences in cheating at cards, I descended from my tribunal, walked to London Bridge, embarked in a steamer, and was carried in her thence to Westminster Bridge for the sum of one penny sterling.

---

[6] The Bill passed the Lords, but was lost by the inefficiency of the Government in the Commons.

She was crowded with decent-looking people of the lower order. Having landed, I entered the House of Lords and there made a speech upon the Patent Law, which was well received. I proposed and carried a clause allowing courts of Common Law to grant an injunction against the infringement of a patent. This is a great era in the history of our jurisprudence. The abolition of the Court of Chancery, or what is called 'the universal fusion of Law and Equity,' I consider nonsense. There must be a peculiar jurisdiction to enforce the performance of trusts, and to dispose of suits to which there are numerous parties with distinct interests. Where the judge is himself to decide fact as well as law, the procedure must be different from what it is where the law is decided by the judge and the fact by the jury. And in a country where, from the quantity of business, there must be many courts, it is much better that one class of causes should be assigned to one court, and another to a different court. But every cause should begin and be finally determined before the same court in which it properly began. The existing practice with respect to the infringement of patents and the infringement of copyright and similar cases—of being obliged to begin by filing a bill in equity for an injunction ; then being sent to a court of law to try an action; then to go back to the Court of Equity ; employing two sets of counsel, and conducting two suits in two different courts for the same grievance—were it not for ' damned custom,' which reconciles us to all enormities, would be considered most oppressive and most disgraceful. I have now got in the fine end of the wedge. Next session I shall bring in a Bill to give to courts of law a general power of granting injunctions in all similar cases.[7]

July 14.—. . . I have hitherto successfully struggled for the true principles on which legal reform should be conducted. There is now a class of *pessimists* who maintain that ' whatever is, is wrong.' They think that all disputes may be settled by calling the parties before the judge and sum-

---

[7] *September* 1860.—This was effected by the Common Law Procedure Act, 1854. I tried last session of Parliament to carry out the principle to all its legitimate consequences, but I was defeated.

marily deciding after the fashion of a Turkish Kadi. I shall continue to stand up for '*special pleading*'—i.e. a written statement of the claim and the defence, evolving the questions of fact or of law to be decided by the jury and the judge. No doubt this art has been dreadfully perverted, and much labour will be required to simplify and improve it.

August 25.—The Western circuit is over, and I am a free man till November. I have had for my brother judge Coleridge, who is very amiable and agreeable, and has a good notion of law. We had no hard work on the circuit, crime being diminished by plenty of employment, good wages and cheap provisions—the result of free trade—and the civil business being curtailed partly by the county courts—still more, I think, by the Great Exhibition of 1851. Diverting into another channel the rills which otherwise would have irrigated litigation, and affording excitement of another sort, the Exhibition prevents people from quarrelling with their neighbours.

To-morrow morning I sail for Antwerp with my wife and three of my daughters on our way to Florence.

I have to record a meeting with my immediate predecessor a few weeks ago. I had never seen him since his first attack of illness. In accordance with his enthusiastic temperament, he strongly disapproved of any legislation to resent the 'Papal Aggression,' and considered it inconsistent with the principles of religious liberty to complain of Pio Nono parcelling out England into dioceses and establishing a Roman hierarchy in this kingdom without the consent of the civil magistrate. He wished to have made a speech upon the subject, but this Sir Benjamin Brodie and his medical advisers would not permit, as the excitement would probably have brought on another paralytic seizure. However, in the debate on the second reading of the Bill, soon after the conclusion of Lord Aberdeen's speech lamenting the absence of the late Chief Justice of the Queen's Bench, 'whose mild wisdom would have made a great impression on your lordships,' Denman himself, supported by Lord Monteagle, entered the house, and took his seat on the woolsack beside the Lord Chancellor—but he had only come to try to pair off, and, if he could not, to give his proxy to be used in the division against the Bill. While I was working up my resolution to go and speak to him, he withdrew from the House, still supported by Lord Monteagle. I followed him, and saw him slowly and painfully descending the steps which lead to the room of the Clerk of the Papers. When he had entered it to sign his proxy, I shook hands with him, and he received me very graciously. Brougham had told me that he now entertained perfect goodwill towards me, and rejoiced in my success as Chief Justice. I found his features unchanged, and his articulation tolerably distinct, but he had a very imperfect use of his limbs. Having conversed with him a few minutes, I bade him a last adieu.

I wish I could get rid of my circuits, of which I am heartily sick. I have no taste for the pleasure which Mr. Justice Allan Park relished so intensely to the last portion of his existence, in meeting the sheriff and being trumpeted into the assize town; in walking up a cathedral clothed in scarlet, under the gaze of boys and old women; or in lecturing the grand jury; and my spirit almost dies away when I think that I am to pass the remainder of my days in hearing witnesses swear that the house was all secure when they went to bed, and next morning they discovered that the window had been broken and their bacon was gone. But I ought not to grumble! What luck for me to practise at the bar in its prosperous days—and to be now in the certain receipt of 8,000l. a year official income! In spite of the efforts of Cobden and Bright, seconded by the discontented Protectionist squires who wished to cut me down according to the price of corn, the Bill has passed and received the Royal assent by which the Chief Justice's salary is fixed at this sum from the death of Lord Tenterden. Lord John bargained with me that I was to be contented with 2,000l. a year less than the Parliamentary salary, as Denman had been.[8] I said I was satisfied so that the arrangement should be sanctioned by Act of Parliament, but I would not stand an abatement depending upon the pleasure of the executive Government.

[8] The salary had been 10,000l. a year.—ED.

For the next two months I shall have my mind filled with rivers and mountains, pictures and statues. Florence is our destination, and I am not without hope that I may see Rome and Naples. Heaven protect me and those who are dear to me in our travels, and bring us back in safety to our native land!

Letter to Sir George Campbell.

Rome: October 7, 1851.

My dear Brother, . . . We are still going on prosperously. On Monday September 29th we went to Leghorn and embarked in the Neapolitan steamer 'Vesuvio,' which arrived next morning at Civita Vecchia, and the following day landed us at Naples. There we spent three days most delightfully, visiting Herculaneum, Pompeii, etc. We had no earthquake, and Vesuvius would not throw out flames to frighten us, but smoked very quietly, like the rest of the inhabitants. Naples certainly is the most wonderful place in the world. 'Vedi Napoli e poi muori.' We left it most reluctantly on Saturday morning, and late at night reached Terracina, not without apprehension of banditti. Next morning we posted at a rapid rate through the Pontine Marshes, and arrived here in the afternoon in time to say our prayers before the high altar of St. Peter's.

I never worked harder than during the last three days, and we already know more of the 'Eternal City' than we should learn by reading about it for seven years. My greatest exploit was, *not* going into the ball of St. Peter's, which I did this morning, *but* having in the evening an audience of the Pope and taking him to task for his anathema against the Irish colleges. I was told that he would consider it a slight if I did not pay my respects to him. Accordingly I intimated to his Chamberlain my desire of an audience, and I was invited to attend at the Vatican this evening at six o'clock. He received me in his private room, dressed in white flannel like a monk, seated at a table with candles upon it. He rose, and when I had made my bow he sat down and desired me to be seated on a stool near him. There was no one else present. He was exceedingly good-humoured, and we

immediately fell into familiar conversation, not in the royal
style of question and answer, but each chatting as to an
equal.   After some small-talk about my tour and my judicial
duties, he thanked me for opposing the amendment to the
Diplomatic Relations Bill forbidding his Holiness to send an
ecclesiastic as ambassador to England, and said he was told
the English believed he wished to eat them all up.   I told
him I hoped there might still be an *entente cordiale* between
the Court of Rome and the Court of London.   He observed
liberally that angry feelings on both sides would die away.
I then got upon the Godless colleges, and, asserting that
Parliament sincerely wished them for the benefit of the
Catholics and desired to guard the faith as well as the
morals of the Catholic youth to be educated there, expressed
deep regret that they did not meet the approbation of his
Holiness.   He made but a poor defence, observing that they
were afraid to trust to any professors who were not Catholic.
He added that they were trying to establish a Catholic
University in Ireland, but he doubted much whether they
had the means.   He then courteously bade me adieu and I
retired.

We have had lovely weather here, and I am persuaded
the air is as wholesome as on the banks of the Eden. . . .

Journal.

Stratheden House: November 30.—I cannot say that
I am by any means as well pleased to be upon my tribunal
in ermine robes as I was to be upon the box of my travelling carriage wearing a wide-awake; but I took to business
naturally enough, and got through the term with comfort.
I have since made my first appearance in the Central
Criminal Court, where, it is said, the Chief Justice of England is expected to attend to try 'great murders;' but I
shall not suffer myself to be dragged speedily there again.
I am now sitting at Nisi Prius, working the new Act which
permits the parties in a cause to give evidence for themselves.
It has made a very inauspicious start,—one party, if not both
parties, having hitherto been forsworn in every cause.   But

I still hope that it may operate favourably for the elucidation of truth.　One unfavourable effect it will permanently have,—to increase the labour of the judge; for trials must last much longer, the new fashion being in every case to examine the plaintiff and defendant *plus* all the witnesses on both sides who would have been examined under the old *régime*.[9]

[9] *October* 1856.—The Bill has since been made to work most admirably : all mankind praise it.

CHAPTER XXXI.

DECEMBER 1851—JUNE 1854.

Coup d'état in Paris—Expulsion of Lord Palmerston from the Cabinet—
Thiers in London—Lord Derby Prime Minister—Sugden Lord Chan-
cellor—Roman Catholic Sheriff at Aylesbury—Norfolk Circuit—Lord
St. Leonards—The Protectionists—Pulling down of the Crystal Palace
—Literary Fund Dinner—Controversy between the Publishers and the
Booksellers—End of the Session of 1852—Fall from his Horse—
Northern Circuit—Hard Work at Liverpool—Assizes at Jedburgh—
Duke of Wellington's Funeral—Overthrow of Lord Derby's Government
—Lord Aberdeen Premier—Lord Cranworth the new Chancellor—
Return of his Second Son from India—Lord Aberdeen as a Leader
—The Eastern Question—King of Hanover—Lord Lyndhurst at eighty-
two—North Wales Circuit—Visits his Estates in Galway—Stays in
London as Vacation Judge—Tiresome Work in Westminster Hall—
War between Russia and Turkey—Resignation and Return to Office
of Lord Palmerston—Lord John Russell's Reform Bill—Trial for
Murder at Aylesbury—War with Russia declared—Last Letters to
his Brother—Death of his Brother—The Funeral.

Journal.

December 16, 1851.—Professional, personal and party
questions have lost their interest, and we can think of nothing
but Louis Napoleon's *coup d'état* of the 2nd of December.
' It is not, nor it cannot come to, good.' For violence and
fraud there is nothing like it in history. Such an absolute
despotism never existed · in Europe before. In the East
custom presents a limit to the freaks of reigning sovereigns,
although they are restrained by no express law. The President, having in a moment annihilated a constitution which
he had sworn to defend, imprisons and massacres at pleasure;
suppresses all the journals in Paris and the departments,
except those which confine themselves to registering his
edicts; puts one half of France in a *state of siege*, and claims
the unheard-of power of framing according to his own fantasy

a new constitution for the purpose of perpetuating bondage
in France. But he says that he gives the French people
'universal suffrage.' I am rather pleased with this bitter
irony. Fully convinced that anarchy or military despotism
must be the result of universal suffrage wherever established,
I like to see it so prominently brought into disgrace and
ridicule. The disposition to tamper with our mixed constitution will thus receive a salutary check, and our children
may continue to enjoy the combined blessings of political
freedom and social order.

December 27.—We have a *coup d'état* at home which
causes nearly as great a sensation as the new Revolution in
France—*the expulsion of Palmerston from the Cabinet.*
The real facts are not yet known, but the presumption is
strongly against Lord John Russell. Whether justifiable or
not, he has done an act which will certainly precipitate his
own fall. The Peelites stand aloof, and, without any coun-
tervailing accession of strength, I hardly see how he can
decently propose to meet Parliament.

Letter to Sir George Campbell.

Stratheden House :
Sunday night, January 18, 1852.

My dear Brother, . . . On Thursday I dined in company
with Thiers in a party of five, and sat next him four hours.
He was very entertaining in his account of his captivity at
Ham, and other adventures. He seems to think there would
not have been much harm in the *coup d'état,* if it had been
his. Indeed, in his History he justifies every *coup d'état*
and revolution in France for sixty years, and he has now no
right to complain. He is going to take a house near us, and
to employ himself in continuing his History. He will not by
any means have so good a reception here as Guizot had.

Journal.

February 15.—Parliament has met; we have had explanations about our *coup d'état,* and poor Palmerston for
the nonce seems to be undone. He committed an egregious

blunder by quarrelling on an occasion when he could neither have the sympathies of the Radicals nor of any other party in his favour. Lord John dexterously seized the critical moment for action, and securely got rid of a formidable rival.

Strange infatuation that Palmerston should not have foreseen the unpopularity he must incur by taking part with *absolutism* in France, after having been so long the leader of *liberalism* over the whole continent of Europe! Lord John has considerably raised his character for boldness, but difficulties so multiply around him that I do not see how he can stand. The Protectionists are becoming formidable by discarding Protection. Luckily for them the price of corn rises and the farmers are less discontented. Motions unconnected with Protection are to be made, upon which Ministers may be left in a minority. Should this happen, we may have a new Cabinet and a new Parliament any day. Lord Derby now declares that he is ready with his list to present to the Queen whenever she may be graciously pleased to send for him, although he failed so sadly when he was last sent for.

Brougham and Lyndhurst have entered into a combination to harass the Chancellor, and they keep up a cross fire upon him every night. With very little inclination to interfere, I have been obliged once or twice to come to the rescue. They may wish to have him back again, if the Great Seal should be delivered to ' the flippant and conceited' Sugden.

February 24.—To 'the flippant and conceited Sugden' in a very few hours the Great Seal will be delivered. Lord Derby's administration is formed, and Sugden is his Chancellor. No one can blame this appointment. Sugden, notwithstanding his disagreeable qualities, has well earned his advancement, and I make no doubt that he will reputably execute the duties of his office. What fun we shall have in the sparring matches between him and Brougham!

I must say that I rejoice in the change of Government. For the sake of Lord John himself and of his party, the event is a happy one. The longer he remained in office the deeper he was getting into disgrace. Parliament and the country are for the present sick of him, and it is only by a course of opposition that he can be again set up in the world. Retributive justice had decreed that he should fall by the hand of Palmerston. The Foreign Secretary was wrong in the quarrel about Louis Napoleon, and the Premier dexterously laid hold of the opportunity to get rid of a rival; but his triumph has been shortlived, and the multitude now say, ' *Sarved him right.*'

We are at present made infinitely merry by the list of the Derby Cabinet. A Ministry of such obscure and weak and incompetent men never existed in England before. I am afraid that the performers may be laughed off the stage before the business of the piece properly begins. This would be a great public calamity, for a disgraceful breakdown of the Protectionists would make the Radicals more encroaching and more dangerous. What I wish is to see Lord Derby fairly try to carry Protection, that he should be beaten, and that a strong Liberal Government should then be formed consisting of Whigs, Peelites, and even a small sprinkling of Radicals—with Lord John, or perhaps rather Palmerston, at the head of it. If we are to have war, the latter would be far the fitter Minister. The old Whig aristocracy I presume would prefer a Russell; but Palmerston, notwithstanding his late hallucination about Louis Napoleon, is considerably more popular in House of Commons.

Lord Lansdowne's valedictory address to the House of Lords last night was one of the most graceful and touching oratorical exhibitions I ever witnessed. I could not refrain from saying to him that I had gone on admiring him more and more as our leader down to the present hour. He gave some good advice to the Peers—that, besides being mild and courteous, they must be more energetic and enterprising, so as to fill a larger space in the public eye, or they will soon be superseded and forgotten. We Peers ought to hold our heads an inch higher at present, as we are for a while to have the Premier amongst us. He certainly is the most stirring orator now in either House, and there is abundance of talent among us if it were properly developed.

Unfortunately, in a few days I go on the circuit, and I shall lose all the fun of the inauguration of the Protectionists, and of the denunciations into which they will be forced against *Free Trade.*

What is Lord Chancellor Sugden to say to the proposed 'fusion of Law and Equity' (about which the House of Commons is now quite mad), considering that no longer ago than last session, being examined before a Committee of the Commons, he declared that the present system of proceeding in the Court of Chancery is a piece of absolute perfection? So thought Cottenham, who never could be made to oppose the 'hourly warrants' in the Master's office;[1] but the rage for Equity reform had not then begun, and now it threatens all our judicial institutions with subversion.

February 28.—I heard the Earl of Derby's *exposé* of the principles on which he means to govern. A few minutes before he rose I met him in the robing-room, and, shaking hands with him, wished him joy. He said (and I believe he was sincere for the moment) that ' he was much more to be pitied than congratulated.' He danced his hornpipe among burning ploughshares with considerable dexterity and felicity. But he cannot keep it up long. The nation has practically tasted the sweets of Free Trade, and never will again endure monopoly. It is idle for him to say that, although his own opinion is for Protection, he will be governed by the opinion of the public. If upon a dissolution of Parliament he is left in a minority on the Corn Law question, he cannot continue in office, abandoning Protection ; and if he makes the attempt he will be turned out with unmixed disgrace.

April 14.—I have gone another circuit, and Easter Term begins to-morrow. At Aylesbury, my first assize town, I had a brush with a Roman Catholic sheriff which has been much discussed in the newspapers. He had written to me that he did not mean to appoint any chaplain, and I had told him I wished him to do nothing which should be at all disagreeable to him on the score of religion. When I first met him, and we entered his carriage while the trumpeters were

---

[1] This refers to the usage in the Master's office, according to which the Master who was the judge could never devote more than one hour any one day to the same cause, so that suits that might have been terminated in a few days, lasted many years.

blowing, I was surprised to see a person jump in after us in the costume of a Roman Catholic priest. Before I had any time to collect my thoughts, the door was shut and the horses moved on. At the judges' lodgings I found that this was a *perverted* clergyman of the Church of England, who had gone over to Rome. I intimated to the sheriff that, although he was not bound to appoint a Protestant chaplain for us, and he was at liberty to appoint a Roman Catholic priest to minister to himself, I could not recognise this priest as the person who was to officiate as chaplain to the judges of the assize, and therefore I must decline his presence in the carriage, and he must not sit by me in his canonicals in court. I explained the matter to the grand jury, who unanimously thanked me for what I had done. The proceeding was fully reported in the newspapers, and was the subject of innumerable commentaries, generally taking part with the Chief Justice. Thereupon a Roman Catholic conclave was held, and Cardinal Wiseman wrote a long letter to me in the name of the sheriff, which I answered, to the great amusement of the public.[2]

In several counties I did all the duty of the assizes single-handed, my colleague Crompton, the new judge, having been taken ill, and obliged to return to London. At Bury St. Edmunds I had thrice to pass sentence of death in murders by stabbing and by poisoning. This is very nervous work, unless the cases are characterised by great atrocity, and rest upon evidence free from all manner of doubt. Then I perform my part in the administration of the criminal law with as little concern as Calcraft the executioner. The most painful of all cases to me are charges against young women for the murder of their illegitimate children, secretly born. Here the inequality of the sexes appears very striking. I always tell the jury that the tests of the child being born alive are very uncertain, and that marks upon the child may be attributed to accidents in the delivery. These charges of murder I really believe are generally unfounded. Where there has been a mere *concealment*, I give a very short imprisonment without hard labour.

[2] See the 'Times' of March 18th.

I was glad to observe that the Acts which I passed last session for the improvement of the criminal law worked well, and this is allowed even by my brother judges who opposed them. E.g. by the old common law an indictment for murder was required to specify the manner in which the murder was committed; hence often a great multiplication of counts describing it in different ways; and sometimes an *acquittal,* because the evidence showed it to be different from any of those specified. Now it is enough for the indictment to allege that the prisoner ' feloniously and of his malice aforesaid murdered the deceased.' The prior proceedings before the coroner and the magistrates always fully inform the prisoner of the charge he has to answer.

I found Parliament, on my return to London, in a very queer state, both Protectionists and Free-traders having come to the agreement that there shall be no party divisions this session, and that there shall be a dissolution *quàm primùm.*

I doubt whether ' Sug,' the new Chancellor,[3] is likely to go on as well as I expected. Notwithstanding my sincere desire to co-operate with him cordially in all matters connected with the law, I had a quarrel with him the first night we met in the House of Lords, which originated in my merely suggesting an amendment (the more effectually to gain his object) in a clause of an Act of Parliament about the execution of wills. They circulate an anecdote of him which if true would be very much to his credit. Someone is supposed lately to have twitted him with being the son of a barber, whereupon he retorted, ' Yes, but if you had been the son of a barber, you would have been a barber yourself.' I don't know how far his father would now be pleased to see him on the woolsack. The old gentleman said to Selwyn, the Queen's Counsel, who told me, ' I tried my son Ned in my own profession; but unfortunately he has no genius for it, so I have been obliged to put him as a pupil with Mr. Duval the conveyancer.'

Brougham has not yet had any open skirmish with the new Chancellor, but he privately complains to me very

[3] Lord St. Leonards.

bitterly of his coxcombry, and there is sure very soon to be
mortal strife between them.   Lyndhurst, near eighty, having
three years ago declared that he was speaking in public for
the last time, speaks every night, and is a devoted ally of
the new Government.   Although in Peel's time he suddenly
found out that ' Protection was all a humbug,' he now says
the same thing of Free Trade.

April 22.—The Easter holidays are over, and Parliament
has reassembled.   Lord Derby feels, and almost confesses, that
Protection is for ever at an end, and the watchword by which
he rallied his party will be heard no more.   He seems now
to be about to adopt the cry of *No Popery*.   For this the
indiscreet conduct of the Roman Catholics has given too
much cause.   All over England, and still more in Scotland,
Protestant feeling, even among the liberal and enlightened,
has been evoked in a manner quite unexampled for more
than half a century.   At the ensuing elections candidates
will be very generally called upon to give a pledge to vote
for repealing the allowance to Maynooth.   There is some
plausibility in the proposal, as this college produces nothing
but bigotry and disloyalty.   But without *Protection* I apprehend that the Derby Ministry cannot stand, whatever
difficulty there may be in forming another.   Although the
public be rather sick of Lord John and his Whigs, some
other combination will be formed which will be preferred to
the apostate Protectionists.   They are so dreadfully open to
reproach for their virulent abuse of poor Peel, whose policy
they adopt, that they will be generally abused and (what is
worse) laughed at.   Were a second Disraeli to arise to attack
Disraeli the First, there would be such an encounter as the
world never witnessed since the days of the Titans.   I look
on with considerable indifference.   If the present men do
not seriously attempt to interfere with Free Trade, they can
do little harm.   The Tories may usefully remain in till a new
wholesome Liberal party is concocted in the crucible of
Opposition.

May 7.—The subject which has lately engrossed all my
interest has been the preservation or pulling down of the
Crystal Palace.   This will hardly be known to posterity, but

for many months it has filled a large space in the public eye. I have been the leader of the *pulling-down* faction, and our triumph has covered me with glory, although I have been scurrilously abused in the newspapers, and at all the public meetings which have been held to agitate for a breach of the national good faith, and the perpetuation of an intolerable nuisance.

May 21.—I have been presiding at the anniversary dinner of the Literary Fund, surrounded by almost the whole *corps diplomatique* and many of the most eminent of my countrymen. I remember well that, exactly fifty-four years ago, when I was eighteen years of age, and just come to London as private tutor to James Wedderburn Webster, I had the present of a ticket to dine at an early anniversary of the institution. This was not nearly equal in splendour to the last, but it seemed to me wonderfully grand. The first Marquis of Bute presided, and I thought I had as little chance to succeed him in the chair of the Literary Fund as to be King of Great Britain and Ireland.

I have since been sitting as Chief Justice, with Milman the Dean of St. Paul's, and Grote the historian of Greece, as my puisnes, upon a grand question between the publishers and the retail booksellers as to the right of the former to dictate a *minimum price* at which new books are to be sold by the latter to their customers. Macaulay and all the great literary men have taken a lively interest in the controversy. The hearing took place at Stratheden House, our court sitting *foribus apertis*, and attended by reporters. The judgment which I delivered in favour of free trade in books will be a curious document two hundred years hence, illustrating the manner in which knowledge was circulated in the reign of Queen Victoria. I never took such pains with any judgment to be delivered in Westminster Hall.

June 28.—Parliament is to be prorogued on Thursday, and dissolved the same evening. The session has been very unexciting in the Lords. It was thought that the reign of Sugden was to be suddenly cut short by 'that fell Serjeant Death,' but he has had a wonderful recovery, and he is now in full vigour. After a few smart brushes with him, we have become apparently good friends, and I am sure I bear him no malice. He is undoubtedly a great master of his judicial work.

I have a real admiration of Lord Derby's oratorical powers and of his intellectual acumen. A profound statesman he is not, and I do not believe that he will have more than a taste of premiership. He appears to much advantage in comparison with his colleagues, who in the House of Lords are laughably bad. If there were the means of forming a new Government, there must be an immediate change; but the Derbyites may go on till they get into some scrape which will make the existing Government worse than no Government at all.

Hartrigge : August 28.—Soon after these speculations, it was thought that my career was closed. Returning on horseback from Guildhall, my horse took fright on Southwark Bridge, reared and dashed me against the pavement. When I recovered my senses I was put into a cab and carried home to Stratheden House. I received a cut on my head three inches long, and some very serious contusions on the shoulder and ribs. My surgeon told me I must not go into court or attend to business for some weeks, but next morning at half-past nine I was again upon the bench at Guildhall, to the great surprise and dismay of Mr. Attorney-General, who for a space had considered himself Chief Justice. I did an imprudent thing, but I avoided the exaggerations which would have gone forth of the damage the Chief Justice had sustained. I got through my special juries, and on Saturday July 3rd I was at York on the arduous undertaking of going the Northern circuit as senior judge.

I spent six weeks most laboriously, and I have not yet recovered from the horrors of the gaol at Liverpool, where I had to try 170 prisoners for grave offences, 150 having been tried for minor offences at quarter sessions the week before we arrived there. Every night since I returned home have I dreamed that I had some shocking criminal case before me, and when awaking I have long doubted whether the evidence and speeches I had been listening to were real or imaginary. Anxious *alibis* make a deep impression on the brain, and I should not be surprised if my last words were, like Lord Tenterden's, ' Now, gentlemen of the jury, you will consider of your verdict.'

But the Northern circuit was not without its *agréments*. The country was not so strange to me as to Lord Chief Justice North in the reign of Charles II., when the inhabitants of Northumberland and Cumberland were considered uncivilised as North American Indians. Still I met with many new characters, and I saw a great deal to excite and interest me. I rather envied the Archbishop of York and his Canons their luxurious indolence. Here I had a delightful visit from my wife and daughter, who accompanied me to Winyard, where we were splendidly entertained by the Marquis and Marchioness of Londonderry. At Durham I found my old friend the Bishop of Exeter in residence as a prebendary. We met cordially, and I had a very satisfactory dinner from him—nothing being said about the Gorham case or the powers of Convocation. The Corporation of Newcastle entertained us free of expense while we were within their jurisdiction, and at our departure the Mayor, according to ancient usage, presented to me a gold Jacobus to buy a dagger with which I might defend myself from Scottish freebooters as I passed along the border. I paid a visit to the Earl of Carlisle at Naworth Castle, which has been restored and reinstated as it stood in the days of ' Belted Will.' Tait,[4] the Dean of Carlisle, gave us a splendid entertainment, and presented a rare instance of a Scotsman promoted in the Church of England on account of his reputation as a classical scholar. This, however, he had acquired at Balliol College, Oxford, not at Aberdeen or St. Andrews. The most ceremonious reception I had was from the Earl of Lonsdale, at Lowther Castle. On approaching his domains two grooms or *piqueurs* magnificently mounted presented themselves, and conducted me to the château. There I was treated as the representative of her Majesty.

There is no longer an hereditary Sheriff of Westmoreland, so that the judges are not now lodged and feasted, as

---

4 The present Archbishop of Canterbury.—ED.

formerly, in Appleby Castle. The last Earl of Thanet was the last legitimate Tufton, and he left his immense estates to an illegitimate son, created Sir Richard Tufton, Bart., in consideration of his surrendering his claim to be sheriff, and consenting to the office being regulated by Act of Parliament. Nevertheless I had a delightful stay at Appleby, which is a beautiful village instead of an assize town, and I alone in a few hours did all the business of the county, civil and criminal, my brother judge being detained by a long trial at Carlisle.

I had dreadful work at Liverpool, sitting at the least nine hours a day, and then almost daily having a public dinner. I should not have been able to stand it had I not risen early, and had a long walk every morning before breakfast. But this was only in the wide streets, which are less odious than the suburbs of Liverpool. How delighted was I when on the 22nd of August a railway train carried me off to Preston. I shall never go the Northern circuit again. I have now 'run the gauntlet,' having gone all the six English circuits, and I can henceforth choose as I please, without any breach of etiquette. I ought to express my gratitude to my colleague, my brother Wightman, who was exceedingly kind and attentive to me, and proved a very pleasant companion, displaying stores of literature for which I had never given him credit.

Travelling by Carlisle and Hawick, I reached this place on Monday the 23rd, and forgot all my troubles in the affectionate joy of my wife and children. Here I mean to remain quietly till I am again called to London by my judicial duties. I stand much in need of repose, and with repose I hope to be able again to encounter the smoke of London and the noise of Westminster Hall.

September 9.—I yesterday attended the assizes held at Jedburgh for the counties of Roxburgh, Selkirk, Peebles, and Berwick, which were all finished at a single sitting, there being no civil cause, and not more than half a dozen prisoners to be tried. As in duty bound, I attended the judges— Lord Justice Clerk and Lord Wood—at their levée and in court. A grand dinner I was to have given to them and the

bar this day has been defeated by a general dispersion last
night. It must be 'sixty years ago' since I, a little boy on
a visit to my uncle at Ancrum, came to Jedburgh to witness
the grand spectacle of the judges entering the town to
hold the assizes. They inspired me with admiration and
awe.

Stratheden House: November 18.—I am returned from
the Duke of Wellington's funeral, having attended it in state
as Chief Justice of England. If not for my high office, I was
much envied for my manifold robes and my full-bottom wig,
which kept me comfortable while others were penetrated
by the cold blasts which were raging around. Many generations may pass away before there is again such a spectacle in
England.

December 18.—Lord Derby's Government is overthrown,
and I rejoice. He has played a very undignified and very
silly part. He ought to have stuck to Protection, which he
says he still believes to be true policy, and, being beaten
upon a vote to restore it, he would have fallen with honour.
The hope of retaining office after abandoning Protection was
a delusion. He and his Cabinet really seem to have been led
away by the absurd notion of Disraeli that a budget might be
framed which, keeping up the public revenue, would relieve
some classes from taxation without burthening others. He
has still great confidence in the belief that another Government cannot be formed. Sitting by him last night in the
House of Commons, he said to me: 'I have been counting
the members of the new Cabinet, and I make out that there
must at least be thirty-two.' I asked him if he included the
leaders of the Radicals, Cobden and Bright. 'No,' said he;
'they will make thirty-four.' He was not without hopes till
the division was announced to him, when he exclaimed: 'Now
we are properly smashed; I must prepare for my journey to
Osborne to resign.'

I enjoy the prospect of a strong and enlightened Government, and I am gratified by the poetical justice now executed
on the vituperators of Peel.

Truro cannot be reappointed, but Cranworth may make a
very tolerable Chancellor, and I shall zealously support him.

He is one of the most honourable as well as amiable of mankind; and he has a good stock of common sense by which he
may steer his way amid formidable difficulties.

Abinger Hall: December 26.—The new Ministry is
formed, and Cranworth is Chancellor. His life must some
day be written, and I should delight to do justice to his un-
sullied honour, his warmth of heart, his instinctive rectitude
of feeling, his legal acquirements, his patient industry and
his devoted desire to do his duty.

Having been here three days, I am going back to London
to witness the installation of Lord Aberdeen. Think of a
Scotsman and a Presbyterian being Prime Minister in these
days of Puseyism! I hope his administration will be more
quiet and more durable than was that of Lord Bute, the only
other Scottish Premier we have had. Lord Derby, to his
mortification, will find that the Cabinet instead of thirty-four
consists of thirteen. That a good many of the excluded will
be dissatisfied and vengefully inclined I doubt not. If the
malcontents had had Palmerston for their leader, an opportunity for doing mischief would probably have soon occurred;
but as he has at last accepted office, I think by themselves
they will be innoxious. The Radicals were in great hopes
that they were coming into power, and they look very sinister,
but I trust they will be made to discover that they had
greatly overrated their own importance. They have been for
the last twenty years a very unreasonable and arrogant race,
and we may now see a Liberal Government with sufficient
Conservative support to be able to disregard them.

February 12, 1853.—I was amused by receiving a circular from the Earl of Aberdeen, the new head of the Liberal
party, soliciting my attendance on the reassembling of
Parliament. I sincerely wish well to his administration. I
really think that *Liberal Conservatism* is the true principle
on which politics should now proceed. A pure despotism has
been established in France by universal suffrage, and free
institutions seem to be of more value than the abstract right
of every man to pop a voting paper into a ballot-box.

My poor friend Rolfe seems likely to be badgered in a
very cruel manner between the three law lords, Brougham,

Truro and St. Leonards, and I almost think he wishes he were again a Vice-Chancellor or a Puisne Baron. I shall stand by him at the risk of personal contests which I would rather now avoid.

February 28.—I served to-day on a Select Committee of the House of Lords, attended by the Lord Chancellor and four ex-Chancellors—Lord Cranworth, Lord Lyndhurst, Lord Brougham, Lord Truro and Lord St. Leonards. Five holders of the Great Seal I suppose never met in deliberation before. The 'Bauble' is now very expensive to the public, there being an extra outfit of 2,000*l.* to each new Chancellor, and a retiring pension of 5,000*l.* a year to each ex-Chancellor.

May 22.—I seldom touch on domestic matters in my journal, but I cannot refrain from noticing the vast enjoyment I have had in the safe return of my second son from India, and the comfort I expect from his acting as my 'Associate' for the rest of my judicial life. He is handsome, well mannered, sprightly, intelligent, well principled and kind-hearted. . . .

July 1.—Lord Aberdeen proves to be a very indifferent leader in the Lords. Never having been a member of the Lower House, he is not much of a debater, and he is exceedingly unhandy in answering questions. But he has a reputation for honesty. 'They think him honest as they know he's dull.'

The *thanes* fly from Derby, and now for the first time since I have been a Parliament man a Liberal Government has a steady majority in the House of Lords.

I have steadily supported Lord Aberdeen except in one debate, about 'transportation,' brought on by Lord Grey, supported by the Derbyites. Notwithstanding my exertions on this occasion, the Government triumphed, and after the division Lord Derby looked like a dethroned sovereign.

Letters to Sir George Campbell.

Stratheden House: Sunday night, July 3, 1853.

My dear Brother, . . . I am sitting at Guildhall, where I have the largest entry there has been for years, and I am

obliged to go to the House of Lords every evening to watch
proceedings there, and to protect my little friend Rolfe.
Upon the whole he gets on very well, but Sugden would be
too much for him in single-handed combat. His chief
failure is not keeping the law officers of the Crown in due
subordination. They are allowed to cast off all allegiance
to him, and to proceed in the House of Commons in direct
violation of his wishes. This I never would have submitted to.

The last division on the India Bill shows the Derbyites in
such a desperate condition that the session, as far as party
struggles are concerned, may be considered over. The
present Government will go on smoothly, I should think,
till the Reform Bill comes in next session. At present
we only think and talk of the *Eastern Question*. It was at
the Queen's ball on Friday night that Bunsen first told me
of the Russians crossing the Pruth. This was confirmed by
Lord Aberdeen, who, to my great astonishment, said it might
lead to negotiations and peace, whereas I consider it flagrant
war. If our fleet does not now enter the Bosphorus there
will be public disappointment and indignation.

I ought to tell you of my presentation the same evening
to the blind King of Hanover. He was intensely civil, saying that he had heard much of my reputation, that he was
delighted to make my acquaintance, and that it was a
proud thing for a Scotsman to be at the head of the law of
England.

I am afraid they think much less of me in Fife!

Stratheden House :
Sunday evening, July 10, 1853.

My dear Brother, . . . My labours at Guildhall will soon
be over. The last week was a very severe one for me, as,
beside my judicial and parliamentary duties, I had to dine
out every day except Thursday, when I had a grand law party
at home. I was sorry that George happened to be engaged,
as I wished to introduce him to Lord Lyndhurst, the most
remarkable man, I think, of this generation. He is eighty-
two, with his mental faculties as vigorous as they were half a

century ago.   He hears as well as ever, and, having undergone the operation of couching, he sees very tolerably.   On this occasion he was quite boyish, giving various toasts, and was the life of the company.   We had, besides, an American Chief Justice and the bar of the North Welsh circuit.

Poor Denman is in a very different and a very deplorable state.   With the use of his limbs he has entirely lost the power of speech, and, as he cannot be communicated with through any medium, it is doubtful whether the ruins of his mind have not perished.

As you look with interest at the career of our *little Chancellor*, I may tell you that the Attorney and Solicitor General conspire his downfall, each having the hope of replacing him.   Their constant habit is to *vilipend* him. Bethell hardly attempts to disguise his eagerness to clutch the Great Seal.   But I have little doubt that Rolfe, though not very gloriously, will keep his ground.

Journal.

August 28.—I am returned to London after going the North Wales circuit, and paying a visit to *my tenantry* in Ireland.   My circuit was an agreeable tour, for I went single judge, accompanied by my wife and my daughter Mary, and, there being little business to do, we spent our time in paying visits and admiring scenery.   I hoped to have mounted Cader Idris and Snowdon, but the weather was only propitious for waterfalls.   At Carnarvon I had to pass sentence of death on a murderer, which caused a great sensation, for there had not been an execution in the Principality for twenty years.   The circuit finished at Chester.   There I was joined by Baron Platt, who had held the assizes in South Wales.   Having finished my own business and given my colleague a good lift, I set off for Ireland, accompanied by my daughter Mary and my sons Hallyburton and Dudley.   We made a short stay in Dublin, which I had not seen since I left it as ex-Chancellor in 1841.   There was now an ardent desire to do honour to the Lord Chief Justice of England.

My visit to Galway was very successful.   I ought to

record that ten or twelve years ago I lent 33,000*l.* on mort-
gage on estates in that county, valued at 60,000*l.*, mine being
represented as the first charge. My interest was paid for a
year or two, and soon came the famine. Since then I have
had only vexation and expense from the concern. My
mortgagor, although a Master in Chancery and member of
Parliament, turned out to have been a swindler, who had
cheated me and many others. Luckily for him, he died
before his frauds were fully detected. I at last bought the
mortgaged property in the Encumbered Estates Court, nom-
inally for the sum I had advanced upon it, although no
purchaser would then have given half so much. Hitherto I
have received no rent, the sum collected from the tenants
not being sufficient to pay rates and the expense of management. There are two estates, containing together about
10,000 acres, and occupied by 330 tenants.

I had a very courteous reception from them all on this
occasion, although about a year before they had refused to
attorn to me, and I had been obliged to call in the sheriff to
put me into possession. On the 22nd of August I gave a
grand dinner to the Moycullen tenantry, and made them a
speech, which has been noticed in all the newspapers of
Great Britain and Ireland. I was glad of an opportunity
of explaining my religious principles. From my having
been obliged to resist the intrusion of a Roman Catholic
priest publicly thrust upon me as judge of assize, it was
supposed by many that I had become a Protestant bigot.
I now explained my wish for religious equality, at the same
time reading to the Irish a lesson against Ultramontane
doctrines and the interference of priests in secular affairs.
I really think that I may have done good in softening
sectarian prejudices and allaying animosities between Celt
and Saxon.

I am now returned to the humble duties of vacation
judge. However, I have only to attend at Serjeants Inn
two days a week. The rest of my time is at my own disposal, and I hope vigorously to resume my biographical
labours.

October 5.—Having got three of my learned brethren to

sit for me successively at chambers, I have been for a fortnight in Scotland. Yesterday I returned, breakfasting comfortably at Hartrigge and drinking tea at Stratheden House. I enjoyed my excursion very much. The growth of my trees gives me particular delight. Not only have I planted large masses, but I have followed the advice of the Laird of Dumbiedikes to his son Jock: 'Stick in a tree wherever it will stand; while you sleep it will grow.' My garden and shrubberies are likewise much improved. I have now only to construct a good house on the property for the future Lords Stratheden and Campbell, and then I think I shall have done my duty to them.

The pleasure I had in seeing my children thriving, happy and affectionate is of a higher nature, and, admitting of no description, can only be conceived by a fortunate father. My dearest daughter Mary, my constant companion and fast friend, sticking by me during the long vacation, has insisted on returning to London with me—cheerfully sacrificing beautiful rides and pleasant visits and gay balls which awaited her in the country. Heaven reward her filial piety!

I find London in a state of great excitement about the war between Turkey and Russia. Our Government seems to me to have managed the negotiation very badly, and I fear has got into a sad scrape. If the combined squadrons of England and France had sailed into the Black Sea when the Russian troops crossed the Pruth, tranquillity would speedily have been restored. The Czar has been justified in counting on the timidity of Lord Aberdeen. Submission to insult is an invitation to fresh insult. The Italian proverb is excellent : 'He who makes himself a sheep is sure to be devoured by a wolf.' 'Chi si fa pecora il lupo mangia.' I care little personally about the present Ministers, but it is for the public good that they should be supported, and I should be very sorry to have to go against them.

December 24.—Having finished Michaelmas term and sittings, my holidays are begun. I find the work very irksome. Setting aside the disgrace, I would as soon be beaten well all the time with a cudgel as preside in Queen's Bench with . . .

on one side and . . . on the other. According to Quevedo's mode of fancying future punishments, a sentence to suffer such torture for a thousand years ought to expiate any venial sin. But I am seriously convinced that in every condition and position there are *désagréments* wisely ordained with a view to prevent us from becoming too fond of this life, and to prepare us for leaving it with less reluctance.

I continue to go on very comfortably with my puisnes, although they sometimes give me trouble and anxiety in differing from me, I of course think, without reason. But none of them ever dissent from a love of differing, or from a desire to gain *éclat,* or from any except the purest and most laudable motive. I consider myself most lucky in my colleagues.

I am much grieved by the present state of political parties in this country. The result of the negotiation on the Eastern Question has been lamentably unfortunate. The national honour is tarnished, and, after all, a general war seems inevitable. After quietly allowing the Czar to pass the Pruth and to seize the principalities of which the Sultan is sovereign, we might have laid our account with a continuation of similar outrages. The destruction by the Russians of the Turkish fleet at Sinope is more disgraceful to us than any event since the surrender of Lord Cornwallis in America. A very moderate share of prudence and spirit would have been quite sufficient to avoid it. The ministerial journals blame the Turks and blame the French ; but the chief share of blame seems to me to rest on the English Cabinet for not long ago having shown a determination to go to war, if necessary, for the protection of our ally. Lord Aberdeen has been afraid of doing anything that might be disagreeable to Austria, and he has had a terrible suspicion of Louis Napoleon, who appears to have acted with perfect good faith since we entered into alliance with him. In the course of my long experience I have never known any minister as unpopular as Lord Aberdeen is at this moment.

We have had an interlude which would be amusing if it did not tend to distract our counsels and lessen our influence at this critical juncture, in the resignation and return to

office of Lord Palmerston. To-day it is understood that the
difference is patched up, after sharp criminations and re-
criminations in the public journals. The rupture showed
the Government to be in a very unsound state, and little
good will be done by the reconciliation. The nation will
say that men who fight and shake hands so foolishly are
unfit to be at the head of affairs. Yet if the ministerialists
can stick together they are safe, for the Protectionists are
annihilated, and there is no other party extant to whom the
Government could be entrusted for a single day.

February 14, 1854.—Last night I went to the House of
Commons, and heard Lord John Russell open his new Reform
Bill. To bring it forward when we are on the brink of a formidable war seems to me wholly unjustifiable, for it must create
much party animosity, and lower the credit and influence of
England with foreign nations. That in the excitement of aggressive hostilities, and the dread of disasters to our allies,
the proposed new reform should be calmly discussed and
deliberately adopted may be expected by those who compare
us to the Romans with Hannibal encamped under the walls
of Rome; but the expectation is known to be absurd by all
sober-minded practical observers. If the war becomes flagrant,
which the electric telegraph may any moment declare it to
be, I presume the Bill will be abandoned without any motion
for a second reading; and then not only will Ministers
incur the suspicion of insincerity, but proclamation is made
that the existing House of Commons, which is still to
legislate for us, does not justly represent the people, and does
not deserve their confidence. There can be no reasonable
chance of the Bill reaching the Lords during the present
session of Parliament. If it should, several of its enact-
ments I should strenuously oppose, more particularly the
amalgamation of the county and borough franchises. This
destroys a fundamental distinction which has subsisted ever
since Parliament sat in England, and inevitably leads to a
representation by uniform numerical constituencies, which
would be fatal to the monarchy.

March 31.—I am returned to London after completing my
ninth circuit, being now in the fifth year of my reign. I had

to try a very remarkable murder at Aylesbury, when there was a conviction on circumstantial evidence which satisfied me of the guilt of the prisoner. Still I was much relieved from anxiety by his subsequent voluntary confession. He had murdered a female, his fellow-servant, and then tried to make it believed that she had been burnt to death by thieves who had broken into the house. There was an ineffectual attempt to show that there were spots of blood upon the clothes he wore when apprehended. I advised the jury to place no reliance on this evidence, but to consider whether, although there might be no blood on those clothes, he might not have changed his clothes after doing the deed. In his confession he said that he had done so, and the clothes which he wore when he did the murder were found saturated with blood in the hole where he said he had hid them. . . .

I find Lord Aberdeen's Government in a very ' staggering state.' Without any formidable opposition, they are guilty of such follies as must speedily prove their ruin. Within a year there are five members of the Administration who have successively sent in their resignation and have returned to office. There is, as far as I have heard, no struggle in the Cabinet between the Whigs and Peelites, but individually they dislike each other, and the chief has no ascendancy to control them.

War is declared, and a new chapter opens of the history of the world. We see a sight which has not been seen since the time of the Crusades—French and English armies fighting side by side against a common enemy.

Letters to Sir George Campbell.

Stratheden House : April 9, 1854.

My dear Brother, . . . My holidays continue to the 19th, and I have been enjoying them very much. Dudley is at home, but Hally is gone to fish in Connemara, and to see how our affairs prosper there.

I have at last ordered the alterations to the house at Hartrigge to be made according to Mr. Bryce's first plan. I can expect little enjoyment in the house myself, but I should

like to leave a decent place of residence for those who are to
come after me—having entailed Hartrigge as a little *majorat*
on the title of Stratheden and Campbell.

It was announced last night at Lady Palmerston's that
the Cabinet have agreed to drop the Reform Bill for the
session. Lord John was very obstinate, and the Government
was very nearly broken up. There is an impression that
there will be no fighting after all. I hope that Charley
Napier may first burn the ships at Revel. . . .

Stratheden House: Easter Monday.
April 16, 1854. Five P.M.

My dear Brother,—I can only give you two lines to say
all is well.

We have a salmon for dinner caught by Hally at Bally-
nahinch. He must be back on Wednesday, the first day of
term.

Ena has got up her pony, Gooseberry, from Hartrigge,
and is gone out riding with Dudley and Cecie. I am not
yet remounted, and I don't know whether I ever shall be.
Walking exercise agrees with me well.

I have not yet heard of Mr. Bryce having *opened the
trenches* before Hartrigge.

I am strongly tempted to buy a very nice house on the
property adjoining Moycullen, which I could get much
cheaper than new Hartrigge will be; but I don't much fancy
transferring the family to Ireland.

I am dreadfully tired of this horrid east wind, and it has
forced me to take a little quinine.

Give me some arguments to support my 'Unauthorised
Communications Bill.'   Yours affectionately,

C.[5]

---

[5] *Hartrigge* : October 4, 1856.—This is the last letter from me to my
brother which has been preserved. On the 22nd of May following I heard
of his death. Our correspondence continued till within a few days of that
melancholy event, but was confined to the details of his health and strictly
domestic matters. As far as affection was concerned, it never knew change ;
but when I was made Chief Justice the vicissitudes of my career were at
an end, and I was withdrawn from party politics, so that my epistolary
topics very much dwindled away.

Journal.

[*May* 22.--I have received the sad news of the sudden death of my brother. This is a dreadful blow to me, and the world now presents quite a different aspect to me—a very gloomy one—which I fear will continue for the remainder of my sojourn here. Although he was nearly two years older than me, we were in the same class at school and college, and have been devotedly attached to each other through life. It was often said that he was the cleverer of the two, and I believe that with the same opportunities he would have gained greater distinction. For the last thirty years he has been settled as a country gentleman in Fife, but we have interchanged yearly visits, and carried on an almost daily correspondence by letter. He took the most lively interest in my career, and my name was never mentioned in any newspaper connected with anything I had done or written or said, that it did not attract his attention and excite his sympathy. Seldom has so long and steady a friendship subsisted between two brothers or two human beings. His must be considered a very prosperous lot, for he has lived very happily with a charming wife, and all his children are very advantageously settled in the world—his three sons being in the civil service of the East India Company, with the prospect of great advancement; one of his daughters being married to the member for Carmarthenshire, a gentleman of very large property; and the other to the Honourable FitzGerald Foley, a distinguished officer in the Royal Navy.

My poor brother cannot be said to have been cut off prematurely, and according to the dictates of reason and religion, I ought calmly to submit to the inevitable bereavement—preparing for the awful event which may overtake myself at any hour, and which in the course of nature cannot now be distant. ' In all time of our tribulation, in all time of our wealth, in the hour of death, and at the day of judgment, Good Lord deliver us.'

June 4.—On Friday, May the 26th, I went down to Scotland to attend my poor brother's funeral, and I got back on Sunday the 28th, the only occasion of my absence from

court since I became a judge. I was deeply affected by the
sad scene which I had to witness. The ceremony was
conducted according to the Presbyterian fashion—solemn
prayers in the house before the procession began, and no
religious service at the grave. The whole was awful and
impressive. But the English Burial Service is very fine, and,
as I think it would be agreeable to the feelings of my family,
I should wish it to be adopted when my turn comes, and
my remains are deposited in Jedburgh Abbey, where a
resting-place is secured to us in very holy ground.

CHAPTER XXXII.

Acts as Judge at Chambers—Procedure Bill of 1854—The Russian War—
Tour in Germany—Letter from Lord Lyndhurst—Death of Lord
Denman—Trial by Jury—The Army in the Crimea—Reconstruction of
the Government under Lord Palmerston—Oxford Circuit with Baron
Martin—Torquay and Saltram—Motions for New Trials—State of
National Affairs—Lord Cranworth and Sir Richard Bethell—Appeal
Business in the House of Lords—Dinner at Lord Brougham's—Death
of Lord Raglan—Willes, the new Judge—Judgment in a Case before
the House of Lords—Resignation of Lord John Russell—South Wales
Circuit—The new House at Hartrigge—News of the Fall of Sebastopol
—Mr. Justice Willes and the Abjuration Oath—Christmas at Abinger
—Macaulay's new Volumes—Committee of Privileges and Debate on
Life Peerages—Peace Conferences in Paris—Visit to his Daughter in
Worcestershire—Scotch Judges in the House of Lords—Dissensions
between the Chancellor and the Law Officers—Treaty of Paris—'Free
Ships, free Goods'—Trial of Palmer for Poisoning—Quarrel with
America—Norfolk Circuit—Dr. Whewell.

Journal.

CHAP.
XXXII.

A.D. 1854.

August 12, 1854.—Instead of going circuit this summer I have remained in town to do the business at chambers, which I have not found so disagreeable as I expected. This is not to be confounded with being 'long vacation Judge,' which I was the year before. The judge at chambers during the circuits sits five or six hours daily. A good deal of troublesome work I have had, no doubt, but I regret it the less as it more thoroughly initiates me in the practice of the courts—a branch of knowledge which it is very comfortable to possess. By remaining in town I have been of considerable service in the House of Lords, and particularly in getting through Parliament the great 'Procedure Bill of 1854,' which brings about, as far as is now practicable, the fusion of Law and Equity, and establishes the principle on which our jurisprudence must henceforth be moulded, ' one court for one cause '—i.e. that the court in which the suit commences shall carry it through all its stages, and finally determine it and everything connected with it. Thus parties will no longer be kept oscillating between Law and Equity till the subject-matter in controversy is wasted in costs.

On one important enactment I have been thwarted and defeated. I wished to do away with the barbarous custom of imprisoning and starving juries to compel unanimity. Accordingly I introduced this proviso, that, after they have deliberated twelve hours if nine or ten have agreed, their verdict shall be taken and shall have the same effect as the verdict of the twelve, subject to any objection which may hereafter be taken to it as being contrary to the evidence. If there is not such a concurrence of opinion at the expiration of twelve hours, the jury to be discharged, and the cause to be tried by another jury. The Commons changed this into an enactment which still required unanimity, but provided that, if at the expiration of twelve hours there is not a unanimous verdict, the jury shall then be discharged. To this I would not agree, as you cannot insist on unanimity without compulsory means of enforcing it, and, according to the proposal, there would frequently be abortive trials . in civil actions, and in criminal trials it would hardly ever be possible to obtain a capital conviction. The result has been that, after an interchange of messages and the Bill having travelled backwards and forwards several times between the two Houses, the clauses upon this subject have been struck out of the Bill altogether, and the law respecting unanimity and compulsion remains as it was. I intend in another session of Parliament to bring in a Bill to carry into effect the principle for which I have been struggling. It is a curious fact that the Lords have become more rational and more liberal on all subjects of law reform than the Commons. That House is now much infested with lawyers. It was said that the Reform Bill would exclude them altogethei, but their number has since been trebled, and they are no longer the quiet, silent nominees of borough proprietors. Nowadays

they have numerous constituents whose prejudices they
must try to flatter; and they hope for the offices of Attorney
and Solicitor General by obtaining notoriety in proposing bad
Bills or opposing good ones. Lord Coke's *parliamentum
indoctum* was much preferable to this *parliamentum doc-
tissimum.*

I feel intense interest in the Russian war, and I could
only wish it were waged more energetically. But I have
had the satisfaction of seeing the rascally Czar defeated by
the unassisted Turks, and obliged to recross the Pruth.
Now for Sebastopol! If it be taken I shall not grudge the
doubled income tax, or any of the sacrifices we are called
upon to make.

I am now going to make a tour in Germany with my
wife, my daughters and one of my sons. I shall probably
keep a journal if I see or hear or think anything worthy of
being remembered.

[He visited Berlin, Dresden, Prague and Vienna, going
down the Danube as far as Pesth; and returned by the
Tyrol, Munich and Paris, keenly enjoying the whole tour,
and displaying as much energy and activity as the youngest
of the party.—ED.]

Stratheden House: October 31.—The journal of my
German tour will show how I have been occupied during
the last two months. I am not at all sorry to return to
my judicial labours.

On my return to London I found the following letter
on my table from an illustrious ex-Chancellor.

> Where'er I roam, whatever realms to see,
> My heart untravelled fondly turns to thee,
> Still to my Queen's Bench turns with ceaseless pain,
> And drags with each remove a lengthening chain.

Dear Lord Campbell,—It is true that the Campbells ran away from
Montrose, but that is long since. They have made ample amends, they
and their gallant commander, by their glorious conduct on the Alma.

Brougham tells me you have been everywhere, from the levées of
Manteuffel and the meetings of the far-famed Bund, to the funeral of
St. Arnaud. You have heard, seen and, with your usual perspicacity,
observed much. Pour a little of the overflowings upon a poor wretch

confined by gout in both feet, unable to move. As the mountain cannot
go to Mahomet, let the prophet kindly come to the mountain.

From three to five o'clock every day it is in a tolerable state of tranquillity.   Yours ever,

George Street: October 19.   LYNDHURST.

I found him in George Street, laid up by a violent fit
of the gout, but talking in his usual agreeable, rollicking
strain. . . .

I likewise found the following letter from the eldest son of
Lord Denman, written immediately after his father's death.

Stoke Albany: September 23, 1854.

Dear Lord Campbell,—You must forgive me for expediting painful
news to you, but you would be more shocked by learning it from a newspaper. My revered father was seized at dinner, just after finishing some
broth, on Thursday, and was carried to a sofa, and thence to his bed, from
which he never rose until Friday at night, when he fell from a disturbed
sleep into his everlasting rest. He regained consciousness before going to
his death-bed, and showed that he knew and thanked my wife and me for
our endeavours to render the last few months of his existence as cheerful
as possible.

He went to church, as soon as he was strong enough, for several
Sundays, and was, it seems to me, a humble Christian whose works will
(please God) follow him.

I am happy to be in possession of one document in which he praises
your efforts as a law reformer, and I recall to mind his once advising a
person in distress to employ you as counsel in a painful but hopeless case
—and your kindly expressions towards him at Leicester in 1850 were not
lost upon his loving spirit ; and I may add that any difference (which his
family may have deplored) between him and his successor arose from his
feelings as almost an advocate upon public questions for what he thought
conscientiously of paramount importance.

With respectful remembrances to Lady Stratheden, believe me, dear
Lord Campbell,   Yours very sincerely,

THOMAS DENMAN.

I returned a kind answer, stating truly the sincere regard
I had ever entertained for the deceased.

I am rather low, having just heard that Lord Cuninghame is dead, and that Lord Truro is dying. Thus my contemporaries drop around me. But, as in the field of battle,
while death rages round, those that are spared must do their
duty.

December 27.—Another term and sittings have passed
away, and Christmas is come again. I have got through my

work satisfactorily. Our new *procedure* (which in truth is a *juridical revolution*) is now established, and people submit to it quietly. Lord Mansfield attempting a fiftieth part of it failed, and drew down much obloquy upon himself. We not only adopt and act upon his ' equitable doctrines,' long so much opposed and sneered at, but we have a complete fusion of Law and Equity as far as is practicable, and litigation between parties is generally conducted and concluded in the court in which it begins. This certainly is a vast improvement.

I rejoice to think that I have effectually thwarted the scheme which was strenuously pressed of doing away with trial by jury in civil causes. From some conditions and qualifications which I introduced, the new enactment on this subject is a dead letter, and not one trial by judge without jury has yet taken place.

There are many cases now brought to the sittings and assizes turning on matters of account, or a multiplicity of disputed items as to the quantity and quality of goods sold or work done. These a jury cannot satisfactorily try, and they should be sent for decision to an officer of the court, or some accountant or expert, as soon as the action is brought. But where grave questions of fact are to be tried on conflicting evidence, a jury assisted by a judge is by far the best tribunal ever invented for their decision. One great advantage it has is that reasons are not publicly given. The judge, I presume, will be expected to give his reasons for believing one witness and disbelieving another. His conclusion may be right, but his reasons will be sure to be thought wrong, and his verdict will by no means be received as respectfully by the parties or the public as that of twelve shopkeepers. For a single judge to decide issues of fact (such as upon a plea to an action on a fire policy, whether the plaintiff fraudulently burned down his own house ; or upon a plea to a libel charging the plaintiff with murder, or some abominable crime, whether the plaintiff actually committed it) I think would be most unconstitutional and most inexpedient. I shall take pretty good care that such a change is not introduced *tempore Campbell*.

I am at present sadly distracted and depressed by the

state of the British army in the Crimea. My brother-in-law, General Scarlett, has acquired great glory by his famous cavalry charge on the 25th of October at Balaclava, and my nephew Captain Scarlett, of the Scots Fusilier Guards, has been promoted for his gallantry in the battle of the Alma. In spite of this good fortune, it is heartrending to me to think of the condition to which our forces before Sebastopol are now reduced. . . .

February 27, 1855.—What a crowd of events for the history of parties in England since the preceding entry in my journal:—Lord John Russell's flight from the Cabinet; a majority of two to one in the House of Commons for an inquiry into the conduct of the expedition to the Crimea; the dissolution of Lord Aberdeen's Government; the successive failures of Lord Derby and Lord John Russell to form a new one; Lord Palmerston's patchwork of Whigs and Peelites, after a preposterous attempt to restore Lord Aberdeen; the immediate disruption which followed, caused by the secession of the Peelites; Lord John's pacific mission to Vienna; his consent to be Colonial Secretary under Palmerston; the reconstruction of the Government from the dregs of Whiggery! This reconstruction, only twenty-four hours old, is the last phase presented in the political sky; but how long it may endure, and by what it is to be succeeded, no sagacity can conjecture. Perhaps it may have some permanence, for the only rule now to go by is, to expect that which is most improbable.

I made a point of attending Lady Palmerston's next reception after the retirement of the Peelites. They all mustered, with Aberdeen at their head. I had a good deal of talk with him, and having been just shown by the Secretary to the Treasury a letter from Lord John, written from Paris, explaining his acceptance of the Colonial Department without prejudice to his proceeding on his peaceful mission to Vienna, I was the first to communicate this arrangement to the ex-Premier. He professed great astonishment at it, but uttered an ardent wish *that it might turn out well!* Aberdeen is certainly a very respectable man, but wholly unfit to pilot the vessel of the State in such a storm.

I sincerely wish well to Palmerston's Government.

May 21.—I have had a very agreeable circuit (the Oxford), my colleague being Baron Martin, an excellent lawyer and an exceedingly good-natured fellow. We got through the whole of our business together extremely well at every place, leaving no remanets, and asking for no assistance. The only visit I paid was to Lord Lyttelton at Hagley. I was pleased to revisit the hills and valleys, the woods and streams with which I had once been so familiar. At Worcester I still saw my name as I carved it on the Water Gate, near the cathedral, when I first joined the circuit in 1809. I was appalled by recognising old attorneys, whom I remembered lads with curly brown locks and blooming cheeks—now wrinkled, with a few straggling grey hairs round their bald pates. At first I had only a confused notion of having seen something like the pallid visage before me; but by degrees I could trace the features of a brisk young solicitor, who had brought me a brief forty years ago; he being then in the eyes of the country girls the rival of the irresistible ensign commanding a recruiting party in the assize town. This brought me to think of the change upon myself, and how I must now be regarded as a venerable judge, in extreme old age.

The circuit having finished at Gloucester, I had a charming meeting with my wife and daughters at Torquay. Having stayed there a few days, we paid a very agreeable visit to Lord and Lady Morley at Saltram, near Plymouth. Notwithstanding all the beauties of Devonshire scenery, I was then contented to return to London and the labours of Easter term. I could not endure to reside permanently in the country, and no rural ramble can please me so much as a walk through Westminster Hall and St. Stephen's Hall to the great pavilion in the 'New Palace,' with the House of Lords on the right and the House of Commons on the left, the long corridors swarming with persons interested in an impending debate.

I got through Easter term comfortably enough. The first few days were rather anxious, from motions for new trials in cases tried before me at the sittings after Hilary Term and on the circuit. I believe I am as little liable to

the charge of 'misdirection' as any judge, but mistakes may
have been made and there is a great danger of the *direction*
being misrepresented. I always feel relieved, therefore,
when the motions for new trials are over. I have very hard
work during term time, as I must devote several hours
every evening to reading papers for arguments that are coming on, and in writing judgments in cases where we have
taken time to consider.

I have had a pleasant 'short vacation' of six days, having
seen the Queen deliver the Crimean medals to the heroes of
the Alma, Inkerman and Balaclava; having attended her
concert and her birthday drawing-room, and having observed
that the woods at 'the voice of spring' have 'flourished
green again.' From the continued rigour of the season we
had begun to fear that nature was henceforth doomed to
perpetual sterility, and that all the races of animals and
vegetables would disappear from the earth, making way for
new formations.

Our national affairs, though still in a very unsatisfactory
condition, look rather better. There is no longer a danger
of the Russians marching into Balaclava and taking our
surviving soldiers prisoners, or driving them into the sea.
Our troops are again in good heart, and another campaign
may make us masters of the Crimea. I am all for a vigorous
prosecution of the war. A safe peace is at present impossible,
and any further negotiation undesirable.

I have taken, and shall take, very little part in the debates
of the Lords this session. The war is all absorbing. Cranworth, having despaired of being able to carry great measures
of legal reform himself, has succumbed to Bethell, the
Solicitor-General, who has introduced Bills into the Commons
which he will not be able to pass. Notwithstanding my
regard for Cranworth, I thought it my duty about three
weeks ago publicly to complain in my place in the House of
Lords of the manner in which measures of legal reform have
been lost by the members of the Government thwarting each
other. I solemnly advised that before they brought forward
any considerable measure of legal reform, it should be discussed by all who are to be concerned in carrying it through,

and that then all the members of the Government should be required to support it, so that when agreed to by one House of Parliament as a Government measure it may not be smashed in the other House of Parliament by the agency of the same Government.

May 26.—I find that Lord Cranworth's annoyance from Lord St. Leonards is even more serious than I had apprehended. Attending a meeting of the Statute Law Commission on Wednesday, Bethell, the Solicitor-General, put into my hand a memorandum he had written at the table, beseeching my attention to the deplorable condition of the appeal business in the House of Lords, which was likely to bring down great discredit on their jurisdiction, and to set all Scotland in a flame. He afterwards explained to me that Cranworth and St. Leonards being the only two law lords attending, they always differ, and that, instead of having the cases reargued when other law lords might attend, they always affirm. By the forms of the House, the question put is: 'that the judgment be reversed,' and on the maxim, 'semper præsumitur pro negante,' the decision is in the negative. Pretty comfort for the appellant, who is thus for ever barred, perhaps, of an estate of 10,000*l.* a year!

Bethell said he had been speaking upon the subject to Lord Palmerston, and proposing that I should be requested to sit on the hearing of appeals, or that Pemberton Leigh should be created a peer.

June 16.—Dined yesterday at Brougham's, where I was told there were to be two ex-Presidents of the United States and three ex-Chancellors. The three ex-Chancellors appeared, Lyndhurst, Brougham, and myself; but we had only one ex-President, Van Buren; Filmer, the other, who is now in England, being kept away by indisposition. We had some interesting talk about the respective merits and demerits of the English and the American constitutions. Lyndhurst, who has a hankering kindness for his native land, rather took the Yankee side.   The most curious discussion was upon Lord Grey's Reform Bill, which had been so furiously supported by Brougham and myself, and opposed by Lyndhurst and Ellenborough, one of the guests. We all agreed

that it had not improved the *matériel* of the House of
Commons, and we regretted the loss of the close boroughs,
which so conveniently introduced young men of talents to
parliamentary life. Brougham said that his scheme was to
have no Schedule A, and to deprive Old Sarum, &c., only of one
member, for the purpose of giving members to Manchester,
&c. However, we pretty well agreed that the Bill could not
have been carried if it had been less sweeping, and that if it
had not been carried we could not have got over the famous
10th of April without a revolution.

I have deserted the Queen's Bench sittings, and have
been attending the hearing of an appeal in the House of
Lords, on account of the unhappy state of affairs there, which
threatened to ruin this once august tribunal. . . .

July 1.—Yesterday we had the news of the death of Lord
Raglan in the Crimea. This is a most melancholy event,
but I know not whether it is to be considered a national misfortune. He was an amiable, excellent and brave man, but
I do not believe that he was a great general. Unfortunately,
there is no one of much name to succeed him. Had he survived till Sebastopol is taken, he would have had an earldom
with a pension for three generations. He dies an unsuccessful commander, and leaves his family nearly destitute.

Mr. Justice Maule has resigned. He is succeeded by a
capital hand, whom I warmly recommended to the Lord
Chancellor—Willes, who is not only an admirable lawyer, but
has delightful manners and a well-regulated mind.

July 8.—I am thrown into despair by a revelation made
by Lord John Russell in the House of Commons two nights
ago: that when he was at Vienna he was for peace with Russia
on the terms proposed by Austria; so that in his opinion
the war which as a Cabinet Minister he is carrying on is no
longer justifiable. The reason he gave for his opinion was
the great power of Russia. This is most astounding! We
had considered him to be an advocate for checking the
aggressive policy of Russia, which had become dangerous to
European civilisation. He now quails and succumbs, and is
worse than Aberdeen, Gladstone and Graham, suspected
always to be of the peace faction. John Russell remaining

a member of the Cabinet, what confidence can there be in
Lord Palmerston's Government ? *Nusquam tuta fides.* In
such hands the nation will be little pleased to leave the conduct of the war. At home and abroad nothing now happens
which is not mortifying and humiliating.

July 11.—I am just returned from the House of Lords,
where I have been delivering my judgment in the great case
of Hawkes *v.* Eastern Counties Railway Company, which I
heard argued for six weary days. I had taken vast pains with
it, but Sugden's was still more elaborate, and was very able.
The appeal was against a decree of his in the Court of
Chancery. He had been afraid of a *conspiracy* among us to
reverse it. The decree was right, and I got it affirmed.

The town is in a state of great ferment about Lord John
Russell and the Vienna negotiations. People thought the
session was virtually over, and that Palmerston was safe till
February 1856, but in all probability he will be out in a few
days. Lord John will acquire to himself the designation of
Cabinet-breaker. This is the second which he has demolished
within six months.

When I return to London I suppose I shall find Lord
Derby again Minister, and Sugden restored to the woolsack.
News of the fall of Sebastopol could hardly ward off the im-
pending catastrophe.

August 15.—The catastrophe I anticipated would certainly have happened if Sir Edward Bulwer Lytton's motion
had come on, Lord John Russell still remaining a member of
the Cabinet. Palmerston had resolved gallantly to stand by
him, and to peril his Government upon the issue. All the
other members of the Cabinet concurred. But the subordinates rebelled. . . . All were well pleased that Lord John was
gone, but all condemned the plot against him. The peccant
prophet being consigned to the deep, the ship righted, and
now proceeds, not unprosperously, on her voyage.

When these events were happening I was in the county
of Cardigan, wearing white gloves presented to me by the
High Sheriff, because there were no prisoners to be tried,
and employing my tranquil leisure in admiring the beautiful
scenery of the Tivy and the Towy.

I had a most agreeable tour, travelling on the box of my carriage from Carmarthen to Cardigan, from Cardigan to Haverfordwest, from Haverfordwest to Stackpole, from Stackpole to Cardiff, from Cardiff to Brecon, and from Brecon to Presteign. In two counties I received white gloves, and everywhere I met with much hospitality and kindness. At Ludlow my wife and daughters left me for Scotland, and on Thursday, August 9, I got back to London to assist at the close of the session of Parliament.

I met Palmerston yesterday at the prorogation. He looked cheerful, as he would do if he were going to the gallows. I congratulated Lady Palmerston as being Prime Ministress. She came to enjoy the sight of Palmerston standing at the bar of the Lords on the Speaker's right hand. I admire her devoted zeal for the glory of her husband.

This morning news has arrived of the bombardment and destruction of Sweaborg; and it would seem as if the tide of fortune were again to turn in our favour. This would give me great joy. I have been depressed by our failures in the Russian war as if some private misfortune had befallen me.

Stratheden House: October 30.—I am returned to London after passing a very delightful vacation in Scotland. My chief pleasure in the North was to see the immense enjoyment of my wife and children with 'new Hartrigge.' The house being rebuilt and the grounds greatly improved, it is now one of the most beautiful places in the island. Although I must soon be snatched away, I have much gratification in thinking that my family will have a comfortable residence when I am gone, and that what they see in looking round may assist in inducing them to remember me with kindness.

During the ten weeks I spent at Hartrigge I slept from home only one night, when on a visit to my neighbour Lord Minto, and I was hardly ever more than three miles from my own door. Such uninterrupted repose I have not enjoyed for half a century.

My most exciting occupation was every day at eleven to walk to Jedburgh for the daily 'Scotsman,' a paper published every morning in Edinburgh, having by means of the electric telegraph all the foreign news contained in the London morning papers of the same day. Thus was I informed first of the capture of the Malakoff Tower, and then of the fall of Sebastopol, twenty-four hours sooner than by the London 'Times.' I had vast delight in this success, after all I had suffered from our disasters, although still mortified that, by mismanagement or ill-luck, we, the British, came in for so small a share of the glory.

Palmerston at this moment seems stronger than any minister since the dissolution of Sir Robert Peel's Government. Whether he can stand will depend much on the chances of war. In the meantime all who could struggle against him are utterly prostrate. John Russell, Graham, Gladstone, Disraeli, are disunited and without followers. Derby is rather well thought of at present, but only because he has not joined in the pusillanimous and deceitful peace-cry, and does not announce any policy contrary to that of the Government.

November 3.—Yesterday being the first day of Michaelmas Term, went to the Chancellor's house, where I gave Mr. Solicitor-General Bethell a good jobation for his attack upon his chief in the House of Commons. He complained bitterly of the manner in which the Chancellor had conducted the judicial business of the House of Lords last session. I told him he ought to have resigned his office, and then made a public complaint. He says that some change must take place before another session begins.

November 4.—Much amused and pleased with a scene yesterday in the Queen's Bench. At the sittings of the court my brother Willes presented himself at the extreme right of the bench to take the oaths. All stood up, judges, barristers and strangers, with much solemnity. When the judicial *juror* came to the oath of ' abjuration,' he did not repeat the words after the officer who, with much emphasis, was reading it. I made a private sign to Willes that he should repeat, but with no effect. At last, the words being pronounced by which he ought to have abjured ' the said James and the descendants of the said James,' and he still uttering no sound, I said, ' Brother Willes, you should repeat these words after the

officer of the court, that we may know that you abjure King
James and his descendants.' *Willes, J.* ' My Lord, I am
abjuring them in my mind.' *Chief Justice.* ' That is not
enough, brother Willes. The statute requires the words to
be " spoken " by you. Although there be no " Pretender,"
and there have long ceased to be any " descendants of the
said James," you are bound with a loud voice to abjure them.
I am sorry that the law should require such a farce, but
while the law exists, the farce must be played.' Brother
Willes then repeated the remainder of the oath to the end of
it, and kissed the book. The abjuration oath certainly is a
monstrous profanation, which ought now to be done away
with. We may safely trust to the simple oath of allegiance.

November 10.—Dined yesterday at Guildhall with Salo-
mons, the first Jewish Lord Mayor of London—a very
memorable occasion. I brought in the Bill which allowed
him to serve the office of sheriff, and Lyndhurst the Bill
which allowed him to be alderman and Lord Mayor. All
passed off so well that I make little doubt we shall soon
have Jews in Parliament.

January 9, 1856.—Have entered on another year, at my
time of life rather a solemn and melancholy occurrence. With
a grateful heart I thank God for all His past goodness to me,
and pray that while life is spared to me I may do my duty.

Having by hard labour cleared off the whole of my paper
of causes at Guildhall on Christmas Eve, I rose next morning
at five, and went by rail to Abinger Hall, where I spent four
days very delightfully in witnessing the happiness of Lord
and Lady Abinger upon the safe return of their only son
from the Crimea. Since then I have been enjoying myself
very quietly in reading Macaulay's third and fourth volumes.
Macaulay fully supports his reputation. He is an historian
sui generis, whom it will be very dangerous to imitate; but
he does give solid information to the understanding, as well
as tickle the fancy by his fresh and glowing imagery. When
I had finished the last chapter, I yesterday called upon him,
and he seemed pleased with my sincere felicitations. He
now limits himself to the reign of Queen Anne, and he very
much approved of a suggestion, that he should thence give

a *postliminous* sketch of subsequent English history to
correspond with his preliminary sketch, prior to the reign of
James II.   He told me that he is immediately to take the
Chiltern Hundreds, which is quite right, for his literary will
greatly eclipse his parliamentary fame.

Bethell, the Solicitor-General, has made Baron Parke a
peer.   The judicial business in the House of Lords could not
go on another session as it did the last.   Pemberton Leigh
was first offered a peerage, and I wish much that he had accepted it, but he positively refused to be *pitchforked*.   I
don't know that anything less exceptionable could be done
than applying next to 'Baron Surrebutter.'   This is the
name given to Parke in an exquisitely witty *jeu d'esprit*
from the pen of Serjeant Hayes, in the form of a ' Dialogue
in the Shades below,' in which the Baron is the principal
interlocutor, and in which his passionate attachment to antiquated forms is very successfully ridiculed.

I have a letter to-day from Lyndhurst, dated at Paris,
where he has been for some months.   He jocularly advises
me to resign my office of Chief Justice, to take an earldom,
and to devote myself to the judicial business of the House of
Lords, so that the peers may retain their jurisdiction and
recover their reputation.   An earldom has very small charms
for me, and I would by no means purchase it at such a price.

February 28.—Since my last entry in this diary I have
been engaged in the struggle against life peerages.   At the
Chancellor's levée on the first day of Hilary Term I asked
him ' if there was any truth in a report that Parke was to
have only a life peerage.'   He said ' it was true.'   ' Then,'
rejoined I, ' sorry am I to say that I must make a row
about it when Parliament meets.'   I then contemplated only
that I should denounce the proceeding as ' unconstitutional
and inexpedient.'   I had relied upon the dictum of Lord
Coke that a peerage might be granted for life, although not
for years; I had never examined the *consuetudo parliamenti*
upon the subject; I was utterly ignorant of the fact (since
clearly established) that no one ever sat and voted in the
House of Peers having in him a life peerage only; and the
distinction between the power of the Crown to grant a mere

dignity and to grant a right to be a member of one of the
Houses of Parliament had never been presented to me. I
therefore did not mean to oppose Lord Wensleydale taking
his seat, although I had made up my mind to refuse to officiate as one of the two barons who were to introduce him,
that I might be free to condemn the precedent about to be
established.

A few days before Parliament met I heard that Lord
Derby had given notice to the Government that the new
peer must not take his seat till the House should have an
opportunity of considering the legality of his patent, and that
Lord St. Leonards had pronounced it to be absolutely illegal.
Lord Derby received for answer that ample time would be
given for objection, and, luckily, the aspirant had a good excuse for staying away, being confined to his bed by the gout.
On the first evening of the session Lord Derby drew the
attention of the House to the new peerage for life, and said
that its legality must be debated by the law lords. I
pointed out the infinite importance of the question, contending that lay lords as well as law lords might fully understand
it, and imploring all sections of the House to devote themselves to its consideration. We agreed that Lyndhurst should
take the lead, and, now in his eighty-fourth year, he was as
eager to do so as if, a boy entering on public life, he had
rejoiced at an early opportunity of gaining notoriety. He
at first contented himself with moving that a copy of the
patent should be laid before the House, but afterwards gave
notice of a motion for referring it to a Committee of Privileges.

I now read all that had been written on the subject, and
examined all the instances of life peerages that had ever
been granted. The result was that no life peerage had been
granted to any man for more than four hundred years; that
almost all those that had before been granted were by authority of Parliament, and that there was no authenticated
instance of a peer ever having sat and voted in the House of
Lords having in him a life peerage only, the life peerages
relied upon being superinduced on pre-existing historic
peerages—e.g., De Vere, Earl of Oxford (a title which had

z 2

been in his family since the Conquest), was created by Richard II. Marquis of Dublin for life. My eyes were opened. The power of the Crown to give a right to vote in the House must depend upon the exercise of the power; and no one had voted in right of a peerage for life more than of a peerage during the pleasure of the king—for the granting of which there was at least one precedent. The peerages for life of the royal mistresses granted in the reigns of Charles II., James II., George I. and George II. proved nothing, as they did not profess to grant more than rank and precedence. Thus it was not necessary to resort to the doctrine of desuetude; but the non-exercise of a prerogative ever since the Constitution was settled afforded a strong inference that it had never lawfully existed.

The grand debate came off on the 7th of February. Lyndhurst's speech was the most wonderful ever heard. It would have been admirable for a man of thirty-five, and for a man of eighty-four it was miraculous. No man of that advanced age ever made such a speech in a deliberative assembly. I followed the Chancellor, and was under the painful necessity of cutting him up most cruelly. To be sure, he laid himself terribly open by denying the jurisdiction of the House, and contending that, although the patent might be bad, the writ of summons issued upon it gave an absolute right to a seat, because such a writ without any patent would have had this operation. There was a tolerable sketch of my speech in the newspapers; but as I had to read many written documents and to reason upon them, no parliamentary reporter could do it justice, so I wrote it out myself and published it.[1]

[1] Letter from Serjeant Goulburn, brother of the Right Honourable Henry Goulburn, and a judge in the Court of Bankruptcy:—

'63 Upper Seymour Street: February 27, 1856.

'My dear Lord Campbell,—I can assure you that I have seldom been more gratified or flattered than by your sending me your speech on life-peerages in the House of Lords.

'It found me suffering from my old foe, the gout, with that agreeable book before me, to wit, Macaulay's fourth volume; but I instantly put down his unilateral account of the debates on Sir John Fenwick's Attainder Bill, and was not a little refreshed by reading your real old-fashioned

We had a glorious majority, there being an eager attend-ance of Conservatives, several Liberals voting with us, and some staying away from disgust.

When the grand night arrived for moving the resolution against the legality of the patent in as far as it professed to grant a right to the life peer to sit in Parliament, the part was very suddenly assigned to me of answering Lord Glenelg, who made a motion for calling in the judges. Luckily I was prepared with 'Thorpe's case,' and various authorities against consulting the judges about parliamentary privileges, or the *lex et consuetudo parliamenti.* Our victory was decisive.

. . . This is a most critical time, the peace conferences having commenced at Paris. All depends upon whether Russia is able to continue the war. If she can, she will; but there is good reason to hope that she is quite exhausted, and, in that case, I think there will be tranquillity in Europe for the rest of my time.

April 4.—Although we know that the definitive treaty has been signed, we are to remain ignorant of the conditions till the ratifications are exchanged. The war has not conferred any glory on us. Yet I think we ought to rejoice that we engaged in it, and to rejoice that it is at an end. Upon the whole it has done us good as a nation, and there is no cer-tainty that another campaign would have improved our posi-tion. If England has not much to boast of, Russia has been worsted and humbled, and all over the world people may now sleep comfortably in their beds without dread of the Cossacks.

I am returned from the Midland circuit, and I must mention the pleasure I had in a visit after the circuit to

argument stating both sides fully and fairly, and leading to a conclusion which it seems to me impossible to gainsay.

'You have indeed done good service in stopping this mischief. And I trust that he who adds your Life to those of your predecessors, which have so often enlivened and amused my evenings, will not fail to do justice to the firmness of purpose and powers of reasoning which have saved the House of Lords and, in truth, the Constitution, from the severest blow aimed at it for many a long year. Believe me, my dear Lord,

'Your much obliged and sincere
'EDWARD GOULBURN.'

my eldest daughter, the wife of the Vicar of Chaddesley
Corbett, in Worcestershire. Lord Chancellor Truro gave
them the living of St. Just in Cornwall, and Lord Chancellor
Cranworth transferred them to their present cure—very laudably, for she and the vicar perform their parochial duties in
the most exemplary manner, and it was very gratifying to
me to see them so comfortably circumstanced and so much
respected.

April 10.—After a sharp debate yesterday I prevailed
on the House of Lords to make an order for the Lord
Justice General and the Lord Justice Clerk of Scotland to
be sworn standing by the woolsack, instead of below the
bar. Hitherto there has been a strong indisposition to treat
Scotch judges when appearing before the House with any
mark of respect, and when their presence has been required
they have been sworn and examined as ordinary witnesses.
Henceforth they will be placed on the woolsack like the
English judges.

These two legal dignitaries were examined to-day before
the Select Committee on the Appellate Jurisdiction of the
House of Lords, and amused us very much, the Lord Justice
General, McNeill, saying that in its present state it is very
unsatisfactory, and the only remedy is to have a Scotch
lawyer a member of the tribunal as a peer for life; while the
Lord Justice Clerk declared that the jurisdiction in its
present state is perfect, and that the proposed addition of a
Scotch lawyer would be the ruin of it. Of the latter opinion
is Lord Brougham, who is now at Cannes, but from whom I
receive letters on the subject almost daily. He will be back
soon to embroil the fray.

I think that my suggestion of a Judicial or Appellate
Committee will be adopted. No good will arise from the
addition of a Scotch lawyer as a member of it, but the proposal is so plausible that I fear it cannot be resisted. The
Government acknowledge that they cannot by the prerogative of the Crown force a peer for life into the House. They
mean to ask for the authority of Parliament to create four
peers for life, with a view to the judicial business of the
House of Lords. This I shall not oppose. Lord Grey means

to move an extension of the power to create life peers. This might be at times very convenient, but would be tampering dangerously with the hereditary character of the peerage.

April 11.—Although I have for some time been denominated the 'Leader of the Opposition,' I really wish to strengthen the Government as much as I can, and, finding it still much weakened by the dissensions between the Lord Chancellor and the law officers of the Crown, I have written the following letter to Lord Palmerston :—

Stratheden House : April 11, 1856.

My dear Lord Palmerston,—As a sincere and warm friend to your Government I wish to explain to you the danger to which it is exposed from the insubordination which prevails among your legal functionaries. You are aware that since I have held my present office I have been merely a calm looker-on, without any personal interest in political changes. But from ancient recollections, and from a regard to the public welfare, I have been earnestly desirous of supporting the party of which you are now the distinguished head. I must therefore beg you to try to compose the strife which subsists between the Lord Chancellor and the law officers of the Crown. For this you are in no degree answerable, for it began with the formation of Lord Aberdeen's Government. The Russian war has hitherto prevented the public from caring much about its consequences. In truth, it has produced the failure of all the measures of law reform which have been brought forward. But the gaze of the nation was on the Crimea, not on Westminster Hall. Now we are entering on a new era, and the credit and stability of Government will to a considerable degree depend on the success of measures about Registration of Deeds, the Ecclesiastical Courts, Divorce, and Church Discipline. But no such measures can succeed in Parliament unless there be a good understanding and co-operation respecting them among all the members of the same Government. There was formerly supposed to be a *necessitudo sortis* between the Lord Chancellor and the Attorney- and Solicitor-General. Indeed, in all my experience, before any important measure connected with the law was brought forward in Parliament, there was a conference among all the members of the Government to be concerned in carrying it through, and when launched as a Government measure all the members of the Government considered it their duty cordially to support it. But the recent practice has been, that Government Bills for amending the law which have passed one House nearly with unanimity have been disparaged by members of the Government in the other, and no single Bill of any importance has passed into a law. Indeed, I must frankly tell you that there seems to me a systematic purpose to *vilipend* the Lord Chancellor.

Your difficulties on this subject are great, but fortunately there is no man so well qualified to cope with them as yourself ; and by a firm and conciliatory course I make no doubt that you will restore a wholesome tone to this department of the State.

Wishing you a good deliverance in this and in all your trials, I remain,

Yours very sincerely,

The Viscount Palmerston.   CAMPBELL.

May 5.—Great events have happened. The ratifications of the Treaty of Paris have been exchanged. Government have had an immense majority in the House of Commons on the motion about 'the fall of Kars,' which it was supposed might turn them out; a similar motion which stood for debate in the Lords has been abandoned in despair; and the address approving of the terms of peace has passed both Houses without a division. Meeting Palmerston at a dinner given to her Majesty's Ministers at the Mansion House, I said to him, 'You are now placed on a pinnacle.' *P.* 'A very dangerous position.' *C.* 'Well, then, you are on velvet.' *P.* 'A great improvement.' *C.* 'Keep your lawyers in order, and you will get on very well.' *P.* 'Yes, I was much obliged to you for that letter. I am attending to it.' *C.* 'Do, if you wish to prosper. The matter now becomes very serious.' We were then marched off in procession to take our seats in the Egyptian Hall.

My health being given, I commented on that part of the treaty which modifies the code of maritime warfare, abolishing *privateering* and establishing the maxim 'free ships, free goods.' I designated our negotiator as 'a great law reformer as well as a great statesman.' Clarendon warmly thanked me, as the alleged abandonment of our belligerent rights (the best part of the treaty) is liable to misrepresentation and obloquy; and he was pleased to say that my opinion would have great weight in the City and throughout the country.

June 28.—Since my last notice in this Journal, the great event has been the trial of William Palmer at the Central Criminal Court for *poisoning*, which began on Wednesday May 14th and did not finish till Tuesday May 27th—the most memorable judicial proceeding for the last fifty years, enjoying the attention not only of this country but of all Europe.

My labour and anxiety were fearful; but I have been rewarded by public approbation. The court sat eight hours a day, and when I got home, renouncing all other engage-ments, I employed myself till midnight in revising my notes and considering the evidence. Luckily I had a Sunday to prepare for my summing up, and to this I devoted fourteen continuous hours. The following day, after reading in court ten hours, I had only got through the proofs for the prosecu-tion. My anxiety was over on the last day when the verdict of *Guilty* was pronounced and I had sentenced the prisoner to die, for I had no doubt of his guilt, and I was conscious that, by God's assistance, I had done my duty. Such was the ex-pressed opinion of the public and of all the respectable part of the press. But a most ruffianlike attempt was made by the friends of the prisoner to abuse me and to obtain a pardon or reprieve, on the ground that the prisoner had not had a fair trial. Having unbounded funds at their command, they corrupted some disreputable journals to admit their *diatribes* against me, and they published a most libellous pamphlet under the title of ' A Letter from the Rev. T. Palmer, the Prisoner's Brother, to Lord Chief Justice Campbell,' in which the Chief Justice was represented to be worse than his predecessor Jeffreys, and it was asserted that there had been nothing in England like the last trial since ' the Bloody Assize.' However, the Home Secretary remained firm and the law took its course.

The Rev. T. Palmer has since disclaimed the pamphlet, and it is said to have been written by a blackguard barrister. I bear him no enmity, and he has done me no harm ; but for the sake of example he ought to be disbarred.

The engrossing subject now is America, and I am much afraid that, with all our forbearance, we shall not be able to prevent our cousins from fastening a quarrel upon us. Our Government got very foolishly into the dispute about *enlist-ment*, but long ago made all reasonable concession. I think it was right not to dismiss Mr. Dallas as retaliation for the dismissal of Mr. Crampton, but this forbearance may only lead to fresh insult. Yesterday at the Queen's levée an American insisted on his right to pass her Majesty in a frock-coat and black neckcloth. He was turned back, and, for anything I know, this may be construed into a *casus belli*.

On the day of Crampton's arrival Mr. Dallas dined with me, and then told me he expected to be recalled.

July 31.—Am returned from my circuit (Norfolk), which has been very light and not disagreeable. It lasted barely three weeks and, there being hardly anything to do at Huntingdon, I was able to come to London for several days.

The weather has been divine and, after being long ' in populous city pent,' I exquisitely enjoy rural sights, sounds and scents. We have got *peace*, and there is every prospect of *plenty*.

Cambridge was a desert, but Dr. Whewell, Master of Trinity, being Vice-Chancellor, was in residence, and I had much lively talk with him on all manner of subjects, from his denial of a plurality of worlds to his dislike of the Bill just passed for reforming the University.

CHAPTER XXXIII.

NOVEMBER 1856—MAY 1859.

Death of Chief Justice Jervis—Sir Alexander Cockburn—The China
Question—General Election—Publication of the Third Volume of
'Lives of the Chief Justices'—Principle of the Divorce Bill—Opposes
Lord John Russell's Plan to admit Jews by a Resolution of the House
of Commons—Obscene Publications Bill—The Indian Mutiny—Visit
from Lord John Russell at Hartrigge—Fall of Delhi—Successful
Working of the Obscene Publications Bill—Christmas Holidays in
Scotland—Lord Derby's Second Administration—Trial of the British
Bank Directors—Bethell and the Law of Conspiracy—Lord Chelmsford
the new Chancellor—Motion for a New Trial of the British Bank
Directors—Trial of Bernard—Prosecutions for Libels—Meets M.
Guizot in Norfolk—Competitive Examinations—Enjoyment of Hart-
rigge—Writes a Dissertation on Shakespeare's Legal Training—Work-
ing of the Divorce Act—Letters from Macaulay, Charles Dickens,
Dean Milman, and Mr. Gladstone on Shakespeare's Legal Attainments
—War in Italy—General Election—Dinner at the Royal Academy—
Harwich Election.

Journal.

Stratheden House: Monday, November 3, 1856.—During
the vacation at Hartrigge I worked upon an average four or
five hours a day in preparing the fourth edition of the Lives
of the Chancellors, and revising the MSS. which I mean to
leave behind me for publication. . . .

While writing this I was interrupted by the news of the
sudden death of Chief Justice Jervis. From his years he
ought long to have survived me—and before long I must
follow him. While living, when dying, and at the day of
judgment, Lord have mercy upon me!

I am going presently to the Chancellor's levée, where I
shall find all absorbed in speculations on Jervis's successor.
Sir Alexander Cockburn, the Attorney-General, has frequently
declared that he would not accept any judicial appointment,

CHAP.
XXXIII.

A.D. 1856.

that he would prefer a political office, and that he would rather remain at the bar without office than become a judge. But now that ' the pillow of the Common Pleas ' is within his grasp, I doubt much whether he will kick it away.

January 12, 1857.—As I suspected, Cockburn's abjuration of the bench turned out to be only *nolo episcopari*. He is now Lord Chief Justice of the Common Pleas, and as yet without a peerage. I have no doubt that he will make a very respectable judge. He is a man of great intellectual ability ; he is capable of keen, though not as yet of continuous, application ; he is ambitious of fame ; and he has very courteous manners both in public and in private.

Palmerston is at present in the ascendant, having compelled Russia, notwithstanding the vacillation of France, to agree to the just construction of the treaty of peace respecting the Danubian boundary. His greatest danger arises from the antagonism between his legal functionaries. . . .

March 1.—We have had a two nights' debate on the China Question. The Ministers very much wished me to speak, but I would not do more than pair off for them. The law of the case is too doubtful for me to give an opinion upon it, and the Lord Chancellor laid down propositions about the impossibility of questioning the professed nationality of a ship which I could not have endorsed. Thinking upon the whole that Ministers ought to be supported, I rejoice in their majority of thirty-six.

I have been calling on Lyndhurst, who is very proud of the speech he made condemning the proceedings at Canton, and is looking forward with intense interest to the division on the same question in the Commons. He says that if they had divided on Thursday or Friday, the first or second night of the debate, Ministers would have been beaten, but that the interposition of Sunday will save them, by giving time to the whipper-in to purchase votes by promises of places and preferments, and for the members with doubtful seats to recollect that a division adverse to the Government may bring about an immediate dissolution of Parliament.

I was last night at Lady Palmerston's reception, when she spoke to me about the attack by the ' Times ' on the

Lord Chancellor, and lamented the disorganised state of the
law department of the Government. I truly told her that
the Premier could do nothing to extricate himself from his
difficulties by *cashiering*, and that he could only try to
moderate the hostility of the conflicting functionaries.

Stratheden House: Sunday, March 15.—While at
Northampton I heard of the unexpected majority in the
House of Commons against the Government on the China
Question, and the determination immediately to appeal
to the people. The time allotted to the assizes for the
county of Rutland I spent at Normanton, on a visit to Lord
Aveland, where I was joined by my wife and my daughter
Mary. At Lincoln I heard that my eldest son was to stand
for Taunton. It was very material that I should be in London
to make arrangements for this object. Having finished my
business in the Nisi Prius court at Lincoln at 4 P.M. on
Thursday March 12th, at 5 I started by an express train, and
having drunk tea at Stratheden House, by 10.45 I was at a
party at Lady Granville's in Bruton Street. Next evening I
paid my respects to Lady Wensleydale, and all our disputes
about the life peerage were forgotten. Last night I was at
Lady Clarendon's, where there was a reunion of all parties in
the State, Lord and Lady Palmerston, Lord and Lady John
Russell, etc. Lord Derby eschews *soirées*, but Lady Derby
was there, and I highly complimented her on her lord's
oratorical powers. We all looked like ' the happy family.'
At first I was rather afraid that as Chief Justice I might have
been called upon to preserve the peace. . . . I had a good
deal of talk with John Russell, and wished him success in
London.

I rise to-morrow morning at five, and, travelling by train
to Leicester, at ten I shall there charge the grand jury,
reminding them that ' property has its duties as well as
its rights.'

Stratheden House: April 2.—The elections on the
whole go in favour of Palmerston, and he will be able to
meet the new Parliament with an imposing front; but he
is in great danger of being speedily upset by ' Parliamentary Reform.' John Russell has openly announced his

intention of working this engine against him, and the Tories
even now cry out for 'extension of the franchise.' A
new Reform Bill, therefore, Palmerston must launch, however unwillingly. This the members of the House of
Commons will in their hearts exceedingly disrelish, knowing
that if successful it must lead to a speedy dissolution; but
they will be afraid openly to oppose it, and the contest may
be who shall go fastest and farthest ahead.

There is no longer a great Conservative party to check
innovation. Yet there is a fund of good sense in the people
of England which may be relied upon, and our monarchical
institutions are more relished in this country by all classes
than American democracy with slavery in its bosom.

May 21.—The new Parliament has met and, in spite of
the threatening aspect of the political horizon, there seems
every prospect of a quiet session.

I have at last published the third volume of my Lives of
the Chief Justices, and have received complimentary letters
from several friends who received presentation copies. The
criticisms in the weekly periodicals have been very favourable. The profuse praise bestowed upon me to my face
does not give me the slightest pleasure. The most valuable
compliment I have received was from Lord John Russell
in a great speech in the House of Commons, in which he
quoted my Life of Lord Ellenborough, with a parenthesis
expressing his high sense of the amusement and instruction
to be derived from the writings of the author. This is what
Gibbon calls 'a compliment in the face of the British
nation.'

July 13.—The campaign in London is over for me, and
to-morrow morning I start upon the circuit. I have been
working very hard during the last month, sitting day by day
to try special jury causes. Six trials have we had for
infringement of patents, these and several others lasting two
or three days apiece. The railways now bring an influx of
country causes to be tried in London, so that as assize business diminishes, my sittings become heavier. But, thank
Heaven, I am as yet equal to the task, and when it is too
much for me I hope I shall contentedly resign my office.

I am happy to say I have uniformly remained on the best terms with Cranworth, and that our friendship is unabated. I have a most sincere desire at all times to see him prosper. He is not only the most amiable of mankind, but no one can be more sincerely desirous to do what is right. Three weeks ago, accompanied by my wife and my daughter Mary, I paid him a most agreeable visit at Holwood, his villa in Kent, once possessed by William Pitt the younger.

I am very glad that the Divorce Bill finally passed the Commons framed almost exactly according to the recommendations of the commission over which I had the honour to preside—preserving the law as it has practically subsisted for 200 years: that a husband who has conducted himself properly may obtain a dissolution of the marriage for the adultery of the wife, and that a wife may obtain a dissolution of the marriage for the adultery of the husband attended by incest or any aggravation which renders it impossible for the connubial union to continue; the law being now to be administered by a regular judicial tribunal, instead of the injured parties being obliged to petition the Legislature for private Acts of Parliament to dissolve the marriage. We were assailed on the one hand by those who hold that according to the divine law marriage cannot be dissolved even for adultery, and on the other by those who think that for this purpose no distinction should be made between the sexes, and that in all cases the wife should be entitled to a divorce on proof of any breach of the marriage vow by the husband. But I think the true principle is, that the marriage ought only to be dissolved when it is impossible for the injured party to *condone,* and that Divine Providence has constituted an essential difference in this respect between the adultery of the husband and the adultery of the wife. I would rather run the risk of cases of great hardship occurring when it would seem desirable that women should be released from the tyranny of profligate and brutal husbands, than give too great a facility to divorce, which has a tendency most demoralising.

August 20.—I have had a very pleasant summer circuit, with my old pupil Vaughan Williams for my colleague. It was rather a tour of pleasure. I visited for the first time the Chequers, once inhabited by Oliver Cromwell; Hampden, which belonged to the illustrious patriot (of that ilk); Wimpole, which I had described in my Life of Lord Hardwicke; and Shrublands, more wonderful than any of them, the seat of Sir William Middleton, who in his gardens has excelled those of Armida, or the Hesperides, and realised the visions of the Arabian Nights.

During the Huntingdon assizes I came to London and made a speech against Lord John Russell's revolutionary project of admitting the Jews to sit in Parliament by a resolution of the House of Commons. I strongly denounced the meditated *coup d'état*, and pointed out the inevitable collision with the courts of law. I likewise wrote a strong representation on the subject both to Palmerston and Lord John. Here are their answers:—

94 Piccadilly : July 22, 1857.

My dear Lord Campbell,—Thank you for your letter. I quite agree with you, and have resolved to have no Resolution. Yours sincerely,

PALMERSTON.

Pembroke Lodge : July 22, 1857.

My dear Lord Campbell,—I have always resisted the proceeding by Resolution. But when the House of Lords, by the advice of all its law lords except the Lord Chancellor, decided to defy the prerogative of the Crown, and to decide by its own authority that a *member of that House, named by the Queen*, should be refused admittance, I foresaw that the example would not be lost. In fact, if the *dictum* of Lord Coke is despised, how can we expect regard to the *dictum* of Lord Campbell? If the most learned of the peers pursue a *reckless and headstrong course*, what are we to expect from the Radical representatives of Radical electors?

Allow me to say that you should have thought of all this before you excluded Lord Wensleydale.

The case of Pease the Quaker appears to me to go a long way, perhaps not the whole way, to justify the course of Resolutions.

What may be done I cannot tell, and I conclude Lord Palmerston does not care. At all events, *liberavi animam meam*. Yours faithfully,

J. RUSSELL.

I replied to Lord John, ' prompted by my regard for the public tranquillity and for his glory,' trying to show him the inapplicability of Pease's case and the Wensleydale peerage case. He then took new ground, someone pretending to have discovered a statute of William IV. supposed to authorise the House of Commons to remodel the Abjuration Oath, and he got a Select Committee appointed to consider how far this statute could be made available ; but his own Committee reported against him, ' that it did not apply to the Houses of Parliament,' and he was obliged to content himself with a notice that he would again bring forward the subject at the commencement of the next session.

CHAP. XXXIII.

A.D. 1857.

Since I returned from the circuit my chief business has been to watch the progress through the House of Commons of my Bill for checking the trade in obscene publications by allowing them to be seized in the dépots of the dealers. Brougham had hardly ventured to oppose the Bill as it passed through the Lords, but afterwards he wrote a violent article against it in the ' Law Magazine,' and he put up Roebuck to assail it in the House of Commons. The Bill being in committee yesterday at a morning meeting of the House of Commons, I showed myself in the Peers' gallery to watch its fate, and that I might be consulted if necessary during the debate. Roebuck contented himself with reading a letter which he had received from Brougham pointing out the danger of country justices perverting the Bill for the punishment of poachers; and it went through the Committee with amendments which I had suggested or assented to. The Speaker then sent me a message by the Chancellor of the Exchequer complaining ' that I had appeared in the House to *overawe their deliberations*, like Cardinal Wolsey and Charles I., and that it would become his duty to protest against such an unconstitutional proceeding.' Denison, the new Speaker, is an old friend of mine. . . .

I have been dreadfully depressed for some weeks by the frightful news from India. Having conquered every foreign foe, our empire there seems to be vanishing like a dream. I do not suffer so much as if my son, Hallyburton, formerly in the service of the East India Company, had still been at Cawnpore, where a massacre of all Europeans is rumoured to have taken place, but I am extremely anxious about my nephews, who are in the disturbed provinces. I think what would have been the sufferings of my poor brother if he had still survived, and look with dread to the danger of Russia, or even of France, taking advantage of our embarrassment, and forcing us into a war, or making us submit to discreditable concessions.

Hartrigge: September 17.—Had a visit here to-day from Lord John Russell, who is at present with his family at Minto. The ex-Minister appears to great advantage in private life. A fall from power generally gives a terrible shock to the spirits. Pitt the younger when out of office was alarmingly dejected, and sadly at a loss how to employ his time. Lord John seems as gay as a lark, and I really believe is very cheerful. He talks very freely and unaffectedly of passing and past politics, including the measures of his own Administration. He is now engaged with his 'Life of Fox.'

I thanked him for the compliment he paid me in the House of Commons last session as a biographer, when quoting my Life of Lord Ellenborough, and I said it was equal to Sheridan's compliment to Gibbon during Hastings's trial—'atrocities of a deeper dye than any recorded in the Annals of Tacitus, or the *luminous page of Gibbon.*' *Lord John* : 'But recollect Sheridan declared that his epithet was the *vo*-luminous page of Gibbon ; and I see you are publishing the tenth volume of your new edition of the Chancellors.'

Hartrigge: October 27.—Since I have been down here this autumn I have chiefly occupied myself with reperusing Sir Walter Scott's novels. 'Anne of Geierstein' and others that he composed merely from books which he read for the task, as a lawyer reads his brief, I could not get on with ; but 'Old Mortality,' 'The Heart of Midlothian,' and such as embody the visions which had been before his eyes and in his imagination from early youth, I could gloat upon for ever. I have likewise read 'Kate Coventry' and several other fashionable novels of the last season ; and I again wish for some serious intellectual labour, but I am determined that I will publish no more in my own lifetime. Although the third volume of my Lives of the Chief Justices has been abundantly praised, there have been flippant criticisms upon it which have annoyed me. A critic in the 'Edinburgh Review,' from malice or stupidity, says that I refer to the *Rolliad* and to *Waverley* as historical authorities, and represents me as more credulous than the Irish bishop who declared that he met with some things in Gulliver's Travels which he could hardly believe to be true.

In Disraeli's 'Curiosities of Literature' I last night met with the statement of several authors of great celebrity who died of a broken heart, by reason of unjust attacks upon their writings. I shall not add to their number; but I shall not again give a defeated suitor against whom I have pronounced a just judgment, or a coxcombical barrister to whom I have rendered it disagreeable to talk nonsense, or an importunate applicant for place or promotion whom in the strict discharge of my duty I have disappointed, an opportunity of being revenged by contending that the Chief Justice is wrong in a date, or is too familiar, or too stately, in his style, or displays an excessive liking for democracy or for arbitrary power. When I am dead and gone, envy and ill-will towards me may cease.

I have to-day heard the important and joyful news of the fall of Delhi. My dreadful depression for some weeks from the state of affairs in India was by no means unreasonable; for if the native population, or the native princes, had taken part against us, or the Sikhs had embraced this opportunity to recover their ascendancy, or the Mutiny had extended to Madras and Bombay—all of these being contingencies by no means improbable—every European in India would have been massacred, and we should have had to encounter difficulties and disasters at home which it is fearful to contemplate. *Barbarus has segetes!* In two years a regiment of Cossacks might have been bivouacking at Hartrigge. Now that Delhi is in our possession all serious danger is over, and the Mutiny will collapse as rapidly as it spread, although years must roll on before the traces of such dire outrages can be obliterated.

Stratheden House: December 17.—I have been too busy since I returned to London to make a single entry in my Journal. My work has been incessant and very severe. The term business I do not so much mind, but to sit at Nisi Prius

A A 2

seven hours a day for a continuous month, listening to tiresome examinations and dull speeches, is too much for me,
and I am afraid I shall not be able to stand it much longer.

We were enlivened for ten days by the short session of
Parliament. I did but little, besides annoying Brougham
and Lyndhurst by moving for a return of the *seizures* under
my Bill for putting down obscene publications, which they
opposed so violently. Its success has been most brilliant.
Holywell Street, which had long set law and decency at
defiance, has capitulated after several assaults. Half the
shops are shut up, and the remainder deal in nothing but
moral and religious books! Under the Bill similar abomin-
ations have been cleared away in Dublin. Even in Paris its
influence has been felt, for the French police, roused by the
accounts of what we are now doing, have been energetically
employed in purifying the Palais Royal and the Rue Vivienne.

January 11, 1858.—I have spent my holidays very
agreeably in Scotland, passing one week in Edinburgh with
Lord Murray. On this occasion I was summoned to preside at a public meeting attended by the leading men of all
parties for the reform of the Scottish Universities. I had
a most hospitable and flattering reception from the Scotch
judges and advocates.

I feel rather depressed when I look forward to the labours
which await me; but, praying for God's help to enable me
to do my duty, I will try to proceed vigorously and cheerfully. May I be ready to meet the close of my career with
resignation and firmness, grateful for the many blessings
showered upon me.

I have a terrible trial coming on, expected to last a month,
—the prosecution against the directors of the Royal British
Bank for a conspiracy to defraud the shareholders and the
public.

March 2.—What a sudden turn of the wheel of fortune!
Ten days ago Palmerston seemed stronger than ever, and I
looked upon him as Minister for life. Yesterday I was present
in the House of Lords at the inauguration of Lord Derby's
second Administration. Ostensibly the omission to answer
Walewski's despatch was the cause of the change. . . .

My great trial of the British Bank directors is over, having lasted thirteen long days. The 'Times' and other journals wrote furiously against the culprits, and demanded that they should be sentenced to transportation. I let one defendant off with a nominal fine, because he had been improperly convicted; and I sentenced the others to various periods of imprisonment according to their degrees of delinquency. The public were made to believe that I had treated them with undue indulgence, but the bar all concurred in thinking that the judge, during the trial and in passing the sentence, had displayed patience, discrimination and firmness.[1]

I have had a fierce war with Sir Richard Bethell, Attorney-General of the late Government. Upon the attempt to assassinate the Emperor of the French, I had laid down the law of conspiracy as it applied to foreigners residing in England. The Government by his advice having determined on legislation, to make out the necessity for legislation Bethell pretended that ' aliens, by conspiring in England to commit an offence beyond the seas, would not be subject to English law.' In the discharge of my duty, and by the advice of Lord Lyndhurst, I exposed this misrepresentation. All the law lords, *seriatim*, agreed with me. Bethell attacked us all scurrilously in the House of Commons, and I was obliged to vindicate myself last night in the House of Lords. This *logomachy* between the Attorney-General and the Chief Justice has amused the town, but will soon be forgotten.

The strange occurrence is that Sugden, Lord St. Leonards, has declined the resumption of the Great Seal, and Sir Frederick Thesiger, under the title of Lord Chelmsford, is now Chancellor. Unfortunately, he is by no means a well-grounded lawyer, but he is a very good fellow, with a large store of mother wit. Everybody is well pleased with his elevation, and I dare say he will get on very decently. In the House of Lords, as a deliberative assembly, he will have a great deal more weight than his predecessor, Lord Cranworth.

CHAP.
XXXIII.

A.D. 1858.

---

[1] By-and-by petitions poured in, complaining that the punishment was too severe; and the periods of imprisonment of some of the defendants were shortened by the Secretary of State.

March 24.—On entering the House of Lords on my return from the Midland circuit, I find the Conservatives on the right of the woolsack and Thesiger presiding upon it. This is the fifth Chancellor who has sat there since I became Chief Justice, eight years ago.

. *May* 9.—Have had the most unpleasant work to go through which I have ever encountered since I became a judge. The six directors of the British Bank, whom after a thirteen days' trial I convicted and sentenced to imprisonment, when term came round all moved for a new trial, and their counsel, by gross misrepresentations which I could not at the moment correct, made an impression upon my puisnes that injustice had been done. I was resolved to declare my entire approbation of the conviction, and my clear opinion against granting the rule. It would not only have been most annoying to me but a public calamity if the court had been divided on such an occasion. For a fortnight I was most wretched, passing sleepless nights and losing my appetite for food. At last the one puisne who still doubted was brought to reason, and sent me a written adhesion. I then prepared a very elaborate judgment in the name of the whole court. It was printed in all the newspapers *verbatim* from my MS., and it brought me more credit than any former judicial performance.

However, the trial that has most fixed public attention was that of *Bernard*, the French refugee, for being an accomplice in the plot to assassinate the Emperor of the French ; the formal shape of the indictment being, that he was accessory to the murder of those who were actually killed by the explosion of the grenades at the door of the Opera House in the Rue Lepelletier at Paris. All Europe looked on with intense curiosity, and all the world was astonished at hearing a verdict of *Not Guilty* pronounced.

I received various anonymous letters abusing me for unfairness to the accused, some of them comparing me to Jeffreys. Although I by no means relished the plan of prosecuting for the capital charge, which was attended with many legal difficulties, I summed up strongly for a conviction, as the evidence was overwhelming to establish the complicity of the accused. Nevertheless, I cared little about the acquittal, and it saved me from considering the points of law reserved for the Court of Criminal Appeal in case of a conviction. The French nation took the acquittal more calmly than I had anticipated. I had the satisfaction to see my summing up at full length in the 'Moniteur,' with some compliments to 'Mons. le Lord Chef Justice.' I have still to try, at the sittings after Trinity Term in the Court of Queen's Bench, two informations for libels charged to have been intended to recommend the assassination of the Emperor.

July 4.—When the day for trying these cases had arrived, the Government pusillanimously agreed to acquittals, on the defendants expressing sorrow for what they had done, and promising not to do the like again. The pamphlets prosecuted recommended in the most express terms the assassination of Louis Napoleon as a tyrant, lauding the attempt of Orsini and Pianori, and lamenting that it had failed. Such publications, as they give just cause of complaint to foreign Governments, and bring the liberty of the press into discredit, ought not to be tolerated; and, notwithstanding the verdict in Bernard's case, I do not believe that I should have now had any difficulty in obtaining a conviction. I had very elaborately studied the proceedings in prosecuting Lord George Gordon for a libel on Marie Antoinette, against Vint for a libel on the Emperor Paul, and against Peltier for a libel on Napoleon the Great, and I was prepared with an exposition of the law upon the subject, which I think would have been of public service. But just as I was entering the court I was told that *it was all settled*. I did venture, nevertheless (for the benefit of the students, as Lord Mansfield used to say), to point out the necessity for considering a direct incitement to crime as criminal, and, one of the defendants being a political refugee, to inculcate the duty of foreigners, while they have an asylum among us, to obey our laws like native-born subjects, glancing at the heterodox doctrine of Sir Richard Bethell, that foreigners in England may do with impunity that for which native-born subjects may be punished.

The session of Parliament may now be considered as over, and Lord Derby is safe till Parliament meets again in 1859.

He has been saved by the dissensions of the Liberals, by truckling to Bright, and by courting the Radicals. I prophesied many years ago that in England the Whigs would be (as in America they are) the only true Conservatives. The Tories as a body are still staunch and sincere, but the Tory leaders are ready to sacrifice the monarchy that they may keep their places. Democracy has made more progress in England during the last three months than during the twenty years of Whig rule. I am myself very indifferent about party politics, and personally I would as soon have Lord Derby for Prime Minister as Palmerston or John Russell, but I begin to be afraid that I may live to see John Bright President of the Anglican Republic. Extreme democracy is tyranny in its worst shape, despising public opinion, and showing no respect for the rights of property or for personal liberty.

Hartrigge: August 23.—On my circuit nothing memorable occurred except that I spent two days at Sir John Boileau's in Norfolk with the celebrated Guizot. I admired as much as ever his wonderful acquirements and powers of conversation, but I must look upon him as the destroyer of Louis Philippe and the Orleans dynasty by his eagerly pushing on the Spanish marriages, and resisting the call for reforming the House of Representatives in France. Like Lord John Russell, he bears his fall from power with equanimity and cheerfulness.

On my return to town I found Parliament still sitting. In a speech against *competitive examination* for office, upon which 'the Commons have gone wild,' I proposed that, as the *property* qualification for members is now abolished, an *education* qualification should be substituted, so that no one shall be allowed to take his seat as a representative of the people till his abilities and stock of knowledge have been tested, and he has exhibited a satisfactory specimen of his oratorical powers. Next day the Chief Justice was severely handled by the Commons for saying that they had 'run wild,' and that they should be subjected to a preliminary examination before being allowed to take their seats. The leading competitive examination journal observed ' that rank had neither conferred upon him [the Chief Justice] dignity nor good manners.' But by the judicious I have been applauded, and my scheme of Parliamentary Reform was much applauded in the 'Saturday Review' and other respectable publications.[2]

Coming down here on the 31st of July, I found Hartrigge perfect; and it is now the most beautiful place in the whole world. The weather having been since divine, I have been in a state of great enjoyment.

My amusement is to read over once more the whole of Shakespeare's plays, marking all the passages in which he introduces legal phraseology or alludes to legal proceedings, that I may consider the question whether the Bard of Avon, before he left Stratford, had not been an attorney's clerk.

I have had a visit here from M. Guizot, and I found him very agreeable and good-humoured.

Hartrigge: October 28.—Alas! the long vacation is over, and to-morrow I return to London.

> My hour is almost come,
> When I to *tiresome and tormenting speeches*
> Must render up myself.

I have accomplished my purpose of writing a dissertation on the question of Shakespeare's legal training, which, if it be approved of by a critical friend to whom I shall submit it, I may bring out in the shape of a shilling's-worth for railways.

January 10, 1859.— . . . I have been sitting two days in the Divorce Court, and, like Frankenstein, I am afraid of the monster I have called into existence. (The new jurisdiction arises from the Report of a Commission over which I had the honour to preside.) Upon an average, I believe there were not in England above three divorces a year *a vinculo matrimonii,* and I had no idea that the number would be materially increased if the dissolution were judicially decreed by a court of justice instead of being enacted by the Legislature. But I understand that there are now 300 cases of divorce pending before the

---

[2] *Punch* had afterwards a very amusing article on the Chief Justice's scheme, with specimens of the examinations and of the speeches. (See *Punch,* February 12, 1859.)

new court. This is rather appalling. In the first place, the business of the court cannot be transacted without the appointment of fresh judges; and there seems some reason to dread that the prophecies of those who opposed the change may be fulfilled by a lamentable multiplication of divorces, and by the corruption of the public morals.

Hilary Term begins to-morrow—Lord Chelmsford being still Chancellor. How Lord Derby is to launch a Reform Bill which will satisfy both divisions of his supporters—the ultra-Tories and the ultra-Radicals—I do not understand.

February 5.—Parliament has met, and Lord Derby's policy is disclosed—to stave off Parliamentary Reform, and to take the chance of remaining in office by delaying his Bill, rather than encounter certain destruction by immediately bringing it forward. The danger is that he may thus get up the democratic steam more effectually than Bright has been able to do, and that, while a moderate measure would now give satisfaction, something more sweeping and dangerous may become necessary.

I have published my 'Shakespeare,' and as yet I do not repent. There are some hostile criticisms, but, generally speaking, I have been treated by the press civilly and respectfully.

[These are a few of the letters which my father received on this subject from his private friends.—ED.]

From Lord Macaulay.

Holly Lodge : January 26, 1859.

Dear Lord Campbell,—Thanks for your interesting little volume. I always thought that Shakespeare had, when a young man, been in the lower ranks of the legal profession; and I am now fully convinced of it. It is impossible, I am certain, to mention any writer, not regularly bred to the law, who has made half as many allusions to tenures of land, to forms of action, to modes of procedure, without committing gross blunders. The mistake which you mention about the words 'to join issue' was made by no less a man than Lord Castlereagh, when leader of the House of Commons. You may observe that the best writers perpetually use the word 'pleading.' incorrectly. They think that it means haranguing a jury. I saw the other day a sentence to this effect: 'It may be doubted whether Erskine or Curran were the greater pleader.' The person who expressed himself thus would have stared if he had been told that Littledale was a far greater pleader than either. Miss Edgeworth's books were carefully revised by her father, a most active magistrate, who ought to have picked up a little law. Yet what monstrous errors there are in every passage which relates to legal proceedings. In a novel of last year a man is taken up and tried in London for a felony committed in the Tyrol. When a writer draws numerous illustrations from legal proceedings, and makes no mistakes, we shall always, if we can learn his history, find that he was of the profession. Fielding is an instance; so is Cowper. In Shakespeare's case the presumption seems to be peculiarly strong. Thanks again and again. Ever, dear Lord Campbell, yours truly,

MACAULAY.

From Mr. Charles Dickens.

Tavistock House, Tavistock Square, London :
Thursday, January 27, 1859.

Dear Lord Campbell,—I must trouble you by thanking you for the very curious and interesting little work for which I am indebted to your kind remembrance, and which I received—and read—yesterday. Apart from the knowledge and ingenuity it evinces, it is so exceedingly graceful and pleasant that I have read it with uncommon satisfaction. It will always hold its place on the shelf in my mind where I keep Morgann's essay on the character of Falstaff : a delicate combination of fancy, whim, good heart, good sense, and good taste, which I am pretty confident is a favourite of yours.

If I know myself at all, I beg to warrant myself not in the least biassed by your flattering mention of me. I am very proud of it, but, I believe, quite honestly. Dear Lord Campbell, yours faithfully and obliged,

CHARLES DICKENS.

From Dr. Milman, Dean of St. Paul's.

Deanery, St. Paul's : January 27, 1859.

My dear Lord Campbell,—I thank you for a pleasant evening. I have read your Shakespeariana with great interest. You have acted Mr. Attorney-General in favour of his legal education with great skill : then subsided with dignity upon the seat of the Chief Justice, and charged us, the jury, with perfect impartiality. It is really a curious though, at present at least, insoluble question. What struck me the most was the fondness for law terms and images in the Poems, his earliest writings. But I fully agree with you that it would be a convincing case as to any other than Shakespeare, who seems to have been strangely endowed with universal knowledge. If I remember right, the late Sir H. Halford was for making him out to be a medical man ; and I think, after a quiet and industrious summer, I could show him to be a very sound and enlightened divine. How much of Christianity is contained in the beautiful passage which you have cited from *Measure for Measure*.

Thanking you again for your very acceptable present, believe me, ever, your lordship's

Very truly,
H. H. MILMAN.

From the Right Hon. W. E. Gladstone.

Hawarden Castle : August 31, 1859.

My dear Lord Chancellor,—I am glad I did not find an opportunity, which could only have been a very summary one, of thanking you at the Cabinet on Monday for your charming book on the legal attainments of Shakespeare : a book, if I may presume to say so much, at once useful and graceful, light and solid.

Your facts, as a whole, leave me in a comfortable persuasion, upon the case as it stands, that our great poet was once an attorney's clerk.

I am seduced into the impertinence of offering two remarks. First, I quite understand your doctrine that the direct forms of law have their own interest and attraction, almost their own proper beauty. But then it seems to me fair to suggest that none of these lie on the outside ; and that they can only be perceived after circumstances have in some manner made us acquainted with the said forms ; that they would not be likely, as natural objects, and even as certain pursuits might be, to draw the spontaneous observation of a man of high poetic temperament ; that he would eschew that very warren of Alsatia, because it was haunted by attorneys ; that, in fact, the existence of such accurate and technical knowledge in such a man requires the hypothesis of a special cause to account for it.

My second remark is yet more daring, for it is in the nature of a comment on one of yours. You state with truth that such a man would pick up rapidly what would cost others much labour, and might therefore gather as an observer what they could only get as practitioners. But is not this also good to show that a very slight and short tenure of the stool inside the attorney's office will *à fortiori* well account for all the knowledge that he shows ; consequently, that he may have done very little in that capacity, and that the negative argument from our not finding any of his signatures as a witness is weakened in proportion ?

My note of interrogation is only meant to give a false air of modesty, not to draw a further reply, which I should open with some fear of having been found to have committed myself in the manner you so justly describe as so common and deplorable. Under no circumstances whatever will I '*join issue*' with you, unless and until you deny me leave to subscribe myself very sincerely yours,

W. E. GLADSTONE.

Sunday, May 1.—Flagrant war in Italy between the Austrians and the Sardinians with their allies the French ! I fear that the Government has been sadly bamboozled by the Emperor Louis Napoleon. Frightful times seem to be at hand.

Meanwhile we have no Parliament to advise the Crown. After the vote on Lord John Russell's motion, Lord Derby had no other choice than to dissolve or resign ; but the latter would have been the patriotic and the constitutional course, for he had no question to take the opinion of the nation upon, and he dissolved in this awful crisis, merely to take the desperate chance of gaining a majority and continuing in office.   It is now supposed that, upon a balance of winning and losing, he will have gained near twenty seats, but this will give him no security against being turned out any day by a coalition of the Liberals.   His only chance is the rivalry between Palmerston and Lord John for the leadership, and no one knows how to reconcile them.

Dined yesterday at the Royal Academy and met several distinguished men, although Palmerston and a good many others are still absent in the country at their elections.   As I was before dinner standing and looking at a picture with Lord Derby, Sir Hamilton Seymour (late Ambassador at Vienna) came up and said to me: 'Lord Campbell, you will lose your pocket-handkerchief.'   Looking round and seeing it depending in rather a tempting fashion, I exclaimed, 'Thank you; but did you really think my pocket would be picked by the Prime Minister?' at which they both laughed.

I sat exactly opposite to Derby at dinner, and he narrated a *bon mot* of Lord Plunket: 'When Lord Campbell in the year 1841 was invading Ireland as Lord Chancellor, he had a most tempestuous passage from Holyhead to Dublin. Lord Plunket, most reluctant to give up his place, was in hopes that his intended successor might be drowned, and asked his private secretary whether he thought there was any chance of this.   *Secretary.* ' If he is not drowned, I am sure he must be very sick.'   *Lord Plunket.* 'Perhaps he may *throw up* the Seals.'

Lord Derby reproached me with putting questions to him in the House of Lords about the great clock at Westminster, which had been wholly inactive for six months, and which I had represented as 'though not a *striking*, a *standing* reproach to Government.'   I said I had been actuated by a regard for his credit, for I was afraid the Government clock might be considered an emblem of the Government; and as the hands on the four dials were all pointing to different hours, it might be thought that there was a split in the

Cabinet, and that our affairs both foreign and domestic were all at sixes and sevens.' The Lord Chancellor, who was sitting close by me, observed, ' I hope that, as we are to be judged by this clock, it will be seen that we have no inclination *to go.*'

He said another good thing: the health of the Lord Mayor of London being given, his lordship, instead of imitating the generality of Mayors of London, who on such an occasion make very long and foolish speeches, spoke a very few sensible words and sat down. *Lord Chancellor.* ' Did you ever see a *mare* with so short a *tail* ? '

In the midst of such rollicking, the toast being given of *Her Majesty's Ministers,* Lord Derby sprang up and made an exceedingly good speech upon ' the alarming state of the Continent,' and ' the beauty of the pictures by which we were surrounded.' Derby certainly is a very extraordinary fellow, but I confess I feel by no means comfortable when I recollect that he is at the helm in such a stormy sea.

To-morrow I shall know whether my son is returned for Harwich, or again defeated.

May 3.—Fred is returned for Harwich, to my unspeakable joy! Yesterday at the rising of the court I went to Brooks's, and found that at 1.30 he was third on the poll, and three behind the second. Another telegram was every moment expected with the close of the poll at four o'clock, but this did not arrive till 5.45. It was immediately opened, and there was a shout ' Campbell is in,' followed by the general acclamations of a crowded room. He stood second, and only three below the first. This unexpected event is most gratifying to me.

CHAPTER XXXIV.

Journal.

Friday, June 17, 1859.—Most important public and private events have happened since the last entry in my Journal. As the day appointed for the meeting of Parliament approached, a plan was proposed at once to try the strength of parties by moving in the House of Commons a vote of 'want of confidence' as an amendment to the Address. I must own I thought this not only hazardous but indiscreet, as, from the divisions of the Liberal party, they could hardly expect a majority. However, it was crowned with brilliant success. After a debate of three nights, Lord Derby was beaten, and next day he resigned with all his Cabinet.

Who was to be sent for by the Queen? As the basis of the operation Palmerston and John Russell, under extreme

CHAP.
XXXIV.

A.D. 1859.

pressure, had at last professed a willingness each to serve
under the other, as circumstances might require. The
Queen sent for neither, wishing to avoid both. Lord Granville was accordingly commissioned to form an Administration; but, although Palmerston would have consented, Lord
John made objections (which amounted to a refusal) to acknowledge Granville as Premier, and the Queen transferred
the commission to Palmerston.

In the natural course of things, Cranworth should have
been restored to the woolsack; but his reputation had been
so much damaged while Chancellor by allowing Bethell to
thwart and insult him, that, notwithstanding the regard
entertained for him, his restoration was understood to be
impossible. Bethell ought to have come next, as a great
Equity lawyer who had been Attorney-General under the
Liberals. He had often openly declared that he was to be
Chancellor as soon as his party should be again in power.
The problem was to keep him under the new Government in
his former office of Attorney-General.

Returning home on Tuesday evening, I found a note
from Palmerston requesting a few minutes' conversation
with me. I went at the appointed hour, thinking it not
improbable that he was going to consult me about who
was the fittest for the vacant office of Solicitor-General, as
former Prime Ministers have several times done since I became
Chief Justice. As soon as I was seated he begged that I
would accept the Great Seal. I answered truly that my
ambition was satisfied, but that if it was really thought that
the proposed arrangement would be serviceable to the Liberal
party and to the public, I was ready to consent. He made a
flattering reply, referring to the times when we had before
sat in the Cabinet together, and to the judicial reputation I
had since gained in the Queen's Bench. Thus in five minutes
I was virtually Lord Chancellor. I suggested that Bethell
might be dissatisfied. *Palmerston.* 'Lord Campbell having
consented, Bethell cannot object.'

However, as I sat in court next morning, I had a note
from Palmerston requesting that for the present I would not
mention what had passed between us the preceding evening.

I saw in a moment that Bethell had exploded at Cambridge House, and, in a few minutes after, I received a note from Brougham asking me to come to him in the House of Lords, and he would tell me what had passed between Bethell and Palmerston, which it was very material I should know immediately.

At the rising of my court, having reached the lobby of the House of Lords going towards Lord Brougham's private room, I met Bethell. He looked rather embarrassed. I walked up to him and shook him by the hand. He then readily recovered himself, and exclaimed amidst a multitude of counsel coming along with him from the bar of the House, ' How d'ye do, my Lord Chancellor ? ' He asked me to go into a private room with him, and he would tell me all that had passed. I said, ' The sooner we come to a full and frank explanation the better.' He said he had calculated with confidence on now being Lord Chancellor ; that having a great respect for me he would not have made any objection to serve under me, although he certainly would not have consented to serve under any of the others whose names had been mentioned (Cockburn, Romilly, Page Wood), but that he was afraid that if he had at once acquiesced, he might be considered to have compromised the rights of the Equity bar; that he had therefore taken the opinion of the four law lords who had been hearing an appeal in the House, Lord Cranworth, Lord Brougham, Lord Wensleydale and Lord Kingsdown ; that they had unanimously answered, ' You cannot with propriety refuse to serve under Lord Campbell ; neither you nor anyone can complain, and your honour is safe, you resuming your office of Attorney-General and Lord Campbell being Chancellor ; ' and that he therefore withdrew all objections to my appointment. We then referred to any differences we might before have had as trifles to be forgotten, and I expressed (what I felt) an entire confidence in our going on harmoniously together.

When I got to Brougham's private room, he repeated to me the accurate statement I had just received of Bethell's question to the four learned pundits, and their response. ' My noble and learned friend,' with very friendly words and,

I really believe, without any feeling of envy or ill will (for he has long ceased to have any wish to hold the Great Seal himself), warmly congratulated me on my elevation, and condescended to ask me to appoint his nephew a Registrar in Bankruptcy, which I very readily promised to do, reminding him that he, when Chancellor, had given a similar appointment to a nephew of mine.

Yesterday was the last day of Trinity Term and the last day of my sitting in the Queen's Bench. I had to deliver judgment in several important causes, and I believe that no abatement in my vigour has been discovered.

To-day the House of Lords meets again after the Whitsuntide adjournment, and we shall have a valedictory harangue from Lord Derby, to which I suppose Granville will make some response, although, as he is not Premier, he will be chary in explaining the views of the new Government. Palmerston cannot do this till after his re-election for Tiverton.

To-morrow we go down to Windsor to kiss hands and receive our seals. In the evening I presume that the *Clavis Regni* will be deposited in Stratheden House.

The list of the new Cabinet was published this morning; and I confess that I shall be proud to be associated with such men as Palmerston, John Russell, Gladstone, &c., &c., in governing this mighty empire.

Monday, June 20.—On Saturday at two o'clock fifteen members of the new Cabinet appeared on the platform of the Great Western at Paddington. Cobden, the intended sixteenth, is not yet returned from America, and it is not exactly known whether the great Free Trade agitator will accept or not. We made a goodly show, and I said to Palmerston that he need not be ashamed to march his new recruits through Coventry, but that all would depend upon his keeping them under proper discipline. We passed an express train bringing back our resigning rivals, who had delivered up to the Queen their insignia of office at Windsor at an earlier hour. What an opening might have been made for aspiring gyoun statesmen if a wicked wag of a railway director had ordered the two trains to be put upon the same line!

After luncheon and some private conferences, the Council was held, and John Lord Campbell having sworn to serve her Majesty truly as Lord Chancellor in the terms of the ancient oath, she motioned to him to take up a huge red velvet bag which lay upon the table before her and contained the Great Seal in its embroidered purse and all its coverings, as described in the 'Lives of the Chancellors.' According to the custom of Queen Elizabeth on such occasions, she ought to have made me a long speech; but she only held out her hand for me to kiss, and I had no opportunity of dwelling upon the felicities of her Majesty's auspicious reign, or my own devoted attachment to her service. Having got our seals, keys, wands, &c., we all came back to London very merrily. But it will not surprise me if before long we have sadly to take another trip to Windsor to surrender our seals, keys, wands, &c., for the benefit of a merry party enjoying our long visages and forced smiles.

Yesterday I went to church, took the Holy Communion, and prayed earnestly to Heaven to enable me to perform the duties of my new office. In the evening I attended a special service in Westminster Abbey.

I am now setting off for my first Cabinet to be held in Downing Street.

Same day, 9.45 *p.m.*—The Cabinet was summoned for 3.30; I was there a few minutes before the time appointed, and for a considerable time I was 'alone in my glory.' By four all had straggled in except Cobden, not returned from America, and Palmerston our chief. He was always the last in John Russell's time, but as chief I now expected him to set a good example. I was told that when he was before at the head of affairs, a Cabinet being summoned for three, he seldom appeared before 4.45. On this occasion he entered the room about 4.10, and we proceeded to business without any apology on his part; and I rather think he was dearer to himself by reason of his extraordinary punctuality. As we were arranging for another Cabinet to meet on Wednesday, I asked what was to be the hour. He said 3.30. *Chancellor.* 'But let us know the real, *bona fide,* true time, for our own comfort and the

public good.' Some others joined me, pointing out how the
business of their departments was deranged by these irregularities, and a resolution was passed unanimously that the
hour should be precisely 3.30. If he be again unpunctual
we must pass a vote of ' want of confidence ' against him.

Present:—Lord Palmerston, Lord John Russell, Mr.
Gladstone, Duke of Newcastle, Duke of Argyll, Duke of
Somerset, Sidney Herbert, Charles Wood, George Grey,
Cornewall Lewis, Milner Gibson, Lord Granville, Lord Elgin,
Cardwell, Campbell. Cobden still beyond sea.

Thursday, June 23.—I dined yesterday with Lyndhurst,
and met two other ex-Chancellors, Brougham and Cranworth,
and two other law lords, Wensleydale and Kingsdown, with a
great number of other notabilities. All were civil to me, and
we were immediately in our old familiar rollicking mood.
Cranworth I really believe has no envious or ill-natured
sensation towards me. As ex-Chancellor Truro was passed
over when Cranworth himself was appointed, he cannot complain.

In the evening I went to a concert at the Palace. Her
Majesty was very gracious to me, and expressed a hope that
I might not find the duties of my new office too laborious. I
could only say, 'Madam, I shall do my best worthily to serve
your Majesty.'

July 3.—Have been sworn in Chancellor at Lincoln's Inn,
with as little parade as possible ; have heard several causes in
the Court of Chancery ; have decided three Scotch appeals in
the House of Lords ; and during several debates have presided
on the woolsack, as yet, I believe, without any discredit. But
I am sometimes very nervous, and almost wish I were at my
ease again in Queen's Bench.

I have already got into great disgrace by disposing of my
judicial patronage on the principle *detur digniori*. Having
occasion for a new judge, to succeed Erle made Chief Justice
of the Common Pleas, I appointed Blackburn, the fittest man
in Westminster Hall, although wearing a stuff gown ; whereas several Whig Queen's Counsel, M.P.'s, were considering
which of them would be the man, not dreaming that they
could all be passed over. They got me well abused in the

'Times' and other newspapers, but Lyndhurst has defended me gallantly in the House of Lords.

Since I received the Great Seal I have dined once at Buckingham Palace, when I had a long discussion on the state of Europe with Leopold, the King of the Belgians, and a violent flirtation with the Princess Alice, who has expressed a strong desire to bring her mamma and papa to visit Teviotdale and to partake of a *disjeune* at Hartrigge. I renewed my acquaintance with the Prince of Wales, who is much improved by his Italian tour.

Last night I was presented at Lady Palmerston's to H.R.H. the Comte de Paris, and had a long chat with him, and I explained to him that my office nearly resembled that of the 'Garde des Sceaux' under the *ancien régime* of France. He is a remarkably fine-looking young man, and seems very intelligent and well informed. So keen a Frenchman is he that he rejoices exceedingly in the victories of Napoleon III. in Italy, although they will protract, if they do not entirely prevent, the restoration of the Orleans line.

July 10.—I still abstain on principle from making a statement in my Journal of the deliberations of the Cabinet, but I may mention that I never before Wednesday last was present at any which had such a direct influence on the destinies of nations. . . . In twenty-four hours we heard by telegram of the armistice between the French and Austrians being actually concluded at Villafranca on the proposal of the Emperor Napoleon, by which another pitched battle within the Quadrilateral is prevented, and peace may be re-established.

We expect that England will be invited to take part in the coming negotiations.

We were alarmed by a rumour, sanctioned by D'Azeglio, the Sardinian Minister, that Savoy is to be surrendered to France. We could not have gone to war to prevent this, but it would have been highly distasteful to Europe, and would have led to war on the Rhine, and ultimately to the invasion of England. But the French ambassador being sounded on the subject, he produced a formal renunciation from the Emperor of this or any other such *arrière pensée.*

If he is sincere, and is contented with the glory of being the Liberator of Italy, the world may again enjoy repose. But I have little faith in his peaceable professions, and I shall not be surprised if before I die I should be again obliged to handle my ' Brown Bess.'

I get on pretty well both in the Court of Chancery and with the judicial business of the House of Lords. But I am quite overwhelmed by the thousands of applications I have, not only for livings and legal appointments, but from persons who are neither in the Church nor the law, and nevertheless press on me to procure for them ' places under Government.' Although the bulk of these letters are acknowledged by my secretaries, I have a good many which I am obliged to answer myself, in such terms as not to appear rude, yet not so civil as to be converted into a promise, and afterwards quoted against me as a proof of perfidy.

I am happy to say that I get on as yet most harmoniously with all my brother law lords. Brougham is perfectly civil. St. Leonards has sent me his ' Handy-book.' The good Cranworth does all he can to help and oblige me. Wensleydale has forgotten that I opposed his admission into the House as a peer for life. Chelmsford and I are loving brothers while hearing appeals in the morning, although a little political asperity shows itself in debate in the evening ; and Kingsdown (Pemberton Leigh), a Derbyite, seems disposed to support my authority as Chancellor. Storms must be expected, but I hope I shall not be shipwrecked.

I have as yet managed Bethell successfully by having a Committee of the Cabinet appointed for legal reform measures, and having these measures all debated privately before they are launched in either House. I have a difficult game to play about the Divorce Court, Bankruptcy, the Statute Law Commission, the Consolidation of the Statutes, and the conundrum about a 'Minister for Justice.' By prudence and discreet reticence, and dealing in generalities, I hope to tide over the session ; and in little more than a month from this time I may declare in the Queen's name that Parliament is prorogued.

August 18.—The latter part of the session was very

quiet for us in the Lords ; Lord Derby and Lord Malmesbury absconded soon after their resignations, and we not only had no party division but no party logomachy. The Divorce Bill encountered no serious opposition, and our fair promises for next session were deemed satisfactory.

As for the appeal business, such a number of cases was hardly ever known to be disposed of in the same time, and with Cranworth, Kingsdown, Wensleydale and Chelmsford for my coadjutors, they were disposed of very satisfactorily.

Luckily, St. Leonards was constantly absent. He is much more familiar with the law of real property than I am, but there is an utter impossibility of acting comfortably with him ; and when I have heard any question, however abstruse, as to a contingent remainder or executory devise well argued, I think I am competent to form a sound opinion and to deliver a good judgment upon it.

Brougham, to my great surprise, regularly attends in the morning as a law lord. One would suppose that the philosophical pursuits by which he expects to rival Newton would be more attractive. But he does no harm, for he is never inclined to differ, and if there be a difference he sides with the present Chancellor.

My experience in the Court of Chancery is as yet very small, but on Saturdays I have sat regularly with the Lords Justices of Appeal, and we have pulled very well together. In one case, on the construction of a will, we were divided. I wrote a long judgment, in which Lord Justice Turner concurred. Lord Justice Knight Bruce was very courteous in his dissent. In and after next term I shall be sitting with them daily, for the fear of an autumnal session of Parliament has died away for the present.

I had a pleasant trip to Osborne for a Council to approve of the Speech closing the session. As the Queen was not to be present, I was rather nervous at the thought of delivering it to the two Houses of Parliament in her name. But, with two Lords Commissioners on my right hand and two on my left, wearing my parliamentary robes, full-bottom wig and cocked hat, I got through the ceremony very well.

I have had a meeting of the law officers of the Crown

and a Committee of the Cabinet on law reforms to be brought forward next session—not at all satisfactory. Strange to say, I get on more harmoniously with Bethell than with other members of the Government. The Chancellor of the Exchequer shows very little deference for our opinion, seems to think that we wish to do jobs by employing our dependents in preparing Bills, and, while a sum of 17,000*l.* has been voted to purify the Serpentine, he grudges a third of the money to clear away the mud that has been accumulating for centuries in Westminster Hall.[1]

And now, with gratitude to Heaven, I look forward to spending a few weeks quietly at my country house in Scotland. Some question my right to carry the Great Seal across the Border; but I am Lord Chancellor of Great Britain, and the Seal which the Queen delivered to me is the Great Seal of the United Kingdom. I may use it lawfully at all events in any part of Great Britain, although my jurisdiction as an Equity judge is confined to England. Cardinal Wolsey was impeached (*inter alia*) for carrying the Great Seal to Calais, and using it there, but it was then the Great Seal of England only, and it could no more be used at Calais than at Pekin or Timbuctoo. When Brougham was Chancellor, he made himself ridiculous by carrying the Great Seal along with him in his ' progress ' through Scotland, but he then only used it by making pancakes upon it at Taymouth to amuse the Marchioness of Breadalbane.

Chaff Wax,[2] that ancient and venerable officer of the Great Seal, is to pay me a weekly visit at Hartrigge, bringing down with him all *sigillanda,* and he will carry back the *sigillata* next day to London. In point of time Hartrigge

[1] A better illustration might have been drawn from the vote of 20,000*l.* for the great bell at Westminster, which has twice cracked and is now again dumb.

[2] His ancient Norman name was 'Chaud cire ' from the hot wax always used for an impression of the Great Seal. *Chaucer* the poet is said to have held the office, and to have taken his name from it. The *Chaud* was gradually corrupted into *Chaff,* and, as the Anglo-Saxon was restored, the ' cire ' was translated into wax. Hence ' Chaff Wax,' who is to be my *Ariel.* I have never seen him, for according to the present division of labour he never officiates except when the Chancellor is at a distance from London.

is not more distant from London than was Encombe, Lord Eldon's country house in Dorsetshire.

August 21.—I have opened the Commission moved by Lyndhurst for inquiring into the manner of taking evidence in Equity suits. Find I have got into a scrape by following Lyndhurst's advice in not including Brougham and St. Leonards as Commissioners, but have tried to pacify them, and have offered now to add their names. Cranworth attended, and comported himself very amiably. The Commission will give me a good deal of trouble.

I have been amusing myself with a cursory inspection of the Lives of the Chancellors, and I cannot find that since the time of St. Swithun the Great Seal has ever been delivered to anyone, ecclesiastical or lay, who had reached my years.

I do not discover anyone who died Chancellor before Cardinal Morton, age not stated. The next of this class is Lord Audley, who died aged 56. Then follows Bishop Gardener, the bloody Chancellor to the bloody Mary, age uncertain. Strange to say, the five following successive holders of the Great Seal all died possessed of it :—Sir Nicholas Bacon, aged   ; Bromley, aged   ; Sir Christopher Hatton, aged 52 ; Puckering, aged   ; Lord Ellesmere, aged 76. We have no other of the class till Lord Coventry, who died at 60. Then comes Lord Nottingham, who died at 61. Next Lord Guildford, who died at 58. Down to the present time there are only two more : Lord Talbot, who was suddenly cut off at 53 ; and the ill-fated Charles Yorke, who put an end to himself two days after he had received the Great Seal, before he had completed his 48th year.

The wonderful octogenarian lawyer connected with the Great Seal is Serjeant Maynard, most famous for his saying to King William, who observed to him that he had survived all the lawyers of his time : ' Yes, sir, and I should have survived the Law itself if your Majesty had not come to deliver us.' At 88 he was made Lord Commissioner of the Great Seal with two colleagues, and so held it for more than a year. But he was never in the category of Lords Chancellors, or sole Lord Keeper of the Great Seal.

No Chancellor has died in office since Charles Yorke. Modern Chancellors have reached a good old age after their resignation. Lord Hardwicke died at 74; Lord Camden at 81; Lord Bathurst at 86; Lord Thurlow at 76; Lord Loughborough at 72; Lord Erskine at 73; Lord Eldon at 87. But Lord Eldon, born 1751, resigned the Great Seal in 1827, when he was only 76. It would therefore appear that no one before Campbell ever held the Great Seal and exercised the functions of Chancellor having entered his 80th year. Thanks to Almighty God, I am, I believe, as able for this task both in body and mind as I ever was.

Stratheden House: October 2.—I thought that long before this there must have been a final settlement of Italy, or a renewal of the war. But the complication only becomes more complicated. In all history there is nothing so surprising as the Peace of Villafranca. We never shall know, or be able to conjecture, what were the motives of Louis Napoleon for stopping suddenly in his victorious career, and agreeing to conditions so discreditable, by which, if fully performed, Italy was again to have been subjected to Austrian rule, all the petty princes, satraps of Austria, were to be restored, and the temporal power of the Pope was to be increased. The new Federation over which Austria would have dominated must have been to her more than a recompense for the loss of Lombardy; and, indeed, Lombardy, being defenceless, might very speedily have been recovered. The French Emperor seems to have been frightened at the revolutionary spirit which was rapidly spreading over the Continent, and which might have been communicated from Hungary to France. He probably had some vague notions that the fulfilment of the article about the restoration of the old dynasties to the Duchies might be prevented without a glaring breach of good faith on his part, and that he might be able to turn the military glory of Magenta and Solferino to account without being made ridiculous by his boast that he would make Italy free from the Alps to the Adriatic.

I went down to Hartrigge on Tuesday, the 23rd of August; found the place in great beauty, and expected to enjoy it quietly for six weeks; but on Saturday the 27th I received a telegram summoning me to a Cabinet in Downing Street for Monday the 29th. I went up by the mail train on Sunday night. We had rather a stormy meeting next day. . . .

. . . Having got back to Hartrigge on the 31st, I was allowed to play at bowls, billiards and croquet till the 15th of September, when I heard of the disaster at the mouth of the Pei Ho, and received a summons for a Cabinet to meet on the 17th. I wrote to Palmerston that I should not come without a peremptory telegram, as I supposed they only met to consider what reinforcements should be sent out to China, about which the Great Seal would be a dumb oracle.

I had the following answer from him:—

94 Piccadilly : September 16, 1859.

My dear Lord Campbell,—I have received your letter of yesterday. I summoned a Cabinet because I thought it would look ill if the Cabinet were not to meet on the receipt of the bad news from China. We should have been accused of taking our disasters too coolly. But we can come at present to no decision on the matter, except to order some moderate reinforcements to China, to make good the casualties, and to provide for the defence of our stations if the Chinese should become aggressors; and for that purpose those members of the Cabinet who are within easy distance will be quite enough.

If we were to determine upon operations on a large scale against Pekin, we could not begin to act in the north of China till the spring.

Yours sincerely,

PALMERSTON.

I found, however, that I was wanted at the Cabinet, for several questions arose as to whether the proceedings of Mr. Bruce, our ambassador, and of Admiral Hope, the commander of the forces, in trying to force a passage up the Pei Ho, could be justified by the law of nations; and that my colleagues could come to no resolution till my opinion was known, and I had decided whether *any* and *what* questions should be put to the law officers of the Crown. Sir George Grey was deputed to write to me from London. . . .

Another Cabinet was called for the 24th. Sir George and Lady Grey were with me at Hartrigge, having arrived on a visit the day before. At four P.M. on the 23rd we started for Berwick, Lady Grey to return to their country house at

Fallodon, and Sir George and I to catch the express train for London. *En route* we found that Lord John Russell and Lord Elgin, who had left Balmoral that morning, were in the train along with us. . . .

We held another Cabinet on Monday the 26th, to which I summoned Bethell, the Attorney-General, who was beginning to be very troublesome, and who showed a disposition to throw blame upon me on the ground that some law reforms he contemplated were not sufficiently supported by the Government. I introduced him and begged that he might have a full hearing. . . .

Stratheden House: October 15.—My Journal does not usually enter into domestic life, but I must mention the auspicious event of the 4th of October—the marriage of my youngest daughter—which is *de omni parte beatum*. She certainly is a little angel, sent to soothe and to bless me. In all her life she never once was naughty that I ever saw or heard of—the most affectionate and pious of children. It was sad to part with her, but I resign her to a husband who is in character very worthy of her.[3]

I have come up to London for this solemnity. The day after the wedding I went to Ampthill, on a visit to Lord Wensleydale. A paragraph which has made the round of the newspapers has celebrated our presence at the Bedford races, where we are said to have made a distinguished figure in the betting ring.

My wife and I then spent a week at Orchardleigh in Somersetshire, the seat of the bride's father-in-law, and were rejoiced to think of the mansion and domain where she is (D.V.) one day to be mistress.

October 20.—Since my return to London I have constantly been attending Cabinets—by no means pleasantly. We have various matters on hand, each of which may produce a war, and render it necessary immediately to assemble the two Houses of Parliament. Besides the Pei Ho and San Juan, we have got into a terrible brangle by a dispute between Spain and Morocco as to the possession of the coast

---

[3] The Rev. W. Arthur Duckworth, of Orchardleigh Park, in Somersetshire.

opposite Gibraltar—England for her own sake taking part with the Moors. . . .

I almost begin to regret that my attention did not continue for the rest of my days to be exclusively directed to the decision of causes in the Queen's Bench.

I have kept up a close correspondence during the vacation with Lyndhurst, that most extraordinary man. He not only makes speeches on foreign politics which fix the attention of Europe, but revels in the *badinage* which might be expected from a boy of eighteen writing to a boy of sixteen. I introduce two or three of his letters as a specimen :—

Cowes : September 5, 1859.

My dear Lord Chancellor,—'Here's to the pilot that weathered the storm'—for I distinctly found a storm brewing—but you have pursued Franklin's advice and poured oil on the troubled waters—'ponto Unda recumbit.' Have you forgotten the lecture read by King William IV. of glorious memory (I say of glorious memory because he was the distinguished patron of the Reform Bill of 1830)—the lecture to Lord Brougham for his irregular conduct in taking the Great Seal to Scotland? You appear to have followed the precedent, but without much fear of the lecture being repeated under a wiser rule. I am wondering when your grand Commission of all the living authorities on Chancery Reform is likely to commence its real business. I am unfortunately getting every day more lame and more inefficient. You must lay in a capital stock of health in your native air, for you will have no light work when Parliament meets and Lord John Russell fires off his blunderbuss. If it should burst in his hands ! Excuse my nonsense, for I am very very idle. Faithfully yours,

LYNDHURST.

Cowes : September 15, 1859.

My dear Lord Chancellor,—. . . There is no difficulty you cannot surmount, so I remain in the same easy tranquil state as before this *contretemps*.

Are the people of the North enrolling themselves in Rifle Corps? and with activity, or sluggishly? We may have much on our hands—and much out of our pockets. A Chinese war, uncomfortable condition of India, a Reform Bill pending, the proposed new constituencies in a state of *strike*, Italy unsettled, Lord John Russell Foreign Minister. What can you want more? But Brougham on the 10th of October will settle all. So be confident and easy. Faithfully yours,

L.

St. Leonards-on-Sea : October 13, 1859.

My dear Lord Chancellor,—I congratulate you warmly on the marriage of your daughter. The marriage of a daughter is both an anxious and a

happy event in a family. I am pleased to find you have returned from
that horrid Scotland. Some people said, as you had taken the Great Seal
with you, that you intended to persuade the Queen to transfer the seat of
government to the modern Athens. I was afraid, as you had accomplished
all the usual objects of a lawyer's ambition, that you intended to settle
down in the country of your birth, recollecting the lines, I think, of
Goldsmith—

> 'And I had hopes, a length of labour past,
> Then to return, and die at home at last.'

But I took a short measure of your ambition. Witness the Bedford Races,
and the gallant figure you are said to have there displayed! Again, why
should not the double coronet be merged in an earldom? You know I am
a bit of a prophet. So something is still to be done! Rest not—

> ' On Moscow's walls till Gothic banners fly,
> And all be mine beneath the Polar sky.'

Your great indefatigable rival is Brougham. He has spoken a world
of social and physical philosophy at Bradford—old Shaftesbury in the
chair; and this while you were betting odds on a race-course!

Yours faithfully,
LYNDHURST.

I have likewise had frequent letters from Brougham.
His last lies before me, and I add it as a specimen:—

Private.   Brougham: October 18, 1859.

My dear Chancellor,—I have just got your kind letter of yesterday,
and let me beg and entreat that you would insert Napier's name in the
Commission, and so make the inquiry extend to Ireland. It is incon-
ceivable how much importance is attached to their being included in
anything which is done with respect to England, and though in some things,
as the Divorce Court, there may be reasons against it, in this of taking
evidence in Equity there can be none.

I saw in the papers your having taken to the turf in your old age.
Whether Jem Parke, besides seducing you, profited by doing you in a
bet, I can only conjecture.

My week at Bradford was by much the hardest week I ever went
through—even at the election of 1830—and I was not the least fatigued;
but when all was over, and I was on my way home, like an army in a
retreat when the excitement is over, I was seized with such a cold as I
never had in my life, and I had to put myself under medical treatment,
which has greatly reduced it,—not, however, in the Scotch law sense of
the word, set it aside—so I hope to get to Edinburgh; but I assure you it
will be a very painful event: a quarter of a century since I last was there
has left me hardly a single one of my old friends.

Many felicitations to Lady Stratheden and the rest of the family on
the Duckworth marriage, which was only *in fieri* when I last wrote, but
has since been executed.   Yours ever truly,

H. BROUGHAM.

October 27.—I have prorogued Parliament to the 15th of
December, and I hope it may not assemble for the despatch
of business till the beginning of February; but we have
several times been within a hair's breadth of a proclamation
to call Parliament together immediately, on account of the
dispute at the Pei Ho; of the dispute with America about
the island of San Juan; and of the attack on Morocco by the
Spaniards. . . .

November 2.—This being the first day of term, the
Chancellor's levée has been at Stratheden House. The day
has been brilliant, and we had a grand procession to Westminster Hall.

I had to begin the day by receiving the Corporation of
London, and delivering her Majesty's approbation of the
new Lord Mayor, who mounts the civic throne on the 9th
of November.

I sat by myself to-day in the Court of Chancery, and disposed of several matters of a light description with ease and
satisfaction. But to-morrow I begin serious work at Lincoln's Inn, sitting with the two Lords Justices, Knight Bruce
and Turner.

To qualify myself, during the vacation I looked over all
the Equity decisions during the last ten years of Lords
Chancellors, Masters of the Rolls, Lords Justices, and Vice-
Chancellors. I did not meet with any case which I did not
understand, or on which, after hearing it well argued, I could
not have given a satisfactory judgment. I have no hope of
being quoted as a great Equity authority; but I trust that
I shall not tarnish my Common Law reputation.

I lately paid a visit to Erle, one of my colleagues in the
Queen's Bench, now Chief Justice of the Common Pleas.
With him I had differed oftener than with any other judge,
and he is one of the sincerest of mankind. Yet he said to
me with great solemnity: 'There is no functionary under
the Crown who during the last ten years performed more
valuable services to the public in quantity and quality than
John Lord Campbell.'

I leave behind me thirteen huge volumes (xv. to xviii. of
Adolphus and Ellis, and i. to ix. of Ellis and Blackburn) of

Queen's Bench Reports, chiefly filled with my judgments while I presided in the Queen's Bench. But from the portentous multiplicity of law reports now published, there seems almost a certainty of all the judgments of every judge, however eminent, being speedily smothered. The whole world is now insufficient to contain all the law reports which are published. I remember the time when one good-sized bookcase would hold all the law books worth consulting —from the Year Books to the last number of the Term Reports. What is the remedy? Perhaps a decennial *auto da fè.*

November 8.—My *alma mater* has sent me the following invitation :—

> United College of St. Andrews :
> November 5, 1859.
>
> My Lord,—At a public meeting of the students of this University, held last night, a committee was appointed to ask your lordship to allow yourself to be proposed for the office of Lord Rector of this University. Should your lordship accede to this request, the committee have good grounds for believing that, from the tone of feeling among the students in reference to your lordship's qualifications for the office, your lordship's election would be all but unanimous.
>
> Our University more than any other requires all the fostering influence which your lordship's exalted position and great political influence would secure for it; and from the deep interest which we know your lordship takes in matters of Scottish education, the committee hope that your lordship will honour the students of the University of St. Andrews by allowing them to elect as their Lord Rector its greatest living *alumnus.*
>
> I am, my Lord, your lordship's most obedient servant,
>
> GEORGE THOMSON.
> (Convener.)

I have refused permission to start me, as there are duties to be performed by a Lord Rector under the new *régime* which, as an absentee, I must have neglected.

December 1.—I sat daily through the whole of Michaelmas Term with the Lords Justices Knight Bruce and Turner. I might have been compared to a wild elephant broken in between two tame ones. My associates were the most experienced Equity lawyers in Westminster Hall. They behaved exceedingly well to me, and I got on marvellously well with them.

Legal tradition reports that Mr. Justice Buller, being

allowed to sit in the Common Pleas for the Chief Justice, so urged on the Serjeants, accustomed to travel at a very slow pace, that he cleared off in one day all the causes entered for trial which ought to have lasted above a week, saying when he got home that ' he had been giving the heavy blocks a gallop.' I am told there have not been such doings in Lincoln's Inn Hall for half a century. We decided offhand most of the matters which came before us, but I delivered four written judgments—in one case differing from Knight Bruce, but having Turner with me.

Now I am out of leading strings. During the next three weeks, I am to sit all alone at Lincoln's Inn : and I am not very nervous. With the assistance of my chief secretary,[*] I get possession of the nature of the case, often from a printed report of the judgment below, and, hearing the arguments on both sides, I conscientiously believe that I shall be able to come to a right conclusion. If I am puzzled, I can resort to Lyndhurst's certain resource—always to affirm, which, he truly said, ' discouraged frivolous appeals ;' he, *of course*, having no desire to save himself trouble and to avoid responsibility !

I have to-day been attending a meeting of all the Equity judges—Master of the Rolls, two Lords Justices, and three Vice-Chancellors—to digest all the orders of all the Chancellors since the time of Lord Bacon ; to prepare a Bill for sweeping away the few remaining Masters in Chancery ; and to introduce the practice of *printing* all answers as well as bills in Chancery ; from which we expect great advantage. We sat five hours.

We have had frequent Cabinets, chiefly upon the affairs of Italy, and as to the conditions on which England should agree to join the Congress resulting from the treaties of Villafranca and Zurich. . . .

My wife and I were invited to dine with her Majesty at Windsor on Saturday the 26th of November, and to stay till Monday. The visit passed off most agreeably. On our arrival on Saturday evening, we were inducted into a nice *appartement* of three *pièces* looking on the Long Walk. As

[*] Henry R. Vaughan Johnson, Esq.

at Buckingham Palace, the Royalties joined the party an instant before dinner was announced, the programme of the procession having been previously intimated to all the guests. I had the honour to take the Princess Alice to dinner, and to sit on the Queen's left hand; her son-in-law, Prince William Frederick of Prussia, being on her right. . . .

On Sunday I attended her Majesty to chapel. By rights I ought to have walked before her with the purse containing the Great Seal in my hand, as Lord Chancellors always attended the Sovereign on Sundays till the reign of George I.

At dinner on Sunday I sat next the Princess William Frederick (Princess Royal), and, getting deep into her confidence, she told me how Prince William Frederick proposed to her as they were riding together over a heathy mountain at Balmoral, and how happily they had lived together, notwithstanding the stories published in the newspapers of her being neglected and ill-used. . . . I do believe that it was a marriage of affection, and that it has turned out very auspiciously.

The Queen was extremely civil to Lady Stratheden, and introduced her to Beatrice, the baby princess. I renewed my acquaintance with the Princess Helena, at whose birth I was present in the year 1849, when I was a member of Lord John Russell's Cabinet, and Chancellor of the Duchy of Lancaster. After breakfast on Monday we returned by the train to London.

December 23.—For three weeks I have been sitting as Lord Chancellor in Lincoln's Inn Hall, hearing, all alone, appeals from the Master of the Rolls and the Vice-Chancellors, and I have got through marvellously. Every appeal ready for hearing has been heard. The two Lords Justices sat by themselves, and cleared off a good deal of business. Lord Justice Knight Bruce, who has known the court for half a century, declared to me that the Christmas adjournment had never before found the court in such a satisfactory state. Unluckily, at the close of the sittings after term in the Queen's Bench there is a tremendous arrear, and a jocular rumour is circulated that as soon as Parliament meets the

Attorney-General is to bring in a Bill to empower Lord Campbell, having disposed of all the business in Chancery, to try causes by jury in the courts of Common Law.

CHAP.
XXXIV.

A.D. 1860.

Mr. Attorney and I have hitherto gone on very amicably; but, in spite of his magniloquent professions about the law reforms he is to bring forward next session, I have not yet been able to get from him a draft of any of his Bills; and I am afraid that when Parliament meets we may fall into disrepute, and may be driven to disparage each other.

When I think of the new Reform Bill, the new Bankruptcy Bill, the new Registration of Titles Bill, the new Common Law Equity Jurisdiction Bill, and the new Criminal Law Consolidation Bill, I look forward to the 24th of January with some dismay! But 'time and the hour run through the roughest day.'

Saturday, January 14, 1860.

Extract from a London Newspaper.

A scene occurred in the Court of Chancery on Thursday morning, such as has not been witnessed since the days of Lord Eldon. The Lord Chancellor sat on that day to administer the oath of allegiance to the Volunteers of the Inns of Court. He commenced the proceedings by delivering a spirit-stirring speech, which will he found elsewhere in our columns, and which excited considerable enthusiasm. It was one of his lordship's happiest efforts, and will, no doubt, find its place in some future edition of the 'Lives of the Chancellors.' Loud demonstrations of applause were with difficulty repressed, and it may be doubted whether in the whole course of the present movement any address has been delivered which produced greater effect than the recent speech of Lord Campbell.

Mr. Selwyn, Q.C., the Commandant, returned thanks to the Lord Chancellor for the honour he had done to the Inns of Court Volunteers by following the example of Lord Eldon on a similar occasion.

Tuesday, January 17.—Sitting in my library reading the newspaper, there being no appeals for me to hear in Lincoln's Inn, I have just received a letter from Bethell, the Attorney-General, in which, after observing on some Bills we have in preparation, he adds :—

Pardon my telling you that the bar misses you in the Court of Chancery. 'Magnum est desiderium tam cari capitis.' We all fully expected that when not presiding in the House of Lords you would preside over the Court of Appeal.

The benefit you have done to that court and to the *habits of the judges*
by your presiding there, has been fully appreciated. In the theory of the
law the Court of Chancery is there where the Lord Chancellor is bodily present, and though that is innovated upon, yet it is good for you to be there.

This is rather a flattering remonstrance. The truth is
that the Lords Justices have been sitting on several half-
heard cases which they began when I was sitting by myself
after last term. But to be of some service to the public,
and for my own credit, I really wish to preside alone in
Chancery when I am not presiding in the House of Lords.

Being at present a lounger about town, I call on Lyndhurst and chat with him. On Saturday last he said to me,
' So there has been a split in the Cabinet, and you were three
to thirteen. It was touch and go with you.' I expressed
some surprise at the news. He said, ' What is more, although the league against Austria won't do, you are going
to have a commercial treaty with France to supply her with
coal and iron to invade us. I know all about it.' *Campbell.*
' Well! when Palmerston is a little mysterious, and I wish
to know what is coming, I will apply to you.' *Lyndhurst.*
' That is right; you shall know all about it.'

Lyndhurst reproached me for want of reciprocity in the
interchange of political news; for, said he, ' although I tell
you so much, I can get nothing out of you.' There certainly
must be some member of the Cabinet much more communi-
cative, more *blabative.*

Wednesday, January 25.—I have recorded in my ' Lives
of the Chancellors' the judgment of King William IV.,
who, there being a dispute between Lord Brougham and
Lord Lyndhurst on the question to which of them the old
Great Seal belonged, like another Solomon ordered the subject in controversy to be cut in twain and divided between
them.

A similar case having arisen upon a new Great Seal being
ordered while Lord Chelmsford was Chancellor, and adopted
when Lord Campbell had succeeded him, we at once agreed
that, with the consent of the Queen, we would be bound by
the former decision. The doubt was, whether it would be
followed by the Sovereign ordering the two halves to be

fitted into handsome silver salvers, to be presented to the Lord Chancellor and his predecessor.

One day about a month ago, paying Lyndhurst a visit, I mentioned the subject to him and he said: 'I wager you that you don't get the silver salver.' I answered, 'I will take your wager if you will write to me such a letter as I require.' At this moment in came Lord Chelmsford, and I told him how much he was interested in the matter we were discussing. *Lyndhurst.* 'No! you will never get your silver salvers as Brougham and I did.' *Campbell.* 'Only write a letter to me stating the judgment of William IV. in the case of Lyndhurst *v.* Brougham, concluding with the present made by the judge to the litigants.' *Lyndhurst.* 'Well, you shall have what you ask, but it won't do.'

He was as good as his promise :—

George Street : January 11, 1860.

My dear Lord Chancellor,—You wish to know what took place when a new Great Seal was ordered on the accession of His Majesty King William IV. It was this. The new Great Seal was ordered immediately upon the accession. I was then Lord Chancellor. Before the order was completed I was succeeded by Lord Brougham. We each of us claimed the old Seal, the usual perquisite of the office. His Majesty condescended to decide between us. He allotted to each of us one of the *sides*, and as the designs were different, his Majesty added with a smile that he would toss up for the choice, which was accordingly done. His Majesty's kindness did not stop here. He graciously added that each part should form the centre of a handsome piece of plate, and that he would give directions to Rundell and Bridge to prepare a design for that purpose. We accordingly in due time received by his Majesty's command our respective portions of the old Seal, thus associated and decorated. Very faithfully yours,

LYNDHURST.

This I enclosed in a letter to the Queen, and I received a gracious answer saying she was ready to follow the precedent of her uncle, and to divide the old Great Seal between the present Chancellor and his predecessor, and that she wished also to follow her uncle's precedent in having the half of the Great Seal worked into a piece of plate for the acceptance of the Lord Chancellor and Lord Chelmsford.

On Monday the 23rd of January the Council was held at which the new Great Seal was adopted, and the old one received the stroke of the mallet by way of defacing it. The

Council being over, the Queen told me she wished to keep
the two halves of the old Great Seal for the present, and that
I should let her know what was the choice made between us
respecting them.

Returning home I wrote a letter to Lord Chelmsford,
informing him what had been done and asking him to choose.
Next morning I received an answer warmly thanking me for
my handsome conduct to him, and choosing ' the Queen
sitting on her throne.'

The first night of the session went off most auspiciously ;
and instead of an ignominious break-up, which I dreaded a
fortnight ago, we are supposed to be the strongest Government since the time of Sir Robert Peel. I introduced a
paragraph into the Queen's Speech about law reform.[5] But
I have serious misgivings, and I must remain prepared for
fatal reverses.

March 18.—The Budget, which was to ruin us, comes off
with brilliant success. We have crushing majorities in the
House of Commons, and our opponents are quarrelling and
abusing each other like pickpockets.

In the House of Lords we have had a debate on the
Commercial Treaty, and a good division. I was called up
by Lord Derby to say whether the treaty would be binding
without an Act of Parliament to ratify it, and whether at all
events there must not be an Act of Parliament to sanction
the eleventh Article, by which the Queen undertakes not
to prohibit the exportation of coal. The first question I
answered triumphantly, and made him ashamed of having
put it, and of having thus confounded the Constitution of
England with that of the United States of America—by
which treaties are not binding till the Senate ratifies them.
And I showed that no legislation was necessary as to the
eleventh Article, as this had commerce only in contemplation, and left untouched the prerogative of the Crown to be
exercised in the case of war, or the apprehension of war.

---

* ' I earnestly recommend you to resume your labours for the improvement of our jurisprudence, and particularly as regards bankruptcy, the
transfer of land, the consolidation of the statutes, and such further fusion
of Law and Equity as may always ensure the satisfactory decision of the
rights of the parties by the court in which the suit was commenced.'

But the fears I had of the annexation of Savoy are likely to be fully realised. Louis Napoleon, taking advantage of the depression of Austria and the mutual jealousies of the other Continental Powers, is determined to set Europe at defiance. . . .

Thursday night, March 22.—I dined to-day at the Palace, and sitting on the Queen's right hand had a great deal of conversation with her about Lord John and Palmerston and the answer to Thouvenel; but I am now indifferent about all such matters; for my beloved wife has been seriously ill, and the doctors, who till now have told me there was no danger, are evidently alarmed.

. . . .

April 4.—Early in the morning of Sunday the 25th of March all was over, and I am now preparing to accompany the remains of my beloved wife to their last resting-place, in Jedburgh Abbey.

Praying that I may think and act as she would wish me to do, I try to attend to my private and public duties; but I still feel the bereavement with increasing bitterness. The worst of it is that at times I cannot persuade myself that the calamity has actually happened, and I hope to awake from a melancholy dream. But I have sad proofs of the reality of my irreparable loss. I have seen her in her last attire, surrounded by our weeping children. I have to bless God for the tender affection of all the seven; above all for the devoted kindness of my beloved child and best of friends, Mary—without whom I could not support this heavy trial, or be reconciled to life.

We have met with much sympathy, from the Queen down to our faithful domestics, Reed, our old butler, and Sims, our old nurse, who both insisted on accompanying the coffin down to Hartrigge, where it awaits our arrival tomorrow.

On Friday evening the 23rd of March, I was sent for to the House of Lords, and obliged to leave the woolsack in the middle of a debate. Since then, Lord Redesdale, Chairman of the Lords' Committees—who has a commission to act as Speaker in the absence of the Lord Chancellor—and one of the law lords chosen by the House have occupied the woolsack for me; and the Duke of Argyll, Lord Privy Seal, has presided in giving the Royal assent to Bills. Lord Granville, the Lord President, is absent on the Continent, having suffered a similar bereavement, which I believe he has almost as severely felt. I received a sweet note from him this morning. He is a most amiable and excellent man. . . .

Sunday evening, April 15.—To-morrow is the first day of Easter Term, and I must again plunge into the turbulent business of life. I decline holding a levée of the judges and Queen's counsel; but I must sit at Lincoln's Inn with the Lords Justices of Appeal.

By the blessing of God I have been supported through the sad duties cast upon me. I had resolved at all risks to be present at the last solemn rite. My children were much pleased at first, but afterwards alarmed; and my very dear Hally wrote me a touching letter to dissuade me. I remained firm in my purpose. . . .

I arrived here from Hartrigge on Tuesday, April 10, and have since seen several persons in my library; and have made a new judge in the Court of Exchequer—Mr. Baron Wilde, the best man I could select.[6]

When left alone I am more depressed than at first, and still I cannot help sometimes hoping that I may awake and find it was a dream. . . .

I do not expect another hour's real happiness in this world. But I ought not to repine. I cannot say

Optima quæque dies miseris mortalibus ævi
Prima fugit.

I have had a long continuation during almost forty years of prosperity and felicity with my beloved wife, without ever meeting, till now, with any serious calamity; having reached a period of life considerably beyond the ordinary age of man, my bodily strength and mental faculties unimpaired. I shall contentedly and gratefully go to my rest in Jedburgh Abbey, and I had rather be laid there, by the side of my beloved

[6] Now Lord Penzance.—ED.

Mary, than be entombed in Westminster Abbey, amid kings,
statesmen, warriors and poets.

April 29.—For a whole fortnight I have, during the busy hours of the day and evening, been immersed in the bickerings of the Court of Chancery and the House of Lords. This, although most revolting to my feelings, has on the whole been of service to me, by necessarily withdrawing my thoughts from the sad contemplation of my irreparable loss. . . .

I have been enabled wonderfully to perform my public duties, and I dare say some think me unfeeling ; but I never expect an hour of real happiness in this world, notwithstanding all the devoted affection and never-ceasing solicitude to comfort me of all my children.

I pray to heaven that I may be enabled properly to perform the duties of the office which I still hold. . . .

May 10.—We are now at that period of the session when there is usually a ' Ministerial crisis.' I do not believe that the Opposition have any immediate intention, or wish, to seize the government. But we are going on very indifferently. Savoy, as I foresaw, poisons everything abroad and at home. There is no longer any confidence in peace continuing a month longer, and we may be fighting France single-handed or (what I really believe would be worse) with a coalition of effete and corrupt Continental States. The present Ministers are supposed to have been outwitted by Louis Napoleon, and to have disabled themselves for any resistance to his aggressive plans by swallowing the bait of his commercial treaty.

The new Reform Bill, although to be read a second time without a division, is still the subject of interminable debates, and nine-tenths of the House of Commons would be delighted, on any decent pretence, immediately to throw it out. They cannot bear the notion of a *dissolution*, which would be the immediate consequence of the Bill being passed. Passing the Bill, therefore, they consider an act of suicide. Even out of doors, instead of the cry in 1831-2, ' The Bill, the whole Bill, and nothing but the Bill,' the cry now is ' Off with the Bill, no part of the Bill, anything but the Bill.'

There being no counterpoise to the strong inclination of

the members of the House, I have not the smallest doubt
that, in some way or another, the Bill will be postponed to
another session, if not absolutely rejected.

May 29.—There has been a sort of ' crisis ' by the Lords
rejecting the Bill passed by the Commons for the repeal
of the paper duty, there being a majority of eighty-nine
against the Government. This part of Gladstone's Budget
had become so unpopular that several of our usual supporters
voted against us, and more stayed away from the division.

In the debate a great question of privilege, or rather
constitutional law, arose—' whether the Lords were justified
in rejecting a Bill sent up by the Commons to repeal a tax
that had been imposed purely for the purposes of revenue,
the Commons having provided a substitute which the Lords
had adopted.'

The truth is that the Lords have the power, and might use
it properly in an extreme case, such as the Commons passing a
Bill to repeal taxes necessary for paying the public creditor, or
the army and navy ; but the Lords were not justified by the
occasion, as no immediate danger to the State would have
arisen from the repeal of the paper duty. A substitute for it
having been provided, the people will now continue to pay a
tax against the will of their representatives ; and, although
there is good reason to believe that there will be a deficit in
the ways and means, this might still have been supplied by
the Commons.

However, the *coup d'état* is a lucky hit for the Lords ;
their usurpation, instead of bringing obloquy upon them, is
rather applauded by the public. Nevertheless, I fear it will
hereafter be brought up against them and they will have
cause to repent it. ' Turno tempus erit,' etc. . . .

While the House of Lords is now adjourned for the
Whitsuntide holidays, Trinity Term is going on, and I sit
daily by myself, hearing appeals in Lincoln's Inn Hall. I
have reversed several decrees of the Master of the Rolls and
of the Vice-Chancellors—I believe, with the approbation of the
bar.

By the 18th of next month I shall have completed my
year as Chancellor. I shall have enjoyed pre-eminence as

long as a Roman Consul or the Lord Mayor of London, and
my ambition ought to be satisfied. I may say with Julius
Cæsar : 'Satis vixi et naturæ et gloriæ.' But from my
constant anxiety, and from the sad bereavement with which I
have been visited, this has been very far indeed from being a
happy year of my life; and what have I now to look forward
to ? Lord, have mercy upon me !

CHAPTER XXXV.

JUNE 1860—JUNE 1861.

Present of a Silver Salver from the Queen—Withdrawal of the Reform
Bill—Foreign Affairs—Last Speech of the Session—State of Business
—Apprehension of Bad Harvest—State of Italy—Funeral of Mr. Tan-
cred—Six Weeks in Scotland—Italian Unity—Taking of the Taku
Forts—Visit to Lord Lansdowne at Bowood—Chancery Appeals—
Princess Alice and Prince Louis of Hesse—Capture of Pekin—Cabinet
Dinner—Letter from Lord Palmerston—Correspondence about the
new Indian Order—Christmas at Torquay—The Session in the House
of Lords—Bankruptcy Bill—Union of Italian States—Civil War in
America—Division in the House of Commons on the Paper Duty—
Majority for the Government—Judgment in the Case of the Emperor
of Austria v. Kossuth—Conclusion.

Journal.

CHAP.
XXXV.
———
A.D. 1860.

June 7.—Have received to-day her Majesty's most
gracious present of my half of the old Great Seal, set in a
most beautiful silver salver with the Royal arms at the top
and the Campbell arms at the bottom. Her Majesty is on
horseback and looks very brave and patriotic. Her Royal
style and title may be read inscribed, 'Victoria Britanniarum
Regina.' It was accompanied by a brief letter to me from
Sir Charles Phipps, her private secretary, expressing her
Majesty's wishes that it might long be an ornament to my
sideboard.

It really is a very handsome piece of plate, and I hope it
may ornament the sideboard of the tenth Lord Stratheden
in the reign of Albert IX. I intend on great occasions, when
grace after meat has been said, to produce it filled with rose-
water 'in city fashion,' every guest to dip his or her napkin
in the rose-water, and to praise the great Queen Victoria and
Lord Chancellor Campbell !

June 14.—At a Cabinet on Saturday, the 9th, the withdrawal of the Reform Bill was determined upon, and, on the following Monday, was successfully accomplished. The whole House rejoiced. Dizzy said, ' The course taken by the Government was prudent and not undignified ; ' and even Bright confessed that it was inevitable. Nor is there the smallest censure or regret expressed either in the metropolis or in the provinces. Considering that, in 1831, 50,000 armed men were ready to march from Birmingham to overawe the Parliament upon the rumoured withdrawal of a single clause from the Bill, allowing the franchise to be acquired by successive weekly hirings of houses, the present apathy is the most extraordinary change in public feeling which has occurred in my time. The four hundred thousand borough *prolétaires* who are to be enfranchised by the Bill, with all 10*l.* leaseholders in counties, seem to be utterly indifferent about continuing to be taxed without being represented in Parliament. While this state of *feeling,* or rather of *apathy,* continues, it would be idle for any Government to propose another Reform Bill, as it must of necessity be distasteful to the actual members of the House of Commons of all parties ; it can only be forced through by pressure from without, and by a conviction by the actual members that to oppose the Bill takes away all chance of re-election.

June 17.—I regard with deep apprehension and dismay the prospect of a new war with France, and most earnestly pray that there may be peace for the rest of my time, although if there should be an invasion I shall still (as I did in the first years of the century) shoulder my Brown Bess, and be ready to fire a volley at the invaders. In the third generation of men with whom I have mixed in public life, by the blessing of God I could still march twenty miles a day with my musket on my shoulder, my bayonet by my side, and my knapsack on my back.

July 15.—Foreign affairs still continue in a most disturbed condition, and no one can tell what new phase Sicily and Italy may any hour assume. The opinion gains ground that a war with France is imminent. I do not believe this myself; for Louis Napoleon could neither lead an invading army himself, nor trust such a command to any of his marshals. But while he lives we shall have no tranquillity, and we shall suffer under an exhausting war expenditure. Our fleet, our army, and our defensive preparations of all sorts must be increased! Such prospects weigh heavily on my spirits, and I fear that my life may be prolonged only to witness disaster and disgrace.

Sunday, August 5.—Another crisis! To-morrow comes on in the House of Commons a grand debate on the Repeal of the Customs Duty on the importation of French paper under the Commercial Treaty.

Sunday, August 19.—We are now in still water, and the session is as good as over. . . . Notwithstanding some Whig defections, the Government had a triumphant majority.

The Conservatives had made a great muster, summoning deer-stalkers from the Scotch Highlands, and members of the Alpine Club from Swisserland. But all dispersed next morning, and we had afterwards to encounter only the carpings of the ultra-Radicals.

I have now a very easy time of it. The Chancery sittings and the judicial sittings of the House of Lords are over, and, the law lords having gone into the country, I have only to lounge for an hour or two on the woolsack and to say, ' The Contents have it.'

However, I have got rather a difficult and delicate task yet before me—to call the attention of the House to the measures of Law Reform introduced by me into their lordships' House during the present session of Parliament. I wish a little to puff, or rather to vindicate myself; but how to do this without blaming the Government, or the House of Commons, or the Attorney-General—' hic labor, hoc opus.'

Sunday, August 26.—This speech came off on Friday evening. I certainly made out a good case for myself and for the House of Lords as far as legislation is concerned, and I showed that the judicial business of the House is in a better state than it has been in since the time of Lord Hardwicke, when appeals were ' few and far between.' Lord Eldon being Chancellor, the appeals were three or four years in arrear.

All that has been aimed at since has been to hear before the end of the session, all that had been set down for hearing at the commencement of the session; and this never once had been accomplished. When I received the Great Seal there was a heavy arrear, but I have now heard and disposed of all that had been set down for hearing at the beginning of the session, together with several set down since the session began; and there are only twenty-four remaining as nest-eggs for the session 1861. To show the despatch which now characterises the Court of Chancery and the House of Lords, I gave as an example Simpson *v.* the Westminster Palace Hotel Company, a very important suit, commenced in April 1860, and finally decided on appeal by the House of Lords in this present month of August.

Nothing now remains but the simple act of prorogation. The Queen is now at Balmoral, this being the first time of her being out of England, Parliament sitting. At a Cabinet yesterday we agreed upon her Speech, which I am to deliver on Tuesday. A Council is to be held at Balmoral to-morrow morning, when the ceremony will take place of reading it in her presence, and her saying ' approved.'

There are now only two grounds of apprehension. The first is the dreadful state of the weather, which continues notwithstanding the prayers offered up in all the churches ' that the world may not again be destroyed by water.' A second deluge I do not dread; but an unexampled failure of the potato and cereal crops, a monetary crisis, a serious decrease of the revenue, a paralysis of trade, general misery and discontent, with a forced meeting of Parliament in the vain hope of a legislative remedy for these evils, are all events which may be coming, and which seem to cast their shadows before.

Secundo : the state of Italy is now so complicated that a general European war may be unavoidable. Garibaldi is the greatest hero we have had since Napoleon I. He has conquered the Two Sicilies as if by magic ! Is Naples to be united to Sardinia ? Are all the Italian States to form one monarchy under Victor Emmanuel ? Or is the union of Italy to be attempted under a Republic according to the plan of

Mazzini ? I do not believe that Piedmont, Lombardy, Tus-
cany, Romagna, and Naples can long cohere under any form
of government. What is to become of the Pope ? I must
own I should much rejoice to see his Holiness stripped of all
his temporal dominions. Recent experience aggravates my
horror of the Popish superstition. Its effect may be perceived
not only in the state of Romagna, but in the present state of
the kingdom of Naples, which for the last forty years has
been governed by the precepts of the Vatican.

Hartrigge, September 4, 1860.—Here I am once more
amidst rural sights and sounds. On Tuesday, August 28,
the Commissions arrived safe from Balmoral for giving the
Royal assent to Bills and for proroguing Parliament, with her
Majesty's warrant for me to put the Great Seal to them, and
the ceremony was performed with all due solemnity.

The following day I had cast upon me the sad duty of
attending the funeral of the oldest and best friend I have
ever had in the world, out of my own family, Henry Tancred,
my fellow-pupil in the office of Tidd, the special pleader, who
has shown a brotherly sympathy for me in all my fortunes
ever since.

I am now not only in the front rank, but a most con-
spicuous object for the dart of the unconquerable foe. Lyndhurst and Brougham are my only seniors in the law, Lyndhurst by seven or eight years, Brougham by one.

I have great enjoyment of this place, the more that there
has been a complete change of weather, that the harvest is
proceeding auspiciously, and that the dread is dissipated of
dearth, monetary crisis, sickness, discontent, and an early
reassembling of Parliament.

Stratheden House, October 22, 1860.—I spent six weeks
most agreeably in Scotland. The weather continued very
fine, and its brilliancy was heightened by accounts of heavy
rains in England. I had a nice ramble in the Highlands,
and visited Balmoral after the Queen had left the place for
her tour in Germany.

I was nearly blown away in crossing from Braemar to the
Spittal of Glenshee by a terrible hurricane which did infinite
mischief all over the north of Scotland and in the Baltic.

I was disposed to forget politics as much as possible, but I could not refrain from looking into the 'Times' to see how Garibaldi was going on in Sicily and in Calabria. . . .

I was brought up here sooner than I intended by a summons to attend a Cabinet on Saturday the 20th. I might as well have remained in the North, for all that we resolved was to continue our preparations, and quietly to look on. This certainly is a great crisis in the history of Italy and of Europe.

Happen what may, I do exceedingly rejoice in the discomfiture of Lamoricière and the Irish brigade. The Ultramontanism of Archbishop Cullen and the Irish Roman Catholic bishops is so extravagant and revolting that I can hardly regard them with a particle of Christian charity.

I must acknowledge that I long believed Italian unity to be quite chimerical as well under a monarchy as under a republic; but the Italian people seem now all of one mind, and ready to obey Victor Emmanuel as King of Italy. Neither Russia nor Austria seems to be in any condition to go to war; and, although Louis Napoleon is by no means to be depended upon, and French politicians are for preserving the temporal power of the Pope that Italy may not become a rival power, I am in hopes that the French Emperor's dread of assassination will induce him to take the popular side.

My greatest anxiety at present is about our expedition to take Pekin. If we had gone alone, the capital of the Celestial Empire would probably have been in our hands; but I am afraid that the delays interposed by our French allies may prove fatal.

October 23.—Good news from China: Taku forts, the scene of our last year's disasters, taken by storm, and our army in full march on Pekin, which seems incapable of any resistance!

October 30.—Have made a very agreeable visit to Lord Lansdowne at Bowood. He is a very wonderful personage, having been a Cabinet Minister in four reigns, and he and his father having been Cabinet Ministers for very near a century, from almost the beginning of the reign of George III. He himself may be considered as having been at the head of the nobility for above half a century. He might have been Prime Minister if he had liked more than once. He has had about him all the men most distinguished in literature, in the arts, and in arms. He has ever behaved most kindly to me, and I should feel his loss most severely.

December 13.—Have long neglected my diary, being completely absorbed in Chancery appeals.

On the 2nd of November I had a levée at Stratheden House, beginning with the Lord Mayor of London, to whose election by his fellow-citizens I gave her Majesty's consent, with an *éloge* on the merits of the new ' chief magistrate of this great metropolis.' I had a very crowded attendance of judges and other legal dignitaries, and a grand procession to Westminster Hall.

Since then I have been sitting by myself in Lincoln's Inn, the Lords Justices having intimated to me that, from the state of the business, they thought this the best arrangement. While they have been engaged with bankruptcy, lunacy, and miscellaneous matters, I have devoted myself to appeals from the Master of the Rolls and the three Vice-Chancellors. Without assistance I have cleared off the whole. When I accepted the Great Seal I had some misgivings as to my ability to discharge this part of my duty, but I really believe that I have got through with considerable credit, boldly reversing when I thought the decree wrong, and never affirming without giving my reasons, generally in a written judgment, but sometimes, in clear cases, off-hand. Without any complaint of impatience or haste, I have induced the Equity counsel to abbreviate their arguments, and I have despatched more business than any of my predecessors in the same space of time for many years past. . . .

I had the honour to pay a visit to her Majesty at Windsor for two days in the end of last month. . . . My stay at Windsor was rather dull, but was a little enlivened by the loves of Prince Louis of Hesse and the Princess Alice. He had arrived the night before, almost a stranger to her, but as her suitor. At first they were very shy, but they soon reminded me of Fernando and Miranda in the ' Tempest,' and I looked on like old Prospero.

I have only paid one visit since, which was to Hackwood Park, a seat of Lord Bolton's in Hampshire, now occupied by Sir Richard Bethell, the Attorney-General; and here he lives *en grand seigneur*.

We have heard by telegram of the capture of Pekin, and the flight of the Emperor into Tartary; but the despatches are not yet arrived. This is rather uncomfortable news, as it removes to an indefinite distance a settlement with China, and indeed threatens a total dissolution of the Chinese empire. We are to have a Cabinet upon the subject immediately.

I should have mentioned that about a fortnight ago I gave a Cabinet dinner at Stratheden House. Cabinet dinners had fallen into desuetude, but a wish being expressed to revive them, at least while Ministers are in London and Parliament is not sitting, the Prime Minister began, and the Lord Chancellor followed. I think it is a good custom, particularly with a heterogeneous Cabinet like ours, that the members may make acquaintance, and drink a glass of wine with one another.

. . . .

January 9, 1861.—It has pleased Providence that I should live to see another year, which is ushered in by three most wonderful events: the taking by an English army of the capital of China; the union of all the states of Italy into one kingdom; and the disruption of the United States of the American Republic, most memorable events in the history of the world.

This is alluded to in the following note from Palmerston in answer to an application from my niece, Mrs. Jones, the wife of the M.P. for Carmarthenshire :—

Broadlands : January 7, 1861.

My dear Lord Campbell,—If the apple is to be given to the fairest, there can be no question as to its disposal; but there are many circumstances to be considered, and I have not yet been able to settle the arrangements.

Our China war has indeed ended satisfactorily, and I hope we may reckon upon the Chinese observing the stipulations of the treaty. If they do, the treaty will be highly advantageous to us by opening a large field to our commerce. Elgin has done his work admirably, and so have our general and our admiral.

It is pleasant to know that, at least in this conjoint operation, we have always led, and our French allies have had to follow;—no, I forget, there was one exception to this; when the object was the plunder of the Summer Palace, the French contrived to be beforehand with us.

I am very sorry to have to give you Sidney Herbert in the Lords, and to lose him in the Commons, but his health would not stand the double work of a most laborious office and House of Commons attendance.

Yours sincerely,

PALMERSTON.

While at Torquay, where I spent the Christmas holidays, I had a correspondence with Sir Charles Wood, Secretary of State for India, which, were it known north of the Tweed, would make me very popular with my countrymen.

India being transferred to the direct government of the Crown, and the Mutiny being effectually suppressed, a new Order of Merit to be given to Indian Chiefs was projected, and a patent creating it under the name of ' *The Eastern Star* ' actually passed the Great Seal. This name being thought objectionable, a new one was resolved upon—' *The Star of England and India*,'—and, without any doubt as to the propriety of the new name, I was asked whether it could be inserted in the patent as a substitution.

India Office : December 29, 1860.

Dear Lord Chancellor,—You passed some time ago Letters Patent creating an Indian order to be designated ' The Eastern Star.' The Queen has determined to alter the name to ' The Star of England and India.'

Is this such an alteration as you would consider yourself justified in making without going through all the forms and proceedings over again— or must we do it all over again ?   Yours truly,

C. WOOD.

My Scotch blood took fire, and this was my answer :—

Torquay : January 1, 1861.

My dear Sir Charles,—Before altering the name given to the new Indian order I would most humbly and dutifully represent to her Majesty that the proposed new name appears to me to be objectionable, and that I am sure it will be very distasteful to many of her Majesty's loyal subjects. In common conversation and in Parliamentary discussions ' England ' is often used to represent the United Kingdom, but never internationally, or between the Crown and people. I presume that by the proposed new title there was no intention to exclude Scotland or Ireland from any connection with India. Such an intention would have been very unjust to the late Marquis of Dalhousie and many other natives of Scotland who have taken a distinguished part in conquering and governing India.

His Majesty King George III., on coming to the throne, said, ' Born and
bred in this country, I glory in the name of *Briton* ;' and the factious
Junius was the only individual who complained that his Majesty had not
said : ' I glory in the name of an Englishman.'

I do not presume to suggest any other title to the Indian order, but
before affixing the Great Seal to that which is now proposed, I shall feel it
my duty, as one of her Majesty's constitutional advisers on such subjects,
to offer my very humble but very earnest advice to her Majesty, that this
title may not be adopted.   I remain, yours truly,

CAMPBELL.

Confidential.—If you think right you may transmit the enclosed to the
Queen. If you think that a more formal representation would be better, I
will prepare one.

' *England and India* ' would set all Scotland in a flame, and the Queen
could hardly after safely cross the Border.

C.

Wood in a private note said he had transmitted my remonstrance to Windsor, but rather treated it with ridicule,
saying that ' England.' was a part representing the whole ;
and asked whether it should be the Star of England, Scotland
and Ireland and Hindostan, Bengal, and the Punjaub.

I jocularly answered that I should be satisfied if he added
to Ireland ' Alderney, Sark, and Man,' and to the Punjaub
' Ceylon and St. Helena.'

But next came what showed me in good earnest that my
remonstrance, being presented to the Queen, had prevailed,
and that I had gained a great triumph for my native land :

India Office : January 7, 1861.

Dear Lord Chancellor,—I must set your Scotch heart at ease by telling
you that we have yielded to your Scotch——(I won't say what). I am in
despair about my order, for I cannot invent a name which will suit
Christian, Mahometan, and Hindoo, Englishman and Scotchman.

I am beginning to wish that I had no order at all ! Yours ever,

C. WOOD.

I cannot say that I passed a merry Christmas at Torquay,
going there on account of the indisposition of my very dear
daughter Mary. But, thanks to Almighty God, she has derived
benefit from the mild air in this place, and although I am
afraid yet to expose her to the London fogs, I hope she will
soon be restored to me in perfect health.   Without her I
should be quite unable to support life.   But I ought to say

that all my children behave to me most kindly and affectionately, and do their best to console me for the irreparable loss
I have sustained.

.   .   .   .

January 28.—I have been on a visit of two days to her
Majesty at Windsor Castle. . . . The second evening we had
theatricals : a play by Bulwer Lytton called ' Richelieu.' . . .

May 5.—I have entirely neglected my Journal for several
months, and since I made my last entry the union of all the
states of Italy, and the disruption of all the states in America
have been consummated. The face of the whole world is
changed. Centuries have elapsed without changes so great.

Parliament met on the 5th of February, and the session
in the House of Lords has been very tranquil. We have not
yet had one party division. Brougham has been detained by
illness at Cannes, so we have had much less twaddle about
the County Courts and paltry Law Reform.

There have been some interesting interpellations on
Foreign Affairs, but the House has hardly ever sat later than
eight o'clock. . I have introduced several bills about Statute
Law Consolidation, Lunacy, the Court of Admiralty, &c., but
nothing of any magnitude. I have only made one long
speech, on moving the second reading of the Bankruptcy
Bill, sent up from the Commons; although I have been
obliged to address the House on different matters almost
every night. Things political have hitherto gone off almost
as smoothly in the evening as the hearing of appeals in the
morning. But I shall have a hard tussle in getting through
the Bankruptcy Bill which, against my will, has been referred
to a Select Committee.

In the House of Commons there has been a division, a
few days ago, on the Budget, when we had a majority of
eighteen. This division, Disraeli says, cannot amount properly to a *majority*, being in its *teens.* But they will not
try their strength again, and I consider the session as good
as over. . . .

I shall have some rough work before the Bankruptcy Bill
passes; but I ought to be satisfied with the session being so
smooth. We have gone on most prosperously with the judicial

business, and now there are hardly any appeals ready for
hearing which have not been disposed of.

I really and truly think little of myself amid the crash of
governments in the new and old world.   I used to think
'Italian union' an improbable fable; but it is an established
reality, and the Italians really seem desirous and capable of
a constitutional monarchy, to be governed by enlightened
public opinion impersonated by an hereditary sovereign.
There have been greater changes in Italy within a few
months than in any one century since the fall of the Roman
Empire.   I shall rejoice when the temporal power of the
Pope is destroyed in name as well as in reality.

We have a frightful spectacle in American disruption, and
an internecine civil war has begun.   What the Americans
are now to suffer is the curse of God upon them for their
reckless adhesion to slavery.   In this respect the North is as
much to blame as the South, for the Free States connived
at Southern slavery, and although they put an end to the
African slave-trade, they tolerated and encouraged a much
worse system at home: the breeding of negroes in some
states, and sending them to the slave-markets in other states.

We have strange questions about privateering and the
right of blockade, arising out of the consideration whether
the seceding states are to be treated as an independent
government.   The circumstances being quite unprecedented,
Grotius and Vattel render us no assistance.

June 12.—This day, representing her Majesty, I gave
the Royal assent to the Bill for the Repeal of the Paper
Duty.   We have had a hard struggle in carrying it, and in
one stage there was a great probability that we should be
beaten and obliged to resign.   In the Commons it was
carried by a majority of eighteen, which was thought decisive.   The session would virtually have been over but for
the casualty of the Government having given mortal um-
brage to the Irish members, by withdrawing a subvention
granted to the Galway Company for carrying the mail to
America.   This gave fresh courage to the Derbyites, and
they resolved to have another division on the Paper Duty in
Committee on the Bill for abolishing it.

When the night for the division arrived, the general expectation was that the Government would be beaten. I went to the House of Commons to be in at the death. For two hours before the House divided I believed firmly that we were gone; for Brand, the existing whipper-in on our side, and Hayter, his predecessor, both told me that a majority of those actually present was against us by one or two, even if our own men all remained true, which was doubtful.

I watched at the door of the House of Commons during the division, till I at last heard a tremendous shout, and a cry of *fifteen majority.* I thought we were crushed indeed! But then came the cry, 'fifteen for the Government!' I was for some time incredulous, but so the fact was; the solution being that of the Derbyites who had been in the House during the evening, sixteen had walked away without voting, some from disgust at the coalition with the Irish members; some hating Disraeli more than they hated the Liberals; and some trembling for their seats, if there should be a dissolution of Parliament.

I should not at all mind being honourably released from the labours and anxieties of the Great Seal. *Pergustavi imperium,* and I should be satisfied to have repose during the remaining short space of my earthly career. But I did not at all relish the notion of being turned out in such a ridiculous manner; and I must add that I felt much for the country, which certainly would have suffered by the transfer of office at this moment to Lord Derby and his associates.

I am now within four days of completing the second year of my reign. Thank heaven, I have got through my work creditably, if not splendidly, and I am not without hope that some of my judgments may hereafter be quoted and relied upon.

This morning I delivered my judgment in the great case of the Emperor of Austria *v.* Kossuth, the famous Hungarian, who contended that he, and not Francis Joseph, is the lawful Sovereign of Hungary, and that he has a right to manufacture in England paper money to the amount of one hundred millions of florins, which he professes to guarantee by the authority of the Hungarian nation, to be introduced into Hungary instead of the paper currency now circulated there by a usurper. An injunction had been granted by Vice-Chancellor Stuart on the absurd ground that the Court of Chancery had a right to prohibit any act which would be a violation of the friendly relations subsisting between Queen Victoria and any foreign sovereign in alliance with her; and it was generally thought that upon appeal the injunction would be dissolved. But I believe that I have satisfactorily supported it on the true ground that Kossuth threatened an act which would be injurious to the property of the recognised King of Hungary and his subjects.

. . . .

The entry of Wednesday, June the 12th, is the last which my father made in his Journal. For ten days he continued doing his daily duties with unabated vigour. On Wednesday, June the 19th, he attended the Queen's Drawing-room and went afterwards to a garden party at Campden Hill. On Thursday afternoon, the House of Lords not sitting, he accompanied his son Hallyburton to the Crystal Palace at Sydenham, and in the evening paid a visit to Sir Charles and Lady Eastlake. On Friday he was kept very late in the House. But on Saturday morning, June the 22nd, he appeared perfectly well. He drove to Lincoln's Inn, accompanied by two of his daughters, and sat in Court till the afternoon, when he went to Downing Street for a meeting of the Cabinet. Thence he walked home to Stratheden House, and, having some spare time before preparing for a dinner party, he sat down to his desk and wrote a judgment.

Among his guests were Lord Granville, Lord Clarendon, the French Ambassador Count de Flahault, Lord and Lady Aveland, Mr. Chichester Fortescue, General Sir James Scarlett, and his old friend Sir David Dundas.[1] Sir David was the first to arrive, and, talking together of an old and valued friend who had long been lying on a sick-bed having lost all his faculties, my father observed: 'I think a clause

[1] Sir David Dundas, who had been a pupil in my father's chambers more than forty years before, writing on the news of his death says: 'How good and kind and true he was to me from my first acquaintance to the very last!' ED.

should be added to the Litany, and after praying against sudden death we should say, " From a lingering illness, Good Lord deliver us." '

Throughout the evening he conversed with his usual animation, and when the guests had departed, remained having a last talk with his children, and bade them Good-night at about twelve o'clock.

At eight next morning his servant went into his room and found him seated in an armchair with no appearance of life. Medical advice was instantly called in, but he had gone to his last rest, and, in his own words, was ' honourably released from the labours and anxieties of the Great Seal.'

This sudden bereavement was an overwhelming shock to his family, unprepared as they were by any sign of illness or infirmity; but when time had softened the effect of the first blow, they were able to feel deeply thankful that he had been spared ' a lingering illness,' and that, with no interval of enforced idleness, he had been permitted to do his duty to the very last day of his long life.

His body was carried to Hartrigge, and on Saturday, June the 29th, we laid it beside that of our dear mother in the Abbey at Jedburgh; carrying out the wish he had expressed at the time of his brother's funeral that the English Burial Service might be used, when ' his remains should be deposited in the resting place secured to him in very holy ground.'

THE END.

LONDON : PRINTED BY
SPOTTISWOODE AND CO., NEW-STREET SQUARE
AND PARLIAMENT STREET